THE FLOWER

Almost immediately following his divorce, Robin snapped his Achilles, nearly died from a resulting blood clot and couldn't walk for six months. So he sat in his garden and wrote this novel. The idea for it might have been inspired by real events but the plot is entirely fictional.

As an actor Robin is probably best known for television comedy with series of Never The Twain, Ffizz, French Fields and Men Behaving Badly. London stage work ranges from Leontes in The Winter's Tale (Time Out Critics Choice Award) to The King and I at the Palladium. He is a well-known 'voice' on TV commercials and documentaries.

Robin was born in Lancashire, brought up in Oxfordshire and now lives in West London.

The Flowerpot Man is his first novel.

ROBIN KERMODE

THE FLOWERPOT MAN

PENDLE

PUBLISHING

A CIP record for this title is available from the
British Library

A Pendle Paperback

ISBN 978-0-9555301-0-4

Pendle Publishing
www.pendlepublishing.co.uk

With thanks to Julian Fellowes and JoAnne Good for their generous quotes, and to Richard Bradbury for his fantastic photographic work.

Special thanks to Damian for his constant support and creative design ideas; and to my team of hard working editors, Anna, Helen, Kate, Roisin, Tacy, Tess and my parents, whose encouragement and attention to detail was boundless.

For my family

Why does my ex-wife always ring me when I'm eating toast? It must have been the fourth time this week. I was sitting quite happily having brunch with my brother when the mobile rang.

"Don't answer it."

I didn't and started to eat. Two bites later it rang again. This time it was a text. 'PICK UP, I KNOW UR THERE.'

I suggested texting back with 'NO I'M NOT' but that would seem to give the game away. What I really wanted to say was, 'WE'RE NOT MARRIED ANYMORE. LET ME EAT MY TOAST IN PEACE.'

Strictly speaking, of course, I was still married to Liz. She moved out three months ago when all the financial stuff had been sorted out and we've been chasing the lawyers ever since. But at ten o'clock this morning, the Decree Nisi was finally stamped. Now we have to wait six weeks and one day for the Decree Absolute. That's 43 days.

The mobile rang again. Another text, 'PLS CALL. URGENT.'

I dialled her number. "Hi." I tried to sound cool, too busy to chat.

"Sorry to bother you, it's just ..." Her voice trailed off. She sounded bad. I could hear her breathing. The sound of silent tears. "I didn't know who else to call."

On another occasion I might have suggested she called Toby but I resisted.

"There's been an accident ..."

On overdrive, I ran through the possibilities. Her mother, her sister, her niece.

"It's Jamie. He's been hit by a car. I'm at the vet's now. Can you come?"

"Liz, I am so sorry. Of course, I'll come straight away."

I left my brother to pay the bill and headed for the tube. Without sounding callous, I could have done without this today. For one thing I was supposed to be working but more importantly I was hoping not to see Liz for a while. Particularly in a supportive capacity. Just when you think you're making headway, something like this happens and you're back to square one.

I saw her car as I emerged from the tube. Parked badly in the usual way, not dangerous, just weird. From the street I saw her back, shoulders down, leaning on the counter. She turned as I opened the door. Her eyes, red from crying, said it all. She looked five years old, lost and needing her father.

A memory shot through me. A memory of an ultrasound scan and the doctor's face, being told our baby hadn't grown properly. Liz lying on the bed, barely covered by a gown. A memory of being strong for her, knowing that the dream was over. Knowing it was the beginning of the end of our marriage.

"I'm sorry, Liz."

"We tried to save him ..."

"I know."

"Stupid bloody driver. I loved him so much."

"I know."

"You don't bloody know. You don't bloody know anything."

I said nothing and let her sob into my chest.

Eventually, "Will you help me bury him?"

"Now?"

"Is that a problem?"

"No. Right. Sure. Where? I mean, had you thought where you'd like to bury him?"

2

"On the top of Pendle Hill."

"You're not serious? That's a five hundred mile round trip."

"It's what I want. It's what Jamie would have wanted."

"What he would have wanted? He doesn't even know where Pendle Hill is. He's a cat, for God's sake."

I agree not totally diplomatic under the circumstances but couldn't we just have had a little ceremony on Hampstead Heath? I'm not actually sure if you're allowed to bury animals on Hampstead Heath, but if you're not allowed to bury them in public places, it would mean that only people with their own gardens could bury them. What about the gardenless? They'd have to take a slow silent walk to the tip with a discreet Tesco bag.

"It's not that far. It's where he was born and I want to take him home. You can understand that?"

"I can, yes. It's just …"

"Just what? Just, you don't want to? Just, you're too busy? Just, you don't want to spend a night in a hotel with me?"

"We wouldn't have to stay overnight, if we shared the driving."

"But it would be dark before we got there. I was thinking we could drive up now, find a B and B and have a little service first thing in the morning."

So now there was a service to organise. Hymns to choose, no doubt. Service sheets to print. A family friend to read a poem. A bit of T.S. Eliot, perhaps? A six hour journey in a hearse and a night in a hotel together. A minefield, especially with raw emotions flying about.

"Please?" She looked up at me as if I was still her Knight in Shining Armour.

"Come on, darling. Let's take Jamie home."

Liz was in no fit state to drive so I went back to pick up the van. I grabbed a spare shirt, a clean pair of boxers and my shaving things. But I couldn't find the overnight bag anywhere. Liz must have taken it when she left. Along with several other prize possessions, including half a dozen CDs that I was convinced I'd bought long before I'd met her. But they were only things. I could always buy more things.

I found a new toothbrush in the drawer, Liz was bound to forget hers, so I threw that in as well. Though why I still felt responsible for her oral hygiene, I didn't know. As I shoved everything into a plastic bag, my foot knocked against something hard under the bed. It was our wedding photo, covered in dust. Although Liz had moved out three months ago, we'd taken it down several months before that, on the evening of The Great Discussion, in a gesture far more symbolic than my solicitor ringing me this morning with news of the Decree Nisi. I wiped the dust off with my sleeve and looked at our happy, smiling faces, blissfully unaware of what life was about to throw at us. But it was still a great shot. And Liz looked amazing. My friend Paul had wanted to publish it as a black and white postcard to sell in bookshops. He even suggested a title, 'Always.' Thank God we stopped him. I turned the frame over and put it back under the bed. Face down in shame.

The windscreen was fogging up. I tried to wipe it with my sleeve, which caused me to swerve.

Liz sighed. "Careful."

"I am being careful, I just want to see the road because I don't particularly want to die."

"Very tactful. Did you have to bring death into it?"

No, I didn't. She was right, as usual. In fact, she was always right. That was half the problem. She started crying again. I pulled over.

"What are you doing now?"

"I think we've got a puncture." I got out and the worst

was confirmed. And then it started raining.

"Can I help?" I suspect she actually meant it. But Knights can't accept help. That was the other half of the problem. Anyway before you could say RAC, one wet driver, one crying passenger and one dead cat were back on the road again heading north.

"You've cut your finger."

"It's not serious."

"Let me have a look." I was in safe hands, Liz was a good nurse. She'd been made a Ward Sister the year before we married. "You'll live."

She leant forward and turned the music down. That was a first. Some couples fight over the control of the TV remote but with us it was the volume. Two choices, loud or unbearably loud. She was holding out the olive branch and I took it with both hands.

"Want some chocolate?" She opened a bar and threw the wrapper on the floor.

"No, thanks, I'll wait for my coffee."

She cheered as a large blue sign loomed up. "Services one mile. Great, I need a pee."

"Can't you wait? There's another one in nineteen miles." I liked to put off stopping as long as I could so there'd be less to go after the break.

"Oh for God's sake, I need a pee and you want a coffee. Just pull over." She bit into the chocolate. "Now I remember why we split up."

I turned off the engine. "Me too."

"Come on, let's be friends. It's my round." She got out and went to open the boot. "Hang on, I'll just get Jamie."

"We can't take a dead cat into a service station. Two coffees please and a bowl of milk for the cat. Oh no sorry, my mistake, he's dead." Her look suggested I'd just used up eight of my nine lives. "He'd be much happier in the boot. It'll be quieter there."

"I can't leave him." Her voice was firm. "If it was your

5

mother in the boot, would you leave her?"

There was no answer to that.

"You get the coffees and I'll wait with Jamie."

"Thanks, you do understand. I knew you would."

She waved as she reached the entrance before disappearing inside. There was still some chemistry left between us. Or was I imagining it? But now, of course, there's Toby. I didn't want to know if she was still seeing him, so I hadn't asked. He's a cocky bastard, Toby. Enough said. Liz was always asking me if I'd met someone. She's obsessed by it. Perhaps I should lie and pretend I'd had several lovers. Great sex, free from the constraints of marriage. She might find that a challenge and fancy me again. I hadn't slept with anyone for months. Not since Liz. But tonight, the two of us in the same hotel, bound to happen. Technically we're still married, after all.

I heard a cat meow behind me. I cricked my neck as my head spun round, adrenalin shooting through me. Realising it wasn't Jamie waking from the dead but a stray cat in the car park, I calmed down.

"I've got you an Americano, a blueberry muffin and some chocolate. I wasn't sure what you wanted. Jamie OK?"

"I'm sure he's fine." The coffee tasted good. Even the pre-packaged plastic muffin was welcome. "How many nurses does it take to change a light bulb?"

She settled back into her seat. "You tell me."

"Only one. But in my dream it takes five. They're wearing stockings and they're all up a ladder."

She looked at me. "We're not going to sleep together, you know. This isn't about that."

"Of course not, it's about Jamie."

Twenty minutes down the road, with my bladder on the point of overflowing, I needed to stop for a pee.

Liz sighed. "Why didn't you go before?"

I was on the graveyard shift, remember?

I drove on in silence for half an hour looking out for the next Service Station, when I saw a car ahead of us on the hard shoulder with its bonnet up. A middle aged woman was hitting a man over his head with her handbag. Other cars were honking their horns. We joined in and got hysterical. It was as if we were 'a couple' again. It felt good. When would we stop being 'a couple'? Would it stop the precise moment the Decree Absolute is sworn? Or stamped, or passed, or whatever the wretched thing has done to it.

We cheered as we crossed the border into Lancashire.

"The Old Rectory. Sounds nice." Liz was reading the guide book. She was big on guide books.

"Maybe the Old Rector could perform the ceremony?"

A disapproving sigh. "This can't be it. There are no lights on." She was getting tetchy, a tone I knew well.

The place was clearly shut. CLOSED OCTOBER TO APRIL.

"Don't worry, Liz. We could always sleep in the car and have a New Age service at dawn."

"Shut up, I want a meal and a hot bath. And I'm sure you do too."

I love hot baths. But of course, when we were trying for babies I wasn't allowed to have them. Kills the sperm apparently.

"Let's head back to the village. There's bound to be a pub with a couple of rooms. It's Friday, so the disco should stop around four. It'll be perfect."

She laughed. Then suddenly there it was, an old coaching inn with smoke drifting from the chimney.

The girl on the desk shook her head. "Sorry, we're full."

"No room at the Inn?"

Liz pushed me aside. "Look, my cat's died and I'm taking him to be buried tomorrow and I have to stay here tonight. It's very important. Please."

Cat lovers of the world unite. The girl leant in closer and lowered her voice. "The Honeymoon Suite? Would that do?"

I leant in too. "Hang on, I thought you had a full house?"

She turned back to Liz. "It's all ready for tomorrow's wedding. We don't normally sell it on a Friday but Mr. Clarke, the Manager, is away tonight and I won't tell him if you won't. You'd have to leave early though, so we can get it ready in time."

"No problem. We'll be out by nine."

"Scouts honour," I added unnecessarily.

Ten minutes later, with Jamie safely tucked up in the Honeymoon Suite, we went downstairs to a roaring log fire and hot food.

"Bangers and mash. Great. And a cider."

I never have cider at home but there's something about a cosy country pub and cider that just seems right.

Liz spotted two chairs by the fire. "Whatever happened to Scampi in the Basket?"

"Yeah, what was it with pubs and their baskets?"

"Goes with the country. That and shooting everything that moves."

Liz often held forth on hunting, shooting and fishing. Not that it ever stopped her consuming the hunted, shot and fished. I always suspected her hatred of those sports had more to do with class than cruelty. In her mind, class was cruelty. I'm the sort who thinks that class doesn't matter anymore as long as we're kind to one another. "That's all very well if you're posh," she'd say. I'm not posh. Just a tiny bit posher than she is.

The food arrived and I felt myself unwind. We used to do this a lot. Country pubs and Sunday lunches. But we'd usually be late because Liz couldn't decide what to wear and I'd forgotten to check the map. I was about to remind her of our famous pub lunch in Milton Keynes, when I noticed she was wiping her eyes with a paper napkin.

"I just can't imagine life without him."

She looked up at me as if I was the only man in the world. The only man who could possibly save her. I felt invincible. We must have looked like Victorian mourners as we left the bar, Liz bent over in pain and I being brave and manly, accepting the consoling glances.

We stopped by our front door and both felt the irony of 'The Honeymoon Suite'. I felt her hand touch mine. It involved almost no movement or sound but it shot through me. A gesture like that could change the world. We stood there for several moments like lovers do. There was an openness of such humility that I wanted it to last forever.

She broke the moment, maybe it was too much for her as well. "Have you got the key? We should go in."

I hadn't got the key, of course. I'd left it by the fire in the bar. Normally I'd have been shouted down for this but tonight there were no raised voices, no recriminations. Marital snakes and ladders. When you're married you fight like cat and dog, and when you're divorcing it's the cat that brings you back together.

I returned with the key and found Liz looking out of the landing window. "I think it'll be a good day tomorrow. Red sky at night, Shepherd's delight."

I opened the door. Liz went over to the foot of the bed and knelt down.

"I'll miss you, my dear little friend. And I always will."

I was woken by a knocking sound. The ancient central heating system was groaning in its sleep. I turned over and drifted off again.

There was a knock at the door. A little boy opened it and walked slowly across the room towards the bed. I'd seen him somewhere before. He stood there for a few moments watching me. Then I realised the little boy was me at the age of five or six.

Eventually he spoke. "How old are we now?"

My throat was dry. "We're forty four."

The little boy laughed. "That's very old. And are we happy?"

"The last couple of years have been pretty tough."

He put his hand in mine. "Don't worry, it'll be fine, you'll see."

"I feel such a failure. I made vows in church and everything."

His eyes were full of compassion. "I'm sure you did your best."

"But I've never failed at anything before. Not at anything that really mattered."

He smiled. "Just be kind to one another. That's all you have to do."

I opened my eyes and looked over at Liz, still asleep next to me. Her hair was sticking up as it always did first thing in the morning. She was definitely still beautiful. It was extraordinary, I used to be married to this woman. She opened her eyes and, for a brief moment, seemed unsure of where she was.

I reached over and stroked her hair. "We should get

up. We promised to be out by nine."

"They won't mind if it's ten past."

I wasn't so sure. But then I'm a 'ten to' person. If you leave the house at ten to nine all the traffic lights are green. At ten past they're all red. Of course, they're not really all red, it just seems that way because you're in a hurry. Liz was a 'ten past' person. She hated arriving early for anything. We'd always be late for the cinema, running in just as the film started. I'd spend the first twenty minutes out of breath with sweat running down my neck. According to Liz I sweat excessively. Another of my little failings. And perhaps that's where the problem lay. A trickle of sweat somewhere between 'ten to' and 'ten past'.

I opted for the carrot not the stick.

"Let's get up and have some breakfast, it'll set us up for the day."

"Today's going to be difficult for me. Don't forget that."

"All the more reason for a hearty breakfast. Come on, it's nearly quarter to."

"It's Jamie's funeral. I need some space to get my head around it. Stop going on about the time."

"It's also another couple's wedding day and they'll need the honeymoon suite, so we should get up and off."

I said this, forgetting that the mention of any other wedding set off a tidal wave of insecurity about ours. After the reception we'd gone straight home before flying out the next day. No first night of wedded bliss in the Honeymoon Suite with chocolates on the pillow and a mini bar full of champagne for us. Liz thought we should use the money to upgrade our hotel in Cape Town. Fine and dandy, I thought. But no, after a few months it had apparently been a huge mistake. And who was responsible? Me, of course. I waited for the tidal wave. I'd learned to set my watch by it. Whoosh.

"You did like our wedding, didn't you? Having it in

11

that pub was OK, wasn't it? I mean, people didn't think we did it on the cheap?"

"No, it was perfect."

And it was. We'd had a Ceili band with singing and dancing, not a white table cloth event for the bride's father's business associates. I loved it and I loved going straight home after. It felt natural. And the Honeymoon Suite would have been a waste of time as we both passed out in an alcoholic stupor as soon as we hit the sheets.

I jumped out of bed. "Anyway don't worry, next time you can do it differently." The breakfast room had the familiar smell of ten past nine. The tables were mostly covered in remnants of half eaten toast, pots of tea and napkins in the marmalade. We found a corner table with a reserved sign on it. Liz sat down in defiance. I palmed the sign and quickly laid it to rest among the debris of the next table. The waitress arrived. A chirpy, blushing girl in her late teens.

"Room number?"

"The Honeymoon Suite."

She giggled. "You'll be wanting the full English then."

I gave her a wink. "I should say so."

Liz shook her napkin. "In your dreams."

I reached over and took her hand. "Let's make today as special for Jamie as we possibly can."

She smiled. "You're not a bad man." It was a saying of her father's. It meant you were King.

"I know I'm not a bad man. I just wish you did."

She squeezed my hand. "I do."

The waitress returned with the orange juice.

"Renewing your vows already? That's nice." She wiggled her bum as she left.

"I wish she wouldn't do that."

"Don't mind me, you go for it. She might fancy a forty four year old gardener. 'Oh what big hands you've got, sir. Oh sir, be gentle with me, sir!'"

12

Liz's phone went. She let it ring three or four times.

"Aren't you going to get that?"

She looked uncomfortable. "It's probably not important."

I could see the display, 'Toby Calling'. She answered it reluctantly.

Why wasn't Toby here instead of me anyway? He could easily have cancelled his trip to Belgium. I'd gone to school with him and he was irritating enough then. He had it all, bedroom eyes and boardroom looks. The fact that he was the son of the local nob didn't do him any harm either. Nor the fact that he was the first one of us to have a car. And rumours as to the size of his manhood did nothing to help the rest of us. But was he happy? He bloody well is now, he's sleeping with my wife.

Liz looked embarrassed as she spoke into the phone. "We drove up yesterday. No, he's been very sweet." Who's he? The cat's father? "Bye, darling."

Did she have to add the 'darling'? It was the first time I'd heard her say it to another man, and I wished I hadn't.

The chirpy girl arrived with our food.

"Thanks, 'darling'." I flashed her a smile.

"My pleasure."

Liz bit into her toast. "I think you're in there."

"Like Toby's in there with you?"

"Don't do this, it'll only do your head in. Sex is just sex. With Toby or anyone else."

But I wished to God it had been with someone else. Someone I'd never heard of. Preferably some unattractive pauper with a small todger.

We drove to Clitheroe in reverent silence. I thought about finding a religious channel on the radio for some quiet organ music. Alleluia FM? Must exist, surely?

"Fancy the Morning Service on Radio Four?"

Her look suggested I should bury myself in my own grave.

"I nearly forgot, we'll need a box. I'm not burying Jamie in an old towel. There must be a shoe shop in Clitheroe with an empty box."

Shoe shopping with Liz was a killer, there was always a problem. The style, the heel, the toe, the zip, the finish. Thank goodness for men's shoes. Thank goodness for men. They may not know much about shoes but they know what they like. We drove into Clitheroe town centre and looked for a sweet little shoe shop with a sweet little man who'd give us an empty box.

"Sorry, the bin men took the lot, I'm afraid." The sweet man smiled ever so sweetly. "But I could show you some boots and if you found something you liked, you'd get the box for free." Under other circumstances I'd have liked the guy.

Liz glanced over to me. "I could always do with an extra pair."

I said nothing. The man was already bringing in boots of all styles, heels, toes, zips and finishes. I'd only put half an hour in the meter, so I left them to it.

"You're not feeding that meter are you? I'd hate to have to give you a ticket."

Yeah, right. I gave the warden a quick version of the story so far. Liz, the divorce, Jamie and the boot box.

"You're better off on your own, mate. You feed that meter all day if you want to, you'll get no ticket from me."

On the way back I popped into a newsagent and bought a Lottery ticket. But then I realised if I won, I'd have to share the winnings with Liz. Until we got the Decree Absolute, we were still legally married. So I bought two tickets. One for me, one for her. But what if her ticket won? Would she share her winnings with me? I seriously doubted it so I decided to keep both tickets myself, just in case, and split any profit with her. But what if I won five million? Would I give her two and a half just to watch her swan off into the sunset with Toby? I wished the Lottery had never been invented.

Outside the shoe shop I passed a bloke selling the Big Issue. I didn't really want a copy and thought about giving him a Lottery ticket instead. But which one?

"Take these. You never know your luck."

"I do know my luck. And it's crap. I'd rather have a sandwich and a cup of tea."

Crisis over. I'd offered them and he'd refused. If I won now I'd be morally in the clear. I reached into my pocket. I only had a ten pound note, so I had no choice but to give him that.

Inside the shop, Liz was strutting around in the sexiest boots I'd ever seen. She was grinning from ear to ear, like the Lancashire cat that got the cream.

The sweet man was beaming too. "That's three hundred and fifty pounds."

Even Liz looked shocked. "I thought these were the ninety five pound ones, I can't possibly afford them."

With the money her solicitor had dragged out of me in the settlement, I suspected she could actually.

"What do you think we should do?" She looked up at me.

We? They're your boots, your cardboard coffin and your dead cat. Where was Toby's Gold Card when we needed it? Nowhere. So we used mine, naturally. It took the balance on my very ordinary, non-Gold card to over seven thousand. The divorce had almost finished me off and now I was subsidising Toby's trips to Belgium.

Liz peeled the ticket off the windscreen. "I thought you fed the meter?"

I caught sight of the warden disappearing round the corner. I legged it after him, screaming. "You promised you wouldn't give me a ticket, you bastard."

The warden turned round. A different warden. So far this cardboard coffin had cost me four hundred and two pounds. Three fifty for the box, ten for the Big Issue seller, two for the Lottery tickets and forty for the parking ticket.

Liz smiled. "Let it go, we've got a difficult time ahead."

It's going to get more difficult? Bring it on.

It had taken us a good hour to climb to the top of Pendle Hill. We could have driven part of the way but Liz felt it was more of a pilgrimage if we did it all on foot. The view from the top was amazing. Straight ahead of us Liz said she could make out Blackpool and St. Annes but she must have better eyes than I have. To the north-west we could see Waddington Fell stretching out toward the Trough of Bowland and immediately below us we could see Clitheroe, dominated by the castle to its left and the Cement works to its right.

"This is a good spot." I started digging.

Liz grabbed the spade out of my hand. "It's facing the Cement works, I want him to face the sea."

"Cats don't like water."

"Well, I do. And I want him to face the sea."

So she chose another site, which looked towards St. Annes. I strained my eyes to see the coast, but even with a telescope I'd have been hard pushed to spot it. I started digging again.

"And it must be at least two feet deep, I don't want him being dug up by a fox or anything."

I'd been hard at it for about fifteen minutes when a police helicopter passed overhead. I froze, assuming that if I kept still I'd go unnoticed. Unfortunately Liz decided that this was the moment to shake our red picnic blanket with a motion that resembled in every way an urgent distress signal. Luckily the chopper flew off.

"Narrow escape." Liz had to shout over the noise of the engine.

But the chopper turned full circle until it hovered

directly overhead.

A police loudspeaker thundered above us. "Do you need help?"

The helicopter began to lower itself and landed fifty yards away.

"Drag the blanket over the hole. Cover it up, quickly."

A policeman jumped out, crouched under the blades and ran towards us. "Are you OK?"

"Fine, we're just having a picnic." Liz stepped back to show off the blanket. But she caught her foot in the newly dug hole and keeled over, screaming in agony.

The officer helped her up. "You'll live but you can't walk on it. We'll fly you down to the bottom and your husband can pick you up later. Is that alright?" Without waiting for an answer he picked her up and whisked her away.

I was left on top of the hill with a large red blanket, a spade, a dead cat, a funeral to arrange and a fifty minute journey back down again. Slowly, I folded up the blanket, took little Jamie in his four hundred and two pound cardboard coffin and laid him to rest in one of the most beautiful places in England.

I covered the box with earth, replaced the topsoil and knelt down. I wanted to say a prayer but nothing came. I was just wondering if The Lord's Prayer was appropriate for a cat, when the mobile rang.

Liz was sobbing. "Have I missed the funeral?"

"No, I'm right here with him. I was about to say The Lord's Prayer."

"Let's say it together then. Hold the phone close to the ground so Jamie can hear me."

I held out her mobile a few inches above the little grave.

"Our Father, who art in Heaven, Hallowed be Thy name." We spoke gently. "Thy kingdom come, Thy will be done, On earth as it is in Heaven."

I eventually found Liz nursing her bandaged ankle in a little café on Castle Street. The lunchtime rush was over and we sat quietly, sharing a sandwich in our own private wake.

She looked out of the window. "Will he be OK up there, all on his own?"

"I'll bring the car round to the front and we'll drive up to the castle. You can see the top of the hill from there."

We passed a memorial to the men who died in the First World War. A bronze statue of a lone soldier, imposing and strong, his head bowed in prayer. Was he saying The Lord's Prayer as well? We got out and I gave her a piggyback up to the castle ramparts. Her ankle had swollen badly. A mist was coming down fast but we could still just see the top of the hill.

Liz put her hand in mine. "It's perfect. Just perfect."

The journey home was uneventful apart from a near miss with an old lady in an even older Morris Minor. She'd been driving at forty five in the outside lane. I was passing her in the middle lane quite politely when she suddenly made a dash for the hard shoulder for no apparent reason, leaving two lanes of traffic in chaos.

We laughed and chattered away together and, as the hours went by, we became the happy couple returning from holiday. Soon we'd be home, rushing in to check the post and clapping. Yes, clapping. When a house has been empty, even for a short while, it can feel sad. The Chinese suggest clapping loudly in every corner to energise the Chi. Very New Age, I know, but it does work. Anyway, that's what we used to do. Only this time we'd be going back to separate houses, separate piles of post and separate claps of separate hands.

It was getting dark as I pulled up outside her house.

"Are you coming in?"

"Better not."

We'd agreed never to go inside each other's places again. At least not for a long time. Not until we'd each met other people and had families and were tottering around on Zimmer frames and buying Stannah stairlifts. It would be too difficult seeing 'his' toothbrush in the bathroom, 'his' smiling face on the mantelpiece and 'his' impression on her heart. We agreed we could meet for coffee if we had to, if we found it too hard, but otherwise we'd try not to see each other for a while.

She touched my cheek and kissed me full on the lips. Just one kiss but with passion and gentleness. "You've been a star."

"Don't forget your boots."

She gave me one final kiss through the window and went inside. I watched the lights go on in her flat. They illuminated a whole new world. A world in which I played no part. I could see her moving about slowly, closing the curtains. Then suddenly she was gone.

I'd slept heavily and woke to the sound of rain on the windows. I'd been sleeping in the loft ever since we'd decided the marriage was over. It seemed sensible for me to move up there until we'd sorted out the legal side. I'm not sure why I was the one to leave the marital bed but I'd grown fond of my little attic nest. It had a small bathroom where I'd lie soaking for hours, looking up at the sky through the Velux window. Passing aircraft passengers could probably see in if they looked hard enough. You never know, there might have been a plane load of single women scouring the London skyline in search of Mr. Right. I waved at each and every one, just in case. Liz had been gone three months and I was still sleeping up there.

I got up, threw some cold water over my face and went downstairs. On the way, I passed our old bedroom on the first floor and peered in. I still had some clothes in the wardrobe but otherwise I'd hardly been in there for six months. I tried the Chinese clapping trick to wake up the room. After three claps, a shaft of sunlight hit the bedspread and I heard a child laughing outside. It was Colin from across the road with his new baby girl in a sling. He was proudly introducing her to the cooing couple from No. 63. Colin looked up and caught me peering out. He waggled his daughter's little hand as if to wave. I made a silly face back. If things had worked out differently, it could have been me standing there, doing the New Man thing, walking to the health food shop for organic baby food and bankrupting myself in Baby Gap.

Suddenly there was a loud screaming from next door. Six month old Max was ready for food. The couple on the other side of me also had a newborn and I was beginning to feel surrounded. In the last five years, seven babies had been born to friends on the street. Liz and I had celebrated with them all. We'd sent congratulations cards and dutifully bought presents for christenings, birthdays and Christmases. Other people's babies were expensive. Of course, we didn't resent them having children. We just wanted it to be our turn.

Colin shouted up. "Fancy a walk?"

I shook my head. I wasn't in the mood to play Happy Neighbours today.

I put the kettle on and got the coffee out of the freezer. Liz said it kept its flavour longer in there. I drank so much coffee that I knew it couldn't possibly hang around long enough to go off but I still followed her advice. I tore open a bill. Had I really spent a hundred and twenty five pounds on the mobile? That's fifteen hundred a year. I checked the numbers and saw that most were to Jack. I should ring and thank him for being such a good brother but he'd probably had enough calls from me already.

The rest of the post went straight in the bin, apart from a formal looking letter from the bank. I poured the coffee before opening it. I liked to drink my first cup in the garden but despite the cosmic shafts of sunlight it was still too wet, so I sat at the kitchen table looking out.

The bank was offering to extend my overdraft. It had started out as an overdraft facility but my gardening work had been so slow during the winter that it had become an overdraft necessity. If things didn't pick up soon, I could lose my house. I needed to land on 'Go' and collect two hundred pounds pretty quickly.

I also needed to stop hiding in the loft. So I made a decision then and there to move down to my old room. I took my coffee upstairs and sat on the bed. The sun had disappeared behind a cloud and the room felt cold again.

At the start of our marriage I used to bring Liz breakfast in bed almost every day. I'm good in the mornings so it was no real hardship, but after a couple of years I did it less and less. It happened slowly, until one day I realised that we never had breakfast in bed anymore and that's when I knew we'd fallen out of love.

I decided to start by repainting the room. It was a 'Project' and I liked 'Projects'. I had to exorcise the ghosts of old memories before I could sleep there. And certainly before I could sleep with anyone else there. But that would be a long way off. I wouldn't allow a new woman to move into the house in case she tried to take it away from me. I could just about afford to get divorced once but twice would be a killer.

I'd set the day aside for doing my tax. I took down the old shoebox where I stored my receipts. I should have emptied it and taken it up to Clitheroe with me, it would have saved me four hundred pounds. But I decided I couldn't face doing the tax on an empty stomach so I made some toast. I was about to take my first bite when the phone rang. Liz must have had a hidden camera in the kitchen.

"OK, you can stop this now. It's not funny any more."

A lady's voice. "Hello, is that The Flowerpot Man?"

Liz had come up with the name for the company. I thought it might be a bit twee but most women seemed reassured by it and they generally booked the gardener.

I made an appointment to visit the lady in Hampstead tomorrow afternoon. I threw away the cold toast and put another slice in the toaster to celebrate my change of luck. I ate in silence with no interruptions, no phone calls and no Liz.

The headline in the Sunday paper screamed, 'DIVORCE RATE AT ALL TIME HIGH'. I wondered how many of my school friends' marriages had also ended in divorce. So I put my tax receipts back in their shoebox and logged on to the Friends Reunited website. Only four members of my year were registered.

Roger Clifford: 'Currently in Moscow. Married Krysha in 1989. One daughter, Nina.'

Sean O'Connor: 'Happily married to Niamh, with four children, Sinead, Aisling, Ciaran and Patrick. Working as a GP in Farnham.'

Dave 'The Rebel' Hughes: 'Still swimming in the sea every Christmas Morning. Wacky or what?! Unfortunately had to join the rat race to put the kids through school. All five of them! But hey, I'm still the rebel!'

Simon Beardsley: 'MD of own corporate finance company. Still in love with my beautiful wife, Arrabella. Three gorgeous girls, Chloe, Minty and Tiff.'

There they all were, with their perfect children and perfect marriages. What could I say about my life? 'Running failing landscape gardening company. Almost bankrupt. Almost divorced. And absolutely no kids.'

I deregistered myself immediately. The rest of my year, with their failed marriages and imperfect lives, had presumably done the same.

I turned to the gardening section of the paper, as I did every Sunday. Liz was always on at me to write my own column. I knew I could do it standing on my head but I'd never got round to it. Maybe if I had done, I'd be up there on the Friends Reunited website proudly displaying my perfect life.

The phone rang again. It was my mother. "Happy Sunday."

She always cheered me up, without being irritating or preachy. It might look like she'd had a smooth ride, with her two healthy sons and a fortieth wedding anniversary on the way. But her mother had died when she was five and she'd never known her father.

"I've found the top layer of your wedding cake in the freezer …"

Baby Max was getting louder next door. Don't they ever feed him?

"We were keeping it for the christening, of course, but …"

Now that I'd had the Decree Nisi, it seemed unrealistically optimistic to hold onto it any longer.

"Just bin it."

"Yes, that's what your Father and I thought. But we didn't want to do anything without asking."

"You could've sold it at the Village Fete. But someone might have choked on it."

I made myself another coffee and flicked on the television. There were the usual ads for hair loss and younger looking skin. Then one caught my eye. A series of African children looked out of the screen, straight at me. "Eight pounds a month could help bring food and fresh drinking water to their village for a year." The children's eyes were still on me. Questioning. "You say you want to be a father. Well, we're orphans." I turned off the TV and sat in silence. Eight pounds a month would hardly break even my beleaguered bank.

I went to their website and was offered a choice of three children. And if I didn't want to sponsor any of those, I could CHOOSE AGAIN. I was being asked to play God from the comfort of my computer. But how could I possibly choose? From their biography? Their smile? Their look of desperation?

Then I found another option, CHOOSE GEOGRAPHICALLY. Was a child from Bangladesh more deserving than one from Iraq? Malawi more than Albania? I couldn't make a geographical choice either. And yet, with limited resources, I knew the decision had to be made by someone. So I decided to covenant sixteen pounds a month to the general fund and let the charity decide. They were the ones on the ground, they would know which cases were more deserving than others. I punched in my bank details and pressed SEND. My finances weren't great but I knew I had far more than those kids would ever have. My parents had always said, "Eat up, there are starving children in Africa." Well finally, I'd done my bit. But I knew it was only a drop in the ocean. I still felt I'd let them all down. And I still felt no nearer to being a father.

From the chart in the DIY shop, I settled on a sort of light cappuccino colour for the bedroom walls. I hoped it would bode well for a new chapter of breakfasts in bed and Sunday mornings of sleepy togetherness. I also bought some white for the ceiling and got straight down to work. Most people use a roller but, Luddite-like, I stubbornly insist on a brush. I always cricked my neck and inevitably missed out a bit, so I generally had to do two coats. Ceilings are really important. You lie there looking up at them, your eye discovering every flaw over the years of sleepless nights and early mornings. It's the same with a dentist's ceiling, you stare up at it hoping to find comfort. Cracks you find there suggest cracks in your teeth. If I spot a flawless ceiling when I'm having a check up, I immediately relax, knowing I'll be fine.

I was only a few strokes away from finishing, when I over-stretched, knocked the paint off the ladder and covered the carpet in a sea of vinyl matt. It was my own fault, I could have stopped after the first coat but I'd insisted on pushing myself. I don't know what the rush was about anyway. I'd been up in the loft for six months, another few days wouldn't have mattered one way or the other, and now I was going to have to buy a new carpet. So I threw down an old dustsheet to cover the mess and pretended it wasn't there. I was shattered and ready for a hot bath.

I lay in the steaming heat and watched a plane cross the sky. I waved, ever hopeful that Miss Right was on the lookout for her new man. But I'd been told I was in the wrong for so long, that I wondered if I'd ever be anybody's Mr. Right again. Liz was convinced that my passion for hot baths had stopped us conceiving. I turned on the tap with my toes, added some more hot water and felt like a naughty schoolboy.

I'd had this dream before. I was at the clinic, getting my sperm tested.

The nurse handed me a huge test tube, "Can you fill this for me?"

Fill it? Who did she think I was, Superman?

She closed the door and left me in a large room with a chair and a sink in the far corner. I could have stood at the door and donated from there but I felt too exposed. So I hid in the far corner. There was a heavily fingered copy of Penthouse and a copy of the Radio Times with Terry Wogan on the cover. I opened the Penthouse but every page had a picture of Liz. She had no clothes on and was posing in the usual way but her eyes were full of tears. I found one picture of her waving her bum in the air, which meant I couldn't see her face. It almost worked until I realised that she was probably still crying so I had to stop. But on the last page, there was a topless photo of a secretary from Nottingham which almost got me going again. I was about to fill the test tube when I caught sight of Terry's smiling face on the cover of the Radio Times and it completely put me off. So I returned my empty test tube to the nurse.

Toby popped his face out of the Gents. He had his trousers round his ankles and was grinning from ear to ear. "I'm going to need a couple more of these tubes, I've filled this one already and I'm still going strong."

I woke to find the paint smell as strong as ever. It encouraged me to leave the house early and join Jack in the local café. Not that I needed much encouragement. Meeting up with him had been a life saver during the three months before Liz had moved out and since then it had become a regular habit.

I ordered my usual. I knew I was eating too many scrambled eggs but what else could I eat for breakfast? The sausages at the café weren't that great and the bacon in the sandwiches wasn't crispy enough. Jack had a full English, with peppermint tea. He reckoned it was better for his singing voice than coffee.

He put down his Racing Post. "So, how is she?"

"Divorce obviously agrees with her."

He'd always liked Liz. When he first saw us walking down the street five years ago, he said he knew we'd end up getting married. We'd met two weeks before and it had been instant fireworks. My grandparents were married after only four days and their marriage had lasted a lifetime, so I wasn't the only impetuous member of the family. Jack was my Best Man and even wrote a song for us as his speech. It could easily have been one of those embarrassing moments at a wedding. But this was different, not just because he's a professional singer but because he sang with such heart. It was a moment of real love between brothers.

I drank my coffee. "And how's my favourite niece?"

"Emma's good. She can't wait to be thirteen."

"Bet you can't wait for her first boyfriend to come along."

"Tell me about it, Cathy's really worried."

"I'm more worried for the boyfriends. One look from her mother will send them running for the hills."

Jack had lived with Cathy for fourteen years but they'd never married. They had survived where we had failed. But then they'd had Emma. If we'd been lucky enough to have had a child, things might have been different.

"I almost forgot. Cathy and I have got you an unbirthday present. What are you doing tomorrow night?"

"Nothing. Why?"

"We've booked you an evening of Speed Dating."

"Yeah, right."

"No, seriously. It'll be great."

"Ten three minute rounds with a succession of unattractive, desperate women. I don't think so."

"Cathy's had several friends who've gone and had a great time. They're not desperate or unattractive. You never know, it might be something to tell the grandchildren."

"I'll think about it."

I said goodbye and headed off to Acton. It was Monday morning and time for my weekly visit to Ivy. I'd first worked for her twelve years ago and now she'd become a friend. She once told me, in an unguarded moment, that her father had been born in 1870 and he was over forty when she came along. So she must be in her early nineties. She was a tiny woman with bright, determined eyes and I suspect her views on life were largely fashioned from the novels of Jane Austen.

Ivy opened the door and smiled. "Better late than never."

I checked my watch. It was eight fifty nine, one minute early. This was our ritual banter and she meant no harm by it. I gave her a peck on the cheek.

"In you come. That's right."

She ushered me in. Every Monday we'd go straight through to the back room, where the silver was carefully laid out on the kitchen table ready for polishing. I'd potter in the garden while she polished in the kitchen and between us we kept her house in order.

She was already shaking the tin of Silvo. "You get started straight away and we'll have tea at a quarter past ten. That's right."

Ivy liked order and was a stickler for punctuality. The clock in her kitchen was permanently set thirty five minutes fast, so she always had time in hand. I know I'm a 'ten to' man but this arrangement made it almost impossible to work out what the real time actually was.

She had a small cottage garden which suited her perfectly. The forget-me-nots and bluebells of early spring gave way to the scented geraniums and bergamot of late summer. A small patch of grass was cut weekly and edged meticulously.

I'd been recommended to her by a neighbour and we'd got on famously from the start. For the first few years I charged for my services but after a while I offered to pop in once a week as a friend. A routine had developed and now I popped in every Monday morning at nine o'clock sharp.

"Fetch the tea. That's right." She took off her apron and I carried out the neatly arranged tray to the little table under the apple tree.

We'd chat about this and that, putting the world to rights as we ate our bourbon biscuits. I looked forward to my Monday mornings and my time with Ivy. If it rained we had hot toast in the kitchen instead to warm us up.

"Same time next week."

"Off you go. That's right."

In the afternoon I'd arranged to meet the lady from Hampstead who'd rung for a quote. I pulled up outside a large town house, which must have been divided into four or five flats. The street was full of them. I rang the bell. Eventually a woman opened the door.

"The Flowerpot Man?"

"At your service, madam." I saluted in a particularly stupid manner. I never do that normally and had no idea what possessed me to do it then.

"Well, you'd better follow me in." I remembered her voice from the phone yesterday. Cultured, confident and friendly.

The hallway was huge. So was the kitchen. And then I remembered there'd only been one bell.

"Is this all one house?"

"Yes, aren't I lucky?"

She showed me her garden. It was big. Not just by London standards, either. It was very big. The grass was in need of serious attention and the borders were overgrown. Bits of fencing could be replaced and the fountain had stopped working.

She threw a stone into the still water. "I'm open to suggestions. It's been a bit neglected, I'm afraid. Rather like me."

Was she flirting? It felt like she was but I was completely out of practice at reading the signals.

"That's too bad." I tried to sound like Sean Connery as Bond. "I'm sure I can work my magic. There's no major landscaping to be done. A good tidy up and a bit of new planting. We could go to Covent Garden Market early one morning and choose some new things."

"When can you start?"

I could have lied and pretended I had a window sometime next September but the truth was, work had almost completely dried up. "Everything I need's in the van right now."

"Go on, you've talked me into it." I turned to go but she called me back. "Sorry, I don't know your name."

"Just call me the Flowerpot Man. Everyone does."

"In that case, you'd better call me Lady Chatterley."

"Very well, m'lady." Before I could stop myself, I saluted again and left to get my boots.

I made a start on the first border. I'm all for dense planting but this had gone completely wild. So I took out the old and twiggy and made room for those needing to stretch. After a few hours I stepped back to admire my work.

Jane came out onto the patio. "You're good."

"I aim to please."

"Tea?"

We sat at a large wooden table on large wooden chairs and looked at her large London garden.

"Whoever originally planned this knew what they were doing."

"My husband loved it and I grew to love it through him, but with the divorce and everything, I've let it slip."

"Should I ask if he's started work on a new garden? Or did he just admire her window boxes?"

"He had a fling with a younger model in the office. I had hoped he'd come back, but he didn't. Thank God. Now he's happy with what's-her-name, so we can all get on with our lives. I made him pay for it big time, of course. I got this house and my freedom, he got the house in Antigua and the yacht. How about you?"

"Divorce isn't funny but you have to laugh."

I told her the story of Jamie, the boots, the parking ticket and the Big Issue seller. I tried to sound like a man of the world.

"When your husband leaves you for another woman it takes a while to find anything funny."

"Not all men are bastards."

"No, just the ones I fancy. Croissant?"

I nodded and followed her inside.

She opened the fridge. "Was it expensive?"

"I didn't think so at the time, the house was mine before we met and we had no children. We tried to have them but they didn't come along. What can you do?"

"Keep on trying?" She smiled. "Perhaps your luck's about to change."

She was definitely flirting. I was sure of it. And she was pretty nearly perfect.

"Maybe I'll win the Lottery this week, you never know. Pigs might fly." Then I remembered the two tickets I'd bought in Clitheroe on Saturday. "I haven't checked these yet."

She flicked the kitchen television on with the remote and found the correct Ceefax page, while bending over to put two croissants in the Aga. She was pretty nearly perfect from that angle, as well. I was transfixed. If you could bottle essence of woman, she had it.

I called out the first number. "Seven?"

"Yes."

"You're joking. Fourteen?"

"Yes again."

"Amazing. If I get three, it's an omen."

She laughed. "The Omen? You haven't got six six six, have you?"

"Yeah, tattooed under my scalp."

"I'm so scared." This was serious flirting.

"Twenty nine?"

"No, sorry. Next."

"Thirty one?"

"Bingo. You've got three." She seemed more excited than I was. "Keep going. See if we can get four."

I liked the 'we'. "Thirty five?"

"I'm afraid not."

"Last one. And the winner goes to …" I paused for dramatic effect, as if opening an imaginary Oscar envelope. "Thirty seven."

She screamed. "You've done it. You've got four numbers." She was bouncing up and down so much you'd think she'd won. I was stunned as much by her enthusiasm as my win.

"It might even pay for the most expensive cardboard coffin of all time."

She took a bite of croissant. It was like watching a porn movie starring a nun. She was Holly Golightly and Mrs. Robinson rolled into one. The sort of woman who could host a dinner party for twenty and make you feel you were the only person there.

"I've just got time to look at the fountain before I go."

The pipe had come away and the water needed changing but it was a simple job. Forty five minutes later it was ready.

I called in through the kitchen window. "Would you like to declare the fountain officially open again?"

"Hang on, I'll get a hat."

Two minutes later she emerged from the house in a stunning wide-brimmed pale yellow number, which framed her face perfectly.

"I declare this fountain open. Let it bring new Life into the garden."

She flicked the switch and the water shot up.

She screamed. "Alleluia. I love it. The Gods are dancing overhead and all is right with the world."

She smiled at me. Zap. A bolt from Heaven. And in that moment, I knew my world was about to change forever.

I lay looking up at the ceiling in the darkened bedroom. The street lamp lit the brickwork on the side of the window where the curtains had been pulled too tight. The bricks must have been there for over a hundred years. I looked at them carefully and tried to imagine the face of the man who laid them. Nothing that I'd worked on would still be around in a hundred years time. All my planting would have been replaced by three more generations of Flowerpot Men. And maybe we'd all be living in a plastic paradise with plastic flowers by then anyway. If nothing was permanent, what was the point of anything? In the grand scheme of things, a failed marriage here or a miscarriage there was no more important than a wave of the sea.

There was such a large pile of post, I thought it must be my birthday. Mostly bills and circulars, together with several letters for Liz. Had she bothered to inform anybody that she'd moved or was I supposed to be the dutiful ex-husband sticking on labels and forwarding her correspondence for the next twenty years? I'd never actually been inside her flat but the address label started off a chain of mental pictures. I didn't want to know where she was or what her daily routine there might be. I didn't want to know that in the summer she'd be sitting on a specific garden bench or that in the winter she'd be all cosy with Toby in front of a specific log fire, lying on the same Indian carpet that we used to roll around on together.

I took the last letter out into the garden with my coffee. I recognised the writing, it was from Christina, Liz's younger sister. It was a card with a black and white photo of a child dressed up as a bride. It was cute but the significance of the picture wasn't yet apparent. Christina and her husband Rob had an eighteen month old daughter, Phoebe, who was born on exactly the same day that Liz and I had discovered we were pregnant. An extraordinary day, poetic and symmetrical. We had been blessed from heaven. Fourteen weeks later our dreams were shattered when we lost our baby. So Phoebe had become our surrogate child and I would have gladly laid down my life for her.

The phone rang and brought me back to life. It was Ivy. I'd left a sweatshirt there yesterday and did I need it? I said I didn't but she asked me to collect it anyway as she was worried about it. It was a ruse for a midweek visit, of course. I didn't mind and said I'd pop in on my way to Hampstead.

I drank my cold coffee and re-read Christina's card. On the back was a PS. 'Phoebe wants you to be her Godfather. What do you think?' What did I think? I ran into the kitchen, searched through a pile of CDs and found Phoebe's tune. I whacked it up full volume. Christina, Rob, Liz and I had all danced her to sleep to it. I danced around the room for the first time in over a year, imagining she was with me.

"I'm going to be Phoebe's Godfather," I told Ivy the moment she opened the door.

"That's wonderful. She's a lucky child."

I couldn't stop smiling all morning.

"I'm going to be Phoebe's Godfather." I beamed at Jane.

"And will Liz be the Godmother?"

I hadn't thought about that. Would it be weird if she was? We both loved Phoebe, and if we were not going to be parents together, we could at least be Godparents, surely? Christina could easily have chosen someone else, someone less controversial. They must have consulted Liz, so she clearly harbours no resentment as far as Phoebe's concerned. Had they thought about it before or after my heroic duty on Pendle Hill with Jamie? It didn't really matter, the point was, they'd chosen me.

I was finishing a section of border with one last weed to go. It was a stubborn son of a bitch and as I tried to pull it out I shot forward catching my eye on a cane support. The pain was excruciating. I yelled out and Jane came running over.

"I'll get some saline. Hang on."

She was back in no time and after pouring several gallons of water over me, the eye was clear but the bruise was already starting to show.

"I don't think there'll be any long term damage." She led me to a wicker sofa in the conservatory and I lay down.

"Have some brandy."

I drank it but it didn't take the pain away.

Jane was wrapping some ice in a dishcloth. "What's your real name? I can't keep calling you The Flowerpot Man."

"Will."

"Sweet William. Suits you. Here you go." She put the ice pack on my eye.

"Ahh."

"It looks worse than it is."

"You're just saying that so I won't sue. I might phone one of those free injury lawyers they advertise on the telly."

Jane smiled. "You've got kind eyes. Well one kind one, anyway."

"Kind?

"Kind is good, believe me. I've had enough unkindness to last a lifetime."

"Sweet and kind? I'm never going to meet anyone if that's how I'm coming across."

"You should try Speed Dating."

"That's only for sad bastards. I'm not that desperate."

I wasn't about to tell her I was supposed to be going tonight.

"OK, you've got three minutes to chat me up. Starting now."

"These distraction techniques won't work, you know. I'm still going to sue."

"I'll go first, then. I'm Jane, Jane Ramsey. 39, ish. Born Midhurst. Went to Roedean. Married at 31. Divorced at 37. No children. Main hobby, photography. Wants to meet single, kind man for regular afternoon sex and laughter."

The distraction therapy had started working.

"Your turn."

"OK. Will Foster, 44. Born Hertfordshire. Went to Hemel Hempstead Grammar School then three years horticulture at Kew Gardens. Married at 39, divorced at 44. Sorry, divorcing at 44. Soon to be Godfather. Possibly blind in one eye. Likes eating out and holidays by water. Wants to meet Lady Chatterley look-alike for feudal encounters of the bedroom kind."

"How are you feeling now?"

"A little less litigious."

In the evening I went to hear Jack sing at The Underground for a bit of Dutch courage before going to my first meeting of Speed Dating Anonymous. It was a bit of a dive but he was really good and had a loyal following, mostly businessmen and locals.

The manager employed particularly pretty waitresses. I called one of them over and put on my best Sean Connery. "Vodka and tonic. Neither shaken, nor stirred."

Nothing. I nodded towards the piano. "He's good, isn't he? You should have heard him the night the Liverpool football team came in. One chorus of 'You'll Never Walk Alone' and they were all in tears. Oh, by the way, I'm Jack's younger brother." I emphasised 'younger'.

"We all love Jack." She spoke in a sexy Polish accent.

"So, you're from Poland? Don't tell me, Warsaw, right?"

"No, Slovakia, Bratislava."

OK, so my ear's not as good as it was.

Jack finished his song and came over. "What the hell happened to your eye, little brother?"

I told him the full story.

"It'll be a good talking point at the Speed Dating."

"Not sure I'm up to it tonight. With my eye and everything."

"Rubbish. You'll have a ball."

I ate a peanut and relished the rush of the first drink of the evening hitting the back of my throat. We were joined by a dark haired woman in a black trouser suit.

"This is Anna, the new assistant manager. I'd better get back to the grindstone. Good luck with the Speed Dating, little brother. I want to hear all about it tomorrow."

He returned to the piano and started playing, 'Hello Young Lovers' from The King and I. What a wag.

Anna turned back to me. "Speed Dating? Sounds interesting." But her dark, brown eyes looked at me with pity.

"And your name is …?" asked the bubbly girl on the door.

"Foster. Will Foster."

"Great." She handed me a badge, a self adhesive address label with 'WILL' written in red felt tip.

"Do I have to wear this?"

"There are some wonderful ladies here. Who knows? Tonight could be the night."

I hated being treated as a charity case.

She handed me a basket. "Pick a card and enter the free competition, Will."

I picked one. It was Posh Spice cut in half. "Have I won?"

"You have to find the other half of Posh Spice and then the two halves of her other half, i.e. David Beckham. Ask around, find all four halves, and you each win a bottle of champagne."

I walked on into the mayhem. I wanted it to be full of losers so I could turn around and walk straight out again. But at first glance, the room was full of people pretty much like me. The men were possibly a bit older and looked like middle managers of high street chains. Some single, some divorced and a few who probably still lived with their mothers, but they almost all looked embarrassed. The women were sharp eyed and altogether more confident.

"Have you got the other half of Kylie?" asked a woman in a cavernous black dress.

"Posh Spice. Sorry."

"Seen anyone you fancy?"

I didn't want to be blatantly rude. "I can't really see with this eye."

"I bumped into my ex at one of these last week. Embarrassing or what?"

I looked round for the bar. "No danger of my ex being here. She's all loved up."

"Time for you to move on then. What are you looking for?"

"How do you mean?"

"What's your type?"

"Don't think I've got one."

"Bollocks. You're a man. You all have a type. Small, thin and blonde. Right."

"Not necessarily. My wife was dark. I like women who smile. That's really important. I couldn't be with someone who didn't smile."

The cavernous black dress woman smiled manically.

"Excuse me. I need to find David Beckham."

Ten minutes later I was sitting opposite speed date number one. We had three minutes to chat before the whistle blew.

"Hi. I'm Will." I read her name tag. "And you must be 'SEX AND THE CITY GIRL'."

"It's not my real name, obviously. I was a bit scared, so I used a code name."

"Have you been to one of these before?"

"First time. You?"

"Yeah. First time."

"Why Sex and the City?"

"I want to find a man who shares my sense of humour. What would your code name be?"

"Some Mothers Do 'Ave 'Em."

"Interesting."

By the time we'd discussed my damaged eye, the whistle blew.

"Nice meeting you."

"You too."

We turned away and marked our cards, with a tick or a cross. If we both ticked each other, the organisers would put us in touch later via email. I was still internally deciding her fate when I was shoved in front of girl number two and the whistle blew for the start of the next three minutes.

"Well, hello again."

I read the label pinned to the cavernous black dress, 'ALL WOMAN'.

"I take it that's not your real name?"

She smiled more manically than before. "I am ALL WOMAN but you can call me Susannah."

"And what are you looking for, Susannah?"

"A real man. I can't stand all this New Man bollocks. What sort of man are you?"

"I hope I'm a Gentleman."

"That sounds like an Officer in wolf's clothing. Woof, woof."

"Do you think you'll find what you're looking for?"

"I think I might have found it already." She put her card on the table and with a flourish, ticked my box. "Well? Do I get a tick as well?"

"It's supposed to be a secret ballot."

"Playing hard to get. I like that."

I had to give her a tick as she was still watching me, but hoped I'd find some Tipp-Ex before handing in my card.

Next in line was 'RABBIT.'

"Hi. I'm Will." Three down, seventeen to go.

"Why Rabbit?"

"I had one as a child. I've got thirty five cuddly ones arranged on my bed at home."

Really? Next.

By the time I got to girl number fifteen, I decided this would be the last date before I made a mad dash for freedom.

"Hi, I'm Will. And you must be …" I looked at her label but was distracted by her chest. Not only was it huge, it was also barely covered.

"Have a good look while you're down there, why don't you?"

I wish I didn't blush so easily. "RACHEL. Suits you."

"Why?"

I didn't know why. "It's biblical, isn't it?"

"And I look like someone who reads the bible?"

"Do you?"

"I did as a child. Not any more. Adults don't, do they?"

"My father does."

The whistle went and I ran for the door. Rachel ran after me. "I've had enough too. You said you lived in Chiswick. You're not heading West are you?"

I ended up dropping her off at Hammersmith. I'd pulled up on the roundabout and cars were already hooting as they tried to avoid me.

She smiled manically. "This is where you ask for my number."

I didn't and so she grabbed my mobile and tapped in her number. "There, it's in your phone. Rachel. Remember?"

She leant forward showing off her massive cleavage, gave me a peck on the cheek and leapt out.

The evening could have been worse, I suppose. But I wasn't interested in Rachel. Or in any of the others. All I could think about was Jane. I'd have ticked her box. And I'd have given her ten gold stars, as well.

I was dreaming of Jane.

She set the kitchen timer, then opened a newspaper and bent over the kitchen table to read it.

"Now get to work and don't come back in till it rings."

I went out into the garden and started digging, occasionally looking up and watching her in the kitchen, still bent over the table. Liz had never suggested anything as sexy as this. But then again, neither had I.

The bell on the timer rang and I walked slowly towards the French windows. I lifted her skirt and felt the curves of her arse. Neither of us spoke a word. Then I turned her round to kiss her on the lips but she resisted.

"No, that's a different game. That's love. This is sex."

Fine by me, I wasn't about to start splitting hairs. But then that's exactly what I did.

When I woke she wasn't there. Of course.

I got up early and logged on to the Speed Dating website. I was intrigued to see if any of last night's women had ticked me. Not that I was interested in any of them, but I needed to know that I was still fanciable. Of course, if I hadn't ticked them, I wouldn't know if they'd ticked me, so before handing in my card I'd ticked them all. There was only one reply, from ALL WOMAN. I thought I'd be God's gift to the Speed Dating Circuit, singled out from all the other sad bastards. Obviously not.

I checked my emails. There was an amazing amount of porn generated spam but amongst it was one from Emma.

'To The Flowerpot Man from the Flowerpot Girl: You promised you'd take me out next Saturday. I haven't had my birthday present from you yet so make it a good one.

I'm your only niece, remember! Meet me at Victoria Station at 2 o'clock. Love you, TFG. xxx'

Where should I take a thirteen year old girl? The London Eye, Go-Karting, boating on the Serpentine? I'd better ring Jack and ask for suggestions, I hadn't got a clue.

I emailed back. 'To The Flowerpot Girl: The surprise is on for next Saturday. See you at two o'clock. Remember to pack your smile. Love you loads and a whole lot more, The Flowerpot Man. xxx'

Good, that's Saturday sorted. I hate weekends, all single people do. At least, single people who don't like being single. And, of course, it's only when you like being single, that you eventually meet someone. Life's a bitch.

I filled the kettle and turned on the CD player. Phoebe's tune was still in the machine. I was about to be a Godfather and next Saturday I'd be a Dad for a Day. Things were looking up.

I caught sight of myself in the mirror, my left eye was still in a bad way. I made the coffee and read the paper. It was all bad news, it always is. I turned to the horoscopes. 'Cancer: Love is in the air, but it's up to you to make the first move.'

I hadn't even put the toast in the toaster when the mobile went. Liz had mistimed it this time and it served her right. It was a text.

'IM NOT GR8. NO MORE TOBY. CALL ME IF U CAN. X.'

I couldn't believe my eyes. No more Toby? That's GR8 in any language. Should I call? No, I wasn't married to her anymore. If she wanted a shoulder to cry on because she's been dumped by her latest bloke, she'd better find someone else.

A few minutes later it rang again. I answered, of course.

"Tonight? The Tiger Bar, eight o'clock? Sure. Bye."

Jane brought me out a glass of water. It was a hot day and I'd worked up quite a sweat. I'd wanted to tell her that no one at the Speed Dating last night was a patch on her but I'd already started blushing. I think she noticed.

I wondered how she felt living in such a big place on her own. My house was small enough to do the Chinese clapping trick to liven it up, but if Jane tried that she'd end up with a repetitive strain injury. Perhaps she held regular dinner parties instead. Did she still wander from room to room feeling her ex-husband's presence? Or had she really moved on as much as she said?

"Off anywhere special?"

She was wearing a tight blue skirt and a funky top. She did a twirl to show it off. "This old thing? I've had it for ages." She was seriously flirting, just waiting for me to make the first move. I was sure of it. It was written in my horoscope this morning, after all.

So I drank the water down in one and tested the ground. "Here's to a new start. For both of us."

"I don't want to fall in love again. Love is messy and painful. I just want to have fun."

I raised my glass. "Here's to uncomplicated fun, then."

"And plenty of it." She had a wicked grin.

She was way out of my league. I could feel my cheeks reddening. Why hadn't this happened as a teenager? When you're young, sex was all about complication. Should we or shouldn't we? What goes where and when? My first girlfriend was the girl next door. We had our first kiss on her sixteenth birthday. I hadn't a clue what to do really. Luckily I found a book called Boys and Sex. It had diagrams and descriptions that made me horny as hell. I would read it for hours alone in the bathroom. As I was the more grown up and responsible one, I bought the companion book, Girls and Sex, for her and soon we were both getting horny in our separate bathrooms reading the theory of pleasures to come. It wasn't long before we joined forces and put the diagrams into practice. At the time it seemed incredible. A whole new world. But the sex was probably distinctly average. Would she remember me as a great lover? I doubt it. I hope, with time, she's forgiven my inexperience. I think I've learned a thing or two over the intervening years and I've never had any complaints so far. But then, of course, my wife has left me now.

It was ten to eight and The Tiger Bar was already buzzing. I knew Liz wouldn't be there till ten past as usual but I couldn't seem to break the habit of arriving early. I sat looking at the cocktail menu trying to look cool. The bloke at the next table was doing the same thing. I'm sure he had no intention of ordering a cocktail either but neither of us wanted to look as if we'd been stood up. The usual suspects were listed, 'Screwdriver', 'White Russian' and 'Snakebite' but strangely no 'Slow, Comfortable Speed Date Up Against The Wall'. A pretty, dark haired waitress put down a bowl of Bombay mix.

"I'll wait, I'm expecting someone. My wife." I hadn't called her that for ages but it felt good to say it.

"I'll be right back." She had a gentle Irish accent. The world was suddenly full of gorgeous women. I went back to the cocktails and was wondering what a 'Manhattan Mudslide' was when Liz arrived. She was wearing the black dress I'd bought her last Christmas and looked stunning.

She took off her coat. "Hello, stranger. Sorry, I'm late."

"You're not, it's exactly ten past."

"Very funny." She gave me a kiss. "Shall we get a

bottle?"

I sensed a drunken evening ahead. I called over the Irish waitress and ordered a bottle of cold Oyster Bay.

Liz took off her coat. "She's pretty."

"Can't say I noticed."

"Lying bastard."

"What the hell happened to your eye?"

"Walked into a lamp post."

We sat looking at each other for a moment, each second guessing the other's thoughts. Anyone could see why I'd married her. She had the looks, the charm and she still made me laugh. What the hell were we doing, throwing it all away?

"Thanks again for last weekend. It's been really hard, I still miss Jamie. And now Toby's gone as well ..." She trailed off and was about to start crying when the wine arrived. We went through the theatrical ritual of being shown the bottle, watching the foil being cut and the cork being pulled. This performance stopped the conversation dead in its tracks and always took much longer than when you did it yourself at home. I got Liz to taste the wine. That way I couldn't be bollocked for approving something she hated.

"Enjoy." The gorgeous Irish waitress put the bottle in the ice bucket.

I tried to think what we could drink a toast to. Jamie? Toby? Life, love and marriage? Better not. So I offered the best toast I could come up with. "To you."

"To us."

The wine was delicious.

"What really happened to your eye?"

I took a large gulp and put my glass on the table. "Now I'm single again, I suddenly seem to be surrounded by beautiful women. They've been after me for years apparently. A fight broke out and a leggy blonde from Sweden hit a scantily clad babe from Essex and I got caught in the crossfire."

"You're getting laid, aren't you? That's all I need. The day I finish with Toby, you tell me you've met the woman of your dreams. I need a fag." She stormed off towards the bar in search of nicotine comfort.

So it was alright for her to be knobbing Toby for months but if I have so much as a sniff, I'm a bastard?

She lit up. "Well are you?"

"I have met someone, yes." I hadn't actually kissed Jane yet, but it was just a matter of time.

"You're unreal, do you know that? You knew I'd be feeling low tonight, you could have waited, told me another time. You could have lied."

"We're not married anymore, we don't have to lie to each other."

"Is she blonde?"

"Is that important?"

"I always knew you'd leave me for a blonde airhead."

Not all blondes are airheads, surely? But to a dark haired divorcee who's just been dumped by Toby, they obviously are.

"She's not actually, no."

"Is she thin?"

I never asked these questions when she was seeing Toby the Wonder Horse.

"Yes, she is." I decided to go for it. "She's thirty nine, absolutely gorgeous, her tits are amazing and the sex is to die for. Any more questions?"

She looked at me with utter contempt, took a last drag on her cigarette and stubbed it out without taking her eyes off me.

"I was joking."

"No you bloody weren't."

"Look, I've had a really shitty six months and now I've met someone. I'm sorry but I'm not going to apologise for it."

She lit another cigarette. "I'm over the moon for you."

"What happened with Toby? Tell me, has he found someone else?"

"Why do you assume he left me? Look, I'm not completely repulsive, am I? Just because you left me it doesn't follow that every man will."

"What the hell are you talking about? You left me. In fact, I think your exact words were, 'Call yourself a proper man? You can't even give me children. If I'd fucked anyone else in London, I'd be pregnant by now.'" I was fuming.

"I never said that."

"Your exact words. And they're not words you forget in a hurry, believe me." I finished off my glass in one go and slammed it down spilling most of the Bombay mix.

"I'm sorry, we were going through a really bad time. We'd just had the miscarriage. I was upset. You are a proper man. Of course, you are." She poured us both another glass. "And I hope it works out with Barbie, I really do."

We drank our wine and calmed down for a second.

"Let's get this straight. You finished it with Toby, then? Is that right?"

"I want to have children. Well, that much we know." She stroked my hand. "Toby can't stand them. Never wanted them, never wants them. So I couldn't stay."

"It must have been hard."

"I loved him so much. He was wonderful. He was perfect." Not exactly what I needed to hear. "He was what I'd been looking for all my life, a man who loved me for who I was, with passion and strength and ..."

OK now she'd gone too far. "I know I may not live up to Toby the Wonder Dong but I'm not a total wally, you know. I may not be a proper man but I was a fucking good husband." I downed another glass. "You weren't the easiest person to live with yourself, you know." I was shouting.

"Oh and you were, I suppose?" she screamed, tossing her cigarette into my wine glass.

"Maybe this wasn't such a good idea." I tried to fish it out.

But she had already gone.

I could just make out the faint sound of Mike Oldfield's Tubular Bells ringing two floors below me. I'd changed the ringtone soon after Liz had moved out. On the way down to answer it, I noticed the paint smell was getting worse and I'd still forgotten to order the new carpet. I filled the kettle and checked the phone. One missed call, one new message. I dialled the answerphone. Liz sounded tired and drunk.

"Hi, it's me. Look I'm really sorry about storming off last night. I know you hate me doing that but I feel so lonely. I don't have anyone. My sister's away. You're all I've got. And I don't really have you anymore. Not properly. And in a month's time we'll be completely divorced and you'll end up marrying Barbie and I'll be an old maid, too old to have children. And you'll have hundreds of them. Life's so unfair. Why aren't you picking up? God, I hate these machines. Look, what I'm really saying is ring me sometime. Please."

The kettle boiled loudly, reached its peak and clicked off. I was in a trance, watching the steam as the Tubular Bells rang out once more.

"Thank God, you're there." She sounded desperate.

"I'm always here." I spoke quietly, as if she'd phoned The Samaritans.

"I can't do this."

"Can't do what?"

"Live on my own. I hate it. We could make it work again, couldn't we? You and me? We could, we just didn't try hard enough."

"You walked out on me, remember? When the going

gets tough, the tough don't go. But you went. And you've been drinking so you're bound to feel low."

"Great. Now you think I'm an alcoholic?"

"Liz, stop. Of course you're not an alcoholic. I know you miss Toby but it doesn't mean we should get back together just because it's over. I love you but I'm not in love with you. Not anymore. And you're not in love with me. You're just low."

"But soon I won't be able to ring you in case Barbie answers."

"She does have a name, you know."

"To me she'll always be Barbie."

"Fine, to me Toby'll always be Ken."

"Could we meet up later?"

"I don't think that's a good idea. You can't come running back every time something goes wrong. I didn't ring you in my hour of need. I talked to friends. It's the best way. Why not ring Paula?"

"Paula's pissed off with me for going on about Toby all the time. I've bored most of my friends senseless since we split up. Look, can I call you if I get bad?"

"Of course. I'm not totally heartless."

"I know, that's why I married you." She started crying again.

I took a deep breath and put the kettle on.

I was about to ring Jane's doorbell when I saw her note. 'Call me, Mr Flowerpot Man.' I rang her mobile.

"Sorry, had to pop out for the day. I've left the key under the third pot by the side gate. Will you be OK?"

"Of course. See you later?"

"Not sure when I'll be back. Might not be back at all. You never know my luck. Bye."

She was out on the town in search of uncomplicated

fun with someone else. I had misread all her signals and convinced myself that she was interested in me. Pathetic.

I missed lunch and worked straight through till three. I kept re-running all the conversations I'd had with her in my head. Had I come on too strong?

By four thirty there was no sign of Jane, so I started packing up my things. And by five I decided I'd been stood up. I hid the keys under the pot where I'd found them, drove home, ran a very hot bath and waved at every passing plane through the Velux window in the loft.

The Underground was quiet for a Thursday. Jack waved hello with his left hand, whilst still playing with his right. He was talking to a bloke who was probably requesting the latest David Gray or Dido. He finished off 'Father and Son' and joined me at the bar.

"I've just been given a tenner for singing "Lady in Red". I hate the wretched song but we'd all do it for a tenner, wouldn't we?"

Karl, the barman, gave him the glass of white he'd been promised earlier by a punter for playing MacArthur Park. It was a difficult song to sing and really deserved a glass of champagne but he seemed happy enough. I ordered my usual.

"Cheers, big brother." The vodka tasted good.

"Still trying to sow your wild oats in Lady Chatterley's garden?"

"I think she's moved on to pastures new. She says she wants uncomplicated fun but I don't think she wants it with me."

"Try suggesting a bit of role play. I had this girl friend once. We'd meet up in a pub as if we were complete strangers. She'd chat me up, take me home and shag me senseless."

"Sounds perfect."

"Didn't last long, of course. Eventually she met a complete stranger, took him home and married him. Another?"

I downed my glass and we had a second round. I told him about last night's fiasco in The Tiger Bar.

"Liz isn't your responsibility anymore."

The Tubular Bells rang out loudly.

"Don't answer it."

I couldn't help myself. It was a reflex. "Hi, Liz."

"Sorry about this morning. Listen, I've got to dash but just wanted to say I've had a good day and I feel much better. Bye."

I'm good too, thanks for asking.

"Do you think she'll get back together with Toby?"

"Only a matter of time. She can't be on her own for ten seconds. Whereas I'm so sorted, it's scary."

He was only eleven months older than me but he looked at me as if I was a child.

"You think you've got no baggage? Sorry to disappoint you, mate, but you're carrying around a complete set of Louis Vuitton on your shoulders."

He was right. Firstly, why did I always choose women with problems and secondly, why did I think I was the one to sort them out? I've sorted quite a few of them out, of course, but the moment they're back on their feet, they're off. I decided that next time it would be different. Next time I'd choose someone to sort me out. Yeah, right. I finished my vodka.

"What should I do with Emma next Saturday for her birthday?"

"She's been banging on about the Moscow State Circus. They're on Clapham Common for a fortnight. She loves her gymnastics. Perfect, I'd say."

Anna joined us at the bar.

"How's the new assistant manager tonight?" She

looked every bit as good as I remembered.

She looked at her watch and then at Jack. "Isn't it about time you entertained us all? This must be the longest performance break in history." He was supposed to play fifty minutes on, ten minutes off.

He took his wine over to the piano, smiled across at her and started playing. "This is for the beautiful Anna."

I wish I was that cool.

"So, Anna, you like to crack the whip, do you?"

She walked off to answer the phone. Maybe one day a woman would stay with me for more than twenty seconds without breaking my heart. And maybe I'd had enough vodka for one night. But I ordered another anyway. Jack was playing 'Somewhere' from West Side Story. Who needs therapy when you've got lyrics like that?

Anna clapped as he reached the end of the song and rejoined me at the bar. I couldn't take my eyes off her.

"Are you a boxer? That's quite a punch you took there."

My eye was getting better but still had the hallmarks of a major bust up.

"I'm a gardener, I was attacked by a particularly vicious lupin. Drink?"

"Sure."

I had a flash of inspiration. "If you put an ad in a Lonely Hearts column and you only had five words to describe yourself, what would they be?" Genius chat up line.

"You go first."

I thought for a moment, pausing for maximum effect, then spoke slowly, "Very. Good. Between. The. Sheets."

"Just between the sheets? What about on the kitchen floor? Or on a pile of coats at a party?"

I could have told her about the time on the beach in Skiathos but I felt I'd misjudged it already.

"My turn." She put down her glass.

How would she play this? Comic, sexy, ironic?

"Optimistic. That's one. Open. Free spirit. That's four." Deep in thought, she wrinkled her nose. I could watch her thinking for hours. "Loving. That's five."

Great answers. All of which made mine look pretty shallow. And I'm not. I'm just not very good at this dating business. When you're married you know where you are, you know what makes the other person tick. But when you're suddenly out there again, you don't know anything. You have to ask questions and when you do, you come across as either pushy or a prat. Or both. I tried another tack.

"What does your husband do?"

"I'm not married."

Bingo. "That makes two of us." I raised my glass, "To being single."

"To being engaged."

Bugger. "What does he do, your Knight in Shining Armour?"

"He sells sea shells on the sea shore. You ask a lot of questions for a man of the soil."

"Just piecing the jigsaw together. Let me guess. You wouldn't go for the stockbroker, city type. He's a penniless poet, right?"

"Something like that."

"Are you always this enigmatic?"

"Only to lupin victims."

Great, now she thinks I'm a victim. "I've got five more words for you."

She finished off her glass. "This had better be good."

"I'm. Not. Really. This. Shallow."

"That's six actually. You can't shorten 'I am' to 'I'm'. But I'll tell you what you are." Here it comes. "You're frightened and you've been hurt. You're recently divorced, I can tell from the white mark on your finger where your wedding ring used to be. You can't hide your secrets from me, Mr. Gardening Man."

"You're very intuitive, Anna. And you're very beautiful."

"And you're very drunk. Now, I've got five words for you."

I'd set myself up for this. Nobody to blame but myself.

She stood up, looked me straight in the eye and said, "It. Will. Get. Better. Soon."

I was in love and decided to go home before I made a complete fool of myself. So I got up, tripped over the bar stool and knocked myself out on the marble floor.

I dreamt I was crushed under a huge piece of granite. I could hardly breathe and was calling for help. But no one came.

Then I saw two little feet by my head.

"Hang on." The stone lifted and I could breathe again.

Standing there was the little boy who looked like me at the age of five. He was dressed in white and held out his hand to help me up.

"I heard you calling for help. I came as soon as I could."

"I thought I was dying."

He laughed. "You're not going to die for a long, long time."

"But everything feels so heavy."

"It does sometimes." He smiled and squeezed my hand. "But don't worry. It. Will. Get. Better. Soon."

I woke and lay motionless, looking up at the ceiling.

I've no idea how I got home. I know I was talking to Anna at The Underground and vaguely remembered falling over. I looked across to the other side of the bed, hoping she'd taken pity on me and stayed the night. No such luck, I was on my own. The bed in the loft was a small double, perfect for one or the occasional two. Not that I'd slept with anyone else there since Liz had left.

Eventually I found the phone and called Jack.

"I thought you were a goner, mate. But you were only out for a few seconds, thank God."

He and Anna had brought me home. They'd stayed with me till I'd gone to sleep, apparently. So she was not only an 'Open, Loving, Free Spirit' but an 'Angel of Mercy' as well. I should call into the bar and buy her a drink. Then I remembered she was already engaged. The best ones were always taken.

My head was throbbing so I decided against coffee and went for the tea and toast option. I was just buttering it when the phone rang. Not Liz but Jane.

"Are you coming in today? You're usually here by eight."

"I fell off a bar stool and hit my head. I've just got out of bed but I'm not sure it was such a good idea."

"Need a visit from the District Nurse? I'm sure I could rustle up a costume somewhere."

"I think that might finish me off completely."

I lay on the sofa and hoped the spinning would stop. The phone rang loudly. I didn't know where I was. I reached out, grabbed the handset and knocked the base to the floor. I thought a bomb had gone off. I could hear a voice but it was very faint.

"Hang on, let me turn this thing around." I'd been listening to the mouthpiece.

It was Liz. "Are you OK? You sound terrible."

"I am terrible. I nearly killed myself last night."

"I'm coming round. Stay there. Don't move."

"No, wait. Don't come round, please. I don't want you to." But it was too late, she'd hung up and was already jumping into the Batmobile.

The house looked like a tip, there was paint all over the bedroom floor and I looked like shit. I really didn't want her to see me like this. My life looked like it was falling apart and now she was going to witness it, in all its pathetic misery. I started to plump up the cushions. But for what? To impress Liz?

I could hear ringing. My head was about to explode. It was the doorbell. I got up slowly and walked the fourteen miles to the front door. It was Liz.

"You look terrible."

She plumped up the cushions and gently laid me down on the sofa. The sofa we'd conceived our baby on.

"What happened? I was so worried, I drove like a maniac."

"Nothing new there, then."

"I'll make us some tea." She had a poke around my fridge. "A carton of milk that's gone off and a bottle of champagne. You're quite the London bachelor, aren't you?"

"It's a dirty job but someone's got to do it." It was easy with Liz. We knew each other so well, we didn't have to try. I watched her busy herself in the kitchen. She was looking good, if a little tired. She would rustle up something from nothing, she always could. It must have been weird for her to be back here, washing our wedding present crockery in her old sink. I'd kept the plates, she'd taken the blender and the casserole dish.

She was standing motionless in front of the sink looking out at the garden.

"You OK?" I got up and put my arms around her waist. I kissed the back of her head and felt a teardrop land on my arm. She was crying quietly. We stood there silently holding on to each other. We didn't need words, we both knew the lyrics to this one.

We must have stood there ten minutes. Each of us in our own world of memories. Occasionally one of us would squeeze the other a bit tighter as images flew back and forth. Sunday breakfasts, dancing on the grass in the moonlight, listening to the rain outside, drinking wine by the fire. And sad times. There were plenty of those but I couldn't picture them now. I panicked, as you do when someone dies, that you'll never remember them again. I had to remind myself of the bad times or I'd go mad.

She dried her eyes. "I loved it so much."

"Being married?"

"That too, but I meant being with Toby."

I pulled away angrily. We'd clearly been in very different places. "Does he really mean that much to you?"

"You don't want to hear about this now, do you?"

"Not particularly, but that's never stopped you before."

"Look, let me pop out and get us some supper. I'll cook. What do you fancy?"

"Comfort food."

"I'll take your keys. Is that OK? You can trust me, you know, I'm still your wife."

She kissed me on my forehead on the exact spot of the bump. It hurt like hell but I don't think it was deliberate.

I must have dozed off, because when I opened my eyes it felt like Christmas. The house was full of candles and Liz was happily cooking away. Why couldn't I do what she does? The house felt alive again. I'd lit candles and cooked for myself but it's not the same when you do it for one. The longer I spent preparing a meal, the sadder I felt when I ate it. So I lived on pasta instead. Bish, bash, bosh and out of the kitchen. She looked over and saw me watching her.

"Welcome back to the land of the living."

"You didn't have to do all this."

"It's a thank you for driving me to Lancashire. I promised I'd repay you one day and I keep my promises."

"Do you?"

"I do."

She'd done sausage and mash. Butchers sausages and spring onion in the mash, like she used to do. We chatted away but steered clear of anything controversial. She filled me in on the hospital gossip and news of mutual friends. I told her about Ivy, Jack and Emma, but decided not to bring up Jane.

"There's something I need to ask you." She spoke gently. "Don't jump down my throat, hear me out, please."

"If you want the house, you can have it. I'm bankrupt

anyway. My wife took me to the cleaners and there's nothing left." I was joking. Sort of.

"Don't be angry. It's nothing major it's just ..."

"Take it, you've already taken my life, what else is there?" I was overacting badly, trying to be funny. It just made me look pathetic.

"I'll come straight out with it. Can I have the low coffee table?"

"You're having a laugh. I use that table every day, it's the centre piece of the room. If you take it, I'll have to buy another one and I've already bought that one."

"No you didn't. I paid for it."

"You were going to pay for it, yes, but you had no cash on you as usual, so I paid for it."

"The point is, I chose it."

"You should have asked for it when you walked out."

"I didn't walk out. We both agreed it was over. Oh, this is ridiculous. Why are we arguing over a silly coffee table?"

"Why is it silly?" I was getting louder.

"It isn't, it's lovely. And I chose it."

"And I paid for it."

Liz picked up a coin from the table. "Let's toss for it, then."

"OK, but I get to toss because I paid for it." I was behaving like a child.

"Child."

"Heads it's mine, tails it's yours." I was behaving like a loser.

"Loser."

I found a coin and spun it in the air. "Heads."

"You're pathetic."

"No, Toby's pathetic."

"This isn't about Toby."

"Heads it is. It stays here. Quite right too, as I paid for it." I put the coin in my pocket.

"All I wanted was a memory, a lousy coffee table, and you even deny me that."

"We agreed everything before you left." I was trying to be reasonable.

"You mean your flash lawyer did?"

"He wasn't flash and he couldn't have agreed it all on his own, could he?" God, she could be irritating. "He was quick, which is what we wanted, so you could buy your flat and we wouldn't have to live under the same roof and end up arguing over a bloody stupid coffee table."

"If it's that bloody stupid, give it to me." She was screaming.

So I did. I even helped carry it into her car. Now I have no money, no wife and no coffee table. It just gets better and better.

It was Saturday, a day for mooching about doing things. Sunday was a day for mooching about not doing things. If ever I felt lonely it was on a Sunday. But Saturday was a day for 'Projects'. So I started a mental checklist. Order the bedroom carpet and look for another coffee table. Also I wanted to find a new mirror for the kitchen. The one I had now belonged to Liz's grandfather. She'd asked me to hang on to it for a while but I didn't want it anymore, especially after last night. I'll put a sticker on the back of the new one, 'I chose and paid for this myself - don't think of asking for it when you leave, as refusal often offends.' And lastly, I had to book the Moscow State Circus for Emma next Saturday. But before any of that, I was off to have brunch with Jack and later we'd probably take Emma on a boat trip to Greenwich. I love Saturdays.

Jack was reading the Racing Post at our usual table.

"Gardener's Boy. Two thirty at Kempton."

"I'm not backing it just for the name. I once painted my front door Sorrento Sky because I'd liked the name but it was still a terrible colour."

"Stick ten quid on Filly's Gold in the two o'clock at Newbury, then. Can't lose, mate."

"Fool's Gold?"

"Trust me, I know the people who know. Have I ever let you down?"

"Yeah, the last three times." But I gave him twenty anyway, I was feeling lucky. A win might even pay for the new table.

We had the usual Full English. I wavered for a second, worrying about my cholesterol level but I gave in quickly.

It was Saturday, after all.

Jack went off to pick up Emma from ballet and we arranged to meet by Westminster Pier at two thirty. "I'll bring your winnings."

I headed off to Portobello Market, stopping off at the cashpoint on the way. A wad of notes might help with the bargaining.

I found a great old mirror. It was the real thing, not that TV make-over show, mock-distressed MDF look. This one was genuinely distressed. It was a mirror that said, "Relax, I've seen it all before." So I bought it for two hundred, having got twenty five knocked off for cash. They probably only expected to get two hundred anyway, but I still felt I'd won.

I'd seen a table as well but as it was even bigger than the one I'd donated last night to the Streatham Home for the Recently Divorced, I tried a couple of other shops. I was about to give up when I spotted the perfect one in a window next to a gold Chaise-long. It was ten inches shorter in length and a little lower than the old one. It was perfect, the elder statesman of coffee tables. Polished enough to command respect but sturdy enough for elder statesman to put their feet on.

"It's a bit small but it might just do." Never look too keen. "How much?"

"Six hundred and seventy pounds, sir."

At that price, I'd quite like the old one back, Liz.

"What about cash?"

"Six hundred and seventy pounds, sir."

"I'm not from the VAT office. Honestly, I'm a gardener." I gave him my card.

"Very interesting, sir." He held my card with contempt. It did have a bit of mud on one corner but he didn't have to take that tone. He handed the card back to me. "If I want some gardening advice, I'll know where to come."

It was a lovely table but I still had to pay for a new bedroom carpet so I had to let it go. If I'd risked fifty quid on Filly's Gold and it had won, I'd have bought it.

I chose a biscuit coloured carpet that rejoiced in the name of Cromer Sand. They could fit and deliver it next Saturday. I'd be taking Emma to the Moscow State Circus that afternoon but they promised they'd come first thing.

I carried the mirror home and held it up on the wall. It looked great, so I marked the height with a pencil and started drilling. There was an almighty flash and I was jolted backwards. I'd gone through a cable. I assumed it would be safe being an outside brick wall but I'd forgotten about the hidden cable for the security light. Now I'd have to rewire that, which would mean chipping away at the wall.

I was covered in plaster when the mobile rang. I pressed the green button with my clean wrist and spoke into it as it lay on the worktop.

It was Jane. "Just checking you're in the land of the living."

"By the skin of my teeth, I nearly killed myself drilling through a cable."

"Take care, that's two of your nine lives gone. Listen, I was going to ask you to a party tomorrow night."

"I'll have to check with my social secretary."

"Wear a dinner jacket. My ex will be there and I want you to look like James Bond."

"I'm only there to make him jealous?"

"Of course. Thanks, Will." She even managed to make my name sound erotic.

I crouched on the floor and looked at myself in the mirror. My eye had almost healed. I just hoped her husband wouldn't get jealous at the party and punch me in the other one. I left the mess in the kitchen and headed off to Westminster.

Emma was waving frantically from the top deck. I was running to the gate as the horn was blowing.

"Hey, it's The Flowerpot Man. You nearly missed the boat."

She flung her arms round me and I felt a million dollars. She had long dark hair and deep brown eyes. It wouldn't be long before she'd be breaking hearts.

"How's my Flowerpot Girl?" I gave her a kiss on the cheek.

"I've just been picked for the school play, I'm going to play the Wicked Witch of the West. Will you come?"

"Of course, but you're too pretty to play a witch."

"They use make-up, silly. Don't you know anything?"

London looked great from the river. We'd been on this trip many times but I preferred it when it was cold, as most people stayed below and we had the deck to ourselves. Today was sunny, so it was packed on top. Mostly tourists with their cameras, snapping away madly as they passed Tower Bridge. Liz and I used to bring Emma here all the time. You could probably spot the three of us in holiday albums all over the world. I used to offer to take pictures for people, but I don't anymore since a Japanese woman hit me in the stomach for dropping her camera overboard by mistake.

The commentary started up. We knew it word for word and it made us laugh. "We're not professional guides, we just point out things on the way," they'd say. "And please feel free to show your appreciation by putting a couple of quid in the old Captain's hat as you leave." They generally stopped the chat once we left the city as there were fewer landmarks. So the journey to Greenwich past Docklands and the Dome was more peaceful.

I bought Emma an ice cream. She offered me a lick.

"You can't have any flake, though. You can just have some ice cream."

"But I thought I was your favourite uncle?"

"You're my only uncle, silly. Where are we going next Saturday?"

"Wait and see, it's a surprise."

"My birthday's on Thursday. I'll be a teenager by then."

"I know your birthday's on Thursday. But you'll have to wait till Saturday for your present. We'll have fun. Just you and me."

"Can Liz come too? I like her and I don't want you to get divorced."

"It's a bit too late to stop now."

"Do you still love her?"

"I'll always love her. But not as much as I love you." I gave her a hug.

"Then why don't you want to be married to her? Have you got a new girlfriend? Is that why she left, did you have an affair?" She sounded like a teenager already.

"No, it's complicated. You'll understand one day."

"I want to understand now."

But how could she when I didn't understand it myself? Jack came to the rescue and handed me a betting slip.

"Filly's Gold romped home, mate. Twenty quid at eight to one. That's a hundred and sixty smackeroonies."

The day was getting better and better. I was twenty five up on the mirror and now this made it a hundred and eighty five up on the day. Tower Bridge had never looked so good.

On the way home, I decided it was time to start cooking properly again. I'd put a new sign on the fridge door, 'No more pasta'. It could replace the current one,

'No more nurses'. Though I suspect that should stay up a bit longer. I stopped off at the supermarket and bought some chicken breasts, potatoes and green beans. Healthy and not that difficult. I used to cook for myself all the time before I was married, but Liz was so good that I generally left it to her. I hoped I still remembered how to do it. I also bought a bottle of wine and some cashew nuts. Saturday night in on my own and a film on the telly. Great.

Liz was standing at the door when I got there.

"I was just passing and wanted to apologise for last night."

"And you thought you'd return the coffee table?" Oscar Wilde couldn't have put it better himself.

"Let me give you a hand." She took the carrier bags and waited for me to open the door. The alarm gave me thirty seconds to punch in my numbers.

"Have you changed the code?"

I nodded, even though I hadn't.

"What on earth … ?" She saw the devastation in the kitchen. I'd forgotten how far plaster dust travels and I hadn't had time to clean up.

I showed her my purchase.

"But I thought you liked Granddad's mirror?" She looked genuinely offended.

"I do, but I think you should have it back."

"You probably want to make a fresh start anyway."

Yes, without my ex wife popping round every five minutes and ruining my Saturday night.

She took out her purse. "Why don't I buy it for you? I'd like to. How much was it?"

I told her.

"Maybe we could go halves?" That's my Liz.

She started busying herself in the kitchen but I wanted to do it myself, that was the whole point of not having pasta. I wanted to see if I could do it on my own.

"Hope I'm not gatecrashing. I can go if you want."

"No, it's OK. It'll stretch to two and you're probably a

better cook anyway."

"How on earth will you cope without me, my poor darling?"

At this rate, I'll never know.

The chicken breasts were cooked to perfection. The portions were a little on the small side being originally bought for one but we were getting on well and the wine was going down a little too easily.

Liz was eyeing up the new mirror. "Looks good, fancy swapping it for mine?"

"Don't push it."

"Is there any more wine?"

"Help yourself."

She'd already got a bottle from the fridge and had started opening it. "I remember when I first saw you at Christina's 30th. You'd broken your arm and asked me to sign the plaster cast."

"What did you write?" I knew perfectly well but I wanted to hear the story again.

"I'm potty about the Flowerpot Man."

"And then you said, 'That's a great name for your company.'"

"I'm a genius."

"Were you potty?"

"I was crazy about you. It's just …"

"That was then and this is now?"

"I had a thing for men in plaster casts, what can I say?"

"I could break my arm again. Do you want me to dive into an empty swimming pool?"

"I want you to be happy."

We were sitting on the floor in front of the fire. She moved closer, took the glass out of my hand and kissed me.

"What are you doing?"

"Have you forgotten?" She kissed me again.

I thought I had. I'd brought down the shutters, bolted the doors and locked away those memories for good. I'd built a ten foot wall around my heart to block them out. But with one kiss she had blown the whole thing to smithereens.

I began to sweat. "I only asked you to blow the bloody doors off."

She continued to kiss me. Please stop. It was so unfair. I was powerless.

She took my hand. "Close your eyes."

"We shouldn't." I was falling fast.

"Shh."

It was no use. I went like a lamb to the slaughter. It would be wonderful. It was wonderful now. But I'd pay for it tomorrow. And the next day. And the day after that.

DAY
10

I woke to find Liz had gone. I looked around for a note but there was nothing, just the indentation in the pillow where she'd been sleeping. She'd got up and left the ex-marital bed without a word, after the best night she'd probably had for ages. It couldn't have been that good with Toby. We knew each other's buttons and they still worked. And it wasn't like the feeble attempts at baby making that had passed for sex over the last few years, it was amazing. I know she was probably still in love with Toby and I was falling for Jane, but none of that seemed important last night.

"Morning." Liz had made some coffee.

"Hi." I was beaming from ear to ear.

"I've still got what it takes, then?"

"Last night was amazing."

She sipped her coffee. "Glad to hear it. But you're not going to turn into a bunny boiler, are you?"

I got her message loud and clear. "No, strictly a one off."

"That way we can stay friends."

Last night had been extraordinary but I knew the same old problems would soon come flooding back and it wouldn't be long before we'd be arguing again over another stupid coffee table.

She stretched her leg out and touched her toes. She was in good shape. "We've never done it here in the loft, have we?"

"We've never done it in the bathroom or the hall, either."

"Remember the lift episode in Dublin?"

We'd stopped between floors and were doing the scene from Fatal Attraction, when the fire alarm went off. It was one of those checklist things. In a lift, tick. On a beach, tick. Mile High Club, tick. They all had to be done. And now, In the loft, tick. I wondered if this would be my last ever tick with Liz?

She'd got back into bed and was sitting next to me drinking her coffee. Her foot was playing with mine.

"What are you after, young lady?"

"It's Sunday morning and I'm in bed with my husband. Any objections?"

"Not from me." I dived below the covers and pretty soon we were swimming in duvet land.

If I smoked, this would be the moment for the post coital fag. Sex hadn't been this good when we were married. It hadn't been this good before we were married. 'Forget Viagra, take Divorce. It reaches the parts other legal processes cannot reach.'

She snuggled into my neck. "Will you marry me?"

"If you divorce me first."

We fell asleep in each other's arms and were woken half an hour later by the Tubular Bells.

"Let's leave it."

She looked at me. "Who is it?"

"How the hell do I know?"

"Aren't you going to answer it?"

"No."

"Got something to hide?" Suddenly I was in bed with the Spanish Inquisition.

"It's probably work."

"On a Sunday?" Now she was Sherlock Holmes.

I threw back the duvet in temper and sent the coffee cup flying, shedding its load down the far wall. I picked up the phone. Withheld number. Great.

"I have no idea who it was. Satisfied?" I sat on the bed and watched the last few drops of coffee reach the skirting board.

"You lost your temper, don't blame me." She was getting out as I was getting in.

"You're not going, are you?" But we both knew the answer to that one.

It was only nine thirty and the long sprawl of an empty Sunday stretched out in front of me. Why did the mobile have to go off when it did? If it hadn't, we might have gone for a lazy walk in the park and watched an afternoon movie. But I knew if it hadn't been the phone it would have been something else. It was as if, with us, the touch paper was always ready to be lit, willing a spark to send the whole thing skywards.

I managed to get the worst of the coffee stain off the wall but it now looked like a damp patch. Why couldn't this have happened in the new cappuccino coloured bedroom downstairs? Mind you, I'll probably repaint the entire house once the divorce comes through anyway and hopefully by then Liz won't stay over every time she's lonely, start a row and force me to repaint it again.

I spent the rest of the day in the garden. I'd planned to do some cutting back but as the sun was shining, I slumped into my old deck chair and read the Sunday papers. I went straight to the gardening section, as usual, to check that no one had pinched my idea for a new column, 'The Seven Ages of Gardening Man'. Each article would be specially designed for a different age group. Toddler, teenager, single, married, parent, divorced and widowed. There would be specific planting suggestions for colour, scent and ease of maintenance. I was still sure it could work really well but I'd never got round to writing it. Instead, I slept in the sunshine after having made love to my wife four times in the last twelve hours. Tick that box,

Toby.

I found my dress shirt hanging at the back of the wardrobe. It really needed a clean but I didn't have time, so I just ironed it instead. I liked wearing a dinner jacket, the only danger was being mistaken for a waiter.

I felt particularly cool driving to Hampstead in my old van, James Bond would have been proud. Halfway there I wished I hadn't driven as I fancied a drink tonight. But I thought I'd better keep my wits about me with Lady Chatterley's ex-husband Jeremy on jealousy patrol.

Jane opened the door. "You can shake me or stir me anytime you like, Mr. Bond. Martini?"

I pretended my right hand was a Walther PPK. "My name is Man. Flowerpot Man." Pathetic.

"You're in good spirits." Yes, I slept with my ex-wife last night.

"You look pretty hot yourself." She was wearing an off the shoulder black cocktail dress that hugged her chest and didn't do her arse any harm either. She had clearly dressed to inflame her ex.

"Let's take my car, I'd hate to get mud on this dress before we get there."

We got into her classic Mercedes 500 SL soft top. Now I was Steed in The Avengers. Lots of boxes were being ticked tonight. She was a good driver but was frighteningly fast. I casually checked my seat belt was firmly in place.

"I thought you liked speed, Mr. Bond?" She accelerated even faster.

"I do, I just don't particularly want to die before we get there."

The party was in Little Chalfont. The drive was impressive but the house took your breath away. How on earth do people end up in such a place? It certainly wasn't bought from the honest toil of gardening. She parked between a Bentley and an Aston. I wished we'd come in my van, it would have stood out well, but I suspect Jane had wanted to make a different impression. She checked her reflection in the car window, took off her sunglasses and set off. She walked like a superstar on a red carpet, full of arrogant sexuality.

"OK. Showtime." She took my arm.

Then she spotted the enemy, a leggy blonde in a long peach number.

"There she is. What's she done to her hair?"

It looked pretty good to me. "I suppose it does look a bit odd."

"Odd? What do you mean? She looks like a poodle."

Ivana, for that must have been her name, was smoking a thin cigar and towering over several shorter men who clearly had no choice but to put her on a pedestal. They were laughing loudly, though I suspect she wasn't that funny.

"I'm afraid we haven't met." Jane offered her hand.

There was an awkward silence as Ivana looked her up and down. Jane held her ground.

"I'm Jane. I used to be married to Jeremy but, of course, you know that."

Ivana was playing the silent card. Maybe she didn't speak English.

I tried to save the situation. "My name is Bond. James Bond." That should have crossed the international divide but Ivana looked at me as if I was a pre-pubescent teenager and still said nothing. I ploughed on. "I'm sorry, I didn't get your name."

She took a long drag on her thin cigar and then blew the smoke in my face. "They call me Pussy. Pussy Galore."

The dwarf acolytes roared with laughter.

Jane adjusted the sunglasses on her head. "Are you sure that's what they call you?"

I decided it was time to play the diplomat. "I think we could all do with a glass of champagne."

"I could do with a Magnum." She led me towards the house.

"Jeremy must be off his head, she's a nightmare."

"That's him over there." She pulled in her stomach a fraction.

He was talking to a couple of the short guys from earlier. He smoked a fat cigar and looked like the Chairman of a public company.

"Jane, darling, you look magnificent. Doesn't she guys?" The little people nodded their approval. "You know, I used to be married to this beauty. Must have been mad to let her go. What went wrong, my angel?"

"You know perfectly well. You couldn't keep yourself zipped up for two seconds."

Jeremy threw his head back and laughed loudly. "You see guys, she found me out. Not my problem if I've got a massive libido."

The little people were beside themselves.

"And who is this?" He put his arm round my shoulders as if we were great buddies. We weren't.

"This is James."

"And what are your intentions, young man?" His volume was unbearable.

"I intend to get very drunk."

Jeremy almost wet himself, the little people shat themselves and Jane was over the moon.

"Game, set and match, I think."

The dining room was as grand as the rest of the house and I found myself, rather unexpectedly, seated next to the hostess who turned out to be very funny. At least she found me funny, which is almost the same thing. On my left was a slightly deaf elderly lady with interesting, if eccentric, political views. She also found me funny but only the second time round, as I had to repeat everything. Jane was stuck between two bankers and when they both lit up after dinner, I thought I'd lost her in a cloud of cigar smoke.

I'd drunk far too much but was still sober enough to give both ladies my card. They probably had their own garden contractors but it was worth a shot. This was the year to build up my business and this was a great opportunity.

The elderly lady read my card. "The Flowerpot Man."

"That's right."

"So you sell flowerpots? Are you wholesale or retail?"

"No, I'm a garden designer."

"Do you have a television programme? They all do nowadays, don't they?"

"Well, I don't, but I am very good."

"You have confidence, I like that in a man. And you're a wholesaler, you say?" Dear God.

The hostess was easier. "My niece has just bought a garden flat in Brook Green, she could probably do with a hand. I'll get her to call you. She's called Charlotte but everyone calls her Charlie."

Jane whispered in my ear. "Shall we go? I've only had two glasses as I'm driving, so I need to get home sharpish and open a bottle."

We drove home almost breaking the sound barrier with the roof down playing Barry White at full volume. She pulled into her drive far too fast, knocking over a flowerpot.

"Don't worry, you can order me another one at wholesale."

We sat back looking up at the sky, listening to the stereo.

"Jeremy looked sad, didn't you think?"

"It's his loss."

"I miss him. He's a pig but I still miss him."

"I wonder if Liz thinks I'm a pig?"

"Probably."

By the time we'd polished off a couple of bottles of

white it was three thirty. I should really have gone home but I was too drunk to drive. I hadn't thought this through. Tomorrow was Monday and I had to be at Ivy's by nine o'clock sharp.

"You can crash in the spare room, but no creeping along the corridor after dark." It almost sounded like an open invitation but after my exploits with Liz last night and this morning, I was ready to keel over.

She showed me into a spare room. It was all white carpets and crisp linen with some great photography on the wall.

"Did you take these?" I was impressed.

"What do you think?"

"They're brilliant."

"I'll take one of you, if you like."

"Great. But maybe not when I'm this pissed."

"Always the best time." She pushed me onto the edge of the bed and grabbed her camera. She clearly knew what she was doing.

I started smiling stupidly. More Jimmy Tarbuck than Jimmy Bond.

"Don't do anything, just look at me. I'm the lens."

I was trying to focus.

"Got it. I've captured your soul, Mr. Flowerpot Man."

"Then take good care of it. It's the only one I've got."

I woke in a strange bed. Everything around me was white. I checked the time on the mobile. Eight thirty six. Shit. I'd set it for ten to eight but I must have slept right through.

I was hopping about on one leg, trying to put a sock on, when a blurry-eyed Jane stuck her head round the door. I was wearing a pair of old boxer shorts, a grey T shirt and one black sock. I hadn't wanted this to be Jane's first glimpse of me in a state of semi-undress.

She pretended to cover her eyes. "Sorry, I should have knocked."

"I'm late for Ivy."

"Don't let her see you like that, you'll give her a heart attack."

"She's ninety three."

"So? I'll be rampant at a hundred and three."

The traffic was terrible. It took me fifteen minutes to get past Spaniards Inn. I was going to be at least forty minutes late and Ivy would convince herself I'd had an accident if I didn't ring. You can change plans at the drop of a hat when you're young but in your nineties, a routine is all there is to hold onto. I tried to plug the hands free cable into my mobile as I drove, but this was so fiddly that I almost caused an accident and a police car pulled me over. Luckily I got off with a verbal warning.

Ivy opened the door, looked at her watch and wagged her finger. She was wearing her apron and had already started polishing. There were only half a dozen silver pieces left now but this routine had been set in childhood, when her life was much grander. Like many women of her generation, she'd never married. In her late teens, the First World War had taken away half the available men, so she became a teacher. In her thirties, the Second World War had taken them away again. As a child I never understood why there were so many elderly spinsters. Only as an adult could I understand their situation, and so my visits to Ivy were in some sense my generation's way of making amends.

Her garden was small in comparison with Jane's but it was cosy and peaceful, and I knew I'd miss coming here when she'd gone. She waved from the kitchen window that the tea was ready. I was almost done anyway and the last bits would keep till next week.

"Fetch the tray. That's right." Everything was laid out in the usual way. There was comfort in Ivy's order, and I'd have worried if the milk jug had been on the wrong side of the pot or if one of the teaspoons had been missing.

She poured the tea. "You look tired."
I took a bourbon biscuit. "I'm fine, really."

I liked the way Ivy worried about me. Everyone should have someone who cares that much.

"You married too quickly. I'd hate you to make that mistake again." When Ivy looked at you like that, you took her seriously.

Four years ago, when I'd told her I was getting married, she'd burst into tears. She had never really approved of Liz but then I doubt she'd have approved of anyone. In some strange way I'd become the gentleman caller from one of her Jane Austen novels.

"Don't worry, I'm not getting remarried in a hurry. I'm concentrating on the business."
"That's right." She poured a second cup. "Stay away from women. Right away from them. It's too soon."
I didn't mention that I'd slept with Liz two night's ago. Or that last night I'd stayed over at Jane's.

"I worry what will happen to you after I've gone."

Was there something she wasn't telling me? "You're not going anywhere, Ivy."

She sat back in her chair. "Now tell me about the dinner party. Was it what I'd call a proper dinner party? Or was it just supper in the kitchen?" She'd told me of some very grand affairs she'd been to as a child before the War.

"You would have approved."

"How wonderful." She clasped her hands together. "I haven't been to a dinner party for twenty three years. Not a proper one." The world of her childhood had gone forever.

"Why don't I take you out for dinner, Ivy? Just the two of us. What do you say?"

You'd think I'd given her the Crown Jewels. But she was worried about getting in and out of cars. "Why don't you come here? I could manage something simple."

"How about this Friday? I'll even wear my dinner jacket."

I thought she was going to start dancing about on her little lawn then and there. She'd been a good dancer in her time and once or twice over the years she'd invited me into the sitting room to play her old seventy eight records and I'd caught a glimpse of her former glory.

"Have another bourbon. That's right." She held out the plate, but she was already in another world.

Jane was out when I got to Hampstead, so I found the key under the usual flowerpot and let myself in. The bottom of the garden had a dark corner which needed something to brighten it up. I remembered spotting an old wooden water barrel in her garage. The wood was a bit dark but I gave it a quick coat of white paint from a half used tin I found next to it. Once I'd planted the New Zealand Flax, it would be all sorted.

I heard a scream from the terrace. "What the hell have you done?"

"Don't you like it?"

"That's Jeremy's mother's water barrel. You've ruined it. What possessed you to go rummaging around the garage destroying family heirlooms?"

I didn't know what to say. "I'm sorry."

"Sorry, isn't good enough. What am I going to tell Jeremy?"

"Did he really love it?"

"His mother gave it to him on his fourteenth birthday. It came from the stables at Chatsworth, apparently. It was worth a small fortune. Winston Churchill's horse drank from it the night before the Second World War started."

"Shit."

Her face was like thunder. I could have offered to strip the paint off but I'd probably damage it further in the process. If I hadn't totally destroyed it already.

Jane could see I was devastated. "I'd better be ready with my camera. Jeremy's face'll be a picture."

"I'm glad you can see the funny side. Jeremy looks like a man who'd be only too happy to take legal action."

"He won't take any action at all. And shall I tell you why?"

"Please do."

"Because in the first place it's not his mother's and in the second place I've been meaning to dump it for ages. It's worthless."

"Worthless?"

"Garbage."

"And it's not his?"

"No."

"So you've been winding me up?"

"I'm afraid I have. Just couldn't help myself. Sorry." She was almost crying with laughter.

"You are a very, very bad girl."

"Aren't I just? You'll have to think of a suitable punishment for me, won't you?"

I thought of several.

I'd made a rough sketch for the new planting and had a list of what we needed to buy, so we arranged to go to Covent Garden at six o'clock the next morning. I still got a buzz from the market and I knew she would too.

The mobile rang in my trouser pocket. A text.

'THIS IS CHARLIE. MY GARDEN NEEDS YOUR HELP. PLS CALL.'

Great. Another job. I was laughing away with my fantasy woman and work was pouring in. I smoked a metaphorical cigar.

It rang again. Another text.

'THKS FOR GR8 EVE. SRRY IT ENDED BDLY. FNCY CFFEE THUR?'

Liz's texts were getting more and more contracted. Was she worried she was getting older and running out of time to write properly? I was about to text back "X". But I thought it would be misconstrued as a kiss and not a contraction of "NO".

I typed in, 'SO YOU CANT LIVE WITHOUT ME AND FANCY BEING FANCIED ON THURSDAY?'

After a few moments she replied, 'I BEG YOUR PARDON?'

That seemed odd, so I checked my Sent Messages. Unfortunately I'd used predictive texting and had actually sent 'FANCY BEING DAMAGED ON THURSDAY?'

Jane popped her head out of the kitchen window. "As it's such an early start in the morning, why not stay over? There are plenty of spare rooms. I could rustle up some dinner and we could go straight from here in your van."

If that wasn't a come on, I didn't know what was. "Can't, I'm afraid, I didn't bring my toothbrush."

"There's a spare one in the bathroom. Any other objections?"

It had to happen sooner or later, sex with another woman. It was a rite of passage, drawing a line under the marriage. And tonight was going to be the night. I just hoped I was ready. She was gorgeous and I'd been dreaming of her for days, but I had no idea how I'd feel when I actually got down to it. I began to sweat.

I heard a champagne cork pop. Chocks away. Oh God.

"I've just been offered an exhibition."

She had to choose twenty five of her best pictures but only had two weeks to get it all together. I looked through the proofs on the table, she was undoubtedly talented. The faces were energetic and alive, caught mid-action. They seemed totally unaware of her presence. Somehow she'd captured the human Life force itself.

"The black and white's are great. Where do you find the models?"

"Just people in the street. On a long lens."

"You take their souls without permission?"

"I believe in reincarnation." She handed me a glass. "To my fourth exhibition."

"Your fourth? I might totally embarrass myself now, but are you incredibly famous?"

"Two of my pictures are in the National Portrait Gallery."

"I'll have to treat you with more respect in future."

"You will come, won't you?"

"My black tie is already winging its way to the Dry Cleaners."

"Fancy a sauna?"

Did she just ask me if I fancied a sauna?

"Don't look so shocked. I'm not about to jump on you." I was trying to keep up with her changing signals. I was seriously out of practice at this flirting game.

She ran upstairs. "In here."

A room off the corridor led to the sauna.

"Last one in's a sissy."

She threw a large yellow beach towel at me and disappeared off to another room to change. This isn't normal behaviour, surely? Jane returned in her towel just as I was hopping on one foot, almost naked, trying to take my last black sock off. She turned her face away.

"This is getting to be a habit."

I wrapped myself up in the beach towel. "OK, you can turn round now."

"Let me give you a tip. There's nothing worse than waiting for a man to take off his socks. Always take them off first."

Five minutes later I was lying back enjoying the heat. Yesterday, James Bond. Today, Hugh Heffner. Tick that box, Toby.

Jane poured some more water on the coals. It fizzed and the heat soared.

She looked amazing in her yellow towel. I could just see the top of her breasts. She'd been flirting with me for days and was probably waiting for me to make the first move. The job was almost over and this might be my last chance.

I tried to make it sound casual. "Have you ever done it in a sauna?" I was sweating so much, she couldn't have noticed the blushing.

She was lying back against the wooden wall with her eyes shut. "Might have done." I moved closer. She stayed still. I leant forward and kissed her on the cheek. I thought I'd better go in slowly.

She opened her eyes. "What was that?"

"Testing the water."

She still made no move so I leant in again and kissed her on the lips.

"You're very forward, young man."

Was that a signal to carry on? Or a gentle warning off? I went for the safe option and pulled back.

She closed her eyes again. Did she want me to make

the first move? Oh God.

My hand strayed over to her thigh. I was behaving like a teenager. Grab the bull by the horns. Be a man. I leapt across and ripped off her towel.

"What the hell are you doing?" She grabbed back her towel.

"I thought you wanted me to."

"I might well have done but there's such a thing a subtlety."

"Sorry, I haven't done this for ages. I mean with anyone other than Liz."

I stood there totally nude, not knowing what to do.

I picked up my towel. "Sorry, I've spoiled everything."

"Where do you think you're going?"

"I reckon I've made a big enough fool of myself for one day."

Jane pulled me back. "Close your eyes. You can imagine it's her if you like."

That would be too weird. "I think I'll keep my eyes open if it's all the same to you."

"It's bound to feel odd. I just thought you'd be up for a bit of fun. But it's cool if you're not."

I kissed her neck. Then her lips. And pretty soon the towels were off again and we were exploring each other's bodies.

In a sauna. Tick.

It was amazing and strange, all at the same time. Jane had smaller hips and Liz had bigger breasts, but this wasn't the time for comparisons.

Eventually The Big Moment came. Should we or shouldn't we?

I thought of putting up a struggle. But for what? And for whom? I was young, free and single. Anyway, why shouldn't I? Liz had been shagging Toby since she left. And probably before that. Now I come to think about it, he'd given her that book three months before she moved out. They must have been at it behind my back for months. They were probably in the middle of it when I called from the solicitor's office to finalise the settlement.

Jane's right hand went down my stomach and the decision was made for me. She opened her legs and tried to guide me in but we were so sweaty I couldn't seem to find her. Then suddenly I was in. It was amazing. We laughed as we tried to keep hold of our sweaty bodies.

"How many other men have you seduced in this sauna?" It was an odd question to ask, being still inside her.

"Only Jeremy. But he never managed the whole hog."

"You always said he was a pig. And I'm not sure if I'm going to manage it in this heat either. I think I'm going to pass out."

I pulled out and collapsed on the seat next to her. She was probably lying about Jeremy not managing it, just to make me feel better. It made me feel worse.

We sat in silence for a few minutes. I looked down at the bench. Jane looked straight ahead. Then she started laughing. Was she laughing with me or at me? "Come on, I'll get us a drink. There's a shower on the right when you're ready."

I stayed in the sauna on my own for a while, reeling from what had just happened. We hadn't used a condom. I'd spent so long trying to get pregnant with Liz that I never even thought about trying not to. Not that there'd been one handy in the sauna at the time anyway.

I must have stayed in too long because even after several cold showers, I still looked like a sweaty tomato. I lay on the bed trying to cool off, and checked my messages. There was an answerphone message and another text from Charlie.

'MY GARDEN'S DESPERATE. TOMORROW EVE ANY GOOD? PLS CALL.'

I replied with 'THE FLOWERPOT MAN WILL CALL AT 7. PANIC OVER.'

"How dare you suggest I want to be damaged?" screamed Liz on the answerphone. "Are you some sort of sadist?"

Jane looked up as I came into the kitchen. "You look like you're having a coronary."

"I think I stayed in there a bit too long."

She picked up her camera and started snapping away.

"That's totally unfair. I look like a beetroot." I ducked behind the table.

"Coming to get you."

"Help. Help." I ran towards the door.

"Where are you?" She was laughing.

I locked myself in the downstairs loo. "Leave my soul alone. I'm serious, you know. I don't want to come back in my next life as a root vegetable."

"Too late." She shouted through the keyhole. "You'll be in that exhibition before you can say Lancashire Hot Pot."

The alarm woke me in Jane's spare room at ten to six. I threw on my clothes in a series of movements that could only be described as ungainly. I turned my socks inside out and got my foot caught in a trouser leg. Men just can't get dressed gracefully. And if they could, women probably wouldn't fancy them anyway.

We fell into my van. It started first time, which was almost a record.

Jane laughed. "You can feel all the bumps in the road." Poverty must be such a giggle.

She told me that she'd once hired a car and called out the RAC because she thought the steering column was broken but the mechanic pointed out that she was probably just used to power steering, which the hire car didn't have. Jane was slumming it in my van and apparently loving every minute of it.

We slowed down to pay our three pounds to enter the Flower Market. I should really get a pass but had never got round to organising one. I parked up in my usual area and we went inside to pick up a bacon sandwich and a take away coffee from the 'Village Café'.

"Do you sleep with all your clients?"

"Technically I'm still married. So no, I don't."

"That makes me the first, then." She slipped her hand through my arm. We both knew that the whole sorry episode in the sauna had been a disaster, but she was trying make it OK. "Do you know how many women you've slept with?"

"I'm too much of a gentleman to say."

"Under ten then."

In fact, I knew the exact number. The night before the wedding I sat down and wrote a list. I expected to be faithful for the rest of my life and wanted to know what my final tally would be. I'm not into numerology but if Liz had been number thirteen, I might have had second thoughts. She turned out to be number seventeen. She would have been sixteen but then I remembered Phillipa, a travel agent I'd dated for a couple of months. We were about to consummate our passion for the first time, when Phillipa's golden Labrador farted and she couldn't carry on. I wasn't sure if that counted as a refusal, but I decided she went through on points.

We found a trolley and started piling on goodies. Purple sage, bronze fennel and the lucky find of the day, Bishop of Landaff dahlias. Pretty soon it looked like a mini garden on wheels. We found another couple of trolleys and filled those as well.

"You're not really going to put my photo in the exhibition, are you?"

"Of course. You'll be famous."

"But I don't want to be famous." That wasn't a box I'd ever wanted to tick.

We drove home singing, "One Man went to Mow" in silly voices. I placed the plants, still in their pots, around the garden to get a sense of how they'd look and sat on the patio wall to inspect my work.

"I got a call from Jeremy just now. He was asking all about you."

"Always good to get them jealous."

"It's pathetic really but I don't like bumping into him unless I'm with someone."

"I invented a fictitious girlfriend called Fiona, so whenever Liz went on about Toby, I could go on about her."

"Why Fiona?"

"Sexier than Madge."

Jane had been developing the prints from last night's session. Maybe in black and white my redness would look like a healthy tan. But what about the excessive sweat?

She handed me two prints. The first one, in my dinner jacket, had a rakish sexy air but I still looked totally legless.

Jane handed me the second one. "What do you think?"

I have rarely seen a less attractive specimen of the human form. The monochrome seemed to have exaggerated my redness and the halogen kitchen lights had picked out every bead of sweat. I looked like I had chicken pox, a drink problem and was about to suffer a heart attack all at the same time. And my hairline had all but receded. What had she done to me?

"Please tell me I don't really look like this."

"The camera never lies. I love it."

"You can't possibly love it. I look like shit. What are you going to call it? My Latest Shag?"

"Sex in the Sauna."

I'd already prepared the ground, so I gave the plants a really good soak and made them feel welcome in their new beds. By tea time, Jane had a new garden.

I said my goodbyes and gave her a kiss on the cheek. She was affectionate enough in return, but the episode in the sauna had definitely taken its toll.

I packed up my van and drove South West towards Charlie's flat in Brook Green. London looked great in the sunshine. Even Shepherds Bush roundabout made me smile. I parked in the quiet, tree lined street, right outside Number 25. I pressed the bell marked 'Garden Flat'. Beside it was a note stuck to the wall with sellotape, 'Ring loudly as I don't always hear the bell. Thanks C.'

A young girl in her mid twenties opened the door. She

had shoulder length, light brown hair and wore no make-up. She was quite cute but far too young for me.

"You're older than I thought you'd be."

"Sorry to disappoint you."

"I'm Charlie and you must be The Flowerpot Man."

"Your aunt passed on my card obviously."

We shook hands.

"It's only a little London strip but I'm sure you can work wonders." She talked enthusiastically about her plans. We were still on the doorstep.

"Perhaps I could see the garden."

"How rude of me, sorry. Come on through."

She showed me into the kitchen.

"Great room."

"You should have seen it before. I've had builders here for the last three months. The garden will be fantastic as well, but before I show it to you, I must warn you it's in need of serious attention."

She wasn't exaggerating. The builders had used it as a dumping ground and there was a load of work simply to clear it. I'd have to bring in a couple of lads with a pick up to do the heavy stuff. The ground was so badly compacted it would take several tons of new soil and weeks of rotovation to get anything to grow there at all.

"It's not exactly an area of great natural beauty, but if I worked around the clock, you'd be amazed how much I could achieve in five years."

She laughed. "I'd keep you going with tea and biscuits."

"What do you fancy? Water features and decking. Or fruit trees and grass?"

She'd torn out some magazine pictures, which gave me a good idea of what she was after. I got out my sketchpad and we talked through the basics. It was south facing, so I suggested a sitting area on the left which would catch the evening sun.

"I must have at least one hammock but I'd like two. They're so decadent and perfect for reading the Sunday papers. And when I finally get a boyfriend who's not a total loser, we can read them together on a lazy summer morning."

"You've got your whole future mapped out then?"

"You have to take control of life before it controls you."

"It doesn't always work out quite the way you planned it."

"Are you saying I'll never get another boyfriend?"

"I'm saying life has a habit of offering you alternatives to your dreams." I tried not to sound too cynical.

"Sounds like you've been disappointed in love."

"I'm getting over it."

"I've got a few Self Help books I could lend you."

"I may be a little jaded but I don't think I need therapy just yet."

"Really?" She looked at me as if she knew me better than I knew myself.

Hairdressers are used to people opening up to them, but I was constantly amazed how much personal information I was given on a first meeting by a client. Charlie told me that her boyfriend had dumped her the day after he proposed. She kept the engagement ring on a hook on the bathroom wall.

"If ever I feel sad and miss him, I look up at that ring and remember what a spineless weasel he was."

I wondered if it would still be hanging there in thirty years covered in cobwebs, like Miss Haversham's wedding cake.

"Mine's in a kitchen drawer. I took off the ring and threw it in there the day Liz moved out."

"It's her loss."

"Possibly. Your bloke must have been off his head too."

"Cheers." She studied me closely.

"What? Have I got mud on my chin?"

"Do you know, you're quite sexy for an older bloke."

"An older bloke? How dare you? Anyway, how old do you think I am?"

"Forty five?"

I know I'm tired and been through a divorce but I used to look thirty five. "I'm forty four."

"Sadness is very aging."

"Thanks. I'll remember that the next time someone offers me their seat on the tube."

I arranged to start work on Thursday. I was looking forward to it. It was always far easier starting from scratch than adapting the bad planting of a previous amateur. More than anything, I liked to work for people who got as excited about their gardens as I did. Charlie could be a fun person to be around, if she gave the therapy a rest.

I drove home to find half the street standing on the pavement outside my house. The alarm was still ringing loudly.

Mike, the neighbour to my left, came out of his front door. "I've looked over the fence at the back but I don't think anyone's broken in."

I put the key in the lock and kicked the door open with my foot, as TV cops do.

I shouted loudly. "I know you're in there, come on out with your hands up."

Mike laughed. But I know that if a burglar had actually come running out, we'd both have legged it.

There was no sign of entry. Just a little wind-up snowman on the floor in front of the fireplace. Emma had given him to me for Christmas and he'd been on show ever since. The mechanism stuck sometimes. He must have suddenly started marching along the mantelpiece, fallen to the floor and set the alarm off. I put him back in the under-stairs cupboard for next Christmas. Hopefully by then I'd have met someone and we could wind him up together. If not, I could always raid Charlie's Self Help Library. She must have something appropriate like 'Solitaire Can Be Fun At Christmas' or 'The Single Person's Religious Holiday Survival Guide'.

I ran a bath but it was stone cold. The boiler had broken. I'd been looking forward to a hot soak but unless I boiled at least twenty five kettles it wasn't going to happen. I thought about driving back to Hampstead and lying in Jane's sauna, but I didn't want to be captured on film again so soon. Also she'd told me not to fall in love with her and that presumably meant her sauna was out of bounds too.

I felt strangely cut off from the world with no hot water and wandered around the house aimlessly. I caught sight of myself in the new kitchen mirror. I studied the face staring back at me. Did I really look forty five? I couldn't tell anymore. Obviously to a twenty six year old, I did. But hey, I'd just been officially declared a 'sexy older man'. Things could be worse.

I dreamt I'd lost my wedding ring and entered a large room with a series of hooks at eye level. There must have been several hundred of them. On each hook was a gold ring and underneath it sat its owner. I tried to find mine, but all the rings looked the same. Eventually I saw Liz with her head in her hands. There was an empty space next to her on the floor and above it I saw my ring hanging on its hook.

She looked up at me, tears rolling down her face. "It wasn't supposed to be like this in my dream."

"Nor in mine."

I was woken by the bin men working noisily outside and decided to check my emails before setting off for Hampstead. I'd advertised in various West London magazines and often got enquiries via email. I'd even invested in my own website, theflowerpotman.com, but it hadn't got me any work. I'd picked up a few elderly clients through Ivy but they wouldn't live forever and unless I tapped into a younger market I'd soon be on the financial dung heap.

The first email was from Emma.

'To the Flowerpot Man from the Flowerpot Girl. Just checking that you've organised something fantastic for Saturday. I can't wait till tomorrow when I become a teenager and I can't wait till Saturday for my surprise. See you at two o'clock. Love you lots, TFG. xxx'

The second email was from Liz.

'Hi darling, are we still on for Thursday? I'm finding it hard not seeing Toby and it would be great to meet up. If it's too weird, I understand, but now you're seeing Barbie you should be OK. Can you make 6 at The Electric? I can't stay long as I'm meeting someone later. Love Liz.'

Someone? A new bloke? I didn't particularly want to see her anyway. What would we talk about? I think we'd pretty much covered the divorce. I considered emailing back my latest joke.

Q: What do you call a forty four year old man with a huge mortgage and a Marks and Spencer's Meal for One?

A: Single.

Q: What do you call a forty four year old man with a huge mortgage, a Marks and Spencer's Meal for One and a bottle of vodka?

A: Divorced.

Sending that would just make me look sad, so I ate my toast instead.

On the way to Hampstead I bought a card for Emma with ballet dancers on the front. Although now she's a teenager she'd probably have preferred a picture of the latest Boy Band in their boxers.

I pulled up outside Jane's house for the last time. By tea time, the job would be over. There was a Post-it note by the bell. 'Had to pop out. Lunch at one. See you, Mr. Flowerpot Man.'

I found the key under the third pot on the left as before and let myself in. By the kettle there was another Post-it note, 'Coffee in the usual place.' And by the Aga, 'Croissants go in here.' On the kitchen table was another, 'Sauna not recommended for root vegetables.' She was obviously cool about what had happened. But I couldn't quite get her out of my mind. I found the pad and left a note for her, 'Divorced gardener, 44, seeks babe to fill his lunchbox.' Why couldn't I let it lie?

I got to work and finished the few bits of trellising on the left hand side and cleaned out the pond on the right. After lunch, there'd just be some edging and a final cut of the lawn.

At ten to one, I looked at my watch. I was getting hungry. By quarter past I was ravenous. I stopped working and went inside. On the kitchen table was a new Post-it note, 'Lunch will be served in the garden.'

Jane must have snuck out of the side door as I'd gone into the kitchen. She was sitting on a green tartan rug in a pair of faded jeans and a bright white T shirt. Women look great in white T shirts. How do they do it? Mine always look grey after the first wash. She'd laid out a picnic lunch of avocado salad and was pouring a couple of glasses of chilled Chablis.

"What kept you?"

"I was stuck under a huge pile of Post-it notes."

"This is a Thank You lunch, for all your hard work."

"Sounds like The Last Supper."

"Let's not put a label on it. Labels are for shoes."

The Chablis tasted good. "Thanks for not making the sauna episode a huge issue."

She looked up. "It wasn't a huge issue. That was the problem, if I remember correctly."

"OK I asked for that, but you know what I mean."

"Don't worry about it. Divorce is supposed to be one of the three hardest things in life to deal with. Second only to getting married and buying a house."

"Yes, but I don't remember going mad and jumping on clients when I did either of the first two."

"I hope I'm more than just a client."

We clinked our glasses. "Friends?"

"Of course."

"So you'll recommend me to your neighbours?"

"For gardening or sauna work?"

"To be honest, things are so bad at the moment I could do with either."

"That bad?"

"A couple of weeks ago the van broke down in Kilburn, right outside Liz's solicitors office. I'd never been there myself but I recognised the name, Morris and Clift. Liz and I had already agreed the divorce terms quite amicably between ourselves but legally she had to see a solicitor, and one of them, either Morris or Clift, had persuaded her that I could afford an extra twenty thousand."

"In a couple of years, you'll be driving past the offices of Morris and Clift in your Aston Martin convertible and holding up two fingers to the legal profession."

"Pigs might fly."

She smiled. "Sometimes they do."

By six thirty I'd put the mower back in my van and the job was complete.

Jane stood by the door. "I'm not good at goodbyes. And let's not say we'll phone because that sounds like we won't."

"Goodbye. You see, it's not that difficult."

She waved from the steps as I drove off hooting my horn. Jane had been the first women I'd had sex with since the divorce. It had been an important landmark, even if we hadn't gone the 'whole hog'. But I knew it had been a fantasy, like being in an episode of Dallas or Dynasty. I belonged in the world of West London, Jane would be happier in Southfork.

I'd been looking forward to a shower but remembered I hadn't done anything about the boiler so I stood in the bath and washed myself down with the shower hose. The water was freezing. I threw on some clean clothes and opened the post. The first was a circular wanting to know if I was worried about hair loss. Who had given my name to the hair loss people? Liz couldn't be that spiteful, surely? The other was a card from Michelle. On the front was a picture of Charlie Chaplin about to fall off a bridge.

'I'm really sorry about your divorce. I've been through it too, remember? So if you ever want to talk, just call me anytime. Love Moo.'

I'd gone out with Michelle for three years but we each had our own places so we never actually lived together. She'd bought a house in Surrey after her divorce and was determined to keep it. She wanted to have something to fall back on if her next relationship broke down. She was great fun, but logic was not her strong point. I was once paying a restaurant bill and left a ten percent tip. "What are you doing? It was ten percent when I was a child," she said, "it must be more than that by now." On another occasion she phoned me to say she had no hot water in the kitchen. I told her to get a plumber to fix the boiler. "No, you don't understand, it's the kitchen tap," she said. "If you've got no hot water it won't come out of any tap," I said patiently. "But I thought you got mains from the kitchen tap?" she said. "Mains cold, yes, but not hot," I replied. "Oh, I thought the Government gave you hot water in the kitchen tap to wash your dishes in, but you had to pay for the hot water in the bathroom to wash yourself in." Good old Moo.

I poured myself a drink, dialled her number and left a message.

"Hello Moo, this is a voice from the past. Just got your card. I'd love to meet up and talk. Sunday any good? I'm in tonight. Bye."

I hadn't spoken to her for ages. We hardly spoke during the marriage, Liz wasn't too keen on me seeing my exes, and I was hoping we could pick up our friendship where we'd left off.

It was seven thirty so I put Coronation Street on and rummaged through the cupboards. A tin of tuna past it's sell by date, a half opened packet of dried pasta, some Demerara sugar that had gone hard and a tin of baked beans. The fridge wasn't much better, some butter and a bottle of champagne. I'd been keeping the bottle for a special occasion but obviously there hadn't been an occasion special enough for at least six months. In the freezer I found some sliced bread and a bottle of vodka. Even the Ready Steady Cook TV chefs would have a problem making anything other than baked beans on toast with that lot. So that's what I made. I quite fancied an evening in with my feet up, watching the telly, eating comfort food. I didn't have to be charming, witty or even particularly attractive. I could just be myself.

I took one bite when the mobile went. It was a text from Liz.

'FELNG LONLY. TEARFL. SAD. SRRY TO TXT. LZ'

Now even her name was abbreviated. Soon marriage services would be conducted in text speak. 'DO U TKE THS WMN 2B UR LWFL WDED WFE?' It didn't bear thinking about. I decided to finish my food and pretend I hadn't got the message.

I sat holding the remote and succeeded in watching all five channels simultaneously. I was restless and the room felt sad, so I lit some candles and it immediately felt better. When I brought someone back here for that bottle of special occasion champagne, I'd light these candles. I looked around the room again. Was this all I'd achieved in my forty four years? My life wasn't supposed to be like this. The television news came on. More carnage. "There's always someone worse off than you," my mother used to say. Then the mobile rang. It was Charlie.

"Hello, is that the Flowerpot Man?"

"Receiving you loud and clear. Is that Charlie, Tango or Foxtrot?"

She laughed. "It's Charlie. Just checking about tomorrow. You'll need a key. I'm off to work at seven thirty."

"I'll be with you by twenty past. No problem."

I went off to bed in the loft. On the way up, I stubbed my toe on the staircase and swore loudly. I lay awake for a while, noticing the coffee stain on the wall. Only four nights ago I'd slept here with my wife. How was it possible to love someone and hate them at the same time? But I realised that life wasn't black and white. It was a sort of coffee stain colour.

I lay there and thought about Jane in the sauna and Charlie with her Self Help books. And then I thought about Liz and her text message.

Eventually I typed in, 'KP UR CHN UP. X' and pressed send.

I'd set the alarm for six twenty but it seemed like the middle of the night when it went off. I threw myself out of bed with mock enthusiasm for the day and splashed my face with cold water. I had to be at Charlie's before she left so there wasn't time for coffee. I turned the key in the van. It wouldn't start. It was badly in need of a service but the mortgage payments had been more urgent. I thought of praying, "Our Father who art in Heaven, please let my engine start now. If you do, I'll stop hating Toby. I'll even stop trying to have sex with women in saunas." I turned over the engine once more. Nothing. Now I was going to be late for Charlie, I wouldn't be able to pick up the key and she'd think I was totally disorganised. I rang her number.

"Charlie, it's me. The van won't start. I'm not going to make it by seven thirty. I'm really sorry."

"No problem, I'll leave the key at number 23."

I tried the engine again and it started first time. Next time I'd pray to Charlie. I collected the key from the old guy at number 23 and let myself in.

Thirty seconds later the alarm went off. I could see the keypad by the front door but had no idea what the code was. I tried 1234, just in case. The noise was deafening. I tried ringing her mobile, it went straight to answerphone.

"Hi this is Charlie. I'm too busy to talk now but I'll call you back if I can. If I don't call you back, I'm either still too busy or I just don't want to talk to you."

The old guy from number 23 was over like a shot. He had the tone of a military officer. "Turn that bell off this minute."

"I would if I knew the code but I don't, do you?"

"Try ringing Miss Clayton." Thanks for stating the obvious.

"It should stop after twenty minutes. I think it has to by law."

Other neighbours were gathering but none of them knew the code. Then I had a brainwave. I entered her house number twice, 2525. It stopped immediately. Sherlock Holmes would have been proud.

I addressed the crowd. "Show's over. But if any of you need help in your gardens, just give me a call. I'm The Flowerpot Man. Miss Clayton has my number."

They looked at me as if I was selling double glazing. I went through to the kitchen and looked out at the garden. I'd been so keen to get the contract that I'd underestimated how much work there was, even for the two Polish lads with their pick-up. I'd used Kris before, he was six foot three and built like an ox. A couple of months ago I'd thought of using him as a hit man to bump off Toby, but now I think I'd finally got that idea out of my head.

I made the coffee and sat down on the step. My head was still ringing from the noise of the alarm. I called Kris on his mobile.

"I thought you didn't need me till Friday?"

I was about to lose it completely. "Don't do this to me. Not today."

He started laughing. He had one of those huge laughs that started in his boots. "Open the back gate and you'll see us. We've been here for half an hour."

I unlocked the gate and there they were, the giants of the garden clearing world. Kris gave me a bear hug and lifted me up off the ground. He was still laughing. "Had you going there, Mr. Flowerpot Man."

We put our backs into it and by midmorning the truck was overflowing. Kris and his lad drove off to the tip and we agreed to meet back at Charlie's after lunch.

I found a little café at the end of the road where I ordered a chicken baguette and a black coffee. There was a free chair in the corner.

"Do you mind if I join you?"

"You're not going to set off any more alarms, are you, young man?" It was Colonel Mustard from number 23. "What have you ordered?" I told him. "No good, old boy. The chicken's too dry. Better off with the tuna." He called over the counter. "Natalie, make that a tuna baguette, there's a good girl."

The natives were friendly, if a little pompous.

"So, you're doing young Charlie's back garden? Pretty young thing, isn't she?" He winked at me. I half expected a nudge but it didn't come. "If I were twenty years younger, what?" Please God, don't let me end up like that. But he was right about the tuna baguette, it was delicious. I said my goodbyes and headed for the door.

"Same time tomorrow, old boy?"

I let myself in to number 25, keyed in 2525, and opened up the back. Her phone was ringing. The answerphone clicked on and I heard the message loudly over the speaker.

"Hi Charlie, it's your mother. Now, about this Flowerpot Man. Don't let him talk you into doing any more than you want. Just get him to clear the rubbish and put down a bit of turf. And make him stick to his quote. He'll take you for everything you've got if you're not careful. And you're a girl, so he'll try to take advantage. And don't go fancying a bit of rough. Look where that got you last time. Come to dinner on Saturday. I've got a lovely young man for you, he's perfect. Call me when you've got a minute. Love you. Bye darling."

She sounded like the kind of woman who called a spade a garden implement. Charlie should play that message to her therapist, it would explain everything.

At four thirty the pick-up was heaving again and I gave Kris his cash. He'd just make the tip before it closed and be back in the morning to clear the rest. I reset the alarm and locked the door.

Colonel Mustard saw me leave. "Hope you've set the alarm, old boy? Can't be too careful, what?"

I joined in his military manner. "Quite right. No worries. All ship shape."

"See you in the mess at thirteen hundred, what?" If he meant the café tomorrow at one, I might be elsewhere.

Charlie turned the corner.

"I can see you've been busy. You off for a hot soak?"

I was so covered in dust, I looked like Dick van Dyke. "Unfortunately not, my boiler's broken."

"And your van doesn't start. What are we going to do with you? Follow me." She walked briskly home and opened the door.

I called out the number. "2525."

"Sorry, I forgot to tell you the code. Did it go off? It's always doing that. I think the neighbours are a bit upset with me."

She had a powerful American shower. I stood there luxuriating in a trance of steam and felt like I was in a five star hotel. I got dressed and went into the kitchen.

"You brush up pretty well for an oldie."

"The plastic surgery was worth it then?"

We looked out at what had been achieved on Day One. It didn't look as if we'd done anything at all, but I knew that by tomorrow evening it would be ready for the real gardening work to begin.

She checked her answerphone and I heard her mother's message booming out from the speaker a second time.

"My mother's always showing me up."

"Mine too."

She smiled. A great smile.

"What did your mother say about you 'fancying a bit of rough'?"

"She thinks any one who lives outside SW3 is on the rough side."

"That would make W4 a War Zone, then?"

"Absolutely."

We were chatting away happily when my mobile went. It was Liz at the Electric.

"I've been waiting for half an hour. Where the hell are you? I've got to go in ten minutes."

Shit, I'd completely forgotten we were supposed to be meeting. "I've been held up on a job. I'm really sorry."

"Why didn't you ring?"

"My battery went down. I've just charged it using a friend's charger."

"You're round at Barbie's, aren't you?" She didn't sound best pleased.

"No."

"Lying bastard."

"I swear. On Barbie's life."

"Piss off." She hung up.

I thought about ringing back and apologising but there'd be no point. I'd messed up and there was nothing I could do about it now.

Charlie opened the fridge door. "Vodka?"

"Better make it a double."

I was determined not to be late for Charlie again, so I ended up getting there too early, just as she was getting into the shower.

"I'll have a coffee if you're making one."

I heard her in the shower, singing 'Dancing Queen' in the erratic way you do when washing yourself and stretching for those hard to reach places.

She joined me in the kitchen, with her hair in a towel. Why do women do that? I've never seen a man walk around the house with his hair in a towel. But then again, I'd never been to a man's flat and seen stringy things on radiators that wouldn't cover a nat's arse.

She soon reappeared in a black city number and sprayed her shoes with Mr. Sheen. She polished them with a tea towel and gave an embarrassed curtsy.

"Will I do?"

"Very Woman in Black."

"See you later, if you're still here when I get back."

I explained that I was having dinner with Ivy and would have to go straight home and get changed.

"But you still haven't got any hot water. Go home at lunchtime, collect your glad rags, then have a shower here after work." It was well beyond the call of duty but I was very grateful for the offer.

I opened up the back to find Kris and his pal waiting patiently in the pick-up. I was glad to see them as the mountain of rubbish seemed to have grown overnight. Kris sang loudly as he worked, but only ever the first line of a song. By the time I joined in, he'd be onto the next one. His partner, Nikolai, didn't sing at all, he just smiled a lot as his English was limited. The truck was full by eleven thirty, so they went off to the tip and I nipped home to get my dinner jacket.

I couldn't be bothered to clap so I just shouted, "Hello house." I looked around for my dress shirt and eventually found it at the bottom of the washing basket. The message light was flashing on the answerphone. Eight messages.

"Hi, this is Moo. I don't have your mobile number but Sunday's not great. Speak soon. Bye.'

"Hi, Moo again. Sunday's fine. Call me."

"Sunday's fine but better make it afternoon. OK? It's Moo, by the way."

"I really need to know about Sunday. Where are you? Are you playing away from home, you naughty boy? Bye."

"Moo again. This is the very last time I'm going to try you. Why don't you leave your mobile number on your outgoing message?"

"I know I said I wouldn't call but this really is the last time. I can do Sunday lunch now, after all. This offer will self destruct in five seconds if you don't reply immediately."

"It's Liz. I can't believe you let me down last night. You know how I hate sitting on my own in a bar. And you knew I was feeling low about Toby. I really expected more from you. So this is just to say that I'm really pissed off with you."

"Hello? Is this working? Hello? It's Ivy. Hello? I am ringing to see if you are still coming to dinner this evening. Please would you ring me. Love, Ivy."

I was about to dial Ivy when the phone rang.

"It's Moo. Oh, you're there. Thank God. I thought you'd been captured by pigmies and were being slowly roasted on a spit over an open fire."

"No, Moo, I'm very much in West London. Sunday lunch would be great. Two o'clock at Julie's?"

"Looking forward to it."

I gave her my mobile number just in case. I called Ivy who was very excited about our dinner party tonight and then left an apologetic message for Liz. We're almost divorced, so why did I still feel so bad?

I collected my dinner jacket, socks, shoes and dirty dress shirt, set my alarm and locked the front door. My code was 0035. It was supposed to be ironic, half James Bond, 003.5. I put the clothes on the back seat and turned the key. It started first time. Perfect. Then I remembered my bow tie. I switched off the engine, ran to the house, reset the alarm and got back in the van. This time it wouldn't start. I should have left it running. Or got it serviced. I tried praying to Charlie, "Your garden needs me." But it obviously didn't need me enough as it still wouldn't start.

My mobile went with a text from Liz.

'THX FR MSG. FL BTR 2DY. LZ. X'

I wanted to come up with the most ridiculously abbreviated message possible. But instead I typed. "MY VAN WON'T START. CAN YOU SEND THE VIBES?' She used to send me 'the vibes' when I was quoting on a garden.

A few seconds later she replied. 'TRY IT NOW, DARLING. X'

It started first time. I texted back with, 'U R A *'.

I parked outside Charlie's flat and nipped up to the dry cleaners at the end of the road with the shirt. They promised to have it ready by five. I grabbed a takeaway tuna baguette from Natalie at the café and picked up some flowers and a bottle of ginger wine for Ivy. I was finishing my sandwich when the Poles returned.

"Still having your lunch?" Kris laughed his hearty laugh. "Work? You don't know the meaning of the word."

"No, but I know the meaning of Life."

He smiled knowingly. "Nobody knows that until they die. And then, of course, it's too late."

At six o'clock, I jumped into Charlie's power shower and used her special conditioning shampoo, which left my hair ridiculously soft. I looked like something from the seventies.

Charlie roared her head off when she saw me. "Groovy Baby, did you back comb and blow dry it? It's hysterical."

"It was your wretched shampoo."

"You should get it cut really short. It would make you look a lot younger."

"I'll think about it."

"I know about hair. Trust me, I'm a woman."

"I know about Life. Trust me, I'm a gynaecologist."

I finished doing up my bow tie and put my jacket on. "Will I do?"

"The hair's a bit camp, but you'll do."

Ivy opened the door. "Good evening, sir." She was grinning like a Cheshire cat.

"You look beautiful, Ivy."

She was wearing a full length black ball gown, straight out of the forties. Her make-up was a bit skew-whiff and she seemed unaware of the aroma of mothballs but she looked wonderful.

"Freesias, how lovely. My father used to give me these on my birthday."

"I remember you telling me."

"Let me put them in water and we can have them on the table as a centrepiece. You go into the front room, and pour us a glass of ginger wine. That's right."

She'd put two glasses on the side table, each on its

own doily. The room smelt of polish. Ivy must have been hard at it for days.

"To you and me." She took a little sip of ginger wine. "You look splendid. I do like a man in black tie. If I were a little younger …"

"… I'd be asking you out on a date."

She almost blushed. We sat down and I told her my news.

"Be careful, this Charlie will find you very attractive, you know. Women like an older man at that age. You'll have to be on your guard."

I told her I wasn't interested in Charlie.

"A single man in his early forties with his own house, who is not homosexual, is something of a rarity. You're quite a catch."

"You make being divorced sound like a positive advantage."

"I don't think you should get married for at least five years."

"But I'll be forty nine by then."

"Never marry too young or in too much haste. Read Jane Austen or Anthony Trollope."

Ivy had never been married. For all I knew, she'd never even been kissed. I took the plunge. "Have you ever been in love?"

"I wasn't born an old woman, you know." She went over to the bureau and took out a large brown envelope. She opened it and handed me a photograph.

"This is me on my seventeenth birthday."

"Ivy, you're gorgeous."

She smiled. "I know. And I had a fair few admirers, I can tell you."

"Do you remember your first kiss?" I'd never dared to have this conversation before, Ivy was very private about such things.

"It was on Christmas Eve, 1928. I was seventeen and

he was twenty two. He wasn't particularly good looking and he kissed rather clumsily but I thought he was wonderful. He brought me flowers and told me I was beautiful."

"You are beautiful."

"But his family moved away. I only knew him for a few months."

I looked through the other photographs. She had long flowing hair and a tiny waist.

"Did you fall in love again?"

"There were two others. Jimmy and Peter. I met Jimmy when I was twenty seven. I once held his hand in St. James Park and when he kissed me, I thought I was in heaven. Sometimes I think it's better never to have loved at all. Being alone would be easier to bear if you had nothing to compare it to."

"What happened to him?"

"He died soon after with a heart attack. He was only twenty eight."

I poured us another drink.

"And Peter? You said you fell in love with Peter?"

Her face was frozen. "We should eat. It's all ready. Leave your glass. That's right."

I followed her into the kitchen. The table had been laid with great care. The cutlery was polished and the glasses sparkled.

She tied her apron at the back. "Will you open the wine?"

The German Piesporter wasn't really cold enough and far too sweet for my taste, but it didn't matter one bit.

"Can I give you a hand?"

"Sit yourself down. That's right."

She brought out an array of serving dishes with gravy, bread sauce and vegetables. It was as good a meal as I'd had for years and the meat was cooked to perfection.

"Ivy, this is amazing. You're amazing."

We had coffee in her front room. It had originally had a rather grand fireplace but she'd blocked it off and changed it to gas several years ago for convenience. It was cosy but looked slightly odd in the otherwise formal surroundings of her Edwardian Semi.

She opened a small cupboard. "Let's have some music? You pick one."

Her records were old seventy eights and were played on a wind up gramophone with a large brass horn. I chose Elgar's Violin Concerto and placed it on the turntable. I wound the handle and set it going. The crackles added to the magic as we sat looking into the flames. I wanted to ask her about Peter, but I decided to leave that for another day.

After the Elgar, Ivy insisted on one final record. It was an old recording of the Blue Danube.

"My father taught me to dance to this."

I lowered the needle onto the record and took her hand.

"May I have the pleasure of this dance?"

I think I saw someone peeping in through the gap in the curtains, but Ivy didn't notice. She was in a world of her own, dancing with her eyes closed. Dancing with Peter.

ROBIN KERMODE

THE FLOWERPOT MAN

A diary of a divorce
from Nisi to Absolute

"VERY FUNNY, VERY TOUCHING"
JULIAN FELLOWES

DAY 16

I'd got up early to clear the old bedroom ready for the carpet fitters. I hadn't realised there was so much furniture. I knew there was a bed, a couple of bedside tables and a chest of drawers, but I also found a couple of chairs and an old stool. God knows what they were doing there. And under the dressing table I found a Self Help book, 'Good People in Bad Relationships.' Liz must have left it behind. I opened the cover and found an inscription.

'L. I find you irresistible. Remember B. Love T.'

Toby must have given it to Liz. But why had she left it behind? Had she subconsciously wanted me to find it? More to the point, what the hell did 'B' stand for? A place they'd been to together? Brighton? Had they had a dirty weekend there? The name of a person? Bridget? Betty? My mind was racing. Perhaps they'd been having a threesome with someone called 'B' behind my back all along. I ran out into the garden and tried to set the book alight but the wind kept blowing out the matches. I took it inside, ripping out pages as I went. I turned on the gas hob and held the book close to the flame. It caught fire so quickly that I had to drop it in the sink. I'd burnt my hand quite badly. Should I put it under a cold tap? Or put butter on it? I was panicking. My mobile rang. I was almost crying with rage. "Go away." It continued to ring. "I'm not eating toast, I've just burnt my hand and you and Toby can piss off and leave me alone."

I inspected the damage. The shock was worse than the burn but I put some antiseptic cream on it anyway. The tube was past its sell by date but if it killed me now, I really didn't care. I checked the answerphone message. It was the carpet fitters saying that as they couldn't get hold of me they'd be coming later in the day. Shit. I couldn't be late for Emma. I wish I'd never found the stupid book. I wish a lot of things. Mostly to do with Toby. And mostly to do with his death.

I rang the carpet people back. The office was closed on a Saturday but I found their number on my mobile and called them. I explained about Emma and I pleaded with them.

"I'll make it worth your while."

"Really? How much?"

Normally, of course, you'd give the lads a tenner as a tip but if I was to make them change their route it would have to be more substantial than that. Twenty five? Fifty? A hundred? I hated this.

"Fifty quid. Cash," I added, as if they'd been expecting anything else.

They said they'd be over in about an hour and a half. It was now nine thirty. If they arrived by eleven and took an hour to do it, I could be away by twelve. But I'd definitely have to leave by one, I couldn't leave a young girl alone on a railway station. On a different day, I might have asked Liz to send the vibes.

I looked in my wallet and realised I didn't have fifty quid on me, so I stuck a note on the door. 'To the carpet men. Just nipped to get cash. Back in five. PLEASE DON'T GO AWAY.' The van started first time and I shot down to the cashpoint on the High Road. I circled a couple of times but couldn't find a parking space. I decided to chance it anyway, put the flashers on and made a dash for the machine. Just as it was delivering my cash I saw a traffic warden approaching the van.

"Hang on, I'm right there." I didn't bother to wait for my receipt.

The warden smiled. He'd probably been caught in a similar situation himself. Or perhaps he had a secret hand

118

signal, to tell other wardens that he was part of the Brethren and therefore not liable for a ticket. Maybe I'd inadvertently just used it. It might be worth joining up for a couple of weeks to find out what the gesture is.

The van started first time and I got home in time to have a quick coffee in the garden.

By eleven fifteen, I was getting worried. At eleven twenty the doorbell rang.

The carpet guys did a great job. It always amazed me what a difference a new carpet makes. All the hard work of painting comes together and suddenly a new room is born. There would be no more ghostly inscriptions in Self Help books under the bed. It was my bedroom again.

I got to Victoria at twenty to two. Normally I'd have been there at ten to, but with Emma being so young I gave myself ten minutes extra. I stood under the Arrivals Board as usual. I double checked that I'd brought the booking reference for the Circus with me. The show started at three and it was only six stops to Clapham Common. We'd be there in plenty of time.

The arrivals board showed that her train was in. I watched the passengers form a human snake from Platform nine. I couldn't see Emma anywhere. I went to the gate but all the passengers had already gone through. I went back to the Arrivals Board. I did this circuit a couple more times. On the third visit to the gate I thought I saw Liz. As I got closer, I realised it was her.

She managed a half smile. "I suppose you're meeting Barbie off a train."

I could have countered with something vicious about Ken but I smiled back instead.

"No, I'm taking Emma to the Circus. She was thirteen yesterday. But I can't find her anywhere."

"You're here to meet Emma?"

"Yes, I'm a bit worried, actually."

"But Emma asked me to take her out today."

"She can't have asked us both. Anyway where the hell is she?"

I called my brother on his landline. "Is Emma with you?"

"Of course. Hang on I'll get her."

Emma came on the phone.

"I thought we were going out today, I've bought tickets and everything."

"I know. I forgot. I'm really sorry."

"And Liz is here too, I don't know what she's organised for you but I'm sure it's a big surprise." Liz nodded to me, implying it was.

Emma took a deep breath. "I thought if you two went out and had a good time together, then you'd fall in love again and everything would be like it was. And I don't want you to marry anyone else, I want you to marry Liz again. I just wanted to help."

Liz heard this too. What could I say?

"It was very kind of you, Emma, but it's complicated."

"You always say that."

"That's because it is."

"What was my surprise going to be anyway?"

"I've got tickets to the Moscow State Circus."

Liz grabbed the phone. "And I've got tickets to the London Eye and then I've booked tea at The Savoy."

"So you've missed quite a day."

"If you two get back together then I don't mind missing out one bit. Promise me you'll go to the Circus and have tea together. It can't be that hard. Please, for me."

How could I refuse a thirteen year old her birthday wish? "Alright. But don't get your hopes up."

We agreed that we'd go to Clapham for three o'clock and see the first half of the show. Liz had booked tea at four thirty and had tickets for the London Eye at six. As we headed off for the station I was desperate to ask Liz what "B" stood for but I decided it could wait.

The tubes were running well and we were in Clapham Common by twenty to three. I was hoping to have a pee but there was such a long queue to collect the tickets that there wasn't time. We took our seats on the front row just as the music started.

Liz put her hand in mine. "Are you OK?"

"I just hope I'm not frightened by the clowns."

A very camp man dressed head to toe in red brocade led the proceedings. He announced jugglers, trapeze artists and comic cyclists with a pronounced lisp and his announcements got even camper with every act he introduced. We joined in with all the whooping and cheering as if we were kids. The music changed to a comic trumpet and on came the first clown. Both Liz and I found clowns rather scary, it was the whole mask thing. He was riding a bicycle with a wobbly wheel and drove straight into the centre pole. Liz almost fell off her chair. She found nothing funnier than people walking into lamp posts. I think she must have some German blood in her. Forget irony, forget wit, if someone slipped on a banana skin and needed a hip replacement, Liz was wetting herself. A second clown came running on with an obligatory custard pie. He pretended to trip over, doing several forward rolls but managed to keep the pie on its plate. This sort of slapstick doesn't really do it for me but the kids around us were laughing in all the right places. The second clown was being chased by the first one on the bicycle and was heading straight for us. He lost his balance in the sand, rolled over in front of Liz and deposited the entire custard pie in my face. Liz was in hysterics and the rest of the audience went mad. It got worse. The clown grabbed my arm and pulled me into the centre of the ring. The crowd applauded and I bowed dutifully. As clowns don't talk, he gestured me onto a small plinth. It seemed churlish and a little public to refuse. I stood there with shaving foam all over me as three more clowns entered, each carrying a custard pie. They asked the audience if they should throw them in my face. The crowd were baying for blood. Nothing had really changed since the Christians faced the lions. It was then that I wished I'd had time for a pee.

The camp Ringmaster entered in a bright spotlight. He walked over to Liz, took her by the hand and led her into the ring.

He pointed at me. "Do you know this man?" He held the microphone to her mouth.

"Intimately." Easy for her, she wasn't on a plinth covered in custard pie.

The ringmaster walked over to me. "And do you know this woman?" He thrust the mic in my face.

"I've never seen her before in my life." I have to say my comic timing was perfection and I got a huge cheer.

Liz walked over and grabbed the mic. "We used to be married."

I grabbed it back. "Technically, we still are."

The Ringmaster was being upstaged and he didn't like it one bit. "I'll do the jokes, thank you very much."

We were ushered back to our seats and each given a huge teddy bear as a thank you from the clowns.

I looked over at Liz. "What are you going to call yours?"

"Bear."

We left in the interval, hailed a cab and headed for The Strand. I'd never been to tea at The Savoy before and was quite excited.

"Will they make me wear a tie?"

"No idea."

"Didn't you think to ask?"

"I thought I was bringing Emma. Girls don't usually wear ties."

We were shown to our table by a very pretty girl in a short black skirt.

Liz opened her napkin. "Down boy."

The sandwiches and cakes were displayed in a three tiered rack that looked like the frame of a circus tent. I spotted a cake with cream in the middle and pretended to throw it at Liz.

"Don't even think about it, sunshine."

The food kept on coming and we kept on eating.

Liz took another egg sandwich. "I arrived as a size eight but I'm going to leave as a size eighteen."

I polished off the last brandy snap. "We'll have to pay an excess weight charge on the Eye at this rate."

When Liz had gone to the loo, I asked the pianist to play 'our tune'. A few minutes later when he started playing 'Fly me to the Moon', Liz kissed my hand.

We said goodbye to the pianist, paid the bill and headed across the river carrying our giant teddy bears. Neither of us had been on the Eye before. London looked fantastic on a sunny day and even better as we reached the top. We pointed out the landmarks of our past. We could just make out Green Park where we'd kissed in the grass and Battersea Power Station where my van had broken down and we'd taken pity on a homeless guy and bought him supper whilst we waited for the RAC. London was littered with our shared memories and from the air they seemed timeless. We were both looking straight ahead but turned to each other at exactly the same moment. She leant her face towards mine and I kissed her.

"I am so sorry."

"What for?"

"For everything."

I held her gaze. "Can I ask you something? What does the letter 'B' stand for?"

She smiled. "B is for Bear."

I let it go. What was the point in beating myself up? Whether it stood for Bognor, Bournemouth or Brent Cross, it didn't matter. I knew that 'B' really stood for Blown it Big time, you silly Boy.

I dreamt I was walking down a road, carrying a newborn baby in a sling.

He looked up at me and smiled. "You don't know who I am, do you?"

I shook my head.

"I'm the baby that you and Liz should have had."

"Why didn't you want to come to us?" I asked, holding his little hand.

"My body didn't grow properly. But my spirit did. I'm here with you always, even if sometimes you can't see me. I love you. And I love Mummy."

I ran to the phone to call Liz. She had to hear this. But I couldn't remember her number. I pressed memory two. That had always been her programmed number but I got the speaking clock. I wanted to tell her that our baby was alright. I wanted to tell her that we'd made something wonderful. That it wasn't all for nothing. We had made a baby.

I was woken by the sunlight streaming in through the open curtains. I lay watching the light for a while, deciding what to do. On Sunday mornings I liked to lie in the bath and listen to the omnibus edition of 'The Archers' but as I hadn't organized a plumber and my radio still had no batteries, I couldn't do either. Liz thought it was too middle class and not edgy enough. If it had been called 'The Tenants of Tower Block Ten', she'd have tuned in like a shot.

I had planned to christen the new bedroom last night, but I hadn't had time to make up the bed before dashing off to meet Emma. It was sweet of her to set us up, and to be fair we'd had a great time. I picked up the phone and called Liz.

"What sort of bollocking time do you call this?"

"And a happy Sunday morning to you too."

She was waking up. "Sorry. You OK?"

"Fine. Sleep well?"

"Mmmm, like a log. What are you up to today?"

"I'm seeing Michelle for lunch." The line went quiet. "Are you still there?"

"I can't believe you've started seeing her again."

"I'm not seeing her again. Calm down."

"You just said you were." She was getting angry.

"This is the first time I've seen her since you left. And anyway I'm allowed to see who I want, I don't have to ask your permission."

"But she's so blonde. She wouldn't know a good conversation if it hit her in her silicone implants."

"Oh and you would?"

"Piss off."

"Very witty, Wilde."

"God help you. Last week it was Barbie, this week it's Miss Big Tits 1986 and next week, no doubt, it'll be the latest Page Three Stunner. You're full of shit, do you know that?"

"Liz, stop it." But the phone had already gone dead.

I put the kettle on, found two new batteries in the kitchen drawer and tuned into 'The Archers'.

I was taking my first bite of toast when the landline rang. Why couldn't she let it rest? We'd had an argument but it wasn't the end of the world. She always had to have the last word and would generally hang up before I had a chance to counter attack.

I picked up the phone but stayed silent.

"Hello?" It was Emma.

"Is that the Flowerpot Girl?"

"No, I'm too old for that now. I'm a teenager,

remember."

"Of course."

"So, how was it yesterday? Are you going to get married again?"

"It's not as easy as that, Emma."

"You always say that."

"No, I usually say, 'It's complicated'."

"Same difference. You two are so stupid. I was your bridesmaid, you know. Have you any idea how that makes me feel? Being involved in a wedding that only lasted five minutes."

"Four years, actually."

"Same difference."

I changed the subject. "You'd have laughed at the Circus, a clown threw a custard pie in my face."

"Serves you right." She was crying.

"Emma, I'll call you later, OK?"

Nothing.

"OK?"

"Mmmm."

"Love you."

"Love you too." She hung up.

I turned 'The Archers' back on just as the signature tune was ending and ate my cold toast in silence. I put on a wash but wasn't sure if washing machines needed hot water. If they heated their own, I could squeeze inside, spin in a foetal position and pretend my life had turned out differently.

I put my head under the cold tap and thought about walking around the house with a towel on my head. I thought about Charlie. She had plenty of hot water, probably loves 'The Archers' and would almost certainly hate 'The Tenants of Tower Block Ten'. But then again, she's far too young.

The bedroom smelt of new carpet. I made up the bed and put all the furniture back. Then I took most of it out again, leaving the room feeling more spacious. Just the bed, the two bedside cabinets and the chest of drawers. From the carpet upwards, there was nothing of Toby here any more. Tonight I would start my new life. I was coming home.

I got to Julie's at ten to two. I'd forgotten to reserve a table so I put my name on the waiting list and ordered a vodka. There were olives on the bar but I've never really liked them, so I ate some peanuts and turned to the gardening section of the Sunday paper. I came up with a new idea for a column, 'Gardening for the Divorced Man'. Firstly, Garden Centres are a great way to meet new women and, secondly, it's a well known fact that women love men who can garden. It's also good if they can cook, are great in bed and earn a fortune. I ordered myself another vodka.

At two twenty five, Michelle bounded into the bar.

She handed her coat to a passing waiter. "Hello, darling," The men at the bar turned to look. My standing with them shot to ten.

I gave her a kiss. "You look fantastic."

"I know, I caught sight of myself in the mirror just now and got quite turned on." She howled with laughter. The other drinkers howled too.

"Sorry to hear about the divorce, darling." Several men nodded their condolences. I nodded back.

The manageress arrived with the menus. "Your table's ready. Follow me."

Michelle raised her eyebrows. "You could do a lot worse than ask her out, she's gorgeous."

"But not as gorgeous as you."

"Goes without saying." She howled again as we sat down.

The people at the next table looked over. I smiled back.

She leant in. "So what happened, darling? Who had the affair?"

The other diners pretended they weren't listening but I knew they were.

"It wasn't like that. Neither of us had an affair."

"When a marriage breaks up, it's always because one or the other has had an affair. Or wants to." She popped an olive in her mouth. "So who was he?"

"He's called Toby. I was at school with him. He beat me in the hundred meters backstroke final and now he's beaten me in life."

"Don't take it personally. He's probably just got a huge knob, that's all."

The whole restaurant was ear wigging.

"Joke."

"No, I think you've hit the nail on the head."

"Hey, listen up. We had the best sex ever. You have a huge knob, whatever Liz thinks. I won't have a word said against it. In fact, I'd like to propose a toast to it." She stood up. The restaurant went silent as she raised her glass. "To your magnificent knob, one of England's finest."

I thought about doing an Oscar style acceptance speech but as the other diners had already heard the citation, I had no reason to guild the knob, as it were.

"Right, shall we order?" She gave me a wink. "What do you fancy, Big Boy?"

I had the Sunday Roast but as she was a vegan she went for the vegetarian sausage. We ordered a bottle of red and filled in the gaps of the last five years.

She'd been living with a property developer who had a penchant for fast cars, but left him after finding out he also had a penchant for fast women. Michelle had kept her little house and had moved back there when it all went wrong.

There was something decadent about Julie's on a

Sunday. We were getting slowly sloshed before we'd even hit the liqueurs. Michelle was good company and provided the diners at adjacent tables with enough overheard stories to fill their week. But one story we kept quietly to ourselves.

"Do you ever feel we did the wrong thing?"

"We made the right decision based on what we felt at the time."

"I think I was losing the baby anyway." She played with her cheese knife. "I'm not sure it would have survived."

Seven years ago, the day after we split up, Michelle had discovered she was pregnant. It had been an amicable break up but we had both been very clear about why we didn't want to be together. It was terrible timing. We slid back into being a couple for a few weeks while we decided what to do. In the end she decided to have a termination. I could remember waiting in the clinic together and paying the bill with my credit card. The payment slip came back with the default heading, 'Thank you for your custom, please call again.' Our lives would have been very different if we'd had the baby. We might have got married and had more children. I might be driving a people carrier and be living in Surbiton. I would never have married Liz and become a London gardener. I wouldn't be sitting here having Sunday lunch with Michelle wondering if there's someone up there with an Almighty board game, playing Snakes and Ladders with our souls. Maybe next time He could let me know what's in store. That way I'd be ready with an umbrella when the shit hit the fan.

"Hello, Mr. Flowerpot Man." Jane had been sitting a couple of tables away and saw me on her way out.

"Jane, Michelle. Michelle, Jane."

The two girls eyed each other up and down. And then up and down again.

"I've just been doing Jane's garden in Hampstead."

"And he's done a great job. He's very talented, you know. Come round and see how it's doing. Bye now."

Michelle watched her disappear down the stairs. "How long has that been going on?"

"Nothing's going on."

"Men haven't got a clue, have they?"

"I don't know much about Art but I know what I like."

"Will you see her again?" I shook my head. "In that case, are you going to invite me back to see your etchings?"

"I don't etch any more. I think I've forgotten how to."

She stroked my thigh. "I could remind you."

"Not tonight Josephine. But thanks for the offer."

"I just thought you might need cheering up. But I see Miss Hampstead Garden Suburb has been doing that already."

We split the bill and walked towards Holland Park, arm in arm. It has everything you'd want in a London park, formal gardens, wooded areas and a couple of great places to eat. We'd had our first date there and found ourselves walking the same route.

"It is good to see you're not falling apart, which is a relief."

"Did you expect me to be?"

"Could have gone either way, you're an old softie."

"I'm fine. And I'm starting a new life tonight, I'm moving back in to my old room."

"Would you like to christen it in style? Just the two of us?"

"I need to do this on my own. Perhaps some other time?"

"Perhaps."

It would have been fun to spend the evening with Michelle but as I opened the front door, I was pleased I'd come home alone. I wasn't sure that a trip down memory lane was what I needed right now. Not that I had the remotest idea what it was that I did need. But, as my Grandfather used to say, sometimes doing nothing is the most courageous thing of all.

I lay on my bed in the newly carpeted bedroom. The curtains were open and the sun was streaming in. It was only six thirty but I closed my eyes and knew that somehow I'd be alright. I woke around midnight still fully clothed. I pulled the duvet over me, turned over and went back to sleep.

I was half asleep in the loft and heard a knock at the door. The little boy came running in and jumped on the bed. "I looked for you upstairs in the loft but I couldn't find you."

"I decided to move back down here. I thought it might feel a bit sad, but it's OK."

"I like this room. It smells of New."

I sat up. I'd been meaning to ask him a question for some time. "Do you believe in God?"

"Of course, don't you?"

"I want to but sometimes it's hard. I can't seem to find Him right now."

"Don't worry, finding Him is like a Treasure Hunt. There are clues everywhere."

"Are there?"

"Yes, you'll see."

My alarm woke me at eight. I jumped out of bed and rang Ivy's bell at two minutes to nine.

"I'm early for once."

"Your watch must be slow. I make it five past."

It wouldn't be the same if we didn't have this little exchange every Monday morning. I gave her a peck on the cheek and handed her a pot of Lavender, as a thank you for the dinner on Friday.

"That's very naughty of you."

I headed off towards the kitchen as usual.

She opened the door to the dining room. "No, I think we'll start off in here today."

I'd only been in there once before. I'd driven her to a friend's funeral and we'd sat in silence together afterwards, nursing a glass of ginger wine in our overcoats.

On the sideboard was a half bottle of champagne, almost lost in an ice bucket and two glasses.

"You open that, my dear. I have an important matter to discuss with you."

I tore off the gold label and untwisted the metal tie.

"This isn't the bottle I gave you three Christmases ago, is it?"

"I've been saving it for a special occasion. Pour it out and leave the glasses on the side. That's right. Now come and sit down. I want to talk to you first."

I joined her at the dining table. She handed me a thick white envelope.

"Open it. And read it carefully."

Inside the envelope was a Will. I could see my name in bold letters next to the words Sole Executor.

"You'd like me to be your executor?"

"Read on. Take your time."

'And I hereby bequeath all my worldly goods to ...' I stopped reading and looked up at her. She was watching me intently, her eyes sparkling.

"You're leaving everything to me?" I could hardly speak. "That's extraordinary, but why? I mean, I don't want to sound ungrateful but ..."

"I have no children, as you know. I have thought about this very carefully. It is my wish. Now, fetch the glasses and we'll seal it with a toast. That's right."

I handed her a glass, my hand was trembling slightly.

"I don't know what to say. I'm amazed."

She put her glass down slowly. "You remember on Friday, I mentioned a man called Peter?"

"Of course." How could I forget?

"I have never told a soul about it until now. And you must swear never to speak of it to anyone."

"You have my word."

"I met Peter in the summer of nineteen forty three. My

father had died and I was living with my mother. Peter was a solicitor and we fell in love. He was so kind and attentive, and my mother adored him too. One night he borrowed a friend's car and we drove into the country. We ended up with two flat tyres and only had one spare. It was late, so we stayed in the car until the morning."

She stopped talking and looked down at the table.

"To cut a long story short it transpired he was married. But it got worse. I found I was expecting his baby. I couldn't tell my mother. I couldn't tell anyone. Not as things were in nineteen forty three."

"What did you do?"

"I thought about seeing someone to lose the baby but I didn't have to. I lost it naturally. So when I say I have no children, it's not strictly true. I did have one, he just didn't stay here long enough for me to know his name."

"I am so sorry, Ivy."

I got up from my chair and put my arms around her. Tears were rolling down her face.

She looked up at me and spoke quietly. "You are my little boy now."

After a few minutes, she pulled herself together. "Let's have another glass of champagne."

She explained that she had planned to change her Will some time ago but had been waiting for the solicitors to finalise the paperwork. It had already been witnessed and she gave me a copy. She also gave me a set of house keys.

"These are the keys to the kingdom. Guard them well."

I kissed her hands. "I will."

"Come along now, this isn't going to get the polishing done."

Ivy started on the silver and I went out to the garden as usual. I found a perfect spot for the lavender where Ivy could sit at her table and feel its leaves. I mowed the lawn and did the edges on automatic pilot, still in shock. If I'd inherited this house while I was still married, Liz would have been entitled to half of it. I wondered if that was why Ivy had waited until now.

She waved from the kitchen window and I joined her inside.

She put the pot on the tray. "I feel a bit tipsy. I'm not used to champagne at nine o'clock in the morning."

"If you can't feel a bit tipsy in your ninetieth decade, when can you?"

She gave me one of her looks. "I'll pretend I didn't hear that. You know how I hate to talk about age."

"I stand corrected." I gave her a little kiss.

"Fetch the tea. That's right."

I carried out the tray, with its usual pot and plate of bourbon biscuits.

"I'll treasure this lavender, thank you." She reached down and felt its leaves.

"Thank you, Ivy. For everything."

"It's my pleasure, believe me."

I'd arranged for my school friend Dan to meet me at Charlie's at eleven thirty. He ran a company putting plants in offices and car showrooms, but occasionally he liked to do some proper gardening. Today he'd be helping me with the brickwork. I'd drawn Charlie a plan of the new garden, which included a paved brick area with two corner borders. The soil would be arriving the day after tomorrow when the real fun would begin.

I keyed in her code, 2525, but it wasn't accepted. Then I saw her note, 'Guess the new code if you can, Mr. Spaceman.' I only had thirty seconds before the alarm would go off, bringing Colonel Mustard and the other neighbours screaming to the front door. Mr. Spaceman? I could only think of Apollo 13. Then it hit me. 2001, A

135

Space Odyssey. Genius. I tapped in 2001 and the pipping stopped. I'd have to get her back for this by programming in another number. I saw a button marked 'Reset' and pressed it. Nothing. Another was marked 'Code Change', so I pressed that and entered 2001. The LED said, 'Enter new Code'. But what should I enter? I hadn't thought that far ahead so I punched in 2001 and left it as it was.

Dan pulled up outside with his van. I waved him around to the back. We unloaded the cement mixer by the back gate and made some coffee.

"I need numbers." I explained the whole alarm scenario. "We should continue the movie theme."

Between us we came up with a new clue. I turned her note over and wrote 'A pair of Bo Dereks'. I entered the new code, 1010. That would teach her to mess with The Flowerpot Man.

Her phone rang and a few seconds later we heard her mother's voice over the speaker.

"Charlie, it's your mother. I've been thinking about what you said and I am sure this Flowerpot Man is 'totally awesome', as you put it, but he's also forty four and divorced. He's going to be in no position to pay school fees. I know it might sound mercenary but there are a lot of very nice men who are the right age, who are not divorced and who make more money than a common or garden gardener. Listen to your mother. Love you. Bye darling."

If her mother knew about Ivy's will, she might have thought about me differently. And I decided not to mention anything about it to Dan, I knew Ivy would like her personal affairs kept private.

"So, you're 'totally awesome', are you?" Dan was laughing.

"If a twenty six year old thinks I am, I am."

"I can hear wedding bells already."

"It's your turn next."

"I can't afford to get married. Let alone divorced. And Sue doesn't want to anyway."

"All women want to get married sooner or later. They're pre-programmed at birth."

"Sue's not like that. She's different."

"Of course she is."

We were almost finished for the day when the doorbell rang. It was Colonel Mustard from number 23.

"I wondered if I could ask a favour, old boy? Don't suppose you've got a table spoon of mortar left over?"

"Sure, no problem."

"Need to fill a hole. Don't want rats getting in, do we? Can't stand rats."

I went next door and sealed it up.

"Any time I can help, old boy. Just say the word. Understood?"

"Understood."

Charlie turned the corner.

"Is the bar open? I'm gasping."

She threw three vodkas together and we inspected the day's progress.

"He's brilliant, isn't he?" She handed Dan a glass.

"I'd say he's totally awesome." He laughed and left after a quick drink.

Charlie poured us another. We did the usual getting to know you stuff. I gave her the short version of the divorce, then we moved on to favourite films, holidays and books. It was easy talking to Charlie but she'd never heard of any of my films. The age gap left us few reference points. She got us another drink and checked her answerphone. We both heard her mother's message loud and clear.

"Did Dan hear it too?" She blushed.

"He thought it was 'totally awesome'. But there's

nothing to be embarrassed about. I'm a forty four year old 'has been' and you're twenty six and gorgeous. I'm flattered."

"Are you?"

"Of course. Especially as I'm just a common or garden gardener."

She smiled. "Is it true what they say about older men?"

"Arthritis, fat tummies and a Peter Pan complex?"

My mobile rang. I was checking who it was when I pressed Answer by mistake.

It was Liz. "Hello, look I need a favour."

"It's not a great time."

"Why? Are you with Barbie?" No, I'm with Lolita, actually.

I knew what it would be about, there'd be some problem with her computer like, "How the hell do you open an attachment?" She hated computers but had finally managed to send the odd email and do some experimental surfing. She'd bought the same model as mine and I'd offered to set it up for her. It was a stupid idea. I became an 'Internet Helpline' available twenty four hours a day. I should have insisted from the start that all calls would be charged at five pounds a minute. Twenty minutes later, with a throbbing ear from using the mobile, I ended the call.

Charlie sighed. "You're too nice, that's your trouble."

That's exactly what Liz used to say. Well, I'm sorry if I'm one of life's good guys but it's just the way I am. The phone rang again. It was Liz.

"Listen, would you like to come round for supper tonight, as a thank you for helping me?"

"No visiting each other's places. We agreed, remember? But thanks, anyway."

I knew she was only asking me over because she didn't have Toby anymore. As soon as she found her next victim, she'd drop me like a shot.

Charlie kicked off her shoes. She was more socially confident than Liz, but underneath the Sloaney bravado she was probably more frightened of life.

I watched her curl up on the sofa. She smiled and raised her glass. I raised mine back. I knew then that if Charlie had been on my Speed dating evening, I would have ticked her box without a moment's hesitation.

I opened Charlie's front door to find a note on the mat.

'You changed the code so I couldn't set the alarm. PS. If I get burgled it's totally your fault. PPS. Who the hell is Bo Derek anyway?'

That's what comes of meddling with someone who was two when the film '10' was released.

Dan turned up and we sat on the new brick wall with our coffee. Colonel Mustard popped his head over the fence. It was quite high so he must have been standing on a chair.

"Hard at it, I see."

I smiled back. "No peace for the wicked."

"Well, I must get on. Can't stand around talking to you chaps all day, what?"

He disappeared behind the fence but I was sure he'd be up on that chair again, spying on Charlie in her new hammock, before the summer was out.

We worked solidly till lunchtime and then headed off to the café. We were half way through our tuna baguettes when we heard a familiar voice.

"Mind if I join you? Course you don't." The Colonel shouted across to Natalie, "My usual, there's a dear." Then he turned back to me. "Your van was still there at midnight last night. Working late? No floodlights, though. Confused me."

"We were discussing the planting." What business was it of his?

"Planting, eh? Nudge, nudge, wink, wink. Of course you were. I'd be discussing planting with young Charlie given half the chance. If I was ten years younger, what?"

We made our excuses and went back to the house. Stupidly we'd left the back door open and hadn't put the alarm on, but luckily there'd been no intruders. We decided to make up a new clue for Charlie. The best we could come up with was 'Catch the Steps'. (Catch 22 and The 39 Steps). I got as far as 'Enter new code' when the mobile rang in my back pocket. It was Liz. The alarm started pipping. I think I'd pressed '22' but I'd been distracted and wasn't totally sure what I'd done. Now I'd buggered it completely. Shit.

"Liz I'll have to call you back."

Dan came to the rescue and suggested starting again by putting in 1010. It worked and the alarm stopped pipping. My phone went again. I screamed into it.

"This is the Internet Helpline. All calls will be charged at five pounds a minute. And your time starts now."

"I think I've got the wrong number." It was Jane.

"Sorry, I thought you were Liz."

"I've got your invitation to the exhibition. I could post it but I was wondering if you'd like to pop over tonight and pick it up in person. I could make us a little supper if you like."

"Go on then, you've talked me into it."

Dan was amazed. "If this is what life is like as a divorced man, I'll marry Sue in the morning."

The mobile went again.

"Were you ever going to call me back? Or has Barbie tied you to the bedpost?"

Liz was having trouble sending an email to her sister. Why couldn't she just pick up the phone and speak to her like any normal person?

After ten minutes of Computer Helpline, her email had been sent and I entered the new alarm code, 2239. Hopefully both of those films were such classics that even someone born in 1980 would have heard of them.

"Get that bar open PDQ." Charlie disappeared into the bedroom. I was opening the tonic when she re-emerged wearing a cut off tight T shirt.

"Nice pair of Bo Derek's," Dan whispered.

"I heard that, but most people say I've got a nice pair of Charlies."

He laughed. "And I can see why."

Charlie blushed slightly. "Right, it's like this. They're all dying to meet you. We're meeting up in The Sloaney Pony at seven."

"Oh we are, are we?"

"Yes. Have you had a better offer?"

I caught Dan's eye. "I've got to quote on a job in Hampstead."

"If you don't come, Lucy will think I've been making you up."

I went into the garden and called Jane sheepishly from the mobile.

"Not sure I can make tonight."

"Supper's in the oven and you WILL be here at eight." She put the phone down. What did she say about no commitment?

"I'm sorry, Charlie, I can't get out of it. Look, get Lucy on the phone and let me speak to her. At least she'll know you haven't been making me up."

Jane was wearing a blue summer dress. She handed me a bottle of champagne.

"Open that and let's get this party pumping."

We sat outside on the terrace and admired my work.

"Do you manage this all by yourself? It's an amazing

garden."

"No, I have a little man that pops in from time to time."

"A 'little' man?"

"Believe me, 'big' is not all that it's cracked up to be."

I laughed. "It's the first time I've heard that from a woman."

"Male paranoia. Jeremy was too bloody big. Hurt me sometimes."

"It must be a great burden for him." I tried not to sound bitter.

"You're an average size. Average is good."

I played with my champagne glass, feeling totally emasculated. I wanted to explain that the heat of the sauna and the embarrassment of the whole thing might have had something to do with her perception of my size.

"You're not sulking, are you?"

"If a woman asks 'Does my bum look big in this?', there is only one answer. 'Of course not, darling'. If a man asks 'Does my cock look small in this?', there is still only one answer. 'Of course not, darling'.

A text arrived from Charlie.

'CHANGE OF PLAN. WE'RE ALL AT THE CHELSEA RAM IF YOU FINISH EARLY.'

"Have you met someone else?"

Yes Jane, I have. She's called Charlie and I know I'm way too old for her but I could be with her right now having my ego massaged, instead of having my manhood insulted by you. "No, of course not."

"You're a terrible liar. How old is she?"

Beam me up, Scotty. "She's called Charlie and she's twenty six."

"That wasn't so hard was it? Dating after a divorce is weird. You meet someone and think this is fun or comforting or sexy or whatever. Then you panic and think what if it's just a rebound thing? The first person you meet is unlikely to be 'the one'. So you play the field and still feel lonely. And sad." She touched my cheek. "Ring any bells?"

"Just a few."

"I've been there remember. I'm a bit further down the line than you, that's all. Also Jeremy was basically a bastard so it was easier for me to hate him and move on."

"Despite him being hung like a Steeplechaser."

"I told you, I'm not looking to find love, I just want to have fun. But you think that falling in love again will heal the pain. It won't. You'll have to deal with the pain first."

"I'll be fine. But thanks for the advice."

"Which you won't take, of course. Look, go and see her now. You know you want to."

"You don't mind?"

I felt I was asking my mother's permission to stay out late. I looked at Jane in her blue sun dress, sitting with her legs up on the chair. She wanted nothing from me. She didn't need me. But as I'd come to realise, I need to be needed.

I managed to park my van on the Kings Road between a Golf and a BMW. I hadn't been to The Chelsea Ram before and didn't know which end of the road it was on. I spotted a Sloaney girl wearing a pink Pashmina who looked as if she knew the area like the back of her hand.

"The Chelsea Ram?"

"Pleased to meet you." She shrieked loudly. "Follow me, I'm going there myself."

It was a busy night but I managed to spot Charlie in the corner. I nipped into the loo and sent her a text.

'MINE'S A LARGE ONE'

I was washing my hands when she replied.

'TOO MUCH INFORMATION'

I emerged from the loo and joined her group.

"Everybody, this is The Flowerpot Man."

There were five or six other girls at the table, apparently all on an outing from St. Trinians.

"I thought you said you were 'The Chelsea Ram'?" shrieked the Sloaney girl from earlier.

"I've been called many things in my time."

"So you picked up Lucy in the street? You're a fast worker." Charlie took a sip of wine. "I said she was a babe, didn't I?"

I got a round in and sat down next to Charlie. She was glowing.

"You're an amazing colour."

"St. Tropez."

"Is that when you stand nude against a wall and get sprayed from a hosepipe?"

"Sounds like one of your fantasies," shrieked Lucy. "What are you older guys like?"

"I'm not on the scrap heap just yet."

"My tan comes out of a bottle, I'm afraid. You have to wear rubber gloves and be a bit of a contortionist."

"Another of your fantasies?" Lucy was getting louder by the minute.

Charlie downed her glass. "I once asked my ex to help but his hands were so big he couldn't get the gloves on."

Lucy laughed. "And you know what they say about men with big hands?"

I folded my arms. "Big overdraft?" The St. Trinians girls howled. I'd had enough of big ex's for one night and decided to counter attack. "You know what they say about women with big hands?"

Lucy was intrigued and the girls from St. Trinians put down their hockey sticks for a moment.

"What do they say?"

"Big moustaches."

Lucy laughed so much she got a round in.

Soon the conversation turned to boyfriends. "Men only want one thing."

I ate a peanut. "And you want something else?"

"We want love, romance and sex. Men just want the

sex."

"At the moment I'd settle for a hot bath, but my boiler's buggered. Anyone know a good plumber?"

Lucy looked at me as if I was asking her if she'd ever been north of Knightsbridge. These were the kind of girls Liz hated. They took life in their stride and made it look easy.

"Why is it all so fucking hard?" sobbed Isabella on the other side of the table. "How could he do this to me?"

Her bloke had just dumped her by text in five letters, 'U R MY X'. Linguistically economic but emotionally harsh.

I said all the right things about there being plenty more fish in the sea and then drove Charlie home.

"Are you going to ask me in?"

"As long as you behave yourself."

I smiled. "If you're not ready to sleep with me just say so. Anyway you're probably still under age."

"Do you make a habit of seducing young girls?"

"Not generally, no."

"How old was the youngest girl you've slept with? Don't tell me. Twenty one."

"Sixteen."

Charlie got out of the van. "That's disgusting."

"I was seventeen at the time. My lower limit's now twenty seven. I couldn't sleep with anyone younger, sorry. When's your birthday?"

"July 3rd."

"Well, you'll just have to wait for my body till then."

She opened her front door and entered the old code, 1010.

"I've changed it to 2239," I shouted as I locked the van.

"There's no point in having a secret code if you're going to shout it from the rooftops. Anyway, what's wrong with a pair of Bo Derricks?"

"Nothing at all."

I changed the code back to 1010 and closed the front door behind us.

By one o'clock, I was too drunk to drive home.

"I should call a cab."

"You could always christen my new sofa bed."

"What would your mother say?"

"We won't tell her."

She made up the makeshift bed and gave me a quick goodnight hug. "What else do they say about women with big hands?"

"Crap kissers."

She held up her small hands and I kissed them.

"Let's have a look at yours." She inspected my hands. "They're way too big for my St. Tropez gloves."

"I'm sure I could squeeze them in. I quite fancy rubbing mousse all over your naked body."

"Sorry, but you'll just have to wait till July 3rd."

"I don't have a lower limit. I was joking. Twenty six is a great age."

She gave me a kiss on the cheek and smiled. "Forty four's not so bad either."

Charlie sat on the edge of the bed. "Sleep well?"

"Mmm."

She shivered. "It's freezing out here."

"You could always pop in for a quick cuddle." The divorce was throwing me seriously off balance and I wouldn't have even suggested it if I hadn't been in a cosy half sleep.

"Are you saying you can't wait till July 3rd?"

I opened my eyes. "It was just an idea."

I could feel her heart pounding. "Are you sure you want to do this? It's just that sex changes everything."

"No, you're probably right."

"I'm not saying I don't want to." She lent in and gave me a kiss, then looked up to see if I was OK with it.

I fancied her, of course, but I panicked slightly, hoping it wouldn't be a repeat of the 'half hog' scenario in the sauna. She was an even better kisser than I'd imagined and pretty soon our passions were rising. We were in danger of crossing the line of employer/employee conduct, when the doorbell rang.

"It's only Dan. He can wait in the car."

The bell rang again. And again.

"Don't stop. They'll go away."

But they didn't go away. Finally I threw off the bedclothes and stormed towards the front door stark naked. I opened it to find the Colonel also standing to attention. He looked more shocked than jealous.

"Sorry, old boy. Not a good moment. My mistake."

As he turned to go, I slammed the door hard, crushing my left bollock as it passed. I screamed in agony.

Charlie ran through to help. "Shall I kiss it better? Or put an ice cube on it?"

"Fucking Colonel, fucking Mustard." I shouted. "This is what comes of having sex before your twenty seventh birthday."

Charlie was in hysterics.

"It's all very well for you to laugh, but imagine if you'd just caught your left tit in a mangle."

"What the hell's a 'mangle'?"

"Oh for God's sake, this is never going to work. You're far too young. Look, I can't be bothered to explain the history of mechanical laundry equipment every time I catch a bollock in a door."

"You're not too old."

"I didn't say I was," I screamed. "I said you were too young. It's totally different."

I was on my knees in pain. The doorbell rang again. I crawled to the letterbox and shouted through it.

"If I never have kids, I'll hold you personally responsible. I've lost a bollock because of you."

"I never touched your bloody bollock." It was Dan.

I reached up and opened the door.

Charlie stood there rooted to the spot in her birthday suit. "Have you never seen a naked woman before?" She made a dash for the bedroom.

I lay on the hall floor, covering my crushed manhood with both hands.

"Anything I can do to help? I did First Aid in the Scouts."

"Piss right off."

Dan went to the kitchen whistling Colonel Bogey. I'd probably have done the same if I'd found him castrated in a young girl's hallway, but it didn't help. I looked down to inspect the damage.

Charlie came out of the bedroom. "Is it broken?"

"Not sure."

"Come and lie down. I could rub it, if you like."

"Very funny."

She helped me onto her bed. She was late for work, so she gave me a quick kiss and said she'd be home at lunchtime to check up on me.

Dan came in to check up on me. "Nice robe. Are you going to nick it when you check out?"

Her flat had felt like a five star hotel, especially as my place was still without hot water. Dan said he knew a plumber so I arranged for him to call round first thing in the morning.

I caught sight of myself in the mirror. The pain had added ten years. Not only did I look over fifty, but now I only had one ball. It was all downhill from here.

We were drinking our coffee in the garden when the Colonel appeared over the fence.

"Sorry about earlier, old boy. Coitus Interruptus, what?"

"More like Bollocks Crushidus."

"I'd like to buy you lunch as an apology. One o'clock any good?"

If my sex life was to be over, I might as well have a free lunch as compensation.

The café was empty when we got there. I checked my watch, ten to one. Even in the midst of pain, I was still a 'ten to' man. The Colonel, with his military training, arrived at twelve fifty nine and fifty nine seconds.

"Tuna baguette, alright?"

"Same for me," added Dan hopefully. He felt that he was also due a free lunch as he'd endured sympathy pains all morning.

The Colonel handed me a coffee. "So you and young Charlie, eh?"

"Yes." I wasn't quite sure what I was saying 'yes' to.

"Make a habit of answering the door in the buff, do you?"

"Not really."

"Nonsense, you love it." Dan was enjoying himself hugely. "Remember that time in Skiathos?"

"Strictly a one off."

The Colonel took a sip of coffee. "I like to do the ironing in the buff."

There was no answer to that. But Dan found one. "Isn't that a bit dangerous? You wouldn't want to catch your little fellow on the hotplate."

He ignored Dan's remark. "In fact, it's how I like to do most of my housework."

The rest of lunch was pretty much eaten in silence. We were saying goodbye when my phone rang. It was Liz and for once I was pleased to hear from her.

She sounded irritated. "I've got an infection."

"Well, I've only got one ball." I explained what had happened.

"You're out of control, you know that, don't you? Are you going to sleep with all your clients now?"

"I can do what I like. I'm a free agent."

"So you felt trapped being married to me?"

I wasn't going to go there today. "What's this about an infection?"

"My computer's got a virus. It keeps crashing."

"Call the shop we bought it from. I can't suggest anything else, I'm afraid."

"I've sent you an email. Have you opened it yet? Because if you have you'll be infected as well."

"I didn't go home last night."

"You told me that already." She hung up.

Charlie had tried to call while I was on the phone with Liz, and had gone straight through to the voicemail.

"Hello you. I hope this morning's episode hasn't put

you off sex for life. I'll be home six thirtyish and we can go to Lucy's together. Really busy at work but I'll come home and put on my nurse's outfit if you need me to. If you don't ring me, I'll assume you're OK. No, I'll call back in two minutes, because you may be in too much agony to pick up the phone. I'm rambling but I'll call you in two."

As I was deleting her message, the phone rang again.

"I'm fine and I think my manhood's still intact."

"Sounds like a hell of a party. I was going to ask how your evening went, but I think you've just told me." It was Jane.

"Sorry I dashed off."

"Glad it was worth it. Look, I'm sending you two tickets to the exhibition next week. Bring young Charlie."

"Does she really want to see me twenty five feet high, sweating like a giant tomato?"

"It's a sexy portrait."

"That's as maybe, but it was taken before I was neutered."

Charlie had rung again while I was talking to Jane.

"It's me. I think I'd better come over in a cab. Maybe you're in a coma or worse. I'm worried."

I rang her back and explained that I wasn't in a coma but said I'd be ready to leave by seven.

Dan was laughing. "On a scale of one to ten, how keen is she?"

"Eight."

I was about to carry on with the brickwork when Charlie's landline went. True to form, her mother's voice blasted out from the speaker.

"Charlie, it's your mother. I'm still worried about this Flowerpot Chap. He's got his eye on your flat, mark my words. I've seen it all before. Look what happened to your Auntie Jean. He's probably penniless after his divorce and when he looks at you, all he sees are pound signs. I know you said he was a nine out of ten but that only makes me worry more. Call me tonight. Love you. Bye darling."

Dan blew out his cheeks. "Nine out of ten. Now that is scary."

We drove to Lucy's flat in my van. I went up and down her road a couple of times, looking for somewhere to park.

"Just leave it outside. People always park there."

"Sure it's not Resident's?"

"We're late, it'll be fine."

Lucy had set the table in her little kitchen. I counted five settings.

"Isabella's just cancelled. Apparently last night's text had been a huge misunderstanding. She hadn't been dumped in five letters with 'U R MY X'. It was supposed to have been a proposal. What he'd meant to say was, 'YOU ARE MINE. X'. And now she feels terrible because she got so drunk, she shagged her boyfriend's best mate."

That's what comes of conducting a relationship in shorthand. I wouldn't be surprised if the next World War was started by a misunderstood text message.

Lucy was so desperate to find a husband that she'd invited not one but two single men, Rupert and Gus, to speed things up. They both worked in the City and I'm sure when she looked at them all she saw were pounds signs. Charlie's mother would have approved.

We started with gazpacho and had pasta for the main but Lucy was more interested in her search for a husband than in the food. As soon as Gus went to the loo, she set about Rupert and arranged another date. When Rupert left the table, she attacked Gus. And when they both had a fag break in the garden, she asked me what I thought.

"Rupert's cute. Don't you think? Maybe a bit overweight but I could always send him to the gym."

153

"I'm not a good arbiter of cute men, I prefer women."

"Gus has got a great smile but is he just too boring?"

"I think Rupert's really sweet." Charlie was trying to help.

"But could you see me being married to him?"

My phone rang. It was Liz.

"I've never asked a favour before. Not a real one. Have I? Well, I'm asking now. No, I'm pleading. You have to help me. I know I've been difficult. But I don't know what to do. I've locked myself out and I've got nowhere to go. I've still got keys to Toby's but he's away and I'd feel too weird staying there. I have to stay with you. Please. I can't even sleep in the car because the car keys are on the same ring. I closed the front door without thinking. My mother has my spares and she's on holiday. I should have given you a set."

"Liz, I'm having dinner and won't be back till late."

"I'll get a cab over to you and wait. Thanks. I knew you wouldn't let me down."

"Liz, I'm not coming home tonight." But she'd already gone.

Charlie looked daggers. "Go back to your wife. See if I care."

I thanked Lucy for the meal and left to find I'd got a bloody parking ticket. I tore it off the windscreen.

"Serves me bloody well right."

Liz was waiting by my front door. She was wearing a tiny skirt with a thin top and was pacing up and down to keep warm.

"Sorry to keep you waiting." Why was I apologising?

"Just open the door, I'm freezing."

I explained about the boiler. Or lack of boiler.

"I can't believe you. I've been standing here for hours

dreaming of a hot bath. Where's the hot water bottle?"

She put the kettle on and made herself at home.

"Can I have these baked beans?" She'd already opened the tin. "How was the dinner party? What was the average age? Twenty two?"

"No, twenty six, but if you included me it would be fifty one."

"Feeling old?"

"I've still got some life left in me."

"I don't want to know. Actually, what really pisses me off is that we had a shit sex life for the last couple of years and now you're at it like a seventeen year old. I definitely got the short straw."

"Oh, for God's sake, do you want me to stay celibate for the next twenty years just so you can feel better about yourself?"

"You know what I mean?"

And I did. I was happy with Charlie, but Liz was on her own and feeling insecure. I knew how she felt. I remembered how bad I'd felt when she was with Toby. I wondered if maybe we could be friends again one day, when we were both secure in other relationships. But for now we sat in silence. Liz ate her baked beans and I drank my vodka.

I dreamt I was playing Happy Families with Liz.

I had Mr. Flowerpot, the gardener, and Mrs. Flowerpot, the gardener's wife. But I couldn't find the other two cards in the set, Master Flowerpot, the gardener's son, and Miss Flowerpot, the gardener's daughter.

Liz kept her hand close to her chest. I think she had Colonel Bogey, the nudist army officer and Mr. Drip, the plumber. She asked me if I'd got Mr. Toby, the male porn star.

I told her I hadn't, but she didn't believe me and grabbed the cards out of my hand. I was desperate to find the Flowerpot children. I put all the families together in sets of four, but couldn't find them anywhere. I went through the cards a second time.

I was screaming. "I have to find my children."

I woke to the smell of new carpet and looked up at the ceiling. No cracks. I was happy to be in my old bed but it was odd knowing that Liz was lying above me in the loft. It was a complete reversal of her last three months here. I wondered how she'd felt then, with my being on top of her, when for the two years before that I'd hardly ever been on top of her. Last night she'd asked if we could sleep together. "Nothing sexual, just friends." But I'd put my foot down on that one.

My alarm clock rang at ten to seven.

"Put it on snooze." Liz was lying next to me.

I sat up. "What are you doing here?"

"And Good Morning to you too."

"I hope you're not expecting breakfast in bed."

"I was cold, that's all. Now, let me have a look at that crushed ball."

"It's fine." I threw on some boxers and a T shirt.

"Come here, I'm a nurse."

She pulled down my boxers and had a good look.

"Just don't ask me to cough."

"It's alright, we are still married or had you forgotten?"

"And don't ask for a magnifying glass."

"Shut up. It's quite swollen but I think you're manhood's still intact." She kissed it better.

"What are you doing?"

She looked up at me. "Do you mind?"

My head was spinning. She wasn't going to stop unless I asked her.

"I'm not sure this is a good idea." My mind was all over the shop.

"How's that? Is that nice?"

I pulled away. "Liz stop."

"It's not too late. We could try again."

"We both know it wouldn't work."

"Fine. It's the last time I try anything like that."

"I'm sorry, come here. It was sweet of you."

"Sweet? Piss off. I'm going home." She threw herself out of bed.

She looked tanned. "You're very brown."

"Sunlamp."

"It's bad for you, you know."

"I know, I tried the St. Tropez mousse out of a bottle. Toby helped rub it in but his hands were so big they ripped the gloves."

That was it, I'd had enough. "Men with big hands aren't always amazing lovers, they aren't always amazing fathers and they don't always stick around when the going gets tough."

"Where the hell did that come from? I was only saying."

"You're always 'only saying' but it's always about Toby and how fucking perfect he is. I've had it up to here with men with big hands. I'm going to start an internet helpline for men with small hands. Men with big hearts. Men who want to be fathers. Men who want to hold all four cards in Happy Families and live happily ever after."

I was crying. Liz put her arms around me.

"Do you think it doesn't hurt for me too?"

The doorbell rang. It was Dan's friend, Mr Drip, the plumber. It only took him five minutes to sort out the problem. Apparently the air vent had become blocked by a bird's nest. If I'd spotted that, it would have saved me the seventy pound call out charge.

"Any reduction for cash? Or for being a friend of Dan's?"

"I could lose the VAT. Call it sixty. Would that help?"

I gave him the cash.

Liz handed him a coffee. "That's two pounds fifty, but I could probably lose the VAT."

He laughed and gave her a fiver. "You've got a great little wife there. Take care someone doesn't come along and take her off your hands."

"You don't fancy servicing my boiler do you?" Liz was flirting outrageously. Only ten minutes ago she was flirting with my manhood.

Mr. Drip, the plumber, offered to drive her home and break a window to get her in. He also had a mate who was a glazier, so it was all sorted. It had cost me sixty quid and Liz had kept his fiver, but at least I had a boiler that worked properly and she had an army of practical men to sort her out when things went wrong. That had to be worth it.

I looked through the post. There was a new Council Tax demand, but as a single occupant I could now apply for a twenty five percent reduction. I filled in the form and had to tick one of three boxes. Single, Married or

Divorced. Why should I have to tick 'Divorced'? If I wasn't Married, I was Single, surely? It was bad enough having to admit to myself that I'd blown it without having to admit it to the local council as well. I'm surprised they don't offer more specific options, Virgin, Single But Sleeps Around, Looking For Love or just plain Lonely. If there was a box marked Failure, I'd have ticked it gladly. Instead, I added my own little box and marked it Mind Your Own Business. It might have cost me my twenty five percent reduction but sometimes you have to stand up and be counted.

I was doing the washing up when Charlie rang me on the mobile.

"How was Liz?"

"She's playing Happy Families with Mr. Drip, the plumber, so we're definitely on for tonight."

"Did you sleep together?"

I assumed she meant in the Biblical sense. "Don't be silly."

"I couldn't sleep, knowing you were with her. I thought she'd try to get you back."

"No chance. See you tonight and I'll make it up to you, I promise."

"Thanks, darling. Can't wait."

Had she just called me darling? I hadn't been called that for ages. Liz used to call me darling before we got married and then again when we decided to get divorced. But she never used it once during the actual marriage. Next time round, I'd insist on no pet names and no darlings, just the plain Christian name. Constantly repeating it could become irritating, of course, but in the interests of making a relationship work, I was prepared to give it a go. Yes Liz, No Liz, Three bags full, Liz.

I noticed my answerphone was flashing with a message. I should have checked it last night.

"Hello? Hello? This is Ivy. Hello? I could do with a

little help, do you mind? Please ring me. Love, Ivy."

I rang her straight away. "What is it, Ivy?"

"Don't worry, it will keep until tonight." I'd never heard that tone in her voice before.

"I'll be with you in five minutes."

"Will you let yourself in, so I don't have to answer the door?"

I called Dan on the way. The topsoil had just arrived and there was a mountain to shift.

"Ivy's just an excuse. You're trying to get out of the shovelling, aren't you?"

"It's not that, I'm frightened Colonel Mustard might ask me to join him in a little light dusting."

I took Ivy's keys out of my pocket. It was the first time I'd used them. I rang the bell three times, which was my code, and opened the front door.

I called down the hall. "Hello. Only me."

"I'm in the kitchen, dear. That's right."

She'd had a fall and was shaken. Why hadn't she rung me on my mobile? She wasn't very good with modern technology and had once asked me, "If it's really urgent, could I fax you on your pager?"

"Have you broken anything?"

"I've seen two World Wars. A little fall in the kitchen isn't going to finish me off."

She had a Zimmer frame but it had got caught on a dodgy piece of lino and she'd gone over. It was an accident waiting to happen, so I measured up and offered to lay a new piece when I called in on Monday. I checked her cupboards and found they were empty apart from one tin of soup and a slice of bread. I heated the soup and toasted the bread. But there would be nothing for supper, so I offered to do a shop for her after work before spending the evening with Charlie.

Dan put down his shovel. "About bloody time."

"Is that all you've done?"

"Don't start."

I put the kettle on and Dan had a roll up.

"They'll be the death of you."

"Shifting an entire lorry load of top soil on my own will be the death of me."

Charlie's landline rang. Dan laughed.

"Standby for another episode of The Archers. What's her mother got to say about you today?"

"Charlie, it's your mother. You sounded drunk last night. Has he upset you, this Flower Power Man? And I had such a nice young chap lined up for you. His mother's delightful. Such a good family. But your head's full of this gardener chap. I just hope you don't come crying home to Mummy when it's all over. Take care, Bobbles. Love you."

"Bobbles?" Dan took another drag. "How the hell did she come up with that one?"

My mobile went. One missed call. Why does it sometimes go straight to the answerphone? It was my mother.

"Just ringing to check you're OK. Your father and I are worried. It's a delicate time after a divorce and we haven't heard from you for a while. I hope you're getting out there and meeting new people. But don't go looking for it, take your time. Love will find you when the time is right. You are very special and we both love you. Bye, Raisin."

Dan laughed. "Does she still call you Raisin? Sweet. My mother still calls me Winkle."

"Let's not go there."

There was a scream from next door.

"I think the Colonel's just caught something in the mangle."

Charlie looked out at her new garden. "Awesome. Let's open the bar. I've bought some champagne."

"Great. Some bubbles from Bobbles."

"My mother's message, right? I wish she wouldn't call me that. And you're not allowed to use it either, I'm serious."

"OK, Bobbles. I'll never call you Bobbles again, Bobbles."

"What does your mother call you?"

"Light of my Life."

"Yeah, right."

I explained that I'd promised to see Ivy first. So Charlie put the champagne on ice and went for a bath, I headed off to the supermarket. I got everything on Ivy's list, including the condensed milk, which no one of my age would even think of buying. I let myself in to find her sitting in the kitchen exactly where I'd left her. She looked cold.

"Have you moved from here since this morning?"

"I'm afraid of falling over again."

I put the food away and made her some scrambled eggs on thin white toast. I prefer really thick brown but extra thin white was easier on her dentures. I sat next to her while she ate it.

"That was lovely, now off you go. That's right. You don't want to be stuck here with me."

"I don't have any plans, Ivy. I'll stay here for a bit if you'd like."

I walked slowly with her to the front room and lit the gas fire to warm her up. She got out her cards and we played Pontoon.

"You don't have a set of Happy Families, do you, Ivy?"

She smiled. "I used to play that with the children from next door. Mrs. Bun, the baker's wife."

"And Mr. Plod, the policeman."

My mobile rang with a text from Charlie.

'I'M HOT. FIZZ IS COLD. X'

Ivy watched me read it. "Was that an important fax?"

"It's fine but I need to make a call."

"Go through to the dining room. That's right."

I called Charlie and explained that I'd had to help Ivy with her supper. She'd never looked after elderly people and didn't understand that even the smallest job took longer than you thought.

"I'll be forty five minutes getting Ivy into bed and then I'll drive over and get into your bed."

"Don't bother. I'll be asleep by then."

"It'll be worth the wait, I promise."

"It better had be." She slammed down the phone.

It took over an hour to get Ivy into bed and I realised there was no way she could manage without nursing care from now on.

"Phone me when you get home. That's right."

I didn't tell her I was off to Brook Green to make it up with Charlie but I called her on my mobile ten minutes later to say I was home safely.

I let myself in to Charlie's flat. The lights were on but she was fast asleep. There was a note on the pillow next to her.

'I can't believe you've let me down AGAIN. Don't think of sleeping here tonight. You've missed your chance. Just finish the garden and NEVER call me.'

She must have been crying as some of the words had run. I thought of waking her up and having the sort of sleepy sex you have in the middle of the night but I was too tired and she was getting too clingy. I found her pen on the bedside table and wrote, 'Sorry Bobbles. Gone back to the Dog House where I belong.' I put it back on the pillow and crept out.

I was supposed to be going to Covent Garden Market but there was no way that Charlie would want to go with me now. And anyway I needed to sort Ivy out first. She couldn't even get out of bed on her own.

I dialled her number. "Shall I pop over and give you a hand?"

"Sorry to be a nuisance."

"I'll be with you in fifteen minutes."

"Let yourself in. That's right."

I left immediately to miss the school run and was turning into Acton High Street when an idiot in a Porsche drove straight in the back of me.

I leapt out. "What the hell were you doing?"

The Porsche driver was still at his wheel. I looked down to check his number plate. TGH 337. I'd always hated personalised plates but if you're going to have one it's got to be TGH 1, anything else looked like you were just trying to hide the year of the car. The driver got out. A knife shot through me and I realised that TGH stood for Toby G. Hopkins.

"Oh, it's you."

"Yes, Toby, it's me." I inspected the damage. "So you're not content with fucking my wife, now you have to bugger my van."

"I think we're supposed to swap numbers."

"I've already got your number, mate." It was a pathetic line and it didn't even make much sense. "What does the G stand for?"

"Giles."

"Nice."

The Porsche would need a new wing but my bumper could be bashed out.

Toby looked at my paintwork. "They usually do 'knock for knock'."

"But it was entirely your fault, Giles. In fact, everything is entirely your fault."

"Let's not involve the insurance, I hate all that form filling. What's yours going to cost? Fifty? I'll give you a hundred but I could probably buy the whole van for that."

He took a wad of notes out of his pocket. There must have been several thousand pounds. He peeled off two fifties and handed them to me.

"Have you robbed a bank, Giles?"

"Just collected some rent. I'm into property now, you know." I didn't know and I didn't care. "Well, that and a bit of art dealing on the side. You still tilling the land?"

"No, I work in the City. This is my company van. It's a bit flashy but the girls love it."

He folded his arms. "And do you still see Liz?"

"Not often, do you?"

"No, we split up. She loves you, you know. She told me so several times."

I didn't need emotional reassurance from the likes of Giles and I didn't need his money either. So I drove off and said nothing.

They'd just brought in resident's parking in Ivy's road but she hadn't applied for any Visitors Vouchers so I left a note explaining the emergency and hoped for the best. I was on an errand of mercy and any God worth his salt would save me from the wrath of the Wardens.

Ivy was still in bed when I got upstairs. I helped her up and let her dress herself. We discussed the idea of having some nursing care until she felt stronger. Eventually we'd have to borrow against her house to pay for it, but that would take several weeks so I offered to help in the short term. I phoned an agency who said they'd send round a young New Zealand girl called Aly at lunchtime.

I made Ivy some tea and toast and arranged to call back at one o'clock. As I approached my van I saw a Warden reading my note. He smiled and walked on. The Almighty had saved The Good Samaritan.

I phoned Dan and asked him to meet me in the café. It was now ten and I was gasping for a coffee. I could have had an instant at Ivy's but it always gave me a headache, and as she only drank tea, the jar of instant coffee was well past its sell by date anyway. Ivy thought we were all too fussy about things like that. She'd once asked me if I preferred stale bread or fresh bread. She said that stale bread toasted better.

As I was carrying my mug to the table, the Colonel passed the open door.

"How's young Casanova this morning?" He slapped me on the back so hard I spilt most of the coffee and had to order another one.

Dan laughed. "He's in the Dog House."

"I noticed Charlie was wearing dark glasses when she left the house an hour ago."

Surveillance is all very well in times of war but on a suburban street in peace time it's just pervy.

"I bet you run the Neighbourhood Watch Scheme."

"Of course I do."

Dan caught my eye. "Shot any burglars lately?"

"Caught a bloke smelling my clematis the other day. He was clearly casing the joint."

I nodded. "You can't be too careful. In Ravenscourt Park there are gangs of Yardies taking illegal cuttings."

The Colonel finished his coffee and left, presumably to check up on his Hibiscus.

I opened Charlie's front door and looked around for a new clue to the alarm. There wasn't a note so I tapped in 1010 but it was rejected. Then I tapped in the original numbers, 2525, and the alarm stopped. She'd obviously changed it back to how it was before I met her. I'd turned her life upside down and now she was regaining control. And here was I thinking we were just having some fun.

"Have a look at this." Dan handed me a letter from Charlie. She'd left it by the kettle knowing it would be the first place I'd go to in the morning. There were several sheets. I read it out to Dan but after the first page he'd had enough and wandered off to the garden. It was a tirade against men. All men. How they always left her. How she was worthless and unattractive. She hated her nose. She hated her hair. But mostly she hated herself for falling for someone who wasn't remotely ready for a relationship. Apparently I was in the mourning period and I'd have six more phases to go through before I was ready. She ended up by giving me the number of a bereavement counsellor.

Dan came in from the garden. "She's clearly a bunny boiler. Let's get the hell out of here before we find a voodoo doll in a flowerpot with a stake through its heart."

A text arrived from Charlie.

'WHEN UV MADE UR APPNTMNT WITH COUNSELLOR, CALL ME'

She was the one who needed to see a counsellor. In fact, she needed to see the men in white coats and sharpish. I wish I'd gone to the Market this morning and finished the job, but now I wouldn't be able to go there till Tuesday. Monday was my day for Ivy and I wasn't prepared to disturb the routine of a ninety three year old for an already disturbed twenty six year old.

I got to Ivy's at ten to one and still had no Visitors Parking Vouchers so I put my old note on the dashboard again. She had taken great care getting ready. Her hair net was a little off centre but she looked very much in control in her light green twin set. She didn't look as if she needed a carer at all. It was a warm day but I lit the gas fire, as Ivy thought it looked more cosy.

"That's right. I want Aby to feel she's coming into a

homely home."

"She's called Aly, with an L. I think it must be short for Alyson."

Ivy looked at her watch and I looked at mine. "Five past."

It was a good job we were in the dining room, according to the kitchen clock Aly would have been forty minutes late.

At ten past, the doorbell rang.

"I'm sorry Miss Thomas. I got off at the wrong tube station."

"That's quite alright, my dear. In you come. Let me have a look at you. You have lovely hair. I used to have hair like yours. Now is there anything you'd like to ask me?"

My mobile rang and I went into the dining room to answer it. It was Liz.

"Can I call you back? I'm at Ivy's."

"I thought you went there on Mondays. She's getting very demanding. You're too nice, I always said that. Ivy'll take advantage unless you put your foot down."

I didn't want to tell her that Ivy had left me everything, just in case she thought she might be entitled to half.

"I hope that when you're ninety three somebody will offer to help you in your hour of need."

"Well, I'm thirty seven and I need help now."

"Has your computer crashed again?"

"No, I wanted to pick your brains about my mortgage. You remember you helped me decide which one to go for?"

But you're not my responsibility any more. "I'll call you tonight."

Aly was delightful. She had a perfect balance of relaxed New Zealand charm and genuine compassion. She'd brought her bags with her and could start immediately. I showed her to her room. The furniture was a little old fashioned but it was bright and clean.

"No worries." I loved her accent.

On the way back I picked up some turf from a local garden centre. It wasn't a huge area but I don't like London gardens that are all decked, bricked or gravelled. Even the smallest lawn makes you feel the city hasn't completely concreted over your soul.

Dan was struggling with the instructions for the hammock.

"It says Easy Assembly. They're having a laugh."

We were down to the last couple of nuts when I dropped one of them. It rolled away and slid down the drain. I sent Dan off to a hardware shop on the Uxbridge Road to match the one remaining nut, while I made a start laying the turf. This was the gardening equivalent of wallpapering. All the hard preparation made it easy. I was using my old boards to tread it in when Charlie's landline rang and I felt obliged to listen to today's sermon.

"Bobbles, it's your mother. Come home for the weekend and forget all about this Flower Powered Man. He sounds frightful. I'm sure you're right to suggest therapy but he's really not your problem. There are plenty of good looking, uncomplicated men out there who are not in denial about their marriage. Make him wait for his money. In fact, I wouldn't even pay his bill at all. He's just a nasty little man."

I didn't think I was either nasty or little. I felt like ringing Ivy and redressing the balance of my self esteem.

Dan returned from the hardware shop. "They didn't have anything that fitted, so I picked up a couple of new nuts and bolts which might do the trick."

They worked a treat and ten minutes later we were sitting in our respective hammocks enjoying the fruits of our labour.

The Colonel put his head over the wall. "Hard at it again, I see."

He'd taken his shirt off and I wondered if he was wearing anything else below the fence. The thought of him standing completely nude on a chair was not a pleasant one.

"Anyway, must get on." He disappeared, presumably he had a pile of ironing that needed urgent attention.

There was nothing more I could do until I picked up the plants, so I wrote Charlie a note.

'Charlie. I'm really sorry you feel upset. I don't think I need to see a Counsellor but it was sweet of you to think of me. I hope you like the garden. I've tested both hammocks and they're completely safe. Can I leave my bill for the work I've done so far? (I have to pay for the materials, and for Kris and Dan etc.) I'm going to go to Covent Garden Flower Market early on Tuesday morning. Come with me if you like. If not, I'll get what we discussed. Take care, Will.'

I thought about putting an 'X' at the end but decided I wouldn't send any mixed messages.

On the way home, I called in to see Ivy. Aly had only been there for a few hours but the house already felt more alive. She made us all a cup of tea and we sat in the kitchen. I only stayed half an hour, as I was in need of a hot bath and some food.

I could see Ivy watching me from the window, as I peeled off a parking ticket from the windscreen. She waved with one hand, while holding onto her Zimmer frame with the other. Aly had put her arm around her and was waving too. In the scheme of things I wouldn't have minded if I'd got a thousand tickets.

I was fast asleep when the phone rang. The clock said twelve thirty so I let it go to answerphone. I thought it might be a drunken Charlie and it was.

"I'm phoning from the back of a cab. I'm really, really sorry about my letter, I must have sounded like a madwoman. I was going to come round to you now, but you're not there. Or maybe you are there and don't want to speak to me. Are you there? Look, forget my note. You're a wonderful gardener and a wonderful person and I'd love to come with you to Covent Garden on Tuesday. I'll take the day off work, I'm owed a couple of days anyway. It's now twelve thirty two. If you get this message in the next five minutes call me and I'll divert the cab back to yours. I don't know your address but I know it's Chiswick. Or is it Ealing? I'm a little tipsy. Sorry if I'm rambling."

If I'd picked up, she'd have come round and we'd probably have slept together. But she was drunk and would almost certainly have ended up crying.

The phone rang again.

"It's now twelve thirty four and I'm almost home. I could so easily drive onto Chiswick. Or Ealing. Well, it's sort of the same direction. I'd love to see you. Call me in two minutes or regret it for the rest of your life. The meter's running and time's running out. Call me."

Three minutes later a text. 'WHDRE RU? IN CBB. I WNT 2KSS U NMW. LNVF CHBLJF. XZX'

I thought about texting back with, 'IF UR 2PSSD 2TXT, UR 2PSSD TO KSS ME'. I started to type but pressed the answer button by mistake just as she rang again.

"Hello? You're there. What's your address? I'm coming round."

I could have said no. But I didn't. Ten minutes later. The doorbell rang.

"Can I borrow twenty for the cab?"

She paid the driver and came in. She was the first woman to cross the threshold since Liz had moved out.

"Great house. You're a dark horse. I expected old pizza boxes and a sink full of washing up."

"I am reasonably civilised."

She opened the fridge door. "Tonic water's a start. Where's the vodka?"

"In the freezer."

I hadn't got round to buying another coffee table so we sat on the rug in front of the fire. She was wearing faded jeans and in the firelight looked almost edible. I reminded myself that she had shown early signs of Bunny Boileritis but when she kissed me it didn't seem to matter. We lay down on the rug. She was cute and twenty six and I was only human.

She looked up at me. "When you were eighteen, I was still in my Mummy's tummy."

"And now I'm forty four, I'm in your tummy. It's the Circle of Life."

Then she started crying.

"What is it?"

"David."

Her tears had stopped our passion dead in its tracks. Great, thank you, David. I'd love to talk about what happened between you and Charlie but maybe some other time, mate. She told me all about it and I stroked her back. As I listened, I realised that the pain of love, whether lost or unrequited, was universal. My particular sadness was no more unique or more painful than hers. I decided to count the number of people I saw tomorrow who looked like they'd been hurt by love. But I suspect it would probably be easier to count the few that hadn't.

Her mascara had almost reached her nose. "I'm not totally unlovable, am I?"

Charlie was still asleep next to me. A streak of sunlight hit the painting by the wardrobe. I'd bought it on holiday with Liz two years ago in Italy. It was an oil of some fishing boats and had cost a small fortune. She'd wanted to buy it to impress the owner of the gallery. He'd been seriously flirting with her and she wanted to look as if she bought art all the time. She'd handed over my credit card as if she was leaving a tip in a five star hotel. But I'd grown to like it and wondered if I'd ever buy a painting on holiday with Charlie.

Her mobile was ringing downstairs. It was probably her mother, setting her up with some chinless wonder with a huge Trust Fund. Still, size isn't everything.

Charlie snuggled into me. "You smell nice."

I stroked her arse. "You feel nice."

She pushed my hand away quickly. "You must be mad. It's horrible."

"It does it for me."

"I hate it."

"Of course you do, you're a woman. Fancy a coffee and some toast? Or would that go straight onto your already fat posterior?"

"I like it here." Charlie had followed me into the kitchen, wearing one of my sweatshirts. "Now I want to see the Gardener's garden."

I opened the French windows.

"Awesome." Charlie sat on the wall. "Let's play Heads or Tails. We get in the car and just drive. Every time we come to a junction, we toss a coin to go left or right. No maps. No plan. Just Heads or Tails."

"Can't today. I'm going home to see my folks."

I hadn't seen my parents since Christmas. Before I was married I used to go home every few weeks. I should see them more often.

She scratched her nose. "OK, Let's play Heads or Tails tomorrow."

"I might stay over with my parents. I'll call you later."

"That's a 'no', then. I hate it when people say they'll call. They never do."

"I'm not 'people'. I will call. Look, it's a great idea and we will do it. But not necessarily tomorrow."

She drank her coffee looking like she'd been dumped. It sounded like a fun idea and I did fancy her. I just wish I hadn't slept with her here. Not that we'd gone the whole hog last night, of course, because her tears had stopped us in dead in our tracks.

My mother saw the van and came running out as she always did.

"You've lost weight." She said that every time she saw me. If I'd actually lost as much weight as she said I'd done over the years, I'd be dead by now.

"Hello, Will." My father joined us on the driveway. I gave him a hug and he kissed my neck. If I'm ever lucky enough to have kids of my own I'd kiss them every day until I was a hundred.

My parents were having some gardening work done and I was asked to inspect the progress.

"What do you think?"

I wanted to say it looked good but I couldn't. "Have you been planning to do this for a while?"

My mother brought out a tray of drinks. "We would have asked your advice but we didn't want to bother you."

I put on my serious professional face. "How much?"

"Two thousand."

I tried not to look astounded. They'd been ripped off big time.

"Your father's very pleased with it."

I should have been there to protect them from the cowboys. I felt so bad, I had to lie through my teeth. "They know their stuff. It's really great."

My father beamed. "Thought you'd like it. I particularly like the new bird bath."

It was hideous. "I can see why."

My mother handed me a drink. "How's my boy?"

"I'm doing well. Work's going well. Yeah, all's well."

"Have you heard from Liz?"

"We don't really speak."

"A clean break's always best. You'll find someone soon."

My father joined in. "But don't go looking for it. It's too soon. There's plenty of time for all that."

"Are you seeing anyone now?" My mother was anxious to marry me off before the summer was out.

Well, in the last three weeks, I've slept with Charlie, Liz and Jane. Although I didn't go the whole hog with Jane and every time I try it with Charlie we get interrupted. So technically I've only slept with my wife, which didn't sound so bad.

"Not really, I'm not that interested."

"Someone will come along. You'll see."

"Also, I'm not sure I can afford to get divorced a second time."

My mother squeezed my hand. She'd never really got on with Liz but my father thought she was the perfect woman. And she probably was. Just not the perfect woman for me.

I drank my gin and tonic and ate some cheese snaps. If I ever came home and my mother offered me anything other than gin and tonic and cheese snaps I'd be completely disorientated. Most people in London had switched to vodka but ever since the Cold War my parents had never quite trusted the Soviets and resolutely stuck to gin. I reached for the cheese snaps. There were only three left, so I placed one out for each of us with great ceremony. It was another family ritual. Like calling the windscreen squirter on a car a 'Norris'. "Squeeze the Norris," my father would say. It was named after Norris McWhirter (Norris McSquirter), the Guinness Book of Records bloke. We spent the day laughing, but they were both looking older and since my father's retirement he'd slowed down considerably. The simplest things seemed to worry them and now they were asking me for advice.

My mother had saved up some jobs for me to do after lunch, as usual. I wired in a new section of cable on the iron and changed over some difficult light bulbs that had got stuck. They weren't really that difficult, but I'd always done them for her and she felt I always should.

Before I left I made a special point of commenting on my father's lawn. "You could be the green-keeper at St. Andrews." It's what I always said. In fact, the whole day had been a series of repeated scenes from my childhood. It was comforting to be there but I worried for my parents. They lived in the safe isolation of Middle England, unaware that the world had moved on.

On the way back I called in on Ivy. I was sure Aly would be a good carer, but it wouldn't harm to pop in unannounced just to check that all was well. I rang the bell with my usual three ring signal, and as soon as Aly opened the door, I knew Ivy was in good hands. I went through to the kitchen and found her sitting at the table.

"You'll have a cup of tea? That's right. Thank you, Aly."

"No worries." She disappeared off to the scullery.

Ivy took my hand. "I am worried about the money, though. Are you sure I can afford to have Aly?"

"It'll be fine. We're lucky to have her."

"She'll make a lovely wife, you know." She gave me a wink. Why was everyone trying to marry me off today? "I think we should go back to arranged marriages. If I'd been allowed to choose your wife, you wouldn't be divorced now."

She knew me as well as anyone and would probably have chosen me a good soul mate.

Aly brought the tea over. "Sugar?"

"No thanks, I'm sweet enough already." She smiled. "It's what my father always says."

I told Ivy about the progress on Charlie's garden. I thought about including the episode of Colonel Mustard and his nude ironing routine but decided against it.

"I like the sound of a hammock. Do you think I could have one?"

"I'm sure you could, Ivy. I'll look into it."

I remembered my grandmother saying how she hated being told she couldn't have something because she was too old. I would try to let Ivy think that anything was still possible. She'd find it difficult to get into a hammock without breaking at least two limbs, but it was good for her to dream.

I held her hand. "Are you sleeping alright?"

"I do so little in the day, I'm not really that tired. The nights are so long."

"Will Aly bring you a cup of tea in the morning?"

"Ten past seven on the dot. She's an angel. I count the hours till then."

I thanked Aly and said goodbye to Ivy.

"You'll phone as soon as you get home? That's right."

Ten minutes later, I called Ivy and my parents to say I was safely in. I drove back from work everyday and never rang to say I was home safely, but seeing them had temporarily put me back in their world. They wanted to know I was alright.

I was taking the top off the vodka when I got a text from Charlie.

'RU UP FR SPRISE DAY 2MROW?'

I texted back with, 'CANT PSSBLY SAY. IT'S A SPRISE'.

I woke to hear my mobile buzzing with a text from Liz. 'OFF 2 GYM. HOPE UR OK?'

I thought about texting back with, 'OFF 2C 26YR OLD BABE. HOPE UR OK WITH THAT'. Why did she have to tell me what she was up to anyway? I was about to go to the bathroom but I still didn't feel the need to text her my every movement. When would she realise that we're not together anymore? In nineteen days our marriage would be over completely. Would the texting stop abruptly on the same day? Was 'OFF 2 GYM' a way of saying she was keeping fit for a new bloke? So I texted back with, 'WHOS JIM?'

I got up and checked my emails. There were five new ones. Two from Emma.

'Hi, Just to say I miss you. Come and see me soon. I promise I won't try to set you up with Liz again. But I still think you are both stupid. Love Emma x'

'Hi, Me again. I meant to say VERY stupid. Love Emma x'

I preferred it when her emails were signed from 'The Flowerpot Girl' and had a whole row of kisses. But now she's growing up, she just thinks I'm VERY stupid.

The other three emails had been redirected from my website, theflowerpotman.com. The first was from a company trying to sell me manure in bulk, the second from a bloke in Tokyo asking if I was anything to do with the Children's TV series and the third from a woman in Birmingham wanting to know if I was interested in a daily contract to water her window boxes. Liz was right, the website was a complete waste of money.

I was biting into my toast when another text came in. The mobile buzzed loudly as if it was highly irritated. I'd changed the ringtone to buzz because I knew I couldn't possibly listen to forty seconds of Tubular Bells every time Liz felt like going to the gym.

'SPRSE. IM OUTSIDE UR HSE'

I opened the door to find Charlie wearing a crisp white shirt, a short skirt and a pair of great boots. I was still in the old T shirt and boxers I'd slept in.

Charlie laughed. "Thanks for making the effort."

Women can take hours getting ready in the evening, but how come they only take a couple of minutes in the morning? And I bet Charlie would stay looking fresh all day. Even if I'd bothered to iron my T shirt, I knew it would be creased again after five minutes.

"Grab a coffee. I'll be two secs."

The only clean thing I could find was a slightly crumpled white shirt.

"Ready for your first day at school?"

"That bad?"

"Take it off, you look ridiculous."

Charlie marched me upstairs and started going through my wardrobe. There were things in there I'd never worn. I often bought clothes thinking they'd change my life but they never did because I never actually wore them. I had an inner wardrobe of close friends that I rotated all the time. New clothes made me nervous, like I was dressed up for church on Christmas Day.

"What the hell is this?" Charlie held up a particularly horrible sweatshirt. "Right, I need a bin liner now."

"Can't we go for our drive?"

"This is more important. I'm going to halve your wardrobe. You've got some nice stuff here but it's squashed under all the rubbish."

I sat there watching my life being thrown away. She was right, of course, most of it was rubbish, but one day I might wake up and want to put on that short sleeved tank top. Even if only for a seventies theme night.

In twenty minutes she'd filled five bin liners. "And none of these are going to Oxfam. People may be homeless and clothesless but they should at least be allowed some dignity. They'd be embarrassed to be seen in this lot."

"If I was sleeping rough I'd rather have a seventies tank top to keep me warm than have no clothes at all."

"That's why you're a gardener and I'm a fashion guru."

She laid out three sets of clothes on the bed. Formal, Relaxed and Chilled. Her choices made me look like I had a reasonable clothes sense. I plumped for the Chilled look.

"Pretty cool." I saw myself in the full length mirror on the inside of the wardrobe door. Not bad for forty four.

"You'll do, but don't fall in love with your own reflection. That way madness lies."

I was wearing the T shirt that Liz hated. I thought about texting, 'U WERE WRONG ABT T SHRT. IT LKS GR8'. But I didn't want to encourage a reply.

We decided to take Charlie's car as the van still badly needed a service. She had a dark blue MX5. Well, she would, wouldn't she? We got to the end of my road and reached our first junction.

"Left or right?"

"Heads it's left, Tails it's Right."

I flipped the coin for the first time that day. Heads. We turned left and drove straight into a cul de sac. Charlie did a seven point turn and then paused at the junction. I flipped the coin again. Tails. We turned right but as the next four coins were all Tails as well, we did a complete circuit and found ourselves back outside the house again.

"This is fun. We could do this all day."

"We carry on until something changes."

I continued to spin the coin and it continued to land on Tails. My neighbours got bored with waving after the first few circuits. On the eighteenth spin, it came up Heads so we turned left into the cul de sac again.

"Couldn't we just follow the signs for Brighton?"

"Where's your sense of adventure?"

I tossed again as Charlie did another seven point turn. Heads. Fantastic, we were on our way. Unfortunately the next three were also heads, which meant we were back where we started again.

"Is this weird or what? Do you think some higher power's telling us not to go?"

"Keep spinning."

I did as I was told and an hour or so later we'd left Chiswick and were in the middle of a housing estate on the edge of Slough.

"Great spot for a picnic."

A text came through as I was spinning to get out of Slough.

'THERES NO JIM. RU CING ANYNE? FNCY A DRNK LTR?'

"Can we turn off your mobile now?"

"I don't want to lose contact with the outside world before we leave Slough."

Charlie gave me a look which said, 'It's her or me.' I switched it off and lost radio contact with Mission Control. After another couple of spins, we were out in the countryside. I saw a sign for a pub that did Sunday lunches. We would have to turn right in five hundred yards.

She gave me that look again. "We can only turn if it lands on Tails."

I spun the coin and snapped it onto my left hand. It was Heads.

"Tails. Fantastic. Roast Beef here we come."

"Show me the coin."

"Keep your eyes on the road. The right turn is coming up any minute."

"We can't turn if you cheated. Swear on your mother's

life."

"That's not fair."

So we drove on past The Speckled Hen in silence.

We reached a T junction. Charlie looked at me. "Go on then, keep flipping."

"You flipping flip."

"Stop sulking."

"I'm hungry."

"I know but the right place will come up. We just have to trust it. That's the game. Those are the rules."

I spun, I flipped, I called out Heads, I called out Tails and Charlie kept on driving. It was half past two.

"No chance of lunch now. It'll be 'Sorry, sir, the kitchen closed half an hour ago'."

"You've lost your faith. Liz was responsible for that."

"That may well be true but you've only known me five minutes and you're only just out of your training bra, so don't start telling me about my marriage."

Charlie bit her lip.

"Sorry, that was bang out of order. Pull into the next place we see and I'll buy us some lunch."

"OK." But she was still visibly hurt by my outburst.

A Little Chef loomed on the left. I spun the coin anyway.

"Heads. Left it is. It's not the Ritz but at least it'll be still serving lunch."

Charlie smiled. "It's what's meant to be."

Before eating I went to the loo to check my messages and felt like I was cheating. Another text from Liz, 'FNCY A GLSS OF BUBBLY LTR? MY TREAT.' What do you mean, your treat? You can only afford it because of the money I gave you in the settlement. But I replied with, 'CANT 2NITE. BUT THANX ANYWY.' I think I was getting the hang of this texting lark.

Fish and chips wasn't the Sunday Roast I'd been hoping for, but I was so hungry that any food was like nectar from the Gods. Charlie ordered a Burger and Fries with a Diet Coke. Women always did that, as if the Diet content of the Coke would burn off the excess calories of the fries. I had asked if they did champagne by the glass but the waitress just laughed and walked off. "I wasn't trying to be funny," I called after her. I think I heard her say, "Yeah, right," which I took to be a 'No'.

Charlie tried to drink the undrinkable coffee. "What did Liz have to say?"

I blushed. "What do you mean?"

"Look, I'm on your side. I want to help you move on. I really like you but it won't work if you keep answering her texts. By replying, you are stopping her from moving on as well. Don't respond. She'll soon get the message."

"I couldn't just blank her, we were married." But I knew she was right. "The next time she texts me. I'll hand the phone to you."

"I can't do it for you. You have to do this yourself."

"I think we've done the coin thing to death. Shall we drive the shortest way home and watch an old movie on video?"

Charlie agreed but as we had no idea where we were, the journey took twice as long as if we'd spun our way home.

We got back at five thirty and collapsed on the sofa. It had just started to rain, so it was the perfect evening for cosy television.

Charlie opened the fridge. "Do you do champagne by the glass?"

"Only by the magnum."

We walked round to the Off Licence and found a cold bottle of Louis Roederer, which was my favourite. I was going to buy some cashews but Charlie thought they were fattening. And champagne wasn't? We got some Corn Chips which were probably far more fattening but they said 'Low' something on the side which seemed to make it

OK. It was probably 'Low in taste'.

I put the champagne glasses in the freezer to cool them down for five minutes. We 'whooped' over the popping of the cork as you do and I set up the film, 'It's a Wonderful Life'. Charlie had never heard of it, which didn't surprise me, but I was sure she'd love it.

James Stewart was just pulling his brother from the ice when the landline went. Charlie shot me a look so I let it ring. Five minutes later it rang again.

"Next time, I'm unplugging it." She was taking no prisoners.

Then my mobile buzzed and rang.

"It might be important."

"If you were in the theatre, would you expect the actors to stop acting while you answered a call?"

It was probably only Liz suggesting a drink anyway, so we went back to the film. It was one of my favourites and made me cry every time. It got Charlie as well. "Heads, we go upstairs to bed here. Tails, we go back to your flat." I spun the coin and hoped it would be Tails. I still felt odd having her in the house. "Tails it is. Straight back to yours, then."

She grabbed the champagne bottle and set off to Brook Green. I tried to keep up with her as I followed in my van.

We fell onto her bed.

"Heads, I take off your boxers. Tails, you take off my bra."

"Heads, I kiss your lips. Tails, you kiss my hips."

"Heads, I kiss your head. Tails, you kiss my tail."

And so it went on.

Heads we won. Tails we won.

Sex with Charlie was fun.

I was tossing and turning, unable to sleep. But I must have drifted off eventually.

There was a knock at the door and the little boy walked in very slowly. He was dressed in black and carried a black top hat. He reached the bed and took my hand.

"I'm very sorry."

"What's wrong?"

"It's Ivy. Her time has come."

I didn't understand.

"It happened a few moments ago. I'm so sorry."

If this was a dream, I wanted it to stop.

He started to leave. "I must go and see her now. She's a new girl and I need to show her round."

He walked out as slowly as he came in. Then he was gone.

Charlie woke me by putting a tray on the bedside table. "It's true what they say about older men. I'm never sleeping with anyone under forty four again."

"I'm not sure Liz would agree with you on that one."

"Well, she doesn't know what she's talking about."

"Actually I'm forty four and a half."

"Now you're just boasting."

She lay back on the pillow. "Happy?"

I sipped my coffee. "On Cloud Nine."

"Not Cloud Ten?"

"You never get to Cloud Ten."

"Never?"

"No. That's the whole point."

Something was nagging at the back of my mind. I had a vague memory of a dream. And the little boy wearing black.

I got out of bed and tried to find my mobile but couldn't find it anywhere.

"Try ringing it from the landline."

I did, but I couldn't hear it anywhere.

"You must have left it at home. Pick it up at lunchtime."

"What day is it?"

"Monday. Why?"

"I should have been at Ivy's hours ago."

I leapt across the room like a madman.

"Ring her and tell her you'll be late."

"You don't understand."

"Ring her anyway."

It rang and rang. There was no reply.

"Maybe she's in the garden?"

A bolt shot through me and I remembered why the little boy had been wearing black. I ran to my van but the bloody thing wouldn't start.

"I'll drive you. Hang on, I'll just get dressed."

"For God's sake, hurry up." I was almost crying.

She held up two pairs of jeans. "Blue or black?"

"Blue."

"Are you sure? I quite fancied the black."

"Can we just go?"

The traffic was worse than usual and every light was on red.

We pulled up outside Ivy's house and Charlie attempted to park. She was still at it as I rang the bell for the third time. No reply. I shouted through the letterbox. Nothing. I had a set of keys but I'd left them at home. We drove back to Chiswick to get them and I finally put the key in Ivy's door at twelve thirty. I rang the bell three times again and went in.

"Hello. Only me."

I wasn't sure if I expected a reply, but none came.

"Aly?"

"In the dining room."

She looked like she'd been crying all night. And then I saw Ivy lying on the floor.

I knelt down but I knew it was too late. I touched her cheek and it was cold. She'd been dead for several hours.

"I tried to call you. I didn't know what to do."

"Why didn't you answer the door?"

"I went to the Surgery. They're going to send someone. A doctor, I think, to give us a certificate or something."

"That's right." I wanted to be alone with Ivy, so I asked Aly to make us some tea.

"I should have been here with you, Ivy. I've let you down. I'm so sorry." I half expected her to tell me not to worry. But, of course, she didn't.

The doctor arrived. He was a locum and had never met Ivy but he was courteous enough. He issued the death certificate and left.

Charlie had joined Aly in the kitchen. She offered me a bourbon biscuit but I couldn't face one today. Aly explained that Ivy had fallen over last night at nine o'clock. She'd tried to ring me but I hadn't answered. I looked over at Charlie who had been silent up to now.

"You should have let me get the phone."

She couldn't look me in the eye. "Sorry, I don't know what to say."

"Then don't say anything. In fact, why don't you just go?" It came out a bit harsh but I couldn't stop myself.

Aly tried to help. "It's nobody's fault. Ivy had a fall. It's what old people do. But it's not your fault."

I looked at Charlie. "Just go. I'll call you later."

"How will you get home?"

"I'll manage."

"OK then." She started crying and left.

Aly turned to me. "You mustn't blame yourself."

"I know." But I totally blamed myself.

I went through the Yellow Pages to find an Undertaker. There were several block ads but how do you know which one to choose? They all used words like 'sympathetic', 'understanding' and 'complete service' and most had a little drawing of a wreath or a cross. Even the company names sounded Victorian. I decided to call the third one down because three is my lucky number. I spoke to a man from Cuthbert and Sons who said he'd be round within half and hour. He sounded kind. It must be hard to be sympathetic and understanding every minute of every day, like a comedian not always feeling funny. But I guess that goes with the territory.

Aly sat down at the kitchen table. "What do we do now?"

"We wait."

I thought about doing some work in the garden but I couldn't leave Ivy. I knocked on the dining room door before I went in. I don't know why. The room felt peaceful and Ivy looked calm. I knelt on the floor next to her. It felt odd kneeling, but sitting didn't feel right either. I closed my eyes and tried to pray but nothing came out right. I remembered kneeling on Pendle Hill by Jamie's grave. If I could say The Lord's Prayer for a cat, why couldn't I manage it for Ivy?

I opened my eyes and saw that Aly was kneeling on the floor next to me.

I closed my eyes again and began slowly. "Our Father, who art in Heaven." She joined in and we spoke quietly together. "Hallowed be Thy name. Thy kingdom come, Thy will be done, On earth as it is in Heaven."

My eyes were still closed when the doorbell rang. A gentle, quiet ring. I looked at Aly and she looked at me. Eventually I said, "It's time."

Daniel Cuthbert, presumably grandson of the founder, stood at the door with an assistant. They were both in black.

"I'm very sorry."

I gave him the death certificate and showed him into the dining room.

"I should probably leave you to it."

Five minutes later they carried Ivy out on a black stretcher in a black plastic body bag. It looked like they were putting her out with the rubbish but I knew there was no other way. I arranged to meet him back at his office at three o'clock. Aly and I stood on the street and watched Ivy being driven off in a black van, marked 'Private Ambulance'. I waved goodbye. Aly noticed this and smiled. She waved as well.

"Goodbye, Ivy."

The house felt empty and I didn't want to go back into the dining room.

"Let's go out for lunch." I didn't want to sound disrespectful but I know Ivy would have understood.

I locked the front door and looked up at Ivy's bedroom window. I'd been coming here every Monday morning for fifteen years. It was the end of an era.

We found a little café and ordered coffee and sandwiches. I could have easily drunk a bottle of wine but it felt too soon. And I still had to go to the Funeral Directors.

I offered to pay Aly a couple of weeks in lieu of notice. "And I can't leave the house empty. You could stay on there for a few weeks if it would help. I wouldn't want any rent."

" I think I'd find it a bit spooky being there on my own. Is that silly?"

"Of course not, but where will you go?"

"I can sleep on a mate's floor. No worries."

I said she could stay at my place for a couple of nights until she sorted herself out. I'd quite like the company. We went back to Ivy's to pick up her things. I'd only been upstairs a couple of times in all the years I'd known Ivy and now I felt I was trespassing. As I went from room to room, it gradually sunk in that Ivy had left it all to me. But that was for another day.

I found the envelope with Ivy's Will and looked through it. There was also a smaller sealed envelope marked, 'My funeral'. She'd been very specific about what she wanted. A 'simple service'. One reading and one hymn, and a burial not a cremation. There was a letter from the cemetery office, she had bought the plot next to her parents.

We walked round to the Funeral Directors together and met up with Daniel Cuthbert. I arranged for the service to be held at St. Stephen's next Monday at eleven. That would allow me an hour to give the garden a really good tidy up before the service and have it looking just right for her big day.

As my van was still parked at Charlie's, we got a taxi to the Town Hall and waited for what seemed like an eternity to register Ivy's death. With the certificate finally in my hand, we hailed a taxi and went home. We'd both done enough for one day.

I opened my front door. "I think we deserve a drink."

"Sure you don't mind my being here?"

"I'm glad of the company."

I was pouring the drinks when a text arrived from Charlie, 'FEL SO BD. CN I HELP? IM NT A BD PERSN. BN CRYNG AL DY. CLL ME SOON. LVE C XXX'.

I felt 'BD' too. I know Ivy had already died when Aly called last night, but if Charlie had let me answer the phone I could have been there sooner. I couldn't reply to her text.

I talked about Ivy as we drank. I told Aly about her exploits in the War. And the time when she had a particularly vocal run in with the local council, after which she'd been remanded in custody for three hours.

In the middle of these stories my mobile rang again. It was Charlie. She didn't leave a message but a few minutes later she sent another text, 'HPE UR STLL UP 4MARKET 2MOROW? X'

Aly refilled our glasses. "She'll be feeling bad enough without you piling on the guilt."

But I couldn't think about that now so I texted back with, 'NOT TOMORROW. POSS LATER IN WEEK.' And then added, 'SORRY I SHOUTED. I WAS UPSET."

Upset? That wasn't it at all. Shocked? Devastated? Overwhelmed? I'd lost a true friend and would miss her more than I could say.

I raised my glass. "To Ivy."

"To Ivy."

I'd hoped the little boy would come to see me again. And he did.

There was a knock at the door and he came running in. He was dressed in white and was holding the hand of a little girl. She wore a white summer dress and had golden flowers in her hair.

"I've brought a friend to meet you. Her name is Ivy."

I went to shake her hand. "Hello, Ivy."

"Oh, she can't speak yet. She's only a new girl."

But her smile told me that everything was fine.

I was woken by my mobile ringing downstairs. For a moment I thought it was Ivy but then I remembered it couldn't be. Aly called out as I passed her room on the first floor.

"Morning."

"Sleep well?"

"Like a baby."

I missed the phone. A minute later I checked the message.

"Hi, it's Jane. Just to remind you it's the opening of my exhibition tonight. Bring young Charlie. See you later. Bye."

Aly joined me in the kitchen. She had that just woken up look, still wearing the long T shirt she'd slept in. Her hair was sticking up at the back and she looked chilled. I caught sight of myself in the mirror. My hair was sticking up at the back too but I just looked crap.

"Fancy an exhibition tonight? My portrait is the star attraction. I look like a sweaty tomato but I could win Best in Show."

I started to make the coffee.

"Could I have tea instead? Coffee gives me the shakes."

I didn't have any tea, so I nipped round to the corner shop to buy her some. On the way back, my mobile rang. I let it go to voicemail.

"My Mother was right, you're so not over your marriage. You're clearly taking it out on me. Whatever sadness you feel about Ivy's death is not my fault. You've been so used to co-dependent relationships that you need to find some separation. If you can learn to open your heart and make room for another human being without blaming them for your past, then I think we could make a go of it. Look in the mirror and take a reality check. I'm not trying to preach or tell you how to feel, but you know I'm right. When you're ready for an adult relationship, call me."

An adult relationship? How dare she? She'd barely graduated from St. Trinians.

I asked Aly if she wanted some toast, but I didn't have any bread in the freezer so I nipped round to the corner shop again. There was a choice of Rich Swiss Malted or regular brown. I went for the regular. On the way back, another call and another voicemail message.

"I understand if you don't want to finish my garden. Just let me have a bill for what you've done so far and I'll pay it. I can always buy some plants at the Garden Centre myself. It can't be that difficult. I mean, it's hardly brain surgery, is it?"

Aly and I ate our toast. I half expected Liz to ring with a computer problem. But the phone remained silent over breakfast.

Aly said she was going to look for somewhere to stay but I told her there was no need. I gave her a set of keys and left to meet Jack. I wanted to ask if he'd play the organ at Ivy's funeral.

"A piano is one thing, but an organ is a totally different animal."

"Couldn't you just play the tune and forget about the pedals and stops and things?"

"I want to come to the service but I think you should use their own organist. He'd be so much better than me, seriously."

A text arrived from Charlie.

'PLS FGVE ME. IT WSNT MY FLT. I MST CU. C. X'.

I showed it to Jack. "What do you think that would score in Scrabble?"

We drank our coffee and I told him about Ivy's Will.

"What will you do with the money? Her house must be worth quite a bit."

"I can't think about it until after the funeral."

"Is Liz entitled to half? You're legally still married, remember."

"I know."

"Well, don't tell her."

I'd kept the moral high ground in the divorce so far, but now I felt I was behaving badly. And I hated myself for it.

I said goodbye and hailed a taxi. My van was still outside Charlie's flat. I wanted to collect it while she was at work.

I got into the van and turned the key but, of course, it wouldn't start.

Colonel Mustard was inspecting his roses. "Careful you don't flood it. Give it a rest for a couple of minutes, usually does the trick." I did know that, Colonel. "Whilst I've got you, can you have a look at these?"

His roses had a bad case of black spot. I gave him my washing up liquid remedy.

He looked delighted. "That's very kind of you, old chap."

I tried the van and it started first time. What goes around, comes around.

In the afternoon I made an appointment to see Ivy's solicitor. In her Will she had specified Philip Buxton, a senior partner in Massey, Buxton and Cape. She'd only made the new Will a few weeks ago, but Philip Buxton had since died. So I saw Anthony James instead. I'm always suspicious of people with 'First Name First Name' Syndrome. He was also arrogant and spotty. Another bad combination. He might have been an Estate Agent in a former life, if he'd been old enough to have had one.

"It seems you are the sole beneficiary." He tried to sound twenty years older than he was.

I didn't answer.

"Will you be wanting some investment advice? We have an expert team led by Mr. Cape, Junior." No, I didn't want any advice. And if I did, I certainly wouldn't get it from some jumped up spiv trying to sell me commission rich products guaranteed to half my money in five years.

"For now, I just need to know what to do regarding the funeral expenses."

"I can arrange for the release of certain funds for specific purposes." He attacked each word with relish, sounding like a young actor trying to make his mark in a remake of David Copperfield.

I resisted copying his speech pattern and gave him the Funeral Director's bill. He must have read it three times before looking up.

"I will release these certain funds for this specific purpose. Is that what you wish me to do?"

"That is indeed my wish, good sir." It was the best Dickensian response I could muster at short notice.

I stood on the street outside his office and breathed in the air on Acton High Street. By comparison with the stagnant air in the offices of Massey, Buxton and Cape it was like being on holiday.

I hadn't been to a Private View before and wasn't sure what the dress code would be. I could have worn the dinner jacket I was wearing in the portrait but I didn't want to be recognised, so I put on some chinos instead.

Aly was getting herself together upstairs. She'd probably be down in a minute asking me which outfit I preferred. Whenever a woman shows me an article of clothing that resembles a duster, I can never tell what it would look like on. I can only give an opinion once she's wearing it, when I can see all the curves. Then I know where I am.

I was more nervous about this evening than I realised and poured myself a stiff vodka and tonic. Aly came down and had made a real effort, but had put on far too much make up and her hair was shooting straight up, stiff as a board from over spraying.

I wanted to tell her she looked better first thing this morning. "You look great."

"You look good too but can I just do something with your hair?"

Please God, don't spray me. "We should be getting off."

But before I had time to make it to the door she'd put her hands through my hair and messed it all up.

"Much better. Quite sexy."

I looked at myself in the mirror. It was so appalling, I couldn't speak. I wanted to put my hands through her hair in retaliation, but I'd need a blow torch to make any impression on it at all.

I escaped upstairs to undo some of her damage. I couldn't make it look too obvious but, to give her credit, it was probably a bit over formal before. I smiled at myself in the mirror. "You good looking, sexy beef tomato."

I grabbed a few business cards and put them in my wallet. It might be a good place to drum up work and with Charlie's garden almost over, I needed to find some more clients. I'd slept with the last two but I put that down to the fall out from the divorce. It mustn't become a habit.

There was nowhere to park in Cork Street so we ended up walking miles. Aly's hair didn't budge an inch in the wind. It looked faintly ridiculous and I was slightly embarrassed to be seen with her, but she was great fun and we laughed most of the way there.

A pretty Sloaney girl was on reception. "Great hair."

I smiled. "Thank you." But she looked at me as if I wouldn't know Nicky Clarke from Vidal Sassoon.

The room was full of beautiful people and amongst the sea of little black dresses I could see Jane.

She kissed Aly on the cheek. "Fab hair. I'm Jane. You must be Charlie."

"No, this is Aly." Did she really think I'd date a girl with hair like that?

Aly smiled. "No worries, I answer to anything."

Jane handed me a catalogue "Your two portraits are numbers 13 and 17."

I looked at the prices in the catalogue. "Nine hundred pounds each. What percentage do I get as the model?"

"I'll cook you dinner."

"Two photos, two dinners."

"It's a deal."

Aly was keen to see Number 13. It was aptly numbered.

She burst out laughing. "Were you on drugs?"

My face was covered in beads of sweat, each one the size of a golf ball. I explained about the sauna. Well, I explained about the excessive heat part. My face looked even more hideous blown up three foot high. What sort of person would buy a picture like that? A bronzed Toby, that's who. He was walking towards me.

"Sorry about the bump the other day. Still mates?" You've never been a mate of mine, Toby, and I don't think now's the time to start dating.

"No worries." I lied.

Toby, the Art Critic, ploughed on. "She's caught the real you. All your neurosis has come to the surface in those little beads of sweat. It's an extraordinary piece of work."

"That's very perceptive of you." I tried to sound like I'd won an argument I'd already lost.

Aly and I went to check out Number 17.

"Wow. Sexy eyes."

I looked bloody good, though I say it myself. I know I was completely pissed at the time but Jane had made me look like a Sex God. Well, by comparison to how I normally look. Check this one out, Toby.

I heard a voice behind me. "You look incredible."

It was Charlie. She was the last person I'd expected to see.

"Hi." I didn't know what else to say. Then I added, "You know Aly, of course."

"Extraordinary hair."

Aly smiled. "Thanks, mate."

Charlie's hair was more conventional, Sloaney even, but she looked good. I'd been stupid to be so angry with her.

"I'm really sorry, you couldn't possibly have known Ivy was dying. Neither of us could."

Toby joined us. "I didn't know you two knew each other."

He put his arm round Charlie in a particularly irritating and possessive way.

"It's OK. She's my second cousin." His second cousin? No, it wasn't OK.

Toby was studying my image. "Jane's a clever photographer. It's amazing how she can make you look almost passable in one and like a total pillock in the other. I think I'll buy the pair as an essay in juxtaposition." Toby, the Art Critic, was getting more irritating by the nanosecond. "It would also be a bloody good investment."

Great, so now Toby can laugh at me all the way to the Bank.

I straightened my bow tie. "How do you know Jane?"

Toby roared with laughter. "Same way you do, mate. We've just been to Paris for a couple of days. She told me all about your antics in the Sauna department. Tell me, do you sleep with all your clients?"

Charlie was not looking best pleased. "Well, do you?"

I tried not to look guilty. "No."

Jane joined the group. "So what do we think?"

Charlie looked her up and down. "About what?"

"About Will's portrait. Sexy or what?"

"You should know the answer to that one, Jane?" Charlie ran towards the door.

Toby looked at me, eyes narrowing, as he followed her out. "You pillock."

Jane watched him go. "You didn't tell Charlie about us then?"

"What the hell are you doing with a prat like Toby?"

"We're having fun. But I had no idea he was the guy who'd been seeing Liz until he told me on holiday. I'm sorry, it must be really weird for you."

Weird wasn't the word. "And please don't tell me there's a nude portrait of him in the exhibition, sitting in front of a giant marrow."

"You're quite safe there. He's classically good looking

but his face isn't nearly as interesting as yours. His looks are too bland."

Bland? Bland. It was worth coming this evening just to hear that.

I turned to Aly. "I might even buy Number 17 for myself. And whenever I'm feeling down, I could look up at it and know that for one brief moment in time, I was almost a Sex God."

"Or you could just look in the mirror and learn to like what you see." She must have swallowed one of Charlie's Self Help books.

I said my farewells to Jane and left with Aly. In the street, we passed Toby trying to calm Charlie. They saw us and I think I heard the word 'pillock' again.

I caught Charlie's eye. "I'll call you."

"Don't bother." Then she added, a bit louder, "And I want my keys back." We'd almost turned the corner when she screamed out, "I should report you to the Flowerpot Association."

Before we reached the van my mobile rang with a text. 'HOWS TRIX?'

Couldn't be better, Liz. Couldn't be better.

I'd been sitting outside on the patio for a while. The idea of inheriting Ivy's house was beginning to sink in. I could pay off my mortgage and still have a good chunk in the bank. I could go travelling. I hadn't had a proper holiday for years. I could do more garden design and less maintenance. I'd still have to work, but the money would be a great help. There, however, one big moral question. 'Should I tell Liz? Would it make a difference when I actually got the money? I'd have to go through probate and then sell the house. That could take six months. By which time I'd be a free man. It would only be a moral dilemma if I received the money while I was technically still married. I could phone my solicitor for advice, but legally he might have to tell Liz's solicitor if he knew. So I decided to phone Paul, my oldest school friend. He's a Barrister and should know what to do.

The landline rang. It was Paul.

"That's too weird. I was about to call you. I need some help."

"So do I. Pippa's gone."

"Gone shopping? Gone fishing? Gone on holiday?"

"Gone for good." He'd never sounded like this. "Can you do lunch tomorrow?"

We arranged to meet in The Windsor Castle at one o'clock and leave the details till then.

Aly joined me on the patio. "Why do people have to have affairs?" She was very young.

"Because there are people like Toby in the world."

"Do you think Liz had an affair while you were together?"

"She told me she'd wanted to but that she hadn't, which left her frustrated and me destroyed. I had suspected three blokes. She might well have had a fling with all three of them."

"Did you ever check her emails?"

I shook my head.

I was lying, of course. But I couldn't admit that to Aly. About a year ago I'd logged into her email account and discovered one from David Hart. He was one of The Three Suspects. The subject was, 'Yesterday.' Had she seen him Yesterday? Slept with him Yesterday? Wanted to sleep with him Yesterday? I was about to read it when I realised that she'd know it had been opened. So I never knew what it said, but I convinced myself that something of a highly sexual nature had taken place. And when I heard Liz singing 'Yesterday' a couple of days later, I knew that our marriage was over.

But after she'd moved out, I realised I could log into her account from my machine undetected. I checked her emails everyday for the first week. Each day I sat at my computer I felt shabbier. By Saturday I told myself it would be the last time. And then I saw it, a message from Toby Hopkins. Subject: Congratulations. 'Well done, darling. You've finally managed to get rid of that LOSER. You are too special to be stuck in a BORING marriage. Let's have some FUN. I'll pick you up at 8. Dress to impress. You could come straight from work in your little nurse's uniform, if you fancy. It won't stay on long anyway. Love T.' I logged off and swore that I'd never check her emails again. I felt enough of a LOSER without acting like one.

I was feeling restless and decided to go and spruce up Ivy's garden. Aly offered to come with me and spring clean the inside. Ivy had high standards and she wouldn't want them to slip just because she'd died.

I rang the bell three times as usual. "Hello. Only me." I knew Ivy wasn't there in person but I thought her spirit might still be.

I was watering the pots when a strident voice called over the left hand fence.

"Who's there? I can phone the police, you know. Who are you? Show yourself."

As I was under six foot and the fence was over seven, I couldn't possibly show myself. Unless I wore stilts.

"It's The Flowerpot Man," I shouted back. "I'm just tidying up Ivy's garden."

The face of the voice popped over the fence. A large lady in her late sixties. "Can't be too careful these days."

"You're right to check. Thank you." It would be good to have someone keeping an eye on the house while it was unoccupied.

"I suppose you'll be selling up now that you've inherited the lot."

"I'm sorry?"

"Don't play the innocent with me, young man. I've read about people like you, who con vulnerable old ladies out of their life savings. Ivy was going to leave the house to my son, Michael. He's looked after her for years. Then you come along and steal his inheritance right from under his nose."

I wasn't having this. "I haven't stolen anything. When Ivy showed me her Will, it was a complete shock to me."

"And one week later she was dead. Funny that, isn't it?" Her red cheeks were getting ruddier by the minute.

"What are you implying? I could have you for Libel."

"Libel is something in writing and I haven't written anything. Yet. But it's not out of the question. I'll be watching you, young man."

"My conscience is clear. Good morning, madam." I turned away.

"Don't you turn your back on me, young man. How dare you?" She was beginning to rock with rage, when she fell off whatever she was standing on and hit the ground with a resounding thud.

I called through the thin slats of the fence. "Are you alright?"

"Go to hell and take the house with you for all I care." Why does inheritance always bring out the worst in people?

My mobile rang. It was Liz.

"Hello." All I could hear was loud classical music in the background. I tried again. "Liz? Hello?" She hated classical music. She wouldn't know a Clarinet from a French Horn.

"Hi, sorry I couldn't hear you. Toby gave me some CDs for my last birthday, The Brandenburg, Mahler's Fifth, The Goldberg Variations, that sort of thing." It was so loud that she had to shout to be heard over it. "This is The Messiah."

"I do know that Liz, I'm the one that liked classical music, remember? But whenever I suggested putting it on, you said I was middle class, elitist and out of touch. Now suddenly Toby suggests it and you're straight down to HMV, blasting it out at full volume." I had to shout. "Can you turn it down a bit?"

"My radio is barely audible," screamed the woman on the other side of the fence.

"I wasn't talking to you."

"Who were you talking to, then?" shouted Liz.

"The neighbour from hell. I'm round at Ivy's."

"I heard that, young man," yelled the voice from the other side. "Listen here. I'll play my music as loud or as soft as I like. I don't take orders from the likes of you. Is that understood?" She'd been listening to Radio Four quietly on her portable radio but now she turned it up so high that it completely distorted. "Is that loud enough for you?"

"Perfectly."

"Why don't you call me back? You're obviously too busy to talk." Liz was getting irritated as well.

"I'll be phoning the police about that inheritance, you mark my words." And with that, as far as I could tell, she went inside.

Liz turned down the music. "What inheritance? Has Ivy died?"

"Yes, she died on Sunday. The funeral is next Monday at St. Stephen's."

"But what was that about the inheritance?"

"God knows. The woman's batty

"What are you doing there if she's died?"

"I want the garden to look perfect. At least until the Funeral."

"You're too nice for your own good."

"Was there a purpose to this call?"

"Toby's seeing someone else." She started crying. "I didn't know who to ring."

"I'm sorry, Liz."

"It'll probably be some twenty one year old bimbo, knowing Toby." No, Jane is thirty nine and pretty gorgeous actually.

"Are you free tonight? I don't want to be on my own. Please."

"Liz, I can't. Aly's staying and …"

"Aly? My God, I can't keep up with you."

"She's not a girlfriend, she's …"

"I don't want to know." Liz ended the call.

Aly had come out to see what all the noise was about. "I should move out, I'm obviously cramping your style."

"I have no style, as far as my wife's concerned."

"Your 'ex' wife."

"I have no 'X' factor as far as she's concerned, either."

It was a warm evening and we decided to have a BBQ to cheer ourselves up. I did my best to light the coals while Aly marinated the chicken in her mother's secret recipe.

"This is amazing."

"Don't thank me, thank my Mum."

"Will you marry me?" It was that good.

Aly blushed. "You're not serious?"

I'd forgotten how young twenty two was. "No, I was joking but you'll make some man very happy with this dish."

"Mum and I used to have it every Sunday after Church at home."

I wondered if Aly went to one of those 'Happy Clappy' churches. Or 'Slap Happy' as Ivy used to call them.

She smiled. "I've been Born Again."

"It was good of your mother to go though all that pain a second time."

"You're a funny man."

"Liz never laughed."

"Will you stop doing that? Putting yourself down. It's cute at first but it could get very irritating."

"I know, I'm terrible."

Aly looked at me. "Do you believe?"

"I believe for every drop of rain a flower grows. I believe the World will keep on turning. I believe Wolverhampton Wanderers will never win the cup. And I believe in a woman's right to shoes."

"You don't have to answer if you don't want to."

"I believe in compassion, I believe we should try to discover the best part of ourselves and I believe we should be happy."

"So do I. But I also know we need help from God to do that."

She spoke with a gentle conviction. Before long I'd be converted and the wine was going to my head.

I took a large gulp of wine. "Do you believe in sex before marriage?"

She was firm. "No, the Bible is very clear on that point."

OK Aly, I won't suggest trying to find your G Spot tonight then. But what if I called it your Gideon Spot?

Would that make it any more palatable?

A text arrived from Charlie, 'PLS FRGVE ME. I MSS U SO MCH. LET ME FLL UR FLWRPT UP WTH LV. C. XXX'

If I believed in a God of Forgiveness, who was I to stand in judgement? So I drove over to Brook Green and forgave her. Twice.

I watched Charlie cross the room. She turned at the door in her nakedness and beamed at me. Not speaking for a few days seemed to have made her keener than ever to make it work. I lifted the duvet and surveyed my ageing body. I didn't want her to think she was having sex with her father.

She returned with the tray. "I'm glad we're OK again."

"I'm really sorry, Charlie."

"I know. You felt guilty about Ivy and blamed it on me. Classic case of Transference. You had to work it through, that's all."

I laughed. "You're a walking Self Help book."

"I've got a couple of really good ones I could lend you."

"I've thought about writing one myself. 'Men Are From Ramsgate, Woman Are From Scunthorpe.' What do you think? And here's another, for people who need help reading a Self Help book. It would be a Help Help book."

"Drink your coffee."

"In fact, I could write a whole series. For people who are just a little depressed, I'd have 'Is This It Or Does It Get Any Worse?' For those seriously panicking about life, 'I'm Up Shit Creek And Need A Paddle.' And for those about to go under completely there'd be, 'Fuck I'm Drowning!'"

"Are you laughing at me?"

"I think laughter is a natural way to stimulate the relationship growing process, enhancing emotional pleasure and increasing physical relaxation."

"Very funny."

"And there'd be an entry level title in the series, for people who don't really need any help at all, 'I'm Fine, I Just Fancy A Tweak.'"

Charlie smiled. "I fancy a tweak."

So I dived beneath the covers and gave her one.

I drove home and checked the post. There was a letter from Anthony James of Massey, Buxton and Cape requesting Ivy's bank statements and pension books. The letter detailed the work involved in granting Probate and the eventual sale of the house. It followed a legal course that was cold and efficient. In a matter of days, Ivy would become just another faceless number on a file in Anthony James' Inbox.

I asked Aly if she'd help me with the Funeral Service. Ivy had specified one Hymn and one reading. We looked at various readings and Aly suggested Psalm 121. 'I will lift up mine eyes unto the hills, from whence cometh my help.' Then I remembered the Mother Abbess quoted it in The Sound Of Music. I suggested 'Climb Every Mountain' as the Hymn.

Aly closed her eyes. I think she was having a sense of humour failure but she might have been praying. "I find all that 'whence cometh' stuff a bit old fashioned."

"What would you rather have? A modern translation like, 'I want a bit of help so I'll stare at a hill'? Ivy would definitely have chosen the King James Version."

I knew her favourite Hymn was Psalm 23, 'The Lord's My Shepherd', so we went for that.

Aly got up. "Would you like me to do a layout for the Service Sheet? I've got certificates in Excel, PowerPoint and Word."

Compared to Liz, I'm a wizard on the keyboard but to anyone under twenty two, I'm completely cack-handed, so

I left Aly to it. While she was typing away, I looked through Ivy's address book to see who I should invite to the Funeral. Over the twenty six pages of her address book, I only found four names. I dialled the first two and got no answer. Neither had an answerphone, so I tried the third. A man's voice answered.

"Hello, is Mrs. Cotterell there please? I'm a friend of Ivy Thomas."

"I'm afraid my mother died last year."

"I am so sorry to have troubled you."

I rang the fourth name hoping to have more luck. It would be a sad Service with just Aly, the Vicar and me.

"Hello, this is Edith Turner."

I told her the news and she cried. She said she would have liked to come on Monday but didn't feel up to the journey. I'd try the other two names again later.

Aly brought in a rough copy of the Service Sheet. She'd got it just right. Simple yet stylish. Ivy would have approved.

Paul was waiting for me, already on his third cigarette.

"As bad as that?"

"Worse." He looked like he hadn't slept in weeks. "And you?"

"Getting there."

He ordered two double Bloody Marys. "I think Pippa's been having an affair for over a year. She doesn't know that I know yet." He lit up again. "Can't decide whether to sit on it or to have it out with her."

"Are you sure? Do you know who it is?"

"Some guy who owns the Fruit and Veg shop round the corner. The fridge is always full of root vegetables but it's no compensation for a marriage, is it?"

"Do the kids suspect?"

"They've both turned vegetarian. What does that tell you?"

He ordered another double.

"We all go through bad patches. You have to work at it, Paul. If someone has an affair, there's usually a reason. And if there's a reason, it can be worked on." I was sounding like one of Charlie's Self Help Books.

"I had a one night stand with my secretary three years ago. How pathetic is that?"

"And Pippa found out?"

"It was only once and it didn't mean anything but she wouldn't let it go. She went on and on about it. She wanted to know why. What was so wrong with her? What had the secretary got that she hadn't? I tried to explain that it had nothing to do with her. She couldn't understand that. What I want to know is, what has Fruit and Veg Man got that I haven't? Whatever it is, it must be worth risking everything we have for, not just once but everyday for over a year. Maybe even longer." He downed his second Bloody Mary in one.

I tried to think of something positive to say but platitudes like 'Time is a great healer' were pointless.

"I'm sure she loves you really." Paul looked at me as if I was a priest saying, "God works in mysterious ways," to someone whose entire family has been wiped out by a falling meteorite.

Luckily my phone rang.

Paul took another gulp. "Go on, answer it. It's probably Pippa wanting to discuss the finer points of Fruit and Veg."

But it was Liz. "Hi. Just wanted to remind you that it's Phoebe's Christening on Sunday. Shall we get a joint present or separate ones? I thought we could go shopping this afternoon."

I told her I was having lunch with Paul.

"Is he still banging that secretary? Pippa told me all

about it. The little shit."

Paul heard this and grabbed the phone. "No, I'm not. It was three years ago and it was only once. And she's been at it behind my back for over a year. So who's the little shit now? I bet she didn't tell you that, did she?"

"Yes, she did actually. And she feels terrible about it."

"Not half as fucking terrible as I feel." Paul was screaming. "Does she love him? I need to know. Please Liz, you have to tell me."

"You'll have to talk to Pippa. I'm really sorry." She couldn't get off the phone fast enough.

Paul now had his proof and was in shock. There'd be no shopping for Christening presents today. Liz would tell Pippa that Paul knows. The little shit was about to hit the fan and I was right in the firing line.

Two minutes later a text arrived from Liz, 'PIPPA KNOWS THAT PAUL KNOWS.'

Then my mobile rang. 'Paul Home'. It must be Pippa.

"Talk to her, for God's sake. Find out what's happening." Paul was beside himself.

I took the phone for a walk outside. "Hello?"

"It's Pippa. I know you're with Paul. He'd have hung up if I'd rung him. I knew he'd find out eventually. I don't know what to do."

"Pippa you've got kids. This is serious. Paul loves you. You can work it out but only if you meet him half way."

"I know."

"Do you want to meet him half way?"

Paul had followed me into the street. He tried to grab the phone but I held onto it. He was shouting. "I'm not meeting her half way. She's got to meet me at least three quarters of the way. I've still got some pride left, you know."

Pippa continued in my ear. "Tell him to come home."

"Go home, Paul. Talk to each other. You have a family to think about. Liz and I weren't lucky enough to have kids, but if we had we might have tried a bit harder. Families are precious. Go home, Paul. It'll be OK."

He looked relieved that it was finally out in the open. He'd been carrying this burden for too long.

On the way home I passed a church and sat quietly at the back. I closed my eyes. It was in a similar church that Liz and I had got married. Had we tried hard enough? The more time passed, the more I couldn't remember why we'd split up in the first place. I opened my eyes and watched the candles by the side altar, each one burning with hope for someone's dream or someone's memory. I lit one for Ivy. I lit another for Paul and Pippa. And I lit one more, for the baby Liz and I had almost had.

I crossed myself with Holy Water and left feeling more peaceful. I couldn't quote the Bible or put my beliefs into clear thoughts as Aly could, but I felt in some strange way connected to the higher part of myself. I sent a text to Liz when I got onto the street. 'LETS GO CHRISTENING PRESENT SHOPPING TOGETHER ON SATURDAY.'

I arrived home and found Aly still on the computer.

"Just emailing Mum. Hope you don't mind?"

"Of course not."

She showed me a copy of Ivy's Service Sheet. "How many should I print?"

"Could be just you, me and the Vicar. Maybe do ten just to be on the safe side."

I tried ringing the other two numbers from Ivy's address book but they were still not answering. Perhaps they had also died.

"What's the custom over here? Should we invite everyone back to Ivy's after the Service?"

"I don't fancy the three of us sharing a ham sandwich

in her Dining Room. Let's see how many are coming. If there are more than half a dozen we'll invite them back here, otherwise we'll go out for lunch. How's that?"

"Sounds good. I'm going to church later. Do you want to come?"

I didn't fancy Clapping Happily so I drove off to see Charlie. On the way I tried to think if Ivy had mentioned any other friends that I should call. I diverted off my route and popped into her house. It felt more unlived in each time I went. I looked through the desk drawers and read the notes stuck on the fridge but found no new names. I called BT and arranged to have her calls forwarded to my mobile, so if anyone rang her I could let them know. I went into the Dining Room where she'd died and sat quietly at the table.

I was jolted by the mobile ringing in my back pocket. I didn't recognise the number.

"Ivy? It's Georgina."

I explained that Ivy's calls were being forwarded to me.

"I've been trying her for a few days. I thought perhaps she'd gone into Hospital."

"No, I'm afraid she's died."

She told me that she had worked with Ivy at the Victoria and Albert Museum during the War and that they'd shared a flat in Ravenscourt Park in the Thirties.

"I don't drive anymore since my operation but my son, Geoffrey, should be able to bring me on Monday. Are you alright for numbers?"

"It's going to be a very small affair."

"That's what Ivy would have wanted."

I said a silent "Goodbye" as I left the house and drove to Brook Green. Classic FM was playing Handel's Messiah. I smiled and turned it up full blast.

Charlie had taken the day off work to buy her plants. We should have gone to Covent Garden Market but we'd overslept, so we went to Syon House Garden Centre instead. They are particularly good for old varieties of cottage garden plants.

As we were loading the last of the delphiniums, Charlie ducked down behind a wheelbarrow.

I looked around to see who she might be hiding from. "Is it your boss?"

"No, it's Mummy."

I scanned the horizon. Her mother didn't know who I was, so I was safe from artillery attack. There were two possibilities, short and dark or tall and blonde.

"Hair colour? Light or dark?"

"Light."

I studied the tall woman more carefully. She was wearing a sheepskin coat and looked much kinder than the voice on Charlie's answerphone had suggested. Clearly a wolf in sheep's clothing.

"Has she seen us?"

"She's looking straight at me but has no idea who I am. Look out, she's coming this way."

Charlie darted off on all fours and hid behind the dwarf conifers.

Her Mother approached me. "Do you work here?"

"No." I shook my head.

She ploughed on regardless. "Delphiniums? I'm trying to find delphiniums, could you help me?" She looked in my trolley and saw seven of them. "I'll take the lot."

"I'm afraid they're sold."

She looked around and took a step closer to me. "Sold to whom? There's nobody here."

"Sold to me. I'm so sorry."

"But you said you worked here."

I explained for a second time that I didn't and left her with her empty trolley. I think she shouted something after me but I kept walking. Charlie and I loaded up the van and headed back to Brook Green.

"She's not that scary. No more than The Exorcist, anyway.'

"Mummy's lovely."

We grabbed a sandwich from the café on the corner and unloaded our bounty. I loved this part of the job. Within a couple of hours there'd be a new garden. We sat in the hammocks and ate our lunch. My phone rang loudly, shattering the silence.

"Hello, is that Miss Thomas?" It was a forwarded call from Ivy's. The chirpy voice didn't wait for an answer. "We're in your area for one day only and we can offer you a complete Home Gym for an exclusive discount of seventy five percent. How does that sound?"

"Faintly ridiculous."

He got even chirpier. "I know it's hard to believe, isn't it?"

I explained that even if Ivy had still been alive, she'd be ninety three and unlikely to benefit from a Home Gym.

"I sold one only last week to a woman of ninety six."

"Now why doesn't that surprise me?" He'd probably got Ivy's number from a database of 'Vulnerable Old Ladies'. I was so angry, I spilt most of my coffee and looked as if I'd wet myself.

It was a hot day so I took off my jeans and worked in my boxers. Charlie wanted to feel she'd had a hand in the garden, so I let her do most of the planting while I coached from the side.

The doorbell rang as the last of the delphiniums were

going in.

"That'll be Colonel Mustard's Nude Ironing Service."

"Leave it, we're not expecting anyone."

It rang again, more boldly than before.

Charlie continued planting. "Can you get it? I'm covered in mud."

"Now you're just talking dirty."

I opened the door in my boxers to be greeted by her mother. I thought she was going to explode.

"You're the chap who took my delphiniums."

"You must be Charlie's mother. Hello, I'm the Flowerpot Man." I did a silly wave. God knows why, nerves I suppose.

She took a careful look at me and then at my state of undress. "So, this is what you call gardening?" She brushed straight passed me as if I was on day release from an Institution.

I nipped into the bedroom to put on my jeans. The coffee stain had dried but now I just looked as if I'd shat myself. I tried to look as if I hadn't.

"You stole my delphiniums." Her mother wouldn't let it drop.

I tried to explain the stain. "I don't usually work without trousers on. I spilt my coffee." She seemed faintly repulsed.

"I thought you'd suspended the services of this man. My car's filled to the brim with plants for you, Charlie. They were supposed to be a surprise."

We'd already run out of space and still had several trays left over. There was literally nowhere for her mother's plants to go.

"We could dig up some of ours and squeeze in a few of yours." Charlie looked at me for help. "What do you think?"

This was not a battleground I wanted to enter but I had no choice. "I could possibly use some of these on one of my other jobs." Not that I had any.

So we dug up our plants and put in her mother's. But it didn't look half as good as it had done before because we'd got to the Garden Centre first and had chosen the best of the lot.

I turned to her mother, "I'm awfully sorry, I don't know your name. I can't keep calling you 'Charlie's mother' forever."

"I'm hoping there won't be a 'forever'." She extended her hand grudgingly. "Sophia."

"You've chosen well, Sophia. But it's a shame not to have the delphiniums, don't you think? Why don't we use the best of both our selections? We're on the same team after all."

Charlie kissed her mother. "They're awesome, aren't they?"

So we dug up half the garden again and peace reigned once more.

I offered to pop out to the Off Licence. I thought it might give Charlie a chance to win her mother over a little.

I bumped into Colonel Mustard. "Champagne, eh? Seducing young Charlie? Good call. Always works." He winked at me knowingly, man to man. "As the bubbles go up, the knickers come down."

"We're celebrating the completion of the garden."

"Of course you are."

Charlie and her mother were testing out the hammocks when I returned.

"Stay there. I'll get the glasses."

"Great, you know where they are." Her mother noted Charlie's familiarity.

I returned with the champagne. "What do you think, Sophia? It's a great improvement, isn't it?"

Her mother took a sip of champagne and then swallowed her pride. "You obviously know your stuff."

"It's not bad, though I say it myself."

Charlie giggled. "It's like one of those gardening make-over programmes on the telly."

"But I suspect Alan Titchmarsh doesn't get so intimately involved with his clients. Charlie's told me you're seeing a good deal of each other these days."

"Yes, we are." I looked at Charlie, who looked at me and then back to her mother again.

"Thanks for the flowers, Mummy."

We headed for the door.

"Good to meet you at last, Sophia."

"Indeed." She shook my hand. I went to kiss her and accidentally banged my forehead hard against hers.

I rubbed my head. "I'm sure in some cultures that's an affectionate gesture."

She rubbed hers. "Possibly. But not in mine."

We waved from the door as she got into her car and drove off.

I gave one final wave. "I think that went pretty well, considering."

"She'll come round, you'll see. I told her about Ivy's house which seemed to help."

"She doesn't mind you dating a prat as long as he's a wealthy prat?"

"She's just concerned for me, that's all."

We polished off the champagne in the garden. I found a copy of Cosmopolitan and read bits out to her as we lay in the hammocks. "Is Your Man Ten Out Of Ten In Bed?"

"No, eleven."

I carried on. "Let's do the quiz. Question One. How often do you make love? (A) less than once a week, (B) two or three times a week or (C) you've lost count."

"A."

"Very funny. Question Two. Does he know where your buttons are? (A) he wouldn't know what to do with them even if he could find them, (B) he knows where they are but usually can't be bothered to press them or (C) he knows where they all are and he's found a few more you didn't know you had."

"A." Charlie was laughing.

"I'm not doing very well here. Question Three. When you make love does he (A) have his eyes closed, (B) have his eyes open or (C) wear a mask?

"A." She took the magazine out of my hand. "Stay there I've got a surprise for you."

She disappeared off to the bedroom and returned wearing a nurse's outfit. "Shall I take your temperature?"

That might well do it for most blokes, but being in the throws of divorcing a real nurse it had the reverse effect. "The thing is you just remind me of Liz in that outfit."

"In that case, I'd better take it off completely." She must have taken the stripping class at St Trinians. She was really good. Finally she stood there stark naked.

"Well?"

"Does it for me." Colonel Mustard had popped his head over the fence. "I think I'm ready for a bed bath."

Charlie pulled back the curtains. "It's Saturday morning and the sun's shining."

It was all a bit bright for me. I looked up at her bedroom ceiling and spotted a crack.

She was banging about in the kitchen. "What are we doing today?"

"I've got to buy a christening present for Phoebe."

She came bounding back and jumped on the bed. "How sweet. I know this brilliant shop just off the Kings Road."

"I've arranged to go shopping with Liz. We wanted to get a joint present as we're joint Godparents."

"That's just great." She grabbed a towel and covered up her naked body.

"Don't be like that. Come back to bed."

"I think I'll go away for the weekend actually. I've been invited to a party in Sussex. I turned it down thinking you'd want to spend it with me. But if you'd rather see your ex-wife, I quite understand."

A few seconds later I heard the bathroom door slam shut and the shower start pumping. I got dressed and took my coffee into the garden. Two seconds later, Charlie joined me.

"Answer me truthfully. Do you still fancy Liz?"

"I fancy you."

"You haven't answered the question, so you obviously do."

"Being Phoebe's Godfather is the best thing that's happened to me for ages."

"What about me? Do I mean nothing?"

"Of course not."

"Look, why don't you go off and meet Liz? Spend the rest of your lives together, for all I care. I'm off to Sussex now, anyway."

I picked up my jacket. "Have fun."

But she'd already gone back to the bathroom.

I hadn't had brunch with Jack for ages, so I called him from the van.

He walked into the café wearing flip-flops, holiday shorts and a Hawaiian shirt. "My God, I'm ready for a holiday. I got a last minute deal, we're off to Greece. Just think, I won't have to sing MacArthur Park for a whole week."

Our breakfasts arrived. Two Full English. The Great War on Cholesterol would have to be fought next week.

"How's it going with young Charlie? Or is there a new kid on the block? I can hardly keep up with you, mate."

"I think I've just pissed her off."

"You piss all women off. That's why they always dump you."

I knew he was joking but it got me thinking. Of my four main relationships, I'd only ended one.

He put some more sugar in his coffee. "I'm really sorry to miss the christening. I like christenings."

"And funerals?"

"Of course, it's Ivy's on Monday, isn't it? I'll be away for that as well. I'm really sorry."

"It looks like there'll only be half a dozen of us there. I was hoping you could have sung something. Ivy would have loved that."

I was buttering my toast when the mobile rang with a text from Liz. '11.30 BY THE FLOWER STALL. OK?'

"Will she still text you when you're buttering your

toast after the divorce comes through?"

"God knows."

I wished him a happy holiday and set off for Notting Hill. I got to the flower stall bang on eleven forty as I assumed Liz would still be in 'ten past' mode.

"Where the hell have you been? I've been waiting here for twenty minutes. You used to be a 'ten to' person."

"I still am but I thought you weren't."

"So now it's my fault?"

I held out my hand. "Shall we start this again? Hello, you must be Liz. Remember me, we used to be married?"

She shook my hand and laughed. "We're still married. For another fourteen days anyway."

"Does that mean I buy lunch?"

"Let's go halves. As we're half married."

We set off towards the market and agreed we didn't want to buy the usual Christening things, like a baby hairbrush set that would never actually get used. And silver photo frames were just naff. Eventually we settled on three eighteenth century silver perfume bottles which were perfect.

"We should fill them with Gold, Frankincense and Myrrh."

We also bought her a little handbag so she'd have something to play with on the day. She'd appreciate the bottles when she was older and hopefully they'd remind her of me. In twenty year's time I might have lost touch with my ex-sister-in-law. Phoebe might have no idea who I was or just how much she'd meant to me on her Christening Day.

We went for a coffee and I told Liz about Ivy's Will.

"That's amazing. All your hard work has paid off."

"That's not why I did it."

"I know but you've had a shit year and this shows that someone up there is smiling down on you."

"I've no idea what to do with the money."

"I'll have it, if you don't want it."

"I'm not sure what Ivy would want me to do with it."

"She wouldn't want you to give it to me, that's for sure. She disapproved of me, didn't she?"

I drank my coffee.

"It's OK. You don't have to give me half, if that's what you're worried about. I wouldn't take it even if I was entitled to it, which I'm probably not anyway."

We hugged as we said goodbye on Elgin Crescent. We stayed there for a few minutes, holding each other tightly and it felt like coming home.

On the way back, I decided to call into Ivy's. It was a Saturday, so I didn't have to face the wrath of the wardens. I rang the bell three times and put the key in the door.

I heard a voice behind me. "Oh it's you. Come to count your thirty pieces of silver?"

"What do you mean? I haven't betrayed anyone. Least of all Ivy."

"Have you any idea what my son meant to her? How much time he spent looking after her? I've got a copy of her last will, made only three years ago. Michael was the sole beneficiary. Now suddenly you get the lot. You must have poisoned her against him. How did you do it? That's what I'd like to know."

I kept my cool. "Ivy's funeral is on Monday at St. Stephen's. You and Michael are very welcome to come and pay your respects, if you'd like to."

"I'll decide if I come on Monday or not and I certainly don't need an invitation from you."

I went inside and closed the door behind me.

"Hello. Only me." The house had the silent energy of a church.

I picked up the post. There was a gas bill and a couple

of circulars. It was weird seeing letters addressed to Ivy. The gas company's giant computer thought she was still alive. Not that it would shed an electronic tear when it heard of her passing. Eventually, of course, her details would be deleted. As if her life had been a clerical error.

I looked through her desk again, hoping to find another address book. With the funeral on Monday I wanted to check I hadn't missed anything. I looked in the bedroom. There was nothing in the chest of drawers and I was about to close the wardrobe door, when I noticed a small brown envelope on the top shelf.

Inside I found three letters, tied up with green ribbon. The first letter was addressed to Miss Ivy Thomas. The stamp had been cut off and most of the date had gone, but I could just make out the year, 1943.

I sat down on her bedroom floor in the bay window and untied the ribbon. I carefully took the letter out of its envelope. Inside I found the remains of what must have been a rose petal. I read the letter, silently.

'My dear Ivy, I said goodbye to you barely ten minutes ago and already my heart is aching. I know you feel as I do. I wish the postman could deliver this immediately so you know I am with you still. You are my soul. You are my inspiration. I cannot wait until tomorrow afternoon when, God willing, we shall see each other again. I remain always yours, with so much love and affection, Peter.'

I looked up, half expecting to see Ivy sitting on her bed. The second letter was also addressed to Ivy. The stamp had been cut off as before but the date was clear, July 17th 1943. I opened it carefully to find the fragile remains of another rose petal.

'My darling Ivy, Like a child discovering its hands, I have found true love. I only wish that we had met five years ago. I cannot bear to think of the lost time we might have had. I will speak to your mother at the beginning of September, by which time I shall have received my promotion. In the meantime, I have been able to borrow a car. Imagine! I will pick you up at nine thirty on Saturday, if that is agreeable with you. What fun we shall have. Until then, I remain always yours, Peter. PS. I looked for you at the station this morning but your train had already gone.'

That must have been the Saturday night when their car had broken down and she had become pregnant. She'd kept those letters for over sixty years, despite losing the baby and finding out that Peter had lied about being married. I opened the last letter but this time there was no petal inside.

'August 19th 1943. My dear Ivy, I would write 'My darling Ivy' but I know I have lost that privilege. I fully expect you to tear this letter into a million pieces, I deserve no less, but I would urge you to read it to the end before consigning it to the fire. I write to you now, not asking for your forgiveness but only that you understand my deep love for you is eternal. I cannot bear the thought that I have caused you hurt or pain. I should have been honest from the start but I did not know how. I married my wife in nineteen thirty six. Two years later she suffered an illness. She barely recognises me anymore and I fear, in her mind, she left me a long time ago. I cannot possibly know the depth of your suffering at this time but I ask only one thing, that you believe me when I say you are my life. In my heart, I remain always yours, Peter.'

Despite the agony that Ivy must have gone through, she hadn't consigned the letters to the fire. The petals had turned to dust but her love had remained. I drove to the Funeral Directors and arranged for the letters to be buried with her. These were her most private memories and they must go with her to the grave.

Aly was making soup when I got home.

"How many are we expecting for the service?"

"You, me and the vicar. That's three. Georgina and her son. That's five. And possibly Charlie. That makes six."

"In that case let's book a table somewhere. It would be too sad, with only half a dozen of us in Ivy's dining room."

I phoned a local gastro pub that had a quiet alcove tucked away at the back and booked a table for six. Ivy wouldn't have known what a gastro pub was, but I hoped she wouldn't object to my choice.

Aly served up the soup. "Here you are, comfort food."

"You know, Ivy gave me these soup spoons as a wedding present. She thought they'd be more special than desert spoons. The knives were from Liz's cousin. Enough said."

The soup hit the spot. "This is amazing."

"Glad you like it. Another of my Mum's secret recipes. This is Dad's favourite."

"It's obviously the secret of a long and happy marriage."

"They've been married for twenty three years. How about your folks?"

"Forty one. Amazing, isn't it?"

"I can't wait to get married. Three children and roses round the door. The whole fairy tale. But in my case it's going to be a reality. I'm not going to walk away at the first sign of trouble."

I looked down at my soup.

"I'm sorry I didn't mean it like that."

"It's OK. I judge myself more harshly than you ever could."

"Next time will be different, you'll see."

"I'm not sure there'll be a next time. Once bitten five times shy."

"You're an old softie. You won't be able to stop yourself falling in love. You'll be married again before you know it."

After dinner we played Connect Four, which she won easily. It had been ages since I'd played games and I was having fun. She was the flat mate I'd never had and because I didn't fancy her, it was easy. I could just be myself.

The alarm went off at ten to seven as usual. Then I remembered it was a Sunday so I turned over and went back to sleep.

Aly shook my shoulders. "Hello, sleepy head, it's nine o'clock. You'll be late."

Phoebe's christening was at ten. I'd arranged to meet Liz outside the church at twenty to but now I'd be hard pushed to make it in time. I stubbed my toe in the shower and cut myself shaving. Aly made some coffee and toast, which I ate on the hoof.

I put on my one and only suit. "What do you think?"

"It's two sizes too small for you. You can't have worn that since the sixth form."

My shoulders had got bigger with all the gardening work but the suit had definitely shrunk.

"What else have you got?"

"Some chinos but they're not smart enough for a Christening. I don't want Phoebe to look back at the photos in twenty years time and think I hadn't made the effort."

Aly marched me to the bedroom cupboard, took out my dinner jacket and held it up against me.

"Cool."

There wasn't time to argue and without a bow tie, it almost looked like an ordinary black suit.

"I've bought Phoebe a little present." She handed me a parcel tied up with silver ribbon. "It's a children's bible. She might have one already but you can't have too many bibles, can you?"

I gave her a hug and ran to the van. Liz was checking

her watch as I pulled up outside the church.

"You need a good woman to sort you out."

"And what makes you think I can't cope on my own?"

"The four bits of tissue stuck to your face."

"It's supposed to look like baby confetti."

"And the dinner jacket?"

"That's supposed to look cool."

We went inside to join the others. Phoebe was standing on the front pew looking back towards the door. At almost eighteen months, she was a little older than usual to be christened, but Christina and Rob had been away in Italy for a year and had only just got round to organising her big day.

She spotted me. "Hewo, Fwowerman." She still couldn't manage her 'l's.

I gave her a kiss. "You look like an angel."

"Wook wike a angel."

I leant over, shook Rob's hand and waved to Christina at the end of the pew.

"How are the proud parents?"

"Proud."

The organ faded away and Father Dominic made his way to the centre. It was almost five years to the day that he had stood on the same spot at the start of our wedding service.

"Hymn number six hundred and two, Praise my soul, the King of Heaven."

I looked at Liz and she touched my arm. It had been the first hymn at our wedding and I hadn't sung it since. As we stood up, Phoebe climbed onto the pew and held my hand.

During the homily, I caught Christina's eye and mouthed a silent "Thank you".   Liz and I took our places facing the congregation with the other Godparents, Greg and Sandra.

"Today is a special day in the life of little Phoebe

Collins."

As Father Dominic poured holy water over her head, Phoebe reached down into the font and sprayed us all.

"Spwish, Spwash." She was giggling away.

Father Dominic made the sign of the cross on her forehead and I prayed that life would be kind to her.

After the service, we gathered in the courtyard for the photos. I hadn't seen Liz's mother for six months but we both behaved as if I was still part of the family, which in a way, I suppose I still was.

I gave her a kiss. "Great dress."

"I was going to wear white lace but I didn't want to upstage Phoebe. And you've come in black tie, I see."

"Nothing but the best for your first grandchild."

Christina joined us. "Wasn't that a great service? Father Dominic was amazing. He made you feel that Phoebe's christening was the most important event in the Universe."

Rob's brother Martin was running around manically with his new camera. The only problem with going digital was there was no limit to how many pictures he could take. I almost got a repetitive strain injury from excessive smiling.

"See you back at the house in ten minutes." Christina closed the car door.

Phoebe waved from the safety of her car seat. "Bye bye, Fwowerman."

Liz hadn't brought her car. She was going to celebrate heavily and stay the night with her sister, so I gave her a lift in the van.

She climbed in, trying not to get mud on her dress. "Some things never change."

"I like this van. Could you really see me driving a Porsche?"

"With Ivy's inheritance and an early mid life crisis looming, quite easily."

We stopped off on the way to get Liz a packet of fags. She knew she'd smoke at least twenty but insisted on only buying a packet of ten. She must have been trying to lull her lungs into a false sense of security.

By the time we got there, everyone was waiting outside on the street. They had locked themselves out.

"Where are your keys?" screamed Christina.

Rob looked sheepish. "In the pocket of my other jacket. The one you hated and made me change, remember?"

"I could always get Colonel Mustard to call out the S.A.S." I forgot that no one here would know what on earth I was talking about.

Rob's brother Martin offered to pop over the side gate and break the back window. Five minutes later he emerged victorious through the front door, with his hand wrapped in a tea towel.

"It's just a scratch."

Liz bandaged it up with a clean tea towel. Her bandages always looked professional. Phoebe watched her intently and insisted she had a little bandage as well.

She held it up to show to me. "Wook, Fwowerman."

I pulled a funny face. "Ouch." She giggled and ran off to show her mother.

Christina had made a mountain of food. She was as good a cook as her sister and I helped myself to seconds. "Presumably you discovered this recipe in Hindustan?"

"Jamie Oliver. Sorry."

Rob was in charge of the bar. He was a good host and would have made the perfect landlord. A rugby playing, beer swilling, joke telling landlord.

He filled my champagne glass. "Here you go, mate. Mind you, I can't stand the stuff. It's like a Jacuzzi in a glass."

Phoebe had started to rip open some of her presents and was having fun playing with the paper, so none of the gifts bore any relation to their tags. I tried explaining that the three silver perfume bottles were from me and Liz, but she was more concerned with tearing the paper. The biggest hit of the day was the handbag we'd bought her. She went round the house collecting things to put in it. My van keys were in there at one point.

Sandra joined me in the garden. "It's quite a responsibility being a Godparent, isn't it? Committing yourself to guiding her spiritual life."

"I can't pretend to have all the answers but I know I'll always be there for her."

"Me too."

I liked Sandra. She'd been in Christina's year at school and had married Greg eighteen months ago.

"How's married life? Good, judging by the size of your tummy."

I hoped she was pregnant. I'd misjudged it once before with another friend of Christina's.

"We're really happy. All four of us."

"Four?"

"I'm expecting twins."

I remember her being very drunk at Liz's thirtieth. She told me she was going to dump Greg for being a terrible kisser. And now they're married and pregnant. Kissing was clearly over rated. I'd always thought of myself as being pretty good in that department but obviously not good enough to save our marriage.

A tall, stern looking lady, who'd already had too much champagne, refilled her own glass and then topped up mine.

"You and I are the only single people here. Fancy a snog?" I didn't. "You don't want to end up on the scrap heap."

"I think I'm quite a catch actually."

"Then make sure someone doesn't drop you from a great height." She downed her glass in one and went off to find some more champagne.

I spotted Liz's mother sitting on a bench.

"Mind if I join you?"

"I hoped we'd have a chat." She shuffled along to make room for me.

"You don't hate me, then? For ruining your daughter's life." I'd wanted to call her for months but I assumed she'd side with Liz.

"I'm divorced too, remember? I'm the last one to stand in judgement."

Her husband had left her ten years ago, 'to find himself'. He went travelling round Asia and ended up marrying a Thai girl.

"I never hear from him. Not even at Christmas. You know he divorced me by postcard? There was a picture of a Bangkok temple on the front and a request for a divorce on the back. You, on the other hand, are a real gentleman."

"I did try, you know. We both did."

"I know."

"I hope Liz finds what she's looking for."

Phoebe ran across the garden and climbed onto the bench.

She held up her little bandage. "Ouch. Fwowerman banige." She'd brought a duster in her handbag so that I could have one as well.

Liz knelt down. "I'll do that, I'm a nurse. Relax, you won't feel a thing."

I pulled another funny face for Phoebe. "Ouch."

She giggled and wandered off with her grandmother. I joined Liz on the grass.

"You OK?"

"The champagne's helping."

"Only thirteen days to go."

"I know."

We watched Phoebe running round the garden shouting, "Hewo."

Liz turned to me. "Do you think we'll ever have kids?"

"Together? I doubt it."

"I hope you do. I'm sorry I couldn't give you children."

"Stop it. We had every test known to man and there wasn't a problem with either of us."

She looked down. "You must blame me."

"Don't be so ridiculous."

"Well, I think I still blame you. A little. I'm sorry but I do."

"Ouch."

Aly was heating the remains of last night's soup when I got home.

"I couldn't eat a thing but thanks anyway."

"So, how was it?"

"Phoebe loved your bible. She insisted on reading it upside down but I think she still got the message."

A text arrived from Charlie. 'STUCK IN SUSSEX. CAR NT WORKNG. WONT MAKE FUNRAL. CLL WEN U CAN. C. X'

"And then there were five. And that includes the vicar."

"It's not about numbers. It's about Ivy."

"I'm going to ask Georgina to do the reading. She knew her longer than any of us."

"Can I wear this suit again tomorrow? Do you think Ivy would mind if I wore a dinner jacket to her funeral? She might think I was celebrating her death."

"She was ninety three. You'll be celebrating her life."

I'd planned to get to Ivy's by seven o'clock to tidy up her garden and make sure it was looking perfect for her big day. Aly had sweetly insisted on coming along to clean the inside as well. We'd have to leave by half eight to be home in time to get cleaned up ready for the service. But judging by the state of Aly's hair, I wasn't sure if we'd left enough time.

I set to work, pruning the clematis and attacking the few weeds that had been stubborn enough to return since my last visit. I mowed the lawn twice and cut some flowers to take to the church. White foxgloves and blue Canterbury Bells. Ivy would have wanted them to come from her own garden.

Aly was cleaning the kitchen windows and waved. I half expected her to say, "Fetch the tea. That's right."

I'd brought fresh coffee, which Aly brought out to the garden. She'd also found one last bourbon biscuit in the tin, which I ceremoniously broke in half.

A little sparrow landed on the table and pecked at the crumbs. I reached down and rubbed the leaves of the lavender that I'd given Ivy just before she died.

Aly sat back in her chair. "I like it here, it's so peaceful."

A harsh voice shouted from the other side of the fence. "Is that you again?"

I shouted back. "It depends on who 'you' is. This is definitely 'me', I can tell you that much."

"Don't try to be clever." She popped her head over the fence. "I'm not letting this drop, you know."

"What exactly are you accusing me of?"

"Murder."

"Murder? I'm sorry, but are you on strong medication? I'm not capable of murder, not even with a loaded gun to my head."

"Now you talk of loaded guns. I'm calling the police."

"Is this still about the inheritance?"

"Michael's inheritance."

"I'm sorry but I'm not having this conversation."

I'd enjoyed sitting in Ivy's garden but her mad neighbour had cut the atmosphere with a knife. I just hoped she wouldn't turn up at the church and ruin the service as well.

I jumped in the shower first, knowing that Aly would spend hours in the bathroom. She washed her hair then immediately covered it in wax and spray again.

I put on my dinner jacket and found a dark blue tie. I used to have a black one but I'd used it to tie up an old suitcase when the handle had broken. I checked myself in the mirror. The suit looked great but I really should have had my hair cut.

Aly looked shocked. "I think I'd better cut it, it'll only take two secs. I can use your kitchen scissors and a comb. Mum taught me. No worries."

"You may have no worries but I do. Anyway, today's not really about haircuts, is it?"

Before I knew it she'd taken off a couple inches.

"There. What do you think?"

I looked in the mirror. "Who the hell is that?"

"That's you. The new you."

Charlie had said it would take years off me and she was right.

"Do you want some gel on it?"

I shook my head. The mobile rang with a text from

Charlie. "RLY SRRY NT 2B WTH U. GD LCK 2DAY. THNKNG OF U SO MCH. LV C. X."

I wasn't in the mood for abbreviated texts '2DAY' so I switched off the mobile.

Aly put her coat on. "Are you ready?"

I picked up the cut flowers and the Service Sheets. "Yes. Let's go."

I prayed the van would start first time. It didn't. I prayed to Ivy, to the little boy in my dreams and to Phoebe. I even thought of asking Liz to send the vibes.

"Let me try." Aly leant over and turned the key. It started immediately. "See, I've got the magic touch."

We arrived at St. Stephen's at ten twenty as planned. I could see two people at the front of the church and went to introduce myself.

"You must be Georgina." She was in a wheel chair and looked tired from the journey.
"And this is my son Geoffrey."

"Thank you so much for coming. I think it'll just be the four of us, I'm afraid."

"I wouldn't have missed it for the world."

"I was wondering if you'd like to read the lesson. You knew Ivy for longer than any of us."

"I couldn't manage to stand at the lectern."

"You could read it from here, as there are so few of us."

The vicar joined us from the side vestry. I'd spoken to him on the phone but I'd never met him in person before. He was young and full of energy.

"Good morning, I'm Stephen Wilkinson. Stephen of St. Stephen's. Easy to remember."

I had thought of asking Father Dominic to take the service but Ivy would have strongly disapproved. She was staunchly Church of England and used to tease me about going over to Rome, but I took it all in good heart.

I gave everyone a Service Sheet as the organist started

playing 'Dear Lord and Father of Mankind'. Aly sat down on the front row and I headed for the door with Stephen to wait for Ivy.

I was surprised at how small her coffin was. It hardly needed the four strong men from Cuthbert and Sons to carry her in. But they carried her carefully and with dignity.

Stephen announced the first hymn. 'The Lord is my Shepherd'. Aly, Geoffrey and I stood up and started singing. Georgina was too frail to produce much volume and as I can't sing in tune, I sort of mumbled. Which only left Aly and Geoffrey. They sang with gusto but it hardly raised the roof. Half way through the second verse we were joined by Stephen, as his microphone clicked in loudly. He overpowered us all with a strong tenor voice but his contribution helped to lift our spirits.

As the hymn finished and we sat down, I heard the door open at the back of the church. An elderly man had come in, presumably he just wanted to sit quietly in a church and was unaware there was a service going on.

Stephen announced the lesson. He carried the large bible over to Georgina's wheelchair and held the book open for her to read Psalm 121.

"I will lift up mine eyes unto the hills, from whence cometh my help."

Aly reached over and held my hand.

After the reading, Stephen closed the bible and spoke a few words about Ivy. He'd never actually met her but I'd given him some notes. He sat on the pew next to us which was much more intimate.

"Now let us say the words that Our Lord has taught us. Our Father, who art in Heaven, Hallowed be Thy name."

At the end of the service, the four strong men from Cuthbert and Sons lifted Ivy on their shoulders and we followed her out.

The elderly man at the back stood up as we passed. He

held a white handkerchief and was crying. Maybe this funeral had set off the memory of a bereavement of his own.

We made our way to the far end of the churchyard. The headstone next to the newly dug grave simply said, 'DOROTHY AND ARTHUR THOMAS, MUCH LOVED PARENTS OF IVY.'

Geoffrey stood next to his mother on one side and Aly and I on the other. The elderly man had followed us out of the church and was now standing on the other side of the path, some distance away.

I also noticed two other men standing to his left. They wore leather jackets and were watching the proceedings carefully. The sight of a funeral touches even the strongest souls.

I watched Ivy's little coffin being gently lowered into the ground.

"In the name of the Father, the Son and the Holy Ghost. Amen."

Stephen of St. Stephen's stood back so we could lay our wreaths. The flowers from Ivy's garden sat comfortably next to the yellow freesias from Georgina and Geoffrey.

We stayed there for a while, as you do after a burial, no one quite knowing when it's acceptable to walk away. Eventually we headed back to the car park.

The two men in leather jackets began to follow us and when I reached the car they held out their ID cards.

"Detective Inspector Hamilton and Sergeant Kidman. Acton Police."

"How can I help?"

"We're investigating the death of Ivy Thomas."

"This is Mad Fence Woman's doing, isn't it? The neighbour from hell who thinks I killed Ivy for the inheritance."

"We'd like you to come to the station to answer some

questions."

"I'll answer all the questions you like. But not today. You must know it's ridiculous. Do I look like a murderer?"

I caught sight of myself in the car window. With Aly's new haircut I looked distinctly dodgy.

Aly came to my rescue. "I know he didn't do it."

The Sergeant looked her straight in the eye. "Then who did?"

"No one. Old age did it. I was there when it happened."

"In that case, we'll need to speak to you as well, Miss."

Geoffrey wandered over. "What's going on?"

I tried to make light of it. "It's nothing. Just a misunderstanding."

I handed the Inspector my card and arranged that Aly and I would be at Acton Police Station at nine thirty in the morning.

I suggested that Geoffrey followed me to the pub, as it was tricky to find.

"I hadn't realised we'd be going to a pub. I'm afraid Mother disapproves of pubs."

"This is quite different. This is a Gastro Pub."

The Crown had been renamed The Old Crown after being refurbished last year and its reputation had spread. I asked Geoffrey to put his mother at the head of the table. The waiter arrived and Georgina ordered a tonic water with Angostura bitters. The rest of us shared a bottle of chilled Church Road Chardonnay.

Aly smiled. "It reminds me of home."

Georgina turned to her. "Tell me, how do you manage to achieve that look with your hair?"

"Wax and spray. It defies gravity, doesn't it? I'm good with hair. I cut Will's this morning. What do you think?"

Georgina looked at me carefully. Then at Geoffrey.

"I think my son could do with a similar cut. Are you free this afternoon?"

Aly laughed. Geoffrey didn't.

The staff at The Old Crown looked after us well and I learned a little more about Ivy's younger days from Georgina.

Eventually I waved them off and as I got in the van, I noticed our little card had fallen on the floor. "For Ivy. Flowers from your garden. With love from me and Aly." I drove back to St. Stephen's.

When I reached the grave, I saw that a new bunch of flowers had been left there. A bunch of perfect Queen Elizabeth roses. I read the card and recognised the writing immediately. It said simply, 'I remain always yours, Peter.'

We got to the Police Station at nine twenty nine. Aly had spent so long doing her hair that she'd almost made us late.

"Is D.I. Hamilton around?" I tried to sound overly innocent.

The Desk Sergeant looked at me suspiciously. "Take a seat."

The minutes ticked away slowly as I read the Wanted posters. Mostly lost relatives and small robberies. Nothing as earth shattering as the murder investigation I'd found myself at the centre of.

Aly seemed less concerned. She just wanted to go for some breakfast when this farce was all over.

Sergeant Kidman buzzed us through to the back. "Sorry to keep you."

We were taken into separate interviewing rooms. Suddenly I felt like a criminal. I sat at the table while D.I. Hamilton stood towering over me.

I forced a smile. "You don't really take this allegation seriously, do you?"

He watched me in silence.

"The woman's clearly angry that her son didn't get Ivy's money, that's all."

D.I. Hamilton's silent treatment must have been designed to make me nervous. If this was a game, I was sure I could play it as well as he could.

I shifted in my seat. I scratched my nose. I stretched my arms. But he stood completely still.

"I can stay silent longer than you can." I looked at him, realising I'd just lost the game.

Eventually he sat down. "Of course, I know you didn't do it, but when a member of the public makes an accusation of murder, we have to take it seriously."

"So I'm free to go?"

"You're free as a bird."

I got up to fly away but he called me back.

"Just one thing, I noticed on the Death Certificate that she'd had a fall."

"Old people do, I'm afraid."

"The question is, did she fall or was she pushed?"

I sat down again.

"There is a substantial amount of money involved here. It's going to be hard to prove that she wasn't pushed."

"Or that she was. I thought in this country you were innocent until proven guilty."

"But it's still my job to check it out."

"Why would I want to kill Ivy? I loved her. And I have no motive. The money was coming to me sooner or later anyway."

"But you've gone through a divorce. That must have left you a bit short."

"I'm coping."

"Yeah, now that you've got this windfall."

"Ask anyone. I could bring you a hundred people who'd swear I'm not the murdering type."

"Friends will say anything for a share of the loot."

"It's not loot."

D.I. Hamilton leant back in his chair. "So it's stalemate, then. Your word against hers."

"I didn't do it."

"They all say that. Come on, let's get this over with. Why don't you tell me what really happened."

I gave him the whole story of Aly trying to ring me and Charlie not letting me answer the phone.

"So you weren't actually there when she died?"

"No. I was at home watching 'It's a Wonderful Life'. That puts me in the clear."

"Unless you got young Aly to do the dirty work for you. Maybe you agreed to split the winnings with her. Is that why she did it? Are you lovers? She's living with you now, isn't she?"

"I'm not listening to any more of this. If you're not going to charge me, I'm going to leave now."

"As I said before. You're free to go. Free as a bird."

I think he'd watched too many episodes of Good Cop, Bad Cop.

I stood up. "Can I ask you something, as one law abiding citizen to another? Do you really think I murdered Ivy?"

His faced softened. "Truthfully? No, I don't."

"Thank you. I think the matter is now closed."

"I'll need you to sign a statement. We could do it now or you could come back this afternoon."

I signed it then and there. I had no desire to be incarcerated in Acton Police Station any longer. Aly was waiting for me in the reception area as D.I. Hamilton buzzed me to freedom.

"Come on, we deserve a slap up breakfast."

D.I. Hamilton watched us leave. I tried to walk out as innocently as I'd walked in. I even think I whistled, but it just made me look more guilty.

The condemned man ate a hearty breakfast. Scrambled eggs had never tasted so good. I was on my second cup of coffee and buttering my toast when the mobile rang. I didn't react. Our marriage and those breakfast interruptions had almost reached their sell by date.

But it wasn't Liz. It was Charlie, preparing to take over as the new Chief Interrupter of Toast.

"Hi. It's me."

"I thought you preferred the impersonal communication of a text at this time in the morning. I'm surprised to hear your voice."

"I wanted to know how it went."

"How what went? Since I last saw you, I've christened a baby, buried a friend and been arrested for murder."

"Murder? I never know when you're joking. Look, I can't talk for long, I'm at work but why don't I take you out for dinner tonight. You can tell me all about it then. And I'm sorry my stupid car packed up. I really wanted to be there for you."

My toast had gone cold, so I put my mobile back in my pocket and ordered another round.

Aly sipped her coffee. "Do you love her?"

"Charlie? God no. Far too early for that. But I really like her."

"You mean you fancy her?"

"I'm a red blooded man, why wouldn't I?"

"I want a soul mate. Sex would be nice but it's not the most important thing in a relationship. If you didn't think you were going to have sex with Charlie tonight, would you be so keen to rush over there?" She might have a point.

Aly had arranged to stay the night with a friend so I dropped her off at the tube on the way home.

I was unlocking my front door when my neighbour, Colin, shouted to me from across the road. We first met ten years ago, when we were both single. We'd pop into each other's houses for a beer and a chat. I'd give him some tips on his garden and he'd help me with my tax. Then he got married to Ruth and the invitations stopped overnight. Of course, as soon as I married Liz, I was round there all the time. We'd go for dinner and they'd come to us. It's what couples do. But as soon as Liz moved out, the invitations stopped as abruptly as before. So for the last six months, when I'd been going through hell, they'd never once asked me over for a cheery bowl of Spag Bol. And I'd detected a certain frostiness since I'd become single again. Perhaps he thought I intended to steal his wife.

Colin crossed the road to join me. "I've got some sad news."

"You've been arrested for murder?"

He looked at me as if I'd lost the plot completely. "No, we're moving. Selling up in search of village life."

"So no more cosy evenings round at yours, then?" It was lost on him.

"Fancy a beer?" Now he was leaving the area it was safe to invite me over.

"Do you think you'll move soon, yourself?"

"I'm a free man. I could sell up and travel round the world."

"But what would you live on?" He was an accountant through and through.

"I'd eat berries and rub sticks together to make a fire."

He laughed. He was in a good mood because he'd just exchanged contracts on his house. I was amazed how much it was worth.

He handed me a beer. "You could travel quite happily on the proceeds of your house sale for a year. But, of course, you'd be homeless when you got back."

"I could always live in the East Wing of your new country mansion and be your full time gardener."

My mobile went. It was Liz. I explained I was round at Colin's.

"I thought you were persona non grata there, now you're a single man again."

She was ringing to see how the funeral had gone but it was too long a story to go into.

"I'll tell you all about it one day. Colin sends his love, by the way."

He hadn't actually, but he smiled his approval after I'd sent it.

"I won't talk now, Liz. I'm a bit knackered. I'll call you later."

Colin took a swig of beer. "Is everything alright between you two?"

"I think we've both moved on."

"It could have got nasty."

"Life's too short. You have to let it go." I was sounding like one of Charlie's Self Help books again.

"So, she's got a flat in Streatham and you kept your house in Chiswick. I'd call that a result."

A failed five year marriage didn't seem like a result to me. But then, of course, I wasn't an accountant.

I watched a bird splashing about in the birdbath. He'd had a drink first and then had a wash. Presumably he didn't want to drink his own bath water. I wondered how birds would handle divorce. Would they have to admit their failure before some sort of Matrimonial Bird Court or would they just fly off at the first sign of trouble?

"Forgive me for asking," Colin asked tentatively, "but I noticed the police knocking at your door yesterday. Nothing serious, I hope?"

"No, just a routine murder investigation."

I was glad to see Charlie again. She'd suggested we met in a little restaurant off the Kings Road. We were about to order a drink when my mobile rang with a text from Liz. 'THKNG OF U TONITE. LVE LZ X'

"Sorry about that, I'll turn it off." I leant over to kiss her. "It's good to see you."

"I was going to suggest a club. I thought a hot sweaty dance might do you good."

"I haven't had a good old bop for ages."

"What the hell is a bop?"

The man at the next table overheard this and smiled.

He was also sitting opposite a much younger girl. I nodded a complicit nod. One mid life crisis male to another.

He nodded back. "My daughter wouldn't know what a bop was, either."

"Oh, Daddy, of course I do."

He turned back to me. "And how old is your daughter?"

Charlie laughed so much she had to leave the table.

"She's not my daughter." I watched Charlie walk towards the Ladies. "She's my girlfriend."

"Oh, I see." He played with his fork in embarrassment.

His daughter got up from her chair and followed Charlie to the Ladies. "That's disgusting."

Her father turned back to me. "Still, I suppose that's what you'd call a result."

Luckily by the time Charlie returned, he was paying his bill.

The daughter put on her coat. "Bye, Charlie." They were on first name terms after only five minutes in the Ladies.

I watched them go. "What did you two talk about?"

"She asked me if we were having an affair."

"And are we?"

"I hope so. An 'illicit affair'. Sounds sexy, doesn't it?"

We ordered another drink and I told her all about this morning's brush with the law.

"I'm just pleased it's over. And I can't tell you how great it is to see you."

"How great?" Charlie ran her hands through her hair.

I stretched out my arms like a fisherman exaggerating the size of his fish.

"This great."

"Really?" She tossed her hair provocatively. "Let's not eat here, then. Let's go home and have dinner in bed. With room service. How does that sound?"

"Sounds like a result."

I dropped Charlie off at the tube and decided to call into an Estate Agent to get an idea of what Ivy's house was worth. I'd had a quick look in the window but there was nothing for sale to compare it with, so I pushed open the modern glass doors and went inside.

I was greeted by a pushy youth in a dark suit, who shook my hand before I'd asked him to. "Hi, I'm Gary." The cut away collar on his white shirt accentuated the size of his tie. It was almost the size of his neck.

"Is that a triple Windsor knot?" I had to ask.

"Great, isn't it? This tie normally sells for ninety five at Liberties. Got it for forty in the sale. What do you think? Got the suit there as well. Not cheap but I hate cheap clothes, don't you?"

I asked him about Ivy's house.

"No prob. I could sell that for you this afternoon. It would walk out the door. Literally. Vacant possession, is it?"

"I'm afraid so, yes."

"Great. Take a seat." He took my details before I knew what had hit me.

"Listen up guys." He shouted to his colleagues across the office. "I've just taken on a house in Whitehall Gardens. I want to shift it by five o'clock today. I'm taking no prisoners on this one, OK?"

He grabbed his camera and headed for the door. "Right, we're in business. I'll drive, it'll be quicker."

In Gary Triple-Windsor's Wacky World of House Sales everything happened at cartoon speed. I'd only gone in to see how much the house was worth but found myself on a rollercoaster I couldn't get off.

He drove at a terrifying speed in an irritatingly bright mini with a ridiculous sunflower on the side. "Fun aren't they?" He crunched the gears, nearly missing a cyclist. "Five points for a bike. Ten for a pedestrian." He treated life like it was a video game.

I wasn't sure that I wanted this man to sell Ivy's house. He certainly wouldn't have been her first choice. He was the sort of man who knew the price of everything and the value of nothing. But if it had to be sold, I knew Ivy would want me to get the best price I could, so I went along with him. Not that Gary Triple-Windsor would have taken 'no' for an answer.

I rang the bell three times before putting the key in the lock as I always had done. This seemed to irritate Gary. Anything that slowed him down seemed to irritate him.

He went through the house like a storm trouper, snapping away and speaking into a little tape recorder as he went.

Suddenly he stopped on the landing, triumphantly. "Half a million."

"Really? I hadn't expected it to be worth that much."

"But we'll put it on at four nine nine five fifty, obviously."

"Obviously."

He smiled, an irritating cocky grin. "And we'll get that by five o'clock this afternoon."

"Look, I think we might have to slow down a little."

"Did you just say 'slow down'?" I thought he was going to have a heart attack. It was a concept as inconceivable to him as only charging one percent commission.

"The thing is, I have to go through probate and sort everything out with the will."

"No prob. We sell it 'Subject to Probate'. I do it all the time. Sold three last week, as it happens."

I couldn't resist a smirk as he peeled the parking ticket off his windscreen.

"Don't they realise I've got a job to do?"

Before I knew it, he'd stuffed the ticket in the side compartment of his door and I was back in his office signing my life away. Or rather signing Ivy's life away.

I worked out that if he sold it this afternoon, he'd make over ten thousand pounds commission. So I thought about putting up a sign and selling it myself, without an agent. But it might take several months and Ivy wouldn't want hoards of nosey neighbours traipsing through her house with no intention to buy. Better to hire a Rottweiller to do the dirty work for me, even if it meant having to unleash his collar.

After an hour in the company of Gary Triple-Windsor, I felt I deserved a coffee. I would have called Jack but he was sunning himself in Greece, so I sat in the sunshine at our usual café on the Chiswick High Road. I tried reading the paper but it was full of depressing statistics about crime, so I chucked it on the seat next to me and watched a fat pigeon getting even fatter on the crumbs of my chicken baguette instead.

The Tubular Bells on my mobile rang loudly, scaring the pigeon off. It was Liz.

"Hi, it's me. I still haven't heard how the funeral went."

"It's been surreal. I was arrested for murder and I've been in a cell all night."

The story was getting more exaggerated with each telling.

"This isn't St. Michael's Mount, is it?"

My exaggerations were a family joke. It all started in Cornwall when I was ten. As we walked across to St. Michael's Mount at low tide, the causeway was made of cobblestones. When we returned the following year it had been rebuilt in sandstone. The rest of the family said it had always been sandstone. But I continued to insist it had been newly rebuilt. Since then, whenever I told an unlikely or exaggerated story, they'd all shout 'St. Michael's Mount'.

"I got off on bail but I had to put the house up as surety." She was laughing. "Anyway, enough about me. How are you doing?"

"I'm OK. Still missing Toby, of course, but I know I've got to move on."

"Not missing your husband, then?"

"That's different."

"Only nine days to go."

"It's going to be really weird. Especially with our wedding anniversary next Tuesday." She paused. "What do you want to do about that?"

"Put on a firework display?"

"Why don't I take you out to dinner? My treat. I can afford it."

We agreed we'd go to hear Jack sing at The Underground and then go on to eat at Julie's, for old time's sake. We could at least try to be civilised.

I sat and watched an elderly lady walk slowly towards me. She reminded me of Ivy. As she reached my table, a teenager shot out from nowhere, pushed her over, swiped her handbag and ran off down a side street.

I sped after him without thinking. It could have been Ivy's handbag and I would have done no less for her. I'd almost caught up with him when I heard a gunshot. I turned round to see who'd shot me when my ankle buckled under me and I screamed in agony. Instantly I knew what had happened. I'd snapped my Achilles tendon. I fell to the ground and watched the teenager escape down an alley.

I rang Liz from the pavement. She told me to call an ambulance and said she'd come round straight after work.

I lay there for what seemed like hours. I just wanted the pain to stop. Eventually I was helped onto a stretcher. I'd never been in the back of an ambulance before and the novelty provided some small distraction from the pain. My ankle felt worse with each speed hump we bumped over and I cursed every town planner in the land.

"How did it happen?" The attractive paramedic was strapped in next to me.

"I was trying to run faster than a seventeen year old."

"You'd be hard pushed to do that. How old are you, forty five?"

"Forty four. Why? How old are you?" I wouldn't normally have been so forward but I hoped she'd make allowances for my pain.

"Twenty five."

"Married?"

"You're quick off the mark, aren't you?"

"I have to be with this ankle."

She held up her left hand and showed off her wedding ring.

"I used to have one of those. I still do actually, it's in the kitchen drawer." My mobile rang. "Am I allowed to answer it?"

I didn't want to cause any medical equipment to explode. The attractive paramedic assured me it was safe to speak.

"Hi, it's Jane. Are you sitting down?"

"No, I'm lying down, actually, in the back of an ambulance on my way to hospital. Snapped my Achilles. It's agony."

"Sorry, this isn't the best time then."

"What is it? You OK?"

"I'm fine." She paused for a few seconds. "And I'm pregnant."

We lurched over a series of high speed bumps.

"Hello? Are you still there?"

I tried to speak but nothing came out.

"I'm sure it's yours. The dates fit and everything. I'm really sorry."

My mouth went dry. "Can I call you back?"

I'd spent the last four years desperately trying to get Liz pregnant. And now, when my body was falling apart, Jane had managed it without even trying. I didn't think I'd been inside her long enough and I thought I hadn't gone the whole hog anyway.

The ambulance came to an abrupt halt.

"Hold on, while we get you out of there."

My head was spinning. The world as I knew it had changed in the twinkling of an eye.

The doctor told me that I'd be in a solid plaster cast for three weeks and that I wouldn't be able to walk properly for about three months. At least, I think that's what he said. It was all a blur.

I was wheeled into the plaster room by an older nurse. "You can choose the colour of your cast nowadays." She held up a selection of lurid colours.

I asked the student nurse next to her. "What do you think?"

"Blue. Goes with your eyes."

It took me ages to get into the taxi. It was the first time I'd ever used crutches and I'd almost keeled over a couple of times between the hospital entrance and the cab door.

The driver helped me in. "Been in the wars?"

"Tried to out run a seventeen year old."

"Not a good idea at our age." He looked at least fifty.

"I'm forty four."

The driver studied me in his rear view mirror. "Seriously? You're only forty four? Then you really have been in the wars."

I tried to call Jane but it went straight to her answerphone.

"Jane, it's me. I'm on my way home. We need to talk,

don't we? Call me or I'll call you. We should meet up tomorrow. Don't you think? It'll be OK, you know. Whatever we decide to do. Not that we need to 'do' anything. I wasn't implying we should, you know, have a … I'm rambling. We'll speak later. Bye."

Then a text arrived from Charlie. 'CING LUCY 2NITE. GRLY DRNKS. U OK? C X.'

I was in too much turmoil to go into the whole story, so I didn't text back. We pulled up outside the house and I saw Liz and Aly, sitting on the front wall together. It was a good job I hadn't asked Charlie to come over as well. Three nurses might have spoiled the broth.

Liz opened the taxi door. "You poor thing."

Aly handed me the crutch as I paid the driver. I couldn't work out how to get the wallet out of my pocket while still holding on to both crutches. It took me five minutes to get inside and onto the sofa. Liz had pilled up the cushions at one end so I could raise my leg comfortably.

"What pain killers have they given you?"

"What ever they are, they're not strong enough." I gave her the packet. "I had two tablets an hour ago." She grabbed a pen and paper and made a note. She'd come straight from the hospital and was still in her uniform. I was in safe hands.

Aly offered to make a surprise supper and went off to the shops for ingredients. Liz got me a vodka and tonic.

"I know you're on pain killers but this might cheer you up. And you're not going to be driving heavy machinery, are you?"

"With one leg, I won't be driving anything for a while."

"I think it's a good idea if Aly stays on here for a while. You won't be able to manage even the smallest things, like carrying a cup of coffee to the sofa. You'll need both hands for the crutches. And shopping will be impossible."

"You don't mind another woman living with your husband?"

"I'm not threatened by that hair. Scared, but not threatened."

I had an itch under the plaster cast, which I couldn't reach.

"Where are your knitting needles?"

"Why the hell would I have a knitting needle?"

The mobile rang. It was Jane. I let it go to answerphone. I was desperate to speak to her but I couldn't have had that conversation in front of Liz. The idea that Jane might be pregnant with my baby would destroy her. Then I panicked. Was I definitely the father or could it possibly be Toby's? I tried to remember what Jane had said on the phone. Something about dates matching. I had to speak to her urgently, so I sent Liz off to the corner shop for some more tonic water.

"Jane, it's me."

"How's your foot?"

"I'll live. How's your baby?"

"It's not a baby. I'm pregnant but it's NOT a baby, OK? I don't know what I'm going to do yet. So if I decide not to keep it, then it NEVER was a baby. OK?"

"Hey, don't worry. We can talk about it. Come round tomorrow. I'd come to you but I'm not very mobile."

My front door opened and Liz dashed in. I hung up quickly and pretended I was watching television.

"Forgot my car keys, sorry." She ran out again.

I pressed redial. "Sorry about that, we got cut off."

"I'll bring supper round tomorrow night."

"Great. And we can talk."

"Yes."

"Can I ask you something now? Is there any possibility that Toby is the father of this baby? I mean, any possibility at all."

"We'll talk tomorrow."

"I need to know now."

"Well, there is a very small, very tiny, outside chance, of a thin, very thin, million to one, extraordinarily unlikely, but ultimately possible … chance."

So it was Toby's. I crawled over to the sink and threw up.

My leg had swollen in the night. The plaster cast was too tight and was constricting the blood flow. I tried to move my ankle but there was no give. I felt claustrophobic and began to panic. I had to get the cast off. I even started to shake. I took some deep breaths and tried to calm down.

I looked down at my crutches lying impotently on the floor next to the bed. I badly needed a pee but didn't know if I could be bothered with the hassle of getting to the bathroom.

I thought of Jane and the baby. That made my breathing worse. I tried to convince myself it was mine. Jane said the dates had matched. And she must know. I looked up at the ceiling. There wasn't a crack anywhere. That must be a good sign.

Aly knocked on the door. "How are you doing?"

"I'm going mad. The cast is too tight. I just want to rip it off."

She helped me onto my crutches and I caught sight of myself in the full length mirror, disabled and dishevelled in my boxer shorts.

I went down the stairs on my bottom, like a baby. I was exhausted by the time I'd reached the kitchen.

Aly joined me. "What do you think you're doing?" I was trying to put the kettle on. "You put your feet up and I'll get the breakfast. We agreed it all last night. OK?"

"OK." I fell onto the sofa. "Thank you."

I was really pleased to have Aly here, but six more weeks of having to say 'thank you' for everything might drive me insane. I heard a pile of letters hit the mat. The postman must have altered his route. Normally I was the last house on his round.

"I'll go. You stay there."

"Thank you."

There was a nasty looking letter from the bank. The cheery coloured logo on the envelope tried to lull me into a false sense that the bank was my friend and that everyone who worked there cared about me personally. The cheery logo was on the letterhead as well, but the computer-generated print out informed me in stark black tones that I'd exceeded the limit on my already extended overdraft. Ivy's money couldn't have come at a better time. Especially as I wouldn't be able to work for two or three months now.

The landline rang. Aly handed me the phone.

"Thank you."

It was Charlie. "Sorry we didn't speak last night. Lucy was in a bit of a state. Boyfriend trouble. The usual things, you know. Commitment, lack of support and an ex-girlfriend in the background."

"As opposed to the usual Girlfriend troubles? Commitment, lack of support and an ex-boyfriend in the background?"

She laughed. "Anyway, how are you?"

I told her about my Achilles. "And I didn't even get the handbag back. Now I'm going to be lying on my back staring at the ceiling for months. Just because some fucking teenage prat tried to nick a week's pension money. If I ever get hold of him, I'll kick his fucking head in."

"You're bound to be angry. Angry's good. Angry's empowering."

"Which poxy Self Help book did you get that pearl of bollocks out of?"

Charlie went silent.

"I'm sorry. I'm just angry. And my leg hurts. And I'm sorry. Really sorry."

"Sorry's good. Sorry's empowering."

Aly brought me some toast and coffee. "This'll cheer you up. No worries."

"Thank you."

I took my first bite of toast when the phone rang. I threw it back on the plate.

"Why can't people just leave me alone to eat my fucking toast in peace."

Aly handed me the phone calmly. "I can see you're going to be a difficult patient."

"Hello, my name is Trevor Dickinson. I'm a reporter for the Evening Standard."

It seemed that news of my heroic adventure had reached beyond the borders of Chiswick.

"How did you track me down?"

"The owner of the café called the police and I persuaded the hospital to give me your number."

"That's against the Hippocratic Oath, isn't it?"

"They didn't exactly give it to me. I happened to see it on a computer screen."

"Look, all I did was chase a teenage mugger, that's all. It's hardly front page news."

"On a day when the Home Secretary's announcing the new crime figures it is. I'll need a photo. What do you say?"

I didn't know if I fancied being a local celebrity and having my five minutes of fame. Still, better to be known as a 'Have A Go Hero' than a failed husband. And it might even drum up some business. I could wear a T shirt with my website address on the front. Suddenly it seemed like a good idea, so I agreed.

"I'll do your hair." Aly was already overexcited at the prospect of waxing me to high heaven. "You've got to look your best in the photo."

"I'm supposed to look like an injured hero not a model in a hair commercial."

I felt my chin. I hadn't shaved since the morning of

Ivy's funeral but decided to leave it. A couple of day's growth might add to the image.

Aly ran upstairs and came down with a white T shirt. She wrote 'theflowerpotman.com' across the front with a black felt pen.

"That should get the punters in. No worries."

Trevor Dickinson and his photographer, Darren, were round in no time. They agreed to push the whole Flowerpot Man thing, so I struggled into the garden and was shot in my natural habitat.

Trevor interviewed me while Darren snapped away. I don't know why he bothered because he'd clearly written the article already. He asked one leading question after another.

"So, let me get this straight. You heard the old lady scream, you let out a roar, kicked over the coffee table and pinned the teenager to the ground?"

"Not exactly, I ..."

"But two of his mates jumped on you, pulled you off and they got away."

"No, it wasn't like that at all ..."

"Then you pursued all three of them for over half a mile till your Achilles finally snapped. Brilliant."

"Got it." Darren put down his camera. "They'll be weeping in Wapping when they see this."

He plugged the digital camera into his laptop and sent the photo via his mobile. It all happened at lightening speed.

Trevor shook my hand. "You're going to be a national hero, mate."

"I thought the Standard was a London paper?"

"The big boys will pick this one up, trust me. You'll be bigger than Beckham."

Darren stopped on the way out. "What about your kids? They'll be very proud. A shot with you and your kids. Now that would be the icing on the cake."

"I don't have any kids. Though, I think there might be one on the way."

"Why didn't you tell this me before? This is the real story." Trevor got out his notebook and started writing furiously. I knew I'd said too much and begged him not to mention Jane's pregnancy in the article, but the damage had already been done.

Aly rushed in with five copies of the Evening Standard. On the front page was a huge picture of me leaning on my crutches. The headline blasted out the words, FLOWER POWER. It wasn't a bad shot, unshaven and rugged. Then I looked more closely at the slogan on my chest. Some of the lettering was lost in the folds of my T shirt. So where my website should have been, was written 'theflopman.com'. I'd never live this down.

The first person to ring was Jane.

"What the hell do you think you're playing at? Now the whole of London knows our business."

"I didn't tell them who the mother is."

"You think that'll stop them trying to find out?"

She hung up. Seconds later Liz was on the line.

"Why didn't you tell me face to face? I can't believe you let me read it in the paper. You're a bloody coward."

"If you want to know the truth, I don't even know that it is mine."

"You mean it might be Toby's? This just gets better and better."

"Jane might not even keep it. She's not sure what she'll do. We're going to talk about it tonight."

"Let me get this straight. You might be a father, Toby might be a father and Jane, the bitch he left me for, may be a mother. Or she may just kill the baby in cold blood. And if that's not bad enough, I have to find out about all this in the Evening Fucking Standard."

"It's not easy for me, you know. Not knowing."

"My heart bleeds." She slammed down the phone.

Two seconds later it went again. It was Charlie.

"I can't quite decide if you're a local hero or just a right bastard."

"You've seen the paper, then?"

"If you're the father, who's the mother? And when were you going to tell me? Or were you going to wait till the christening?"

"Charlie, let me explain."

But she'd already gone.

I heard the bell but it took me five minutes to get to the door. Aly had diplomatically made herself scarce for the evening.

Jane looked tired. "I thought you must have gone out."

"Everything takes so long on these crutches. But don't worry, I'll be able to kick a football about with the young chap before he's up and running, you'll see." I patted her stomach.

"We need to talk." She'd been crying. "And I think we both need a drink."

"That bad?"

"I've already lost it." She sobbed into my chest. "I don't know why I'm crying. I know I didn't want it really. But now it's gone ..."

I didn't know what to say.

"Let's get drunk. I mean, paralytically drunk."

The first bottle went down like water. The second hit the spot and by the time Jane opened the third, we were away with the fairies.

"We could have got married. Moved to the country. Maybe had a couple more children."

"Then got divorced, fought a custody battle and be right back to where we started."

"Except there'd be the kids."

Jane downed her glass. "I don't think I'll ever have sex again."

"I don't think I'll ever have sex again either. Whether I want to or not. I've seriously pissed off Charlie and Liz'll never speak to me again as long as I live."

Jane was beginning to slur her words. "Well, you're my hero. Do you know that? Do you? Do you really? It's people like you, who count up and be standed, that make the safe a worlder place. It's people like you who show us that handbags matter more than pensioners. You're my hero. Did I tell you that? Did I? You tried to save a teenager from being mugged by an old lady. I'm proud to know you. And friend to call you my proud."

She stood up unsteadily and took a swig from the bottle.

"So here's to you, Mr. Flopman."

I couldn't have put it better myself.

I woke with a sore arm. Jane had turned over in the night and had been lying on it ever since. I pulled it free. My arm hurt. My leg hurt. But mostly my head hurt.

Jane opened one eye. She groaned and closed it again.

Aly had already come down and was putting the kettle on. She looked over at the two of us, hung-over on the sofa where she'd left us last night.

"You're not supposed to drink alcohol with those painkillers."

"They weren't strong enough to kill the pain. But don't worry, I won't make a habit of it."

She made us some strong coffee, which Jane drank with her eyes closed. Aly handed me a plate of toast. The phone rang. It was Liz, right on cue.

"Well?"

"Well what?" I knew what.

"Is it yours?"

"It isn't anyone's. It isn't even Jane's anymore."

Liz changed her tone. She'd been through it herself, of course.

I fancied a long hot soak to clear my head but I had to keep my plaster cast dry, so I sat on the edge of the bath and had a wash with a wet face flannel instead. It was hardly the same thing. I left Jane to have the soak. She needed it more than I did anyway.

It must have done the trick because half an hour later she came down with her hair in a towel, and was looking a bit happier. "What are you doing today?"

Aly was tidying up. "He's got to keep his foot up. Doctor's orders."

"Well, My Gold Card's burning a hole in my handbag, I feel some retail therapy coming on."

She got herself together quickly, kissed me goodbye and left in search of material comfort. Her calm exterior didn't fool either of us.

Aly was about to win the second game of Connect Four when the phone rang. It was Gary Triple-Windsor.

"I've got three offers at the full asking price. So now it's Auction City."

"That's good news."

"Good News Gary. That's what they call me."

"I can see why."

"Talking of news. It was you in the paper, wasn't it? The Flop Man?"

"It's not a name I usually answer to. But yes, it was me."

"This is perfect. It's more than perfect. It's going to get you an extra twenty percent over the asking price."

"Miss Thomas was a very private woman. I don't want her affairs discussed in public."

"Sorry, I'm taking no prisoners on this one. My job is to get you the best possible price."

He was gone before I had time to argue. Two minutes later, the phone rang again. Presumably Good News Gary had some more good news. But it was Paul.

"Hi, you'll never guess what's happened. Pippa's locked me out of the house. 'My' house. Well, I suppose technically it's 'our' house now, even though I bought it before I met her, but it certainly isn't 'hers'. How dare she lock me out? And where the hell am I supposed to sleep tonight? It's a bloody nightmare. I could call the police but they'd only laugh. I'll have to sleep in the car." He stopped to take a breath. "Are you still there?"

"Yes, mate. I'm here."

"Could I stay at yours?"

"Have you tried talking to her? I mean really talking?"

"She won't listen. She just throws things instead."

"What did she lock you out for?"

"Nothing. I haven't done anything."

I told him about the Achilles and explained that Aly was staying in the loft to help me out. But he seemed happy enough to sleep on the sofa, so we agreed he'd come round after work.

I lay there, looking up at the ceiling and spotted a crack. The phone rang again. This time it was Pippa. I let it go to the answerphone.

"Look, I'm sure Paul's already called you. And yes, I have locked him out. But what I bet he hasn't told you, is why. He's been completely out of order. I won't have him telling our children I'm a whore. It's not true and it's not fair. I wanted you to hear my side of it. I had to lock him out. And anyway he's got that huge status symbol of a car, he might as well spend a bit more time in it, if he loves it so much. I think he loves it more than he loves me, actually." She'd started crying and eventually hung up.

My leg was getting worse so I took a couple of pain killers an hour earlier than I should have done. It was unlikely they'd do me too much harm.

I must have slept for a good hour when the phone rang again.

Aly handed me the phone. "Some girl from BBC Radio London."

"How do you fancy coming on The Danny Baker Breakfast show on Monday morning?"

"I'm not sure."

"It's a good news story."

"Not for me, it isn't. I won't be able to walk for months."

"Why does every news summary have to be so depressing? You'd think there was no good news at all. Well, you've just proved them wrong. And I know our listeners would want to hear your story."

"It was nothing, really. I was just sitting having my coffee ..."

"Save it for Danny on Monday morning. OK?"

She said they'd send a car and would pick me up at six thirty.

Aly was laughing. "You pretend to hate this but you're loving it, aren't you?"

"It beats lying on my back being anonymous."

Secretly, I'd always wanted to be a radio DJ. I used to line up two tape decks in my bedroom, as a teenager, and announce the tracks. All kids do it. I bet Danny Baker had a whole studio set up in his room. I could ask him on Monday morning.

Aly handed me my mobile. It had rung with a text from Charlie.

'HOW'S DADDY 2DAY?'

I started texting back and got as far as, 'THE BABY DECIDED NOT TO COME' when I had to stop. I sent what I'd typed anyway.

Two minutes later Charlie rang me on the landline.

"I'm really sorry. I've been a cow."

"It's been a really weird twenty four hours."

"I could come hospital visiting tonight, if you like."

"I like."

Paul rang the bell at six thirty. I answered the door on my crutches.

He gave me a hug. "How's Long John Silver? What a bugger, eh? Still, at least you're a national hero. I'm just a local twat."

He looked like he'd slept in the car for weeks.

"You're looking better than I expected."

"Liar."

He threw himself on the sofa and moaned about

Pippa. I stood on my crutches.

Aly came down and saw me standing in the middle of the room.

"Hi, I'm Aly. You must be Paul. You're going to have to give up the sofa for the invalid, I'm afraid. Nurse's orders."

I was glad of Aly's directness. My leg had started to hurt and I might have been standing there for another couple of hours before Paul realised that I was in more pain than he was.

At seven o'clock Charlie rang the bell. And at ten past Liz joined the party.

Aly was banging about in the kitchen. "So it's dinner for five now, is it?"

"Could be six if Colonel Mustard fancies a spot of home cooking."

Charlie laughed. "No, Friday night is ironing night."

Paul looked confused. "Are you two speaking in code?"

Liz had perched on one end of the sofa. The opposite end to Charlie. They sat there like bookends not speaking. Paul lay on the floor with his head in his hands.

I surveyed the scene. "This is nice. All friends together."

Liz stood up. "I just wanted to check you weren't on your own. But now I see you've got the entire sixth form running round after you, I'll leave you to it."

Aly offered to show her out but Liz pushed past her.

"I know the way. I used to live here remember." Two seconds later the front door slammed shut.

"That'll be supper for four then."

Aly had made a comforting tuna fish pie. We all had seconds and Paul had thirds.

After supper, Aly organised a Connect Four Tournament. First we played singles, which Charlie won by a mile, much to Aly's annoyance. Then in the doubles,

Charlie and I beat the other two hands down.

"Aly usually beats me."

Charlie was collecting the pieces. "Do you two play this together a lot?"

"He has to lie on the sofa, it keeps his mind off the pain."

I laughed. "Also, she likes to win."

Charlie joined me on the sofa.

Aly stood up. "Mind his leg."

"Don't worry, I'll be careful of your precious patient. He's quite safe with me." She ran her fingers through my hair territorially and gave me a kiss.

Paul sighed. "I thought I was coming round to a mate's for some support. If I'd wanted to watch soft porn I'd have checked into a hotel."

Charlie blushed. "It was only a kiss."

Paul's phone went. It was Pippa. He threw his mobile across the room.

Charlie smiled. "Anger's good. Anger's empowering."

"Fuck Anger. And fuck you." Paul was shouting.

"That's right. That's good. Let it out."

I didn't think it was such a good idea to encourage him. Paul had kept the lid on this for too long to risk a sudden explosion. But with the inexperience of youth, Charlie kept on going.

"Sometimes it's better to get really angry with an inanimate object. That way you don't hurt the people you love." She handed Paul a cushion. "Now, imagine this cushion is your wife. What would you want to say to her?"

"Can I sit on your face?"

"You're not taking this seriously."

Aly joined in. "Charlie's just trying to help."

"I know perfectly well what's going on here. You think I have anger issues from my childhood that have nothing to with my anger issues towards my wife. And you think that talking to a fucking cushion is going to make it all better. Well, we'll see, shall we?" He walked around the room, holding the cushion at arms length in front of him. I hadn't seen him this wired before. "So, Mrs Cushion. Let's get a few things off my chest."

Charlie spoke quietly. "That's good."

Aly leant forward. "Well done."

"Shut up, all of you, I'm trying to think what to say."

"Don't block it. Don't filter it. Just let it out."

"I would, if you'd stop talking for one fucking second."

"That's it. There's no right or wrong. Just say the first thing that comes into your head."

"Shut up right now. Before I lose it completely."

"Connect Four, anyone?" I was trying to be helpful.

Paul took a strong, deep breath and then let out an earth shattering primal scream as he hurled the cushion to the ground. I prayed that the Self Help Twins wouldn't start applauding. Paul stood there for a few minutes, swaying silently.

Eventually, "I couldn't find the words."

"Find them." Self Help Twin number one put an arm round his shoulder.

"Let them out." Self Help Twin number two put an arm round the other shoulder.

He took some more deep breaths. "I just want to go home." Tears were rolling down his face.

Charlie gave him a hug. "Tears are good. Tears are empowering."

Paul collected up his things and I phoned Pippa to say that her husband was coming home.

Aly kindly went upstairs to watch TV, so I could be alone with Charlie.

"Fancy an early night? I've missed you and I'm feeling frisky."

"I don't think I'll be up to much with this leg. I can hardly make it up the stairs."

"Come on, last one up pays a forfeit."

I started the slow climb to the bedroom. One step at a time on my bottom. It was surprisingly exhausting and did nothing to enhance my libido. Charlie had taken up the crutches ahead of me and had left them by the top step. I hobbled into the bedroom to find her lying naked on the bed, waiting.

I caught sight of myself in the full length mirror.

"I'm falling apart."

Charlie laughed. "Crutches are good. Crutches are empowering."

But I didn't feel empowered. Even a ton of Viagra wouldn't have helped. I sat on the edge of the bed.

"Sorry."

"It's OK."

But I knew it wasn't really.

The phone woke me at ten past nine. I was still half asleep. "Good morning, it's Gary."

I didn't even know what day it was. The pain killers had knocked me out completely.

"Have I got Good News for you or what? Guess the offer I've just had in."

It was too early for guessing games. "Surprise me."

"Five hundred and sixty five thousand. That's sixty five over the asking. I told you I'd take no prisoners on this one."

"That's amazing."

"We should bite their hands off quick sharp, before they get cold feet."

I could hear Charlie and Aly having breakfast downstairs. So I started the arduous journey down Mount Everest on my bottom, carrying the crutches in one hand and holding onto the banister rail with the other. When I reached Base Camp, I struggled to my feet carefully, balanced myself on the crutches and went into the kitchen.

"I think I've just sold Ivy's house."

Aly helped me onto the sofa. "That must feel a bit weird."

I'd just got comfortable when the phone rang again.

"Hello, I'm from The Evening Standard. We'd like to do a feature on you for next week's ES Magazine. Your Favourite bits of London, that sort of thing. It's quite an honour. What do you say?"

"I'd be honoured."

The reporter took my email address so she could send over a questionnaire for me to fill in.

Charlie was laughing. "You're loving this, aren't you?"

Aly made some toast and handed me the plate as the phone rang again.

"Hello, son. Your mother and I wanted to see how your leg's getting on. We could drive up tomorrow if you like. It's Father's Day."

We arranged we'd all go for Sunday lunch at Julie's. Jack would be back from Greece by then and I hoped he'd be able to join us, with Emma and Cathy.

I put the phone down and took a bite of toast. "I'm supposed to be going to a friend's wedding this afternoon. Well, she's more of an ex-client than a friend. I did her garden three years ago. I said I'd see how my leg was on the day. But I think I'll go."

Aly looked worried. "Sure you're up to it?"

"It'll cheer me up. And I can always find a chair to put my leg on." I turned to Charlie. "Fancy getting all dressed up?"

"You could have asked me yesterday. I'm supposed to be meeting Lucy for a drink later. And I've got nothing to wear."

Aly shouted from the kitchen. "I'll go, I've never been to an English wedding before. I've seen Four Weddings and a Funeral, of course. Will it be anything like that?"

"Without three of the weddings and the funeral, exactly like that."

Charlie checked her hair in the mirror. "I suppose I could wear the red dress at a pinch. What do you think?"

"I haven't seen it, have I?"

"I wore it for dinner at Lucy's. It's very tight and very short. You must remember. Don't you notice anything?"

"Oh, that red dress. Yes, I love that one."

Aly joined us. "I've got a red dress as well."

I took out a coin. "Let's toss for it then, and see which red dress goes to the Ball."

Charlie slammed down her coffee mug. "Why not just

take Aly? You obviously want to."

"I'm in the way, sorry. No worries."

I watched Aly go. "She's been brilliant, you know."

"Take Cinders to the wedding then."

I looked up at Charlie. "What's wrong?"

"I heard you last night. In your sleep. You were talking about Jane. I know it's been hard for you but it's hard for me too. You'd have dropped me like a shot if she'd kept the baby."

"That's hardly fair."

"Do you want us to finish?"

"No, I want you to come to the wedding with me. And I want to show off your fantastic body in that fantastic red dress."

"So I'm only there as eye candy?"

"I can't win, can I? If I say you have a fantastic body, I'm sexist. If I say I love you for your soul, you think I don't fancy you."

"Well, I'm a woman. I love you for your body and for your soul. I love you equally for both."

"Sorry, I'm confused. Does that mean you're coming or not?"

"Of course I'm coming. I just wanted you to ask me."

I thought I'd done that five minutes ago.

It would have been impossible to park in Chelsea on a Saturday afternoon so we took a cab. Charlie handed me my crutches and got a wolf whistle before we'd even paid the fare. She didn't wear the red dress in the end. No shoes. But the green number she had on was spectacular. I couldn't get the trouser leg of my D.J. over the plaster cast, so I wore baggy chinos and a sports jacket instead.

"Bride or Groom?"

"Bride."

The whole congregation seemed to be watching us as we made our way slowly up the aisle. I was on crutches and Charlie looked stunning, so we were bound to get some interest. But I heard "The Flopman" once too often for my liking. I smiled at my public as I hobbled along. It was the price of fame. A little girl of five even asked me to sign her Service Sheet.

"Who shall I make it out to?"

"My name is Ivy."

"That's nice. I used to have a friend called Ivy."

"Is she not your friend any more?"

I looked around at the other guests in their Sunday best and spotted a large lady with an extraordinarily exotic creation on her head. It must have taken the feathers of an entire flock to make it.

I whispered in Charlie's ear. "I think there's a bird's nest in the Lady Mayoress's Hat."

We stood up as the organ played the traditional Mendelssohn. Claudia and her father walked up the aisle, beaming back at their smiling friends.

Charlie held my hand. "Awesome dress. I can't wait to get married."

They were followed up the aisle by Claudia's friend, Jackie, who I'd briefly dated years ago. She looked uncomfortable in purple silk but still managed a smile as she passed me. The two bridesmaids were skipping happily behind her, holding hands.

Matt, the groom, was already waiting by the altar steps. He was over six foot five and towered over his tiny bride.

It was the first wedding I'd been to since the divorce. I felt a knot in my stomach as Claudia and Matt said their vows. Each one twisted it a little tighter. Liz and I had said the same words five years ago, in a similar church on a similar Saturday.

Charlie caught my eye. "You OK?" I managed a nod.

I couldn't kneel for the prayers with my leg in plaster,

so I bowed my head instead.

"Our Father, who art in Heaven, Hallowed be Thy name."

As I said the familiar words, I felt a surge of energy. An energy of extraordinary forgiveness.

"For ever and ever. Amen."

Then the two bridesmaids spoke loudly, a beat after everyone else. "Amen."

We stood on the pavement outside the church for a series of unending photographs. I seemed to feature in most of them. A combination of the crutches and my five minutes of fame had clearly made me photogenic.

Charlie hailed a cab and I rested my foot across the back seat for the short journey to the Mandarin Oriental Hotel on Park Lane. I was negotiating the huge door with my crutches when I bumped into Angela, the mother of the bride.

"I don't think you've met Charlie."

"Pleased to meet you." She eyed her up and down. "That's a lovely dress you're almost wearing."

"Well, I'm gasping for a drink. And I'm sure you are too, Angela. What with all the Mother of the Bride nerves and everything."

"Frank and I are tee-total. But of course, we've had to lay on alcoholic drinks for those who need that sort of thing." She left us, to join her husband.

I couldn't walk fast, so by the time we'd reached the function room we were practically at the end of the Reception Line. Twenty minutes later, with my leg in agony we reached the front.

We shook hands with Angela. "You've met Charlie already."

Her husband Frank gave Charlie the once over. "Great dress." Angela gave him an old fashioned look. We continued down the line

I kissed the blushing bride. "Congratulations."

"Isn't this all just too fantastic? Do you know, you can see Harvey Nichols from the reception?"

"Maybe that's where Liz and I went wrong."

"I don't like to economise on the really important things in life, do you? It pays to spend on quality. Things last longer that way."

I tried to shake Matt's hand whilst balancing on my crutches. "Congratulations."

"And congratulations to you. Chasing that mugger. Well done, mate."

"Hi, I'm Charlie." She offered Matt her hand.

He gave her the twice over. "Great dress."

Claudia dragged her new husband away. "Time to eat."

The first two glasses of champagne went down far too easily.

Charlie checked the table plan, impersonating Claudia. "We're on ten. I hope we get a good view of Harvey Nichols from the window."

"Claudia's OK. She's just got ideas above her station."

"Who has?" Claudia popped her head round a pillar. She came closer and lowered her voice. "You haven't got any Paracetamol, have you? I've got the worst tummy ache ever. India Charlie Oscar, I'm afraid."

She'd only been married for five minutes and was already speaking in tongues. I hadn't a clue what she was going on about.

She spelt it out. "I've Come On. You know, time of the month."

I gave her a couple of the strong pain killers intended for snapped tendons.

Charlie watched her go. "It's so unfair to have your period turn up on your wedding day. Still Mother Nature doesn't stand on ceremony. She carries on popping out those little eggs month in, month out." She stopped, realising what she'd said. "Sorry, that was tactless of me."

Table ten was full of cheery people, all of whom had read about me in the Evening Standard.

Charlie was clearly proud. "He's the main guest on Danny Baker's Breakfast Show on Monday."

"And I've been asked to do the 'My London' column in next week's ES magazine." I took out the email from my jacket pocket. "Let's all do it together."

It was a great ice breaker. We discussed our favourite pubs, parks and pizza restaurants. The whole table joined in.

"Most favourite shop?"

"Harvey Nichols?" Charlie was giggling.

But staying with the gardening theme, I went for the Syon Park Garden Centre.

"Place I'd most like to get married in?"

"Harvey Nichols?" screamed Charlie again. We'd been throwing back the champagne and were now almost hysterical. The rest of the table looked confused, which made us laugh even more.

"How about The Tower of London?" I poured another glass. "Symbolic of the chains of Matrimony."

I was too drunk to finish the questionnaire seriously so I crumpled up the email and stuffed it in my pocket. I'd think of something witty in the morning.

Charlie and I, in our inebriated state, found the speeches surprisingly funny. Frank's father of the bride speech was borderline risqué, which seemed to infuriate Angela, and the Best Man's speech was downright blue. At one point I thought Angela was going to unplug the microphone.

Then Matt stood up, all six foot five of him. A gentle giant of a man. His speech was only fifteen words long and was delivered, slowly and from the heart. He paused between his three sentences.

"I love my wife. I love loving my wife. And I love her loving me."

He spoke with such life affirming humanity. Claudia was a lucky girl. He sat down and kissed his beaming bride. Just as the applause was dying down he stood up again and added, "See you all at the Christening next year."

I raised my glass and envied his certainty. As Charlie clapped loudly, I leant over and whispered in her ear.

"Tango Tango Golf Hotel."

"Sorry?"

"Time To Go Home."

Charlie brought a tray of coffee. "So, have you decided yet?"

"Decided what?" My head was spinning.

"Where you'd most like to get married?

Eventually I realised she was referring to the ES Magazine questionnaire. "The Hanging Gardens of Babylon?"

"It has to be in London, remember?"

"Kew Gardens? The Kensington Roof Gardens? The Blue Peter Garden?"

"Do you actually want to get married again? That's the real question."

"If I met the right woman."

"And have you?"

I drank my coffee. "What's this? The Spanish Inquisition."

"I'd like to get married on a beach in Jamaica."

"In a white silk dress? Or an incy wincey teeny weenie yellow polka dot bikini?"

"Depends if you were in traditional Morning Dress or not."

"So, I'd be there, would I?"

She blushed. "Plan the wedding and the right groom will magically appear. That's what my mother always says."

"Eighteen years is quite an age gap. She'd never approve. I'm speaking hypothetically, of course. There's been no proposal yet."

"Are you saying there might be one?"

"I'm saying, I'm still married."

"Only for five more days."

Charlie liked these conversations. It was harmless flirting that usually resulted in a dive under the duvet. Which, of course, it did. It was all going swimmingly until we were interrupted by the landline.

"I'd better get it. It might be my parents changing the arrangements."

But it was Jack hot foot from Greece.

"It was brilliant. I went fishing and Emma and Cathy learned to water ski. But don't worry, I haven't forgotten you. I've brought your usual, a giant stick of Toblerone and a miniature Metaxa. Anyway how have you been getting on?"

I gave him the highlights of my week in short sound bites. The christening, Ivy's funeral, being arrested for murder, snapping my Achilles and becoming a local hero.

He was laughing. "Stop. Now that's definitely St. Michael's Mount."

"I wish it were. You can see the proof at lunchtime. I won't be able to walk for months."

"Bring a copy of that Evening Standard article. Emma will want you to sign it."

I found Charlie soaking in a hot bath.

"Jump in. You know you want to."

"I've got to keep the plaster cast dry."

"Live dangerously. Dip your big toe in."

But I sat on the loo and washed myself down with a face flannel instead. Charlie got out of the bath and did my back.

"Sorry you're dating an invalid."

She kissed the back of my neck. "Dating? I thought we were getting married. A beach in Jamaica, remember?"

I lay on the bed with my foot raised on two pillows while Charlie tried on outfit after outfit. She was meeting her parents for a Father's Day lunch.

"Can I wear black shoes with a brown belt?"

"You're twenty six. You can wear anything."

She changed her shoes for the third time. "What do you think?"

"Good enough to eat."

Charlie got my clothes out for me and then dashed off to meet her folks in Chelsea. Half an hour later I was dressed and downstairs ready to be picked up by my parents. Snapping my Achilles had turned me back into a school boy again. I was eight years old and totally dependent.

At twelve thirty on the dot, the bell rang.

My mother greeted me with a kiss. "Look at those shoulder muscles. Another month on those crutches and you'll be Mr. Universe."

My father stood in the doorway proudly wearing his "BEST DAD IN THE WORLD' badge. I'd given it to him when I was ten and he'd worn it every year since. He went to inspect the lawn.

"Leave it today, Dad. You're all dressed up. It's fine, really." But he ploughed ahead anyway.

My mother made some coffee and we sat and watched my father at work. When he did a job, he did it properly. My little London lawn was cut three times, each in a different direction.

It was my father who'd got me into gardening in the first place. On my sixth birthday he'd given me a piece of land. It was a two foot by three foot patch of soil by the side of his vegetable garden, which he'd roped off to form a little fence. I was so excited, you'd think he'd given me the whole of Hertfordshire. For the next seven years, I experimented with all manner of bulbs and seeds. And then on my thirteenth birthday, he gave me the keys to his shed and I helped run his vegetable garden. We prided ourselves on never using insecticides. "A dollop of compost is worth a ton of chemicals."

He put his jacket back on. "That looks better. You've got all these ladies running about after you, feeding you up.

But I'm glad to say you still need your old dad to keep your lawn in order."

Emma saw us first. She ran up to the car and opened the door to help me out.

She handed me the crutches. "Let me see you walk on them."

I got out and leapt up and down the street showing off.

My mother shouted after us. "Careful, there'll be tears before bedtime."

And there were. I caught the left crutch in a loose paving slab and went crashing down.

Emma helped me up. "It's all my fault. You're bleeding."

It was only a bump on my nose and the flow soon stopped. My father had insisted on holding his car keys on the back of my neck but I don't think it really helped.

I limped into Julie's and received a polite round of applause from the men at the bar.

"Caught any burglars today?"

"Took on four of them single-handed before breakfast."

"For he's a jolly good fellow." The girl behind the bar started singing with great gusto. But no one joined in, so she stopped after the first line.

Jack picked up the baton. "For he's a jolly good fellow." Then Emma joined in and by the end, the whole bar was cheering.

Emma took my hand. "Will you ever be able to walk again? Or will you always be on stilts?"

My parents were happy to have their family around them, and Jack and his family were glowing from their holiday.

Jack held up his glass. "To our Dad. However old we get, you'll always be our Dad."

Then it was Emma's turn. "To my Daddy. You're the best Daddy in the world."

Cathy raised her glass too. "Here, here."

I'd brought a card for my father with a cartoon of a golfing green on the front. 'Relax on Father's Day.' A young boy was cutting the grass by the eighteenth hole with a pair of nail scissors while his father, the groundsman, sat watching in a deckchair.

Then Emma turned to me and raised her glass again. "To my surrogate Dad. Happy Surrogate Father's Day."

It was the sweetest thing she'd ever said.

"You'll make a great Dad."

"I know."

"Why don't you ring up Liz and get back together and then you can have lots of babies."

"Just like that?"

"Yes."

I heard a familiar voice from the next table. "Hello." It was Jane. If I'd been standing, my legs would have gone from under me.

"Hello?"

She smiled. "Is this your family?"

I introduced everyone and we all shook hands.

My mother shot me a look. "How do you two know each other?"

"He made my garden grow."

She was sitting on her own but I noticed two wine glasses on the table.

My mother clocked her left hand. She whispered to my father. "No ring."

Jane's friend came back from the loo and I turned back to our table.

My mother's eyes were laughing. "She's lovely. And she obviously likes you."

Emma put down her water. "He still likes Liz."

I poured a glass of wine and caught Jane's eye. She was trying hard to smile but her eyes couldn't quite make it.

Emma handed me my presents. "Bet you can't guess what these are?" They were wrapped up in tissue paper but their shapes gave them away.

"An umbrella and a key ring?"

"No, Toblerone and some metal drink."

"Metaxa?"

"That's it, yes."

"Wow, thank you. And I've got a little present for you."

I handed her an envelope.

She opened it and read the letter out loud. "I hereby bequeath six square foot of my garden to Emma, the Flowerpot Girl, so she may grow plants of great wonder. Signed, with love, The Flowerpot Man."

She threw her arms around me. "Can I grow anything I want?"

"Anything."

Jack poured himself another glass of Merlot. "Or you could just sell the land for development."

"There are too many empty office blocks in London already. And not enough magical gardens. I want to grow Sweet Peas. Can I?"

"It's a little late for planting but I'm sure they'll be fine."

She went off giggling with Cathy. They'd spotted a little boutique just round the corner that was open on a Sunday.

"Talking of wills, son. Your mother and I have made new ones."

Jack looked uncomfortable. He hated discussing anything to do with death.

"They're on the top right hand shelf in the landing cupboard. You're both executors, as before. The only change is that we've left Emma ten thousand pounds."

My mother took my hand. "You don't mind, do you?"

"No, it's brilliant."

"Of course, if you ever have children we'll do the same for them."

"What do you mean, 'ever'? Have you given up on me altogether?" I raised my voice a bit too loudly and immediately regretted it.

"You know we'd be over the moon." She was clearly upset.

"And when you do, we'll all crack open the bubbly." Jack was trying to help.

I apologised to my mother for my outburst, which I hope she put down to the frustration of my leg.

Jane had paid her bill and waved goodbye as she passed our table.

My mother turned back to me. "I hope you see her again. Do you know if she wants to have children?"

"It hasn't come up."

Emma came back with us so she could see her garden. Aly had helped me mark it out with four short canes at each corner and we'd joined them up with pink ribbon.

"What do we do first?"

"It's your garden, you must do it yourself. But don't worry, I'll teach you. We can make a start after school tomorrow, if you like."

"Can't I start now?"

My parents drank their tea and watched Emma digging away. One generation of gardeners, passing their love of the soil on to the next.

"I've found some treasure. It's a little tin box." She ran over and showed it to me.

"It's probably been there for years."

I shook the tin. "Hang on, I think there's something inside."

She struggled with the lid and finally managed to get it open.

She screamed. "It's a key."

I caught my father's eye. "How extraordinary."

Emma looked at me. "You put it there, didn't you?"

"I might have done. I couldn't possibly say."

"I know what this is for." She ran over to the shed and tried the key. "Hooray. It fits."

It was the same tin that my father had hidden his key in, twenty four years earlier.

Inside the shed she found her parcel. I'd wrapped up a trowel with a wooden handle, some Delft Blue Hyacinth bulbs and a packet of Sweat Pea seeds.

"I want to be a real gardener when I grow up. Just like you. We could be partners. The Flowerpot Man and his Niece." What do you think?"

She wiped some mud off her nose.

"I love it."

I knew I was dreaming when I heard a knock at the door and the little boy came running in. He was carrying a white orchid.

He took my hand. "Follow me."

He led me into a field of exotic plants. The colours were overwhelming.

"Is this your garden?"

The little boy laughed. "Of course not, it belongs to everyone."

He handed me a fork and we started digging. After a couple of minutes I hit something hard. A small tin box. "There's something inside."

I tried to open it but the lid was too tight. The more I struggled, the more the little boy laughed.

"What do you think is inside?"

I didn't know.

"What do you want to be inside?"

"I don't understand."

I tried the lid again but it still wouldn't shift.

I handed him the box. "Can you open it?"

He shook his head and gave it back to me. "You have to know what you want to be inside. And when you do, the lid will spring open. It's as simple as that."

The alarm rang loudly at ten to six. I couldn't remember why I'd set it that early, so I turned it off. At ten past six, Aly knocked on my door.

"Time to get up. You're on the air at seven."

I lay there for a few minutes trying to remember why I'd agreed to go on the Danny Baker Breakfast Show in the first place. I didn't have a book to sell and I wasn't promoting my latest film. I was just some bloke who'd snapped his Achilles trying to get an old lady's handbag back. Anyone would have done it. I'm sure Danny would have had a go if he'd been there. It didn't make me a hero or even particularly interesting, and I was worried that I'd come across as either self satisfied or boring. Or both.

Aly handed me my crutches. "Got a few anecdotes up your sleeve?"

"I'm a landscape gardener, not a stand up comedian. I don't even know why I'm doing it."

She spotted the Nissan Sunny double parked outside. "I thought they'd send a limousine."

I climbed into the back. The driver must have recognised me. "You're that Flopman, aren't you?"

It was too early to explain that 'Flopman' was not my preferred form of address.

Aly strained to see herself in the rear view mirror. "How's my hair?"

"This is radio, no one's going to see your hair."

"They've got a webcam. My parents will be watching on-line. In fact, I think the whole of Wellington will be tuning in. I've brought my harmonica just in case."

We got to Marylebone High Street in no time.

I got out my wallet. "What do I owe you?"

"It's all paid for by the BBC licence payer. Just make sure we get our money's worth."

"No pressure there, then."

The guy on the door handed me a security pass. He'd already signed me in as 'The Flopman'.

"Sorry mate, but I don't know your real name."

A tall blonde girl in her early twenties came to greet us. "Hi, I'm Ellie. Thanks for coming in. We'll go to the news in five and then cut to you straight after traffic."

"Is that radio speak for 'You've got time for a coffee?'"

She smiled. "Black or white?"

"Can you do me a grandé decaf cappuccino with semi-skimmed goats milk and a hint of nutmeg?" I was psyching myself up to being as funny as Danny Baker.

Aly checked her hair. "Sorry, he's just nervous. Two blacks would be great."

Ellie clocked the outrageous creation on Aly's head. "Fab hair. Spray, mousse, putty or gel?"

"All four, actually."

Ellie turned to me. "Has anyone told you? Unfortunately Danny's off today."

"You mean I got up at the crack of dawn for nothing?"

"Not at all, you've got the lovely JoAnne Good."

"Who?"

"Don't worry. She's fab."

"Not 'the' JoAnne Good? The one I went out with for six days in '93?"

"Was she a DJ then?" Aly caught sight of her reflection in the glass door and quickly tweaked her hair.

"No, an actress."

Ellie showed us into the studio but I caught my plaster cast in the heavy soundproofed door and nearly keeled over.

JoAnne pulled off her headphones. "Are you OK? Let's get you a chair."

It was definitely the same JoAnne Good, but this wasn't the time to play catch up. She put her headphones back on and turned up the traffic. "Don't know why we bother, the traffic black spots are pretty much identical every day."

"You could have it on a continuous loop. Cut your costs and save on the licence fee."

"I'll do the jokes, thank you." JoAnne was laughing.

"Hi, I'm Aly." They shook hands.

"She's brought her harmonica, just in case."

Ellie handed us our two coffees and suddenly we were

live on air.

"Good morning. This is JoAnne Good, standing in for Danny Baker. Now my first guest is none other than the Have A Go Hero himself, Mr. Flopman."

Ellie clapped and cheered, but this only encouraged an already over excited Aly to let out a series of piercing screams. JoAnne shot forward and pulled the microphone away from her. She pushed it closer to me. I wasn't sure what I was supposed to say, so I leant in to it and said, "Hello, London", adopting the ironic tones of a visiting pop star.

"I suppose I should explain that my guest is also my ex-boyfriend, isn't that right?"

I nodded.

JoAnne laughed. "This is radio. We can't hear a nod."

"It lasted six days and was way back in '93."

"Touching isn't it? He remembers it like it was yesterday. And eleven years later, I'm a radio presenter and you're a national hero. Who'd have thought it? Tell me, how does it feel to be known as the Flopman?"

I'd thought of several witty one liners lying in bed last night but sitting in front of a live microphone, my mind went blank.

Aly grabbed the microphone again. "It was an advertising stunt that went wrong. The T shirt was supposed to say 'theflowerpotman.com'."

JoAnne pushed the mike back to me but Aly followed its path and continued talking. "Can I say hi to my folks in Wellington?"

"If your parents are listening, they've just doubled our audience down Under."

"Love you Mum. Love you Dad." Aly was waving madly at the camera.

"For the benefit of those of you not watching on-line Aly, can you describe your hair style this morning?"

"Retro Elizabethan."

"It is truly extraordinary, listeners. And I mean that kindly."

Aly leant into my mike again. "Can I ask you something?"

"I doubt I could stop you, anyway?"

"Why did you two split up?"

"Not because he was the flop man, if that's what you're thinking. The exact opposite, if I remember correctly."

"You left me on Crete with a two line Dear John letter written on a cigarette packet, if I remember correctly."

JoAnne laughed for the benefit of the radio listeners. But in the studio she looked more sheepish. "Time for some Dusty Springfield and 'I Just Don't Know What To Do With Myself'." She faded out her microphone. "Ellie, could you show Aly to the Green Room? Sorry, but we've got the paper review in a sec and we need your chair."

I waved goodbye as Ellie escorted her out. "At least your folks will have seen you on line."

JoAnne turned to me. "What's with her hair?"

"What's with the Dear John letter on a cigarette packet?"

"Panic. I panicked. It was getting too serious too soon."

JoAnne faded up her mike again as the record finished.

"This is JoAnne Good with my very special guest, The Flopman. Now, a little bird tells me you're almost divorced."

I nodded.

"This is radio remember? No nodding."

"Yes, after five … nearly five years." I cleared my throat.

"So you're single now? Girls, check him out on the webcam. He's gorgeous."

I stayed on air for almost an hour, and after a shaky start I really enjoyed it. JoAnne got me to do the traffic report and review the papers.

She handed me a pair of headphones, "Before you go, we've got a surprise for you. I bet you can't guess who's on Line One?"

"The Dhali Llama? The Thane of Cawdor? My ex-wife? I give up."

"Mrs. Dorothy Newton, the lady who's handbag you tried to save. Hello, Dorothy. Are you there? You'd like to say a big Thank You to the Flopman, wouldn't you?"

"Yes."

"We all think he's amazing, don't we, Ellie?"

She clapped and cheered again.

"Tell me, Dorothy, what was in your handbag?"

"A packet of cigarettes."

JoAnne laughed. "You mean he snapped his Achilles for a packet of cigarettes?"

"I'm afraid so, yes."

While she was talking to Dorothy, JoAnne tapped away on her computer and called up the next piece of music.

"And so for Dorothy and the Flopman, here's 'Smoke Gets In Your Eyes'."

The music started and she took off her headphones. "That wasn't too scary was it?"

"My first radio interview or bumping into you again?"

"Fancy a coffee after the show? I can't be too long, I'm opening a curtain shop in West Hampstead at eleven thirty."

"Are you big in West Hampstead."

"Huge."

An overexcited Aly was waiting for me in the Green Room. "They all saw me on the webcam in Wellington."

Ellie arranged for a taxi to take Aly home. "You're lucky. The usual cab company were busy, so you get the star treatment."

Aly gave us a regal wave as she swanned off in her

black Mercedes. I listened to the rest of the show in the Green Room.

"I love live radio." JoAnne was hyped up after the show and was power walking down Marylebone High Street towards the café. I was struggling to keep up with her on my crutches. I looked down to avoid a wobbly paving stone and when I looked up, she'd gone.

"In here." She'd already ordered coffee and orange juice for two and was waiting by the door, holding it open for me. "Make way for a distressed celebrity."

The staff duly obliged with a round of applause.

"I would have brought the cigarette packet with your Dear John note on it, if I'd known I was going to see you."

"You haven't really kept it, have you?"

"I had it framed as a constant reminder of the cruelty of women. It's hanging in the downstairs loo."

She stirred her coffee. "Men can be cruel too, you know."

We compared scars and put the world to rights. But mostly we laughed. We'd shared the same sense of humour eleven years ago and picked up exactly where we'd left off.

"Are you seeing anyone now?" I told her about Charlie. "She's twenty six? My God you should have a T shirt with WALKING CLICHÉ on it."

"HOBBLING CLICHÉ."

"Or CLICHÉ ON CRUTCHES."

"And you could have CLICHÉ DJ."

"I hope I'll never be that."

We ordered more coffee and I told her about my divorce.

"What are you going to do when it comes through on Friday?"

"Do I have to do anything?"

"Think of your favourite place and go there. On your own. Mark the start of your new life in a place you feel totally at peace." She looked at her watch. "Got to fly. Got a shop to open."

She paid the bill and we hugged goodbye on the pavement.

"Did you really keep that Dear John note all these years?"

"In your dreams."

Aly was making soup again when I got home.

"Mum was thrilled with the show. She thinks I'm looking after a huge star."

"Well, I'm very big in West London. I might even be asked to turn on the Christmas lights in Turnham Green Terrace this year, you never know."

She helped me onto the sofa and insisted that I keep my feet up for the rest of the day. My leg was hurting a bit, but the thought of a whole day on my back was too depressing to contemplate.

"I could always invite Gary Triple-Windsor round to play Monopoly. Or Alan Titchmarsh to discuss winter planting. Or the Dhali Llama to discuss the finer points of Buddhism."

"Calm down, you're not on the radio now. Relax for half an hour, then I'll beat you at Connect Four."

I closed my eyes and tried to think where I'd go on Friday to escape the realities of the Decree Absolute.

I thought of family holidays in North Cornwall and days by the sea in Brighton. I'd had a magical weekend on the Isle of Skye and even visited the Taj Mahal one Christmas. I'd had a great time in New York and Boston. But a city would be too noisy. And I wanted to find somewhere that didn't have associated memories.

I must have drifted off because when I opened my eyes again it was supper time.

"You needed that. Ready for some soup?"

"What would I do without you?"

"You'd survive. No worries."

Her soup was delicious as usual but Charlie rang just as I was buttering my toast. With four days to go, Liz had already handed over the reigns of power.

"You didn't tell me you'd dated JoAnne Good."

"It was only for six days and it was eleven years ago."

"How many days have we been going out?" I didn't know. "See what I mean? JoAnne must have been pretty special if you can remember exactly how many days you went out after eleven years. And I bet you haven't remembered that today's our anniversary."

"Really, which one?"

"Twenty one days, since we first kissed."

"Of course I knew that, I was just waiting for the anniversary of something more intimate."

She laughed. "It must have been very glamorous going out with a radio star."

"She wasn't a radio star then. But I did love her."

"Like you love me?"

"JoAnne only managed six days. You're fifteen days ahead of her already."

"I've got to go to a drinks party tonight but we could have dinner tomorrow night. My treat. What do you say?"

"I can't tomorrow, it's my fifth wedding anniversary." Charlie went silent. "I know it's a bit weird but we're trying to be civilised about it."

"You're going to have to cut the umbilical cord sooner or later, you know."

"I know. But I'm not really that good with blood."

I sat with my leg resting on a garden chair, basking in the sunshine. Aly carried our breakfast out onto the patio.

"I wish my Dad had taught me about plants. Your garden's brilliant."

It always looked good in June. The honeysuckle was coming through and the lupins and foxtail lilies were in full bloom. At the bottom of the garden, I could see a single white rose.

"On our wedding day, two rose buds opened up side by side. But now on our fifth anniversary, there's only one. What does that tell you?"

"Life goes on?"

My mobile rang from the kitchen. Aly ran in to get it for me.

"Hi, it's Paul. Remember me? Or are you too famous to talk to me now?"

"Paul who?"

"Very funny."

"How are things with you and Pippa?"

"Bit better, thanks. We're taking it day by day. But I was hoping you could do me a favour. If Pippa calls, I'm staying the night with you, OK?"

"Are you?"

"No, of course not. You're just the alibi."

"So what's the crime?"

"I need to see an old flame. Pippa wouldn't understand."

"Is that wise?"

"Probably not. But thanks. I'll do the same for you one day."

At eleven thirty I went to see Ivy's solicitor, Anthony James of Massey, Buxton and Cape. Their offices were on the first floor, above a Pizza Delivery Restaurant on Acton High Street. I just about managed to hop up the stairs one step at a time, holding tightly onto the rail, sweating profusely. I pushed the door open with my left crutch.

The receptionist looked up. "You don't look at all well."

"I know how Edmund Hilary must have felt."

She looked at me as if I was speaking a foreign language.

"He climbed Everest,"

"And you're here to see …?" she trailed off, expecting me to finish the sentence for her.

"Anthony. James. Or James Anthony. I'm not sure which order the names go in but I know it's a combination of the two."

"Of course." She looked closer at me. "It's you, isn't it?"

"I hope so."

"You're that Mr. Flopman, aren't you?"

I couldn't even manage a smile. "Will Mr. Anthony be long?"

"Mr. James will be out in a moment."

I sat reading 'Hello!' magazine. It was so old that I assumed most of the people I was reading about were either dead or divorced by now. I was pleased that my own wedding photos weren't there immortalised for all to see, forever consigned to waiting room hell.

The receptionist continued. "I heard you on the radio yesterday morning. You were quite funny for a gardener."

"Are you saying that gardeners aren't funny? Are you implying that Alan Titchmarsh isn't hysterical?"

Anthony James popped his head round the door of his office.

"I'm so sorry to keep you waiting. We should look

after our celebrity clients more carefully, shouldn't we? Please come in."

He held open the door for me as I stumbled past on my crutches.

"The Estate of the late Ivy Thomas." He spoke in a reverential tone, as he tapped the buff coloured file on his desk. "I am pleased to tell you that I have today received notification of receipt of our letter of the tenth instant, requesting speedy expedition of Probate."

He paused to look up at me and lowered his voice. "You will find the majority of solicitors pursue a local Probate Office, but I have made it my business to discover that Winchester has a particularly speedy expedition rate."

I looked suitably impressed. "That's good, is it?"

He nodded as sagely as his twenty five years would allow.

"I just wanted to check that I was able to sell Miss Thomas's house 'Subject to Probate'."

"That is indeed the situation."

He took me through a maze of legal information, which he made sound as complicated as possible. But I felt satisfied he knew what he was doing and that Ivy's affairs were being properly looked after.

I shook his limp hand and I got out onto the street as quickly as I could, without endangering myself on the stairs.

I stood waiting for a taxi for what seemed like an eternity, when I got a text from Charlie. I'd just started to read it as an empty cab passed by. I saw the orange light too late but hailed it anyway, shot putting the mobile in the process. It bounced off the pavement and landed in the path of an oncoming British Telecom van.

A passer-by handed me the pieces of my phone. "It's you, isn't it? Look everyone. It's The Flopman." A small crowd had gathered but they didn't look particularly impressed.

I now had no way of contacting Charlie, as her number was stored in the phone and I hadn't backed it up. I sifted through the pieces of black plastic and found the SIM card. Luckily, it hadn't been damaged and I hoped that, like the black box recorder in a plane crash, it still held its information.

I got the taxi to go via a mobile phone shop on the way home. A young guy, who might easily have been Gary Triple-Windsor's younger brother, snapped my SIM card into another phone to check it for me.

"We're in business. Right, let's find you a new model. What do you mostly use your phone for? Video? Photos? Games?"

"Calls."

"Do you text?"

"Only in longhand."

He sold me a new phone that was so small, I'd probably lose it in my jacket pocket. It had so many features that it would take me at least ten years just to read the manual. A moment later it buzzed and bleeped so loudly that I dropped it on the counter.

Gary's younger brother laughed. "It's just a SIM update from the network, no need to panic." The young girl by the till laughed as well.

"It's all very well for you, but you try updating your SIM card while balancing on crutches."

I'd just got home when it bleeped again with a text from Liz.

'HPY ANVSRY. CU AT THE UNDRGRND 8PM. L.X'

I wanted to reply back with, 'JE NE REGRETTE RIEN' but I hadn't worked out how the new phone worked. And by the time I had, it didn't seem that funny. So I sent 'XXXXX' instead. One 'X' for each year of our marriage.

I'd forgotten that The Underground was in the basement down a long flight of steps. By the time I made it to a table, I was sweating badly.

Jack looked up. "You OK?"

"I could have done with a Stannah Stairlift."

A few minutes later Liz wafted down the stairs, powdered to perfection. She was wearing black stockings and a short black skirt.

Jack started to play 'You Look Wonderful Tonight.'

"Well? What do you think?" She did a twirl.

"Still does it for me."

"Glad to hear it. Now, this evening's on me so you can have whatever you like."

"Have you won the lottery or just banked your divorce cheque?"

She smiled and ordered some champagne. "Do you think you'll ever get married again?"

"No chance, I couldn't afford to."

She looked genuinely upset. "That's not fair and it's not true. I could have taken you to the cleaners, you know."

"As opposed to the launderette?"

"You know what I mean." She laughed. "I heard you on the radio yesterday. You were very funny."

"Funny peculiar or funny ha ha?"

"Weren't you scared that mugger might have turned on you?"

"I've got a black belt in Origami. If he'd tried anything, I'd have folded him in half."

Jack took a break and joined our table.

"Where's Anna, the gorgeous assistant manager?"

Liz raised an eyebrow.

"Gone back to Ireland. Shame really, she had the hots

for you big time." Jack and I both knew she hadn't, but it was kind of him to build me up in front of Liz.

A Sloaney couple on the next table were giggling loudly. They'd been on the Happy Hour champagne since five thirty and were now ecstatic.

"It's our anniversary." The blonde wife held up her wedding ring for us all to see. "We're seven today." She laughed like a hyena.

Her husband barked loudly. "Hey, Mr. Piano Man, play a song for me." He had City Banker written all over him.

The wife stood up and staggered over to the piano and almost fell on Jack. "You're bloody gorgeous. And I love your voice. You know, I would rather listen to you sing than have to make love to my husband."

Her husband got up from his chair. "Time to go, Tiggy." He slapped his wife hard on the backside. "No dirty flirty wirty with Mr. Piano Man. Come along now, it's time for little Tiggy Wiggy to see her Hubby's piggy wiggy."

He put his coat on and left. She followed him out sheepishly.

I turned to Liz. "That could have been us."

"You wouldn't have lasted one day if you'd behaved like that."

The mobile rang in my jacket pocket. It was Pippa.

I started panicking. "I can't answer it. Paul's told her that he's here with me."

Liz laughed. "And Pippa's supposed to be here with me."

Then her phone rang. It was Paul.

"We could answer both phones and let them talk to each other, top to tail on the table."

But we let both calls go straight to voicemail.

"If you'd had an affair, would Pippa have covered up for you?"

She drank some more champagne. "I didn't have an affair."

"Sorry I haven't got you an Anniversary present. It's supposed to be wood, apparently. I looked it up on the internet."

"How sad is that?"

"I could have got a giant rolling pin, to remind you of Toby."

"Very funny."

"This next song is for The Flowerpot Man and his Wife on their fifth wedding Anniversary. I love them both."

A few people clapped and we raised our glasses to them in appreciation as Jack played 'Fly Me To The Moon'.

"Will this always be our tune?"

"Always."

I'd forgotten to ask for a ground floor table at Julie's so I had to climb the stairs and worked up a sweat for the second time that evening. I'd hoped for a quiet table in the corner but we found ourselves squashed between a dewy eyed couple on one side and four loud estate agent types on the other.

"I thought it was you." Gary Triple-Windsor stood up unsteadily and shook my hand. "And is this your good lady wife?"

"Yes, but only for another two and a half days."

"Does that mean I can ask her out on Friday night?" His friends guffawed.

We turned our backs and ordered a fantastic Rioja, spinach filo starters and two sirloin steaks.

I really fancied a steak. "Got to keep my strength up."

"For your twenty six year old?"

"For my leg."

Liz watched the dewy eyed couple on the left. They were still holding hands.

"Married or dating?"

"Dating, definitely. They're still holding hands."

Liz dipped her bread in the olive oil. "I think I might have met someone."

"Really?"

"Mmm, it's quite serious."

"And you chose our fifth wedding anniversary to tell me?"

"You've been seeing Barbie for ages, so don't make me feel bad. You haven't got a leg to stand on."

She looked at my plaster cast and laughed.

I took a gulp of Rioja. "How serious is serious?"

"Serious."

"You've only known the guy ten minutes."

"My clock's ticking."

Gary had asked for the bill at the next table and was chatting up the waitress. He held out his hand. "People call me Gary. But you can call me later."

His friends roared with laughter as they left.

Liz finished her Rioja. "I can't stand men like that. He's the sort of man who takes Viagra, then goes home and plays with himself."

I filled her glass. "What does he do, your new Mr. Right?"

"Don't laugh. He's a gynaecologist."

"No jokes about G spots then?"

"Or H spots."

"I didn't know there was an H spot. That's where I went wrong, obviously." "There isn't an H spot, you idiot."

"Could you see him being the father of your children?"

"You're not still obsessing about kids, are you?"

"You're the one marrying the gynaecologist."

We ate the spinach filo starter in silence and as I

307

poured us both another glass of wine, the little candle on our table flickered and went out.

The dewy eyed couple on our left separated their hands. The lady got up and went off to the loo. Once she'd closed the door, the man took out a small jewel case from his jacket pocket and laid it carefully on the centre of her place mat.

Liz leant over. "Is that what I think it is?"

The man nodded. The longer he waited, the more he adjusted its position. Ten minutes later, his girlfriend was still in the loo.

Liz got up. "I'll go and see if she's OK."

The man fiddled with the box again. "She must have known I was going to ask her tonight. She's been acting strangely all day."

Liz came back from the Ladies. "She's not there, I'm afraid."

He blew out his candle, put the jewel box back in his pocket and asked for the bill.

Liz gave him a hug. "I know you don't think so now, but one day you'll look back on all this and laugh."

"Hope so."

The waitress brought us a new candle and we sat looking at each other in the glowing light.

Liz reached over and held my hand. "Do you think we'll look back on all this one day and laugh?"

"What do you think?"

"Hope so."

"Me too."

DAY 41

I was woken by Aly knocking on the door and handing me my crutches. "I think you might need these. I found them in the hall."

I'd been too drunk to carry them upstairs when I staggered in last night. It had been hard enough going up one step at a time on my bottom after the cocktail of champagne, Rioja and pain killers, without coping with the crutches as well. I'd tried hopping to the bathroom on one foot but I was so worried about snapping my other Achilles that I'd crawled there on my hands and knees.

Aly left me to get dressed and went downstairs to put the kettle on.

Ten minutes later, I joined her downstairs.

She poured the coffee. "What's the plan today?"

I didn't have one. I couldn't work, so everyday was a holiday.

"Just mooching about."

"You can't just mooch about for the next two months. You'll go mad."

She was right. I needed a project. I also needed to earn some money. I knew I'd have the proceeds of Ivy's house sale but I didn't want to fritter that away.

Aly poured my coffee. "Think of all the things you could do without using your legs."

"Knitting, crochet, macramé?"

"You could learn a language."

"Serbo-croat. Only trouble is I don't know any Serbo-croats."

"You could learn a Shakespeare sonnet every day."

"To woo my next Lady Friend?"

"I thought you already had a Lady Friend. What's happened to Charlie?"

"She's twenty six. It can't last much longer."

"You could read the five books you'd always wanted to read but never got round to."

That seemed like a winner so we started compiling a list. I felt like a guest on Desert Island Discs. Finally we came up with five. For starters, Catch 22 and Crime and Punishment, two classics I'd never actually read. I'd been given Vernon God Little by an American friend last Christmas, so that made three. Fourth was Fear and Loathing in Las Vegas which I'd given to Liz but never read myself and lastly, Aly suggested The Da Vinci Code.

Aly made some toast. "We could start our own book club. Just the two of us. And how about watching five films you missed first time round?"

"My top five films. Easy."

"You've got to choose ones you haven't already seen, so you're not allowed any old favourites."

I came up with two quite quickly. John Huston's The Dead, and Disney's Dumbo The Flying Elephant. I thought I'd seen Dumbo as a child but I couldn't remember it at all, so I put it on the list. Then came the Mexican classic Amores Perros. Liz had banned the use of subtitles in the marriage, so Il Postino went in as well. We cheated on the fifth, The Godfather Trilogy. It should have counted as three films but we were making up the rules, so we allowed it in.

"Of course, in my condition, I could have had My Left Foot or Reach For The Sky. And Alan Titchmarsh's 1000 Handy Gardening Hints could have made it into the book category, but you can't have everything."

The landline rang as I was eating my toast. Aly answered it.

"If it's 'Hello!', tell them I'm talking to 'OK!' on the other line."

It was Paul. "Did Pippa ring you last night?"

"Yes but I didn't answer it. I'll see if she's left a message and call you back."

I picked up the mobile and noticed another missed call from Pippa so I dialled the answerphone and listened to both messages.

"Hi, it's Pippa. Tuesday evening, nine fifteen. Where the hell are you? I'm with Sally at A and E. She's cut her hand quite badly and wants her father. Tell Paul to come straight to the hospital. If he's with you, that is, which I very much doubt."

"It's Pippa again, Wednesday morning. Sally's OK but I haven't heard from Paul so I guess he wasn't with you after all. When you speak to the lying bastard, tell him not to bother to come home. Ever."

I rang Paul back. "Where are you?"

He'd stayed over with his ex and was too drunk to drive home.

I could hear the terror in his voice. "Call Pippa now. Tell her your mobile wasn't working. You've got to do this for me or my marriage is over."

"Hi, Pippa. It's Will. Sorry I missed you, the phone was on silent. I've only just got your message. How's Sally?"

"Never mind about that. I want to speak to Paul. Put him on."

"He left ten minutes ago."

"Why didn't you answer your mobile last night?"

"I had it turned off."

"No you didn't. If it was off it would have gone straight to answerphone but it didn't. It rang several times. Be honest. Was he with you or not?"

"Of course he was."

"Yeah right." She put the phone down.

I heard the post fall on the mat. Aly handed me a postcard from Paris.

'Just heard that Jeremy and Ivana got married last Saturday in Antigua. So I guess that's what you call closure. Hope you're smiling, love Jane. xxx   PS. Toby's buggered off to Bolivia. God knows what he's doing there. Quite a few ladies, I expect."

I finished eating my cold toast and drank my coffee.

My mobile rang with a text from Charlie. 'WE NEED TO TALK.'

It was the first time she'd sent a text in longhand so I knew it must be serious.

I replied with, 'SOUNDS OMINOUS.'

'IT IS. TONITE AT 8. THE CHELSEA RAM.'

'I'M ON CRUTCHES. CAN YOU COME TO ME?'

'IF YOU WANT TO SAVE THIS, YOU'LL BE THERE.'

'8 IT IS THEN.'

At seven thirty, I left the house to answer Charlie's summons. I was on my way to the local mini cab office when a black cab went past with its orange light on. I'd never seen one on my road before, so I took it to be a good omen and hopped in. But the traffic in West London had ground to a halt with the rain and it ended up costing me almost twice as much as it should have done.

I opened the door to The Chelsea Ram, already smarting from the cost. The place was packed and I couldn't see Charlie anywhere. I stood waiting at the bar for twenty minutes and despite being on crutches, not one person offered to give up their seat. Finally I rang Charlie.

"Now you know what it's like being made a fool of." She was screaming down the phone.

"Hang on, you've left me standing on crutches in a crowded pub and it's my fault? Am I being punished for something here?"

"Too right. I sent you a text yesterday and you never replied."

"I never got it. My mobile was crushed by a British Telecom van."

"Do you think I'm stupid?"

"It's true. I was trying to open your message when I hailed a cab and it went under the truck."

"You just said it was a van. Now it's a truck. Get your story straight."

"Charlie, where are you? Let's talk about this face to face."

"Oh, what's the point." She slammed down the phone.

I left the pub and hailed a cab. Two minutes later, she called me back.

"I'm by the bar. Where the hell are you?"

"In a cab trying to figure out what the point is."

"Stop behaving like a child and get back here now."

I turned the cab round, which cost me another five pounds. Charlie had got us a couple of drinks and had found a table in the corner.

"I went through hell last night thinking you'd gone home with Liz. You've got two minutes to apologise."

"I never got your text. Honestly. What did it say?"

She opened the Sent Messages on her mobile and showed it me.

'FELNG BD. CLL ME B4 U C LIZ. URGNT. C. X.'

"So I definitely sent it and you didn't reply. And to cap it all, Lucy's just got engaged to Rupert. I don't want to be the last one left on the shelf."

"You're only twenty six."

"Look, the way I see it is this. You don't return my texts, you're still in love with your ex-wife, my mother doesn't approve of you and you're way too old for me anyway."

"Do you want me to go then?" I downed my vodka and tonic.

"I think we should end it."

I got up to leave. "Charlie, the way I see it is this. Yes, I'm too old. Yes, I have the occasional dinner with my ex-wife. And yes, I'm fully aware that I'm not your mother's ideal choice as a son-in-law. You also forgot to mention that I'm not a millionaire and I don't look like a movie star. But what I am, is one of the good guys. There aren't many of us left. I may not be cool. I may not be awesome. But that's what I am. Just an ordinary man. If that's not enough for you, then I'd better go now."

I got into my third cab of the day and headed home to Chiswick. I thought about turning my phone off, knowing the rest of the evening would be conducted via text, but Charlie was too quick and a message arrived before I'd worked out how to switch my new phone off.

'CAN WE TALK? TKE CAB 2 MINE. 10 MINS. C'

If I had a coin in my pocket I'd have spun it. Heads, go to Charlie's, have two hours of aggro and end up sleeping together. Or Tails, go home, play Connect Four with Aly and sleep soundly on my own. But I didn't have a coin.

I shouted through the glass screen to the driver. "Brook Green, please. Or do you think I should go straight home?"

He caught my eye in his rear view mirror. "Woman trouble?" I nodded. "What do you want me to say? Better the devil you know? Treat 'em mean, keep 'em keen? Plenty more fish in the sea? Sorry mate, it's your call, I'm afraid."

I tapped two letters into my phone and sent them back to Charlie. 'OK'

I sat on the wall outside her house already regretting my decision, when Colonel Mustard walked past and saw my plaster cast.

"Been in the wars? And you've come round to Nurse Charlie for a bit of TLC? Quite right. I bet she even puts the uniform on, doesn't she? You lucky chap."

Charlie's taxi pulled up.

The Colonel winked at me. "The nurse will see you now."

"I've run out of cash. Can you sort it?"

Luckily I'd stopped off at a cashpoint machine on my way out, but if I'd known the evening was going to cost me an emotional arm and a leg, I'd have stayed at home.

Charlie stood and looked at me. "Well? You wanted to talk."

I thought she wanted to talk. I didn't know what to say. I didn't even know why I was here.

She opened a bottle of tonic, which shot everywhere. "Bugger." She threw it in the sink.

I looked for a cloth. "Sorry for sounding off in the pub, but you and I both know this can't last forever."

"I know. I've known for a while. But I don't know if I'm strong enough to be on my own again."

I thought she'd have had an army of Self Help books on the subject.

"You'll soon find a tall, dark, handsome banker who'll give you all the things you think you want."

"Will you stay tonight? One last night. Just to show there are no hard feelings?"

"I should get a cab home."

"Please?"

"It doesn't solve anything. In the long term."

Against my better judgement, I stayed. And as last nights go, it went with a bang.

I lay looking up at Charlie's ceiling and counted four cracks. They were small but clearly visible. She was still asleep, snuggled into me, when her alarm buzzed loudly.

Her sleepy hand stretched out to turn it off. "Do I have to go into work today?"

"Don't ask me, I'm just your ex."

She headed for the bathroom, avoiding eye contact, and I got dressed slowly. I'd have loved one last soak in her American power shower but I had to keep my plaster cast dry and anyway it was time to go. So I splashed my face with cold water in the kitchen sink and put the kettle on.

I could hear Charlie in the shower. But there was no singing of 'Dancing Queen' this morning.

"You realise, this could be our last coffee together. We should hold a two minutes silence."

Charlie tightened the belt on her dressing gown. "It's not a laughing matter."

"You're right. We should be wearing black arm bands."

"I mean it. Especially after last night. How can you take it so lightly? Or was this whole thing just a way of getting back at Liz?"

I told her how much she meant to me. It was nothing I hadn't said before but she needed to hear it all over again.

Charlie got a small green parcel out of the drawer. "I bought you a present last week. You might as well have it anyway."

I started reading her writing on the gift tag but she grabbed it and tore it off.

"Same present, different words." She was fighting back

the tears.

Inside I found a little silver flowerpot, about an inch high. "Will it grow silver flowers?"

Charlie started crying as we said goodbye in the kitchen. We said goodbye again in the hall. And again on the street. Colonel Mustard walked by and waved but neither of us waved back. I watched Charlie walk away. She didn't look back. Two minutes later she reached the top of the road, turned left and disappeared from my life.

I sat on her wall for a few minutes before getting up slowly. It didn't look that far to the main road but on crutches it seemed endless. I made it to the little coffee shop and collapsed onto a chair. I was sweating badly.

A pretty waitress came over. She looked Eastern European. "You OK?"

"I've snapped my Achilles, just broken up with my girlfriend and I'm getting divorced tomorrow. Apart from that I'm on top of the world."

"Sorry. English not very bad."

Luckily she understood the two magic words, 'black' and 'coffee'. I thought Americano might have been too much for her, but to be honest anything that even vaguely looked like coffee would have been welcome.

Colonel Mustard spotted me at my outside table and sat down.

"Everything alright, old chap?"

"I've snapped my Achilles, just broken up with my girlfriend and I'm getting divorced tomorrow. Apart from that I'm on top of the world." I thought it might get a better response second time round.

"God works in mysterious ways."

"I can't believe the Almighty wastes his time playing practical jokes on the likes of you and me."

The Colonel found me a cab. And as I drove through the streets of West London, it finally dawned on me that I was a single man again.

I got home and collapsed on the sofa. Aly was mopping the kitchen floor.

"You don't have to do that."

"Well, you can't do it on crutches. And also you're paying me, remember?"

With everything that had happened I'd forgotten to give Aly any cash, and she'd been too polite to ask for it.

"We'll stop off at the cashpoint on the way to Ivy's. I'm really sorry."

"No worries."

The cost of cabs was mounting, so I asked Aly if she'd like to drive the van. I phoned my insurance company and added her to my policy.

"Did you take your test in New Zealand?"

"Never took it." She revved the engine hard with her right foot. "Relax, I'm joking."

She was an over confident driver but we made it to Ivy's, via the cashpoint, without a hitch.

I stood on Ivy's doorstep and rang the bell three times as usual.

I heard a familiar voice behind me. "You got away with it then, I see."

I turned on my crutches to see the Mad Fence Woman from next door.

She carried on. "You can break as many legs as you like, chasing as many muggers as you like, but it doesn't fool me."

Aly came to my defence. "I suggest you go back inside before I do something I might regret."

"Are you threatening me?"

"Yes, I've got a black belt, you know."

The Mad Fence Woman turned her back on us and went inside.

I looked at Aly. "A black belt in what?"

She laughed. "Nothing. It's just a black belt."

"Hello. Only us." The house felt cold as we went in. Ivy's Zimmer frame was standing redundantly in the hall and her coat still hung on its hook by the door. I thought about doing my Chinese clapping trick to wake up the house but it would have felt like shouting in a library.

I made a start on the kitchen, sorting out the pots and pans while Aly went through the clothes in the bedroom. We soon had two piles, one for the charity shop and one for the tip. I hated the idea of disposing of Ivy's life in a series of black plastic bags but I knew it had to be done.

The wardrobes in the two spare rooms had some clothes that were so old they must have been Ivy's mother's.

Aly held up an evening gown in front of the mirror. "These are amazing, they should be in a museum."

We decided they'd go to a theatrical costumiers and any proceeds from their sale would go to The Gardeners' Royal Benevolent Society.

In the top drawer of her bedside table, wrapped in a piece of black velvet, I found Ivy's dress watch. I sat on her stripped bed and checked it over.

Aly was admiring it. "It must be worth a fortune."

"I think Ivy would have liked you to have it." I put it on her hand.

"You're not serious?"

"Positive."

I was checking the room before turning the lights out when I looked up and noticed the hatch to a loft above my head. I couldn't have got up there myself but Aly kindly shinned up the ladder and took a quick look.

"Just a couple of suitcases, that's all."

She brought them down. They were covered in travel labels. I brushed away the dust to see the names more clearly. Cairo, New York, Lima, Calcutta, and Kathmandu.

I opened the smaller of the two cases and found a bundle of papers inside, loosely tied with string. 'The travel diaries of Arthur Thomas. August 1885.'

"Her father's diaries. This is amazing. It can be the sixth book on the reading list of our book club."

I checked the timer switches, so that various lights would come on and off during the night. There wasn't much of any value left in the house but I didn't want an unwanted intruder rummaging about through Ivy's remaining worldly goods.

I'd just loaded the last of the plastic bags into the back of the van when I noticed a parking ticket on the windscreen. I looked up to see the Mad Fence Woman smiling smugly from her window. Aly did a ridiculous Kung Fu style kick in her direction, which sent her scurrying behind the safety of the net curtains.

We drove to the tip and threw five of the plastic bags into a huge skip. A few seconds later I saw Ivy's possessions being spewed out and crushed by the giant mechanical hand. It roared loudly as they disappeared into the void.

Chiswick High Road had several charity shops so we split the rest of Ivy's things equally between them and went for a well-earned coffee.

"I think we should get our book club up and running."

I was looking forward to reading Ivy's father's newly discovered travel diaries but as we only had one copy, we decided our first book should be read together.

Aly carried the bag and held the book shop door open for me. "What shall we kick off with?"

"Let's toss for it."

"We've got three books but a coin only has two sides."

"OK. Heads, Crime and Punishment. Tails, The Da Vinci Code. And if we see a red London bus before we toss it, then it's Catch 22."

Two red busses went by before I'd even found a coin.

We'd bought some French bread to go with Aly's famous soup.

She looked at the television guide. "It's always the same on British TV. Cookery, crime and D.I.Y."

"I'm surprised they don't combine them in a new format. Hammer and Chisel, the D.I.Y. Detectives. Or the crime and cookery show, Ready Steady Coroner."

Aly lit the fire and we sat at either end of my large sofa with our first book. She read faster than I did and seemed to be turning the pages at an alarming rate.

"It's not against the clock, you know."

I'd just started page three when the landline went. It was Good News Gary.

"We're exchanging on July 30th and completing two weeks later."

"That's sooner than I thought."

"I don't hang about. I've got bonuses to hit."

"I'd better let you hit them, then."

I returned to my book. Aly was racing towards the end of her first chapter but I was only on page four when the mobile rang.

"How's my invalid brother?"

"The leg's a bit sore, but I'm fine, thanks."

"Tomorrow's the big day, isn't it? I thought you might like breakfast at the cafe."

Aly looked up from her book. "Is this going to go on all evening?"

I was trying to remember how to turn off the new phone when it rang again.

"Hi, it's Moo. Just wanted to wish you luck for tomorrow. I've been through it too, remember? Don't think of it as a bad ending but a new beginning."

"Have you swallowed one of Charlie's Self Help

books?"

"Who's Charlie?"

"My ex-girlfriend."

"You're not even divorced and you've got an ex-girlfriend? You'll be fine."

Aly eyeballed me over her book.

"Sorry about that, I'll turn it off."

I turned it off and was on page ten when the landline rang. Aly let out an exaggerated sigh and handed me the phone.

"Hello, it's Emma."

"How's my favourite niece?"

"Dad tells me you're getting divorced tomorrow. But I thought you were already divorced."

"We've had the Decree Nisi. We get the Decree Absolute tomorrow."

"So it's not too late?"

"I'm sorry, Emma, but it is."

"I love Liz. And you do too."

"I know."

"Well, I think you're making the biggest mistake of your life."

"Liz and I have thought about it very carefully. We think it's the right thing to do."

"Will she stop being my Aunt tomorrow?"

"Of course not."

I said goodbye to Emma and unplugged the phone.

I'd finished the first chapter and decided to take a loo break. I was about to start the long, slow climb up the stairs on my bottom when the letterbox snapped shut and a card landed on the mat.

'To The Flowerpot Man. Something for your new pot. Miss you. Love, Charlie xxx'. It was written in silver handwriting. There was no stamp on it, so she must have driven round specially to deliver it. I opened the envelope but couldn't find anything inside. I looked closer and found a tiny stemmed rose, made out of cardboard. Charlie had cut it with a Stanley knife and coloured it in with crayons. I planted it in her silver flowerpot and it fitted perfectly.

Aly smiled. "You should text her back a flower."

I'd just about mastered the basics of texting but anything horticultural was still way beyond me. Needless to say, Aly did it in two seconds.

I never thought the day would come when I'd be texting flowers. But then again, I never thought the day would come when my divorce would be made Absolute.

"I thought you deserved a cup of coffee in bed this morning." Aly handed me a mug. "I know it's going to be a difficult day for you."

"Doesn't have to be difficult, I'm going to have a great day."

"Good for you."

She sat on the edge of the bed and we drank our coffee together.

"I've been thinking about what to do. JoAnne said I should go to my favourite place, somewhere really peaceful and calm."

"Have you come up with anywhere?"

"We used to go to the Norfolk Broads as children. My favourite bit was the River Ant, north of Ludham Bridge. It's a really narrow stretch, with open fields on either side. Of course, I haven't been there since I was eleven, and it might have all changed, but that's where I want to go. I was hoping you'd drive me."

She was delighted and went off to do something exotic with her hair.

As I was getting dressed, I spotted a folder on the top shelf of the wardrobe. All the legal stuff to do with the divorce had ended up in there. I sat on the bed sifting through the papers and found the photocopy of Liz's passport. Next to her photograph, under 'a relative or friend who may be contacted in the event of accident', was my name and address. Her passport didn't run out till 2012. Did that mean that even if we got divorced today, I'd still be responsible for her till then?

Aly kindly drove me to the café. I'd asked her if she

324

wanted to join us but she felt we should have a Boy's Only Breakfast.

Jack got up from his chair. "How's Hop-along-Cassidy?"

"Hopping along nicely."

"This one's on me, so have whatever you want."

"In that case, I'll have a large glass of champagne."

"Your wish is my command." He took out an ice cold bottle of Louis Roederer from a freezer bag in his rucksack. "I thought we should celebrate in style."

"You're an amazing brother."

"I know."

Marco, the owner, came running out. "You'll have me shut down. I don't have a licence."

"I'm getting divorced today, normal rules don't apply."

"So how are you feeling, little brother?"

"Ask me after another couple of glasses." I told him about my planned trip to the River Ant.

"You can't go there without me. Two Brothers Against The World, remember? I'm not working tonight, I'll drive you. It'll be great."

"I've already asked Aly."

"And will Liz be joining us?"

"Not today, no."

Marco brought out our two cooked breakfasts and we tucked in. There was something decadent about champagne and a full English, which seemed totally appropriate.

Our toast arrived and I started buttering it. I took one bite and looked at my mobile. It neither rang nor buzzed. I took a second bite. And a third.

Jack was struggling to open a plastic tub of marmalade. "Looks like you still want her to ring."

"She won't. Not now she's found happiness in Harley Street."

I sat back and drank my coffee, when the phone rang

loudly. It was Liz.

"Have I made it in time for the toast?"

"You just got in under the wire."

"How are you doing?"

"Fine. A bit weird. How about you?"

"Same really. But Sam was so sweet, he gave me a present this morning."

"Too much information. Is that Sam as in Sam the Gynaecologist?"

"He's bought me a pair of black and white kittens."

"Does that make you Pusssy Galore?"

"You should see them. They're gorgeous."

"I'm sure they are, but don't ask me to bury them on Pendle Hill. I think I'll pass that responsibility over to Sam, Sam the Forceps Man."

"They'll live for years. And anyway, we might be friends again by then."

"We're friends now."

"Sure."

I put the mobile down and went back to my toast.

Jack looked over. "You OK?" I nodded and took a sip of coffee. "Oh, I nearly forgot. I've got something for you."

He handed me an envelope. Inside was a handmade card from Emma. She'd drawn a terracotta flowerpot full of soil. Underneath she'd written 'Somewhere to plant your dreams'.

I opened the card.

'I think you're making a huge mistake but I'll support you in your stupid decision. Love Emma. PS. I love you lots and a whole lot more. xxx.'

We set off straight after breakfast. Aly drove and Jack was Chief Map Reader. I sat in the back with my foot stretched out on the muddy floor. It was a comfortable position for my leg but it did mean that I was nowhere near the controls of the radio.

Aly turned up the volume. "Have you never thought of putting in a CD player?"

"It would be worth more than the van. Anyway I like the radio, at least the stations I usually listen to."

"You should broaden your musical horizons, now you're a single man." She'd tuned into some unknown station, playing unspeakable music.

"I'm not quite single yet. My solicitor has to apply for the Decree Absolute first."

We'd just passed the Muswell Hill exit on the North Circular, when a text arrived from Charlie.

'THNX 4 FLWER. THNKG OF U 2DAY. HVE WE MDE HGE MSTAKE? MSS U. LVE C. X'

I tried texting her from the back of the van but it made me feel sick.

"You know, I had thought about going to the church we got married in and lighting a candle or something."

Jack handed me some chocolate. "No point putting yourself through all that grief."

"I hope they've got a boat free. It's a long way to drive just to stand on the river bank."

"Have faith." Aly turned up the radio even louder. She saw me wince in her rear view mirror and turned it down. "Bit loud for the over seventies?"

We decided to play 'I Spy'. Aly started us off. "I spy with my little eye something beginning with C."

"Car?"

"Carburettor?"

"Carbuncle?"

"Carbon monoxide?"

"No, C is for Chocolate." She laughed. "Don't you men know anything?"

We gave up on that game and started singing 'One Man Went To Mow'.

Jack spotted a sign for the next Service Station. "Fag break alert."

"I thought you'd given up?"

"I'm always giving up."

Motorway service stations are one of the great levellers of our time. Neon shrines to ordinariness. Airports make us feel important, we're international travellers making the world go round. But motorway service stations make us feel small. Pond life struggling to rise above its hygienic blandness. We queued up for our pre-packaged sandwiches and found a table.

I tried to break into a shrink-wrapped muffin. "A glass of champagne would be nice."

My phone rang from deep inside my jacket pocket. It was so small that I cut the call off by mistake. My solicitor had left a message.

"Good morning, Barry Rogers here at ten to twelve. We arranged that I'd call you today before applying for your Decree Absolute. I assume you'd still like me to go ahead, but I need to check with you first. I'm out of the office for the next hour and I'll call you again when I get back."

"Doesn't look like we'll get it processed today. I was hoping to have it all done and dusted before we got to the Broads."

"It's pretty much a rubber stamp, isn't it?"

"I've never got divorced before, but I think that's how it works."

Aly told Jack about our book club and I told him about finding Ivy's father's travel diaries.

Jack was intrigued. "When your leg's better you could follow his route round the world. But you should always travel westwards, apparently. I read it somewhere. The jet lag is much worse if you go eastwards. God knows why, time zones probably. Anyway, I can't think of a better way to spend Ivy's money."

"Round The World tickets aren't as expensive as you'd think." Aly was talking from experience. "Seriously, you should go for it."

I felt reckless at the prospect and if it hadn't been for my leg, I'd have cart-wheeled all the way to Ludham Bridge.

I checked my watch. "We should be there by two thirty. That's plenty of time to hire a boat and get to Barton Broad before dark."

We were singing 'Ten Green Bottles' loudly, for the tenth time, when we ran out of petrol and Aly had to steer us onto the hard shoulder.

"What do we do now? Drill for oil?" I'd had enough of being in the back of the van.

"I spy with my little eye something beginning with M."

"Mud? Motorway? Madness?" I wasn't in the mood for Aly's games.

She laughed. "No, Mobile phone. Call the AA."

"I don't think they do petrol runs, do they?"

"You're on crutches, so you're technically disabled. I'm sure they'll help."

The others got out and sat on the grass, which is apparently what you're supposed to do, but I couldn't be bothered with the hassle of the crutches, so I stayed on my own in the back of the van. The motorway traffic was so loud that I almost didn't hear the mobile ring.

"Hello, Barry Rogers again. Everything alright?"

"I'm stuck on the hard shoulder, but apart from that I'm fine."

"Jolly good. Now are you sure you'd like me to go ahead and apply for your divorce to be made Absolute."

The moment had finally arrived. After forty three days, the waiting was over.

I took a deep breath and said, "Quite sure, thanks."

I put the phone back in my pocket and looked out of the back window at the speeding traffic. I'd never have guessed that my five year marriage would have ended in the back of a van, on the hard shoulder of the M11. It had started with the two words, 'I do', and ended with the three words, 'Quite sure, thanks.'

Five words. One for each of our five years.

I thought about calling Liz to tell her the news but I knew my voice would crack. I hadn't expected to feel so shaky. I banged on the side of the van and Jack let me out. I needed some air.

"The deed is done."

Aly spotted the yellow AA van and waved madly. Ten minutes later we were on our way, with Aly at the wheel.

"Ludham Bridge, driver, and don't spare the horses."

We were only five minutes down the road when the mobile rang again. It was a bloke from the Evening Standard asking me if I'd like to write a weekly gardening column. It couldn't have come at a better time. I wouldn't be able to do any manual work for a while because of my leg, but I could write. So, as Gary Triple-Windsor would have said, I bit his hand off.

We didn't get to Ludham till four o'clock, but that didn't matter, we were in the fresh Norfolk air by my favourite river.

Aly headed for the shop. "Just getting some chocolate for our journey up the Amazon."

"Let's see if we can get a boat first."

We were in luck and hired 'The Captain Pugwash' for an hour. The two able bodied seamen, Jack and Aly, carefully helped me aboard and we set off upstream.

By the bank, a family of ducks were searching for food. I only had Aly's chocolate, so I threw them a stick of Kit Kat.

"I Spy with my little eye, something beginning with F," said Jack.

I was still watching the ducks. "Family?"

"Fly? Fish? Farmer? Frog?" suggested Aly.

"No. Free man. Here's to you, little brother."

Yes, I did feel like a free man. But I also felt like a

complete Failure.

We were just entering Barton Broad when the mobile rang. It was Liz.

"The kittens have just eaten some ice cream. They're so cute. I had to ring and tell you."

"I was going to ring you too. My solicitor's applied for the Decree Absolute. There's no going back."

She went silent.

Eventually, "So that's it? It's all over?"

I took another deep breath. "Absolutely over."

The water gently lapped against the side of the boat.

"Look, can I call you back? One of the kittens has just been sick."

Jack put his hand on my shoulder. "You OK?"

"I'm fine."

I switched off the mobile and split the last piece of Kit Kat with my brother.